Dollarbird

AT SEA WITH A SONG

Catherine Monnet is an American author living in Paris, who has worked as a teacher, philosophical counsellor, translator, script analyst for Canal Plus and freelance journalist. Her professional writing experience includes collaborating on writing French film scripts and authoring a nonfiction book, *Recognition: The Key to Identity*. She divides her time between Paris and the island of Koh Samui in Thailand, where she owns a home in the village of Lamai.

AT SEA WITH A SONG

Catherine Monnet

Dollarbird

Dollarbird

First published in 2021
by Dollarbird, an imprint of Monsoon Books Ltd
www.dollarbird.co.uk
www.monsoonbooks.co.uk

No.1 The Lodge, Burrough Court, Burrough on the Hill,
Melton Mowbray LE14 2QS, UK

First edition.

ISBN (paperback): 9781912049806
ISBN (ebook): 9781912049813

Cover design by Cover Kitchen.

A Cataloguing-in-Publication data record is available from the British
Library.

Printed and bound in Great Britain by Clays Ltd, Elcograf S.p.A.
23 22 21   1 2 3

1

It was another sunny, hot day in March. As Thanikarn trudged up the unpaved hill to her house, she couldn't wait to be home and change out of her school uniform. Besides, she had good news: top marks in her class for the third time in a row. Her father would be proud. They had already begun talking about which school she would go to after she graduated, and if she continued to work this well, she could go most anywhere, Chulalongkorn or Kasetsart in Bangkok, or Prince of Songkla in Hat Yai. Maybe she'd study to be a doctor or a lawyer, or some other important job that helped people.

When Thanikarn turned the bend in the road leading to her home, her thoughts were interrupted when she sighted a red-and-white police truck in front of the house, its roof lights still flashing. She quickened her pace, worry tightening her chest. She scampered up the steps and threw open the door. Her grandmother was sitting in her armchair, crying, while her uncle Trin sat on a stool beside her holding his head in his hands, rocking back and forth as his mouth formed a silent wail.

Thanikarn recognized Katcha, one of the policemen. He was a friend of her father's.

'I'm sorry, Karn,' he said to her. 'There's been an accident. Your father ... He tripped on a cord, fell off the roof his men were working on.'

'How is he?'

Katcha slowly shook his head.

* * *

Nearly ten years later, the day's April heat stubbornly persisted as Thanikarn climbed up her concrete stairway. She silently counted each step just as she had done when she was young, counting footsteps walking home from school. As everyone said, success came by taking one step at a time. The landing in front of her flat was on the second floor of a dilapidated building, its green-painted exterior flaking and peeling, disappearing into its tropical surroundings like a camouflaged uniform. A rusty clothes rack with Thanikarn's drying laundry hid a collection of the owner's stored objects: a broken bicycle, misshapen cooking pots, an old tarnished mirror. They'd been there ever since she'd moved in three years before.

Reaching her door, she paused to see if her little aloe plant needed watering. She smiled; it was a modest barometer of success, and she was proud to have kept it so green. A Hindu calendar with a glossy picture of the god Ganesha was thumbtacked on her front door, greeting Thanikarn with his multiple outstretched arms and tranquil half-closed eyes. It was a gift from the old man who ran an outdoor launderette down the road where she went once a week to wash her clothes. 'For a prosperous new year,

Karn,' he had said, stuffing it into her laundry bag. Like most Thais, they were both Buddhists, but it didn't matter – all gods were the same.

Once inside, Thanikarn flopped off her sandals and walked across the small, bare room to the makeshift kitchen, a white sink stuck into a long, waist-high concrete slab. She pulled down a plastic basket from a shelf above the sink and took out three eggs, a couple of spring onions and a bunch of wilted basil. She scooped out a cup of rice from an old tin box and dumped it into her ageless rice cooker. As she poured in some bottled water, she winced, remembering the comment from her last client.

'What's your name, sweetie?' the paunchy American man had asked as he handed her a five-hundred-baht note.

'Ta-ni-ka,' she said, pronouncing each syllable of her given name. Something she often did when introducing herself to foreigners.

'You're too pretty to be doing this job, Ta-ni-ka,' he said, flashing a self-confident smile. His empty compliment was like a piece of cheap candy. 'Here's my card with my cell number. Give me a call,' he added.

She took his card. '*Kap koun ka,*' she said, bowing her head politely, her hands pressed together above her chest. He gave her a good tip, but not good enough to make her feel guilty for throwing his card in the trash.

At the Golden Gecko, propositions such as his were rare. Most of the guests at the small beach hotel, many of whom were French, were families looking for a low-scale retreat rather than a five-star palace. Though seldom fully booked, the hotel had guests all year long, and they tipped as much as the tourists in the big luxury hotels like the Muang Kulaypan or the Dara Samui. Fortunately, the Golden Gecko didn't lodge too many lone male travellers, and when it did, they were usually friends of the owner. Thanikarn was relieved not to be solicited by the island's frequent sex tourists, who relentlessly washed up on Koh Samui's sandy white shores like unwanted debris.

Faithful to Thanikarn's Thai upbringing, it was her nature to be respectful to everyone. She was taught that kindness, generosity and offers of goodwill would be one day rewarded. But working as a masseuse, she soon learned the downside of such optimism. Some men, like her last client, misinterpreted her gentleness as an invitation, presuming that being a masseuse was a euphemism for another service. Then her sweet smile would freeze, and though her lips continued to turn up, the misplaced proposition felt like a slap of reality: her job didn't earn much respect.

Being a masseuse was so far from what she had wanted to become. But the sudden death of her father had left her few options. One day, a high-school friend, Sawitti, a silly girl whose only plan in life was to get married to a rich foreigner, had asked Thanikarn if she wanted to replace her one day at the beach stand where she gave massages. Sawitti had plans to spend the afternoon with a potential prince charming. It was Thanikarn's day off from work at the supermarket, the first job she found after high school, and she saw no reason to refuse. It would be a welcome diversion, and she knew that with lots of experience soothing her grandmother Preeda's stiff neck and swollen feet, she had a natural talent for massaging.

The day she replaced Sawitti went quite well. The customers were complimentary, and they boosted her morale with appreciative words she'd never heard at the checkout stand. Adding to the unexpected recognition, she got some generous tips.

Sawitti, who had a professional license, sold Thanikarn on the virtues of being her own boss. She explained how Thanikarn could get a certificate where she'd earned hers, at the WatPo School in Salaya. Thanikarn had always been a good student, and if Sawitti could get a license, so could she. Thanikarn's uncle Trin advanced her the tuition money, part of a secret savings he'd been keeping aside. It was a generous action she repaid many times over, allowing Trin to move into her room in her parents' house. When she returned from her five-week training course in Salaya, Thanikarn was lucky, or as she reasoned, rewarded, for her sacrifices, and she was offered a spot at the Golden Gecko's massage stand that had recently been vacated.

Now, as Thanikarn was preparing her dinner, she suddenly remembered that Amnat had slipped something into her bag before she left the hotel. What would be tonight's surprise? She pried open the plastic box he'd given her and smiled to find some fresh, cooked shrimp. Amnat was such a dear man. The Golden Gecko's chef found her too thin and constantly gave her surplus food from the kitchen. She whisked up the eggs in a bowl and tossed in Amnat's shrimp along with some chopped spring onion, the basil leaves and a little fish sauce. She put some oil into her one and only wok, heated it up on a little electric hot plate, and once the oil was sizzling, poured in her improvised version of *kyaw kai jiaw*.

Hungry, tired, and having little reason not to, she ate her dinner right out of the wok while watching TV: the next best thing to eating with friends. If she was lucky, she would find something in English, a language she still struggled to improve. While listening to Westerners talk, she hoped their vocabulary would magically ooze into her brain by osmosis.

The program she half-watched was some stupid game show. The bow-tied, hair-gelled host talked excitedly about his fantastic guests that evening, several young just-married Thai couples, dressed formally enough for a royal ball. Each one of the partners had to answer intimate questions about the other: their past relationships, childhood secrets, embarrassing moments, qualities and faults. Thanikarn was not amused; she was beginning to think that for her, any romantic relationship would remain forever out of reach.

'Couple number one, where was your first date, and how much money did your boyfriend spend?' the slick TV host asked the first wide-eyed young lady.

'Oh, he took me to see a movie, and then we went to dinner at McDonald's.' The bridegroom looked barely old enough to drive.

'McDonald's?' The host chuckled. The young man looked sheepish, and his lovely new wife blushed. They were young, it was excusable.

Thanikarn smiled, trying to remember her first date. It wasn't a real date, just a meetup with a boy from school that began with a meal at the outdoor market and ended with a little flirting next to the lake in Chaweng. One thing she did remember was her grandmother telling her no respectable Thai girl should be going out with a young man alone. Preeda was so protective, overcompensating for Thanikarn's education ever since her granddaughter had lost her mother. Preeda was old and her brain too cluttered with tradition to notice that times were changing. Modern Thai women were highly educated; they had careers, travelled and sometimes made as much money as men did.

Thanikarn was only nine years old when her mother died from uterine cancer, and once Thanikarn was old enough to understand what a uterus was, she felt guilty, as if her birth had something to do with her mother's death. After her mother was gone, her father and maternal grandmother took over raising her. They did the best they could, but going through the tender years of puberty without her mother, Thanikarn never had a clear picture of womanhood. Because of this, a casual statement made by her grandfather before he died stuck in her mind like inevitable fate. He predicted she would never bear a child.

'Couple number two, have you ever discussed how many children you're going to have?' the slick TV host asked.

'Well, at least one,' the spry bride answered, looking down at her tummy. An answer that made bridegroom number two jump as if he'd received an electric shock. The audience laughed raucously.

Thanikarn switched the channel. She didn't want to hear any more about marriage and babies. After finishing up her meal, licking the last bits of rice out of the pan with her fingers, she lay down on her little floor mattress that served as a bed and a sofa, propping up one of its gaudy flower-print pillows behind her head. She looked at the books lying on the floor by her bed, a law book, *Introduction to Corporate Law*, and an English book, *I Speak English: Level 3*. She picked up the law book, began reading where she had left off, and frowned. It had been a month since she'd sent any work to the Open University, Sakhothai Thammathirat. She tossed *Corporate Law* on the floor, as if tossing away a broken dream, and picked up her English book. The bookmarked page began 'Lesson 6: At the Hospital'. Narrowing her eyes, she concentrated. 'Hello, I would like to see a doctor please.' She repeated the words out loud, then scowled; her accent was terrible. 'Doctor, doctor, doctor,' she repeated straining to pronounce the *r* at the end. It would have been so much easier if she had a friend who spoke English. She shut the book and closed her eyes. What was the use? Her motivation had waned as she waited day after day for something or someone to come along and give her a magical shot of ambition.

She got up, went to the window and looked out, as if the answer to her hopes might be found outside. It comforted her whenever she let her eyes scan the distance, the starry sky, the silhouettes of towering coconut trees and the little stretch of sea that she could barely see from her second-floor apartment on a sunlit day.

People came from all over the world to Koh Samui to enjoy its postcard clichés of sunny skies, warm blue sea and endless palm trees. But for Thanikarn, her beautiful island was like a golden cage. Like Thanikarn's, most of her friends' livelihoods depended upon tourism: working in hotels, restaurants or spas. They rented out fishing rods and ski jets, hawked straw hats, bathing suits and scarves. They drove taxis or buses; they shuffled the tourists through the temples and led them through the tropical forests, took them on boat excursions and escorted them on elephant rides.

And some of them, like Thanikarn, gave massages. Every day.

It was hard work and tiring but a lot more gratifying than her supermarket job, and at least she was her own boss. It also accommodated her grandmother. After losing a husband, a daughter and a son-in-law, Preeda was reassured by her granddaughter's steady income and freedom to come and see her whenever needed. The only problem, one that Preeda reminded her of often, was that Thanikarn's chances of meeting a good Thai man were limited. Men her age who worked catering to tourists couldn't offer her a promising future, and foreigners couldn't be trusted.

Leaning out the window, Thanikarn looked up at the moon, its glow reflecting the sadness in her eyes. The prospect of turning twenty-nine next month felt like Damocles' sword. She'd been working at the Golden Gecko and living alone too long. She still fantasized about continuing her education, if for no other reason than to meet someone. But she was too old for university, and correspondence school was uninspiring, especially when she always felt so tired.

After cleaning up her dishes, washing out her underwear in the sink and spending another hour in front of the television, Thanikarn undressed and slipped into bed. She felt very much alone. If she had someone to share her thoughts, they might untangle. As she lay there on her bed, she looked for sleep, stretching out her feet, twisting around her ankles to make them crack. Her body was longing for warm, comforting hands like her own. She reached down and caressed herself gently, but finding no pleasure, she censored her search for self-satisfaction. Thanikarn rolled over on her side, pulled her knees up to her chest, and hugged her pillow as if it were a child's stuffed toy. The moist, tropical air drifted into her room, carrying sounds from outside. Her imagination slipped into night-time dreams, and she drifted off to sleep.

2

The next morning, while the sun slowly rose toward its midday peak, Thanikarn swerved her faded pink scooter around trucks, cars and *songthaew*, converted pickup trucks with two rows of seats in the back for paying passengers, circumventing street vendors, dogs and inattentive pedestrians. It wasn't as if she had to rush to work – there was no worry about arriving on time – but the traffic on Koh Samui was like a frenzied arcade game, and she enjoyed the challenge like any other local island driver.

It was a typical day on Koh Samui, balmy and warm, tented by a beautiful sky spotted with little puffed clouds. When she arrived at the hotel, the restaurant was still full of late-rising tourists lolling over their breakfast and making plans for the day, which often consisted of tanning in the sun, swimming in the ocean, getting a massage, eating lunch, swimming in the pool ... more tanning, another massage, drinks on the terrace, a relaxing shower, dinner and a late drink in a bar.

Before heading to her outdoor massage stand, Thanikarn popped into the hotel's kitchen. It was a habit she had acquired ever since she started working there. Her mother used to work in a beach restaurant when Thanikarn was very young, and the smell of spicy broth and the sound of clanking pots continued to bring her comfort. Amnat already had his head bowed over a simmering pot of stew. He acknowledged her presence with a smile and twinkling eyes.

'Smells like *massaman* chicken curry,' she said, standing behind him, wafting the fragrant steam in her direction.

'*Panang* beef curry,' he said, shaking his head, feigning dismay. Amnat was a proud if not arrogant cook.

'Well, I was close.'

Every day she floated in like a little bubble of joy to brighten his lonely kitchen. In exchange, he fed her a late lunch and slipped little goodies in her bag to take home. Amnat, old enough to be Thanikarn's father, could pass for much younger, not one wrinkle on his smooth, beardless face. But neither did Thanikarn look her age. She still had the glow of youth: creamy, brown skin; deep, brown, almond-shaped eyes; a small, shapely nose, full rose-coloured lips that quickly broke into a wistful smile, and shiny dark hair that she often kept pulled back in a ponytail, giving her the innocent look of a teenager.

Thanikarn crossed the terrace restaurant on her way to the massage stand, giving a sweeping glance at the new hotel guests, her potential clients. Lots of families.

The stand wasn't attached to the Golden Gecko hotel. It was independent, but the land, which belonged to the hotel owners, Philippe and his Thai partner, was rented to the masseuses for a monthly fee. The little square platform was built on low wooden pillars with a sturdy, thatched awning lined with plastic, in case of rain. It was perched between the hotel swimming pool and the beach, only a minute's walk to the shore and shaded by a couple of towering palm trees. It was ideally located for hotel guests who wanted to get massaged in the open air, refreshed by a cool sea breeze and surrounded by lush vegetation. The little stand was an added asset to the hotel, and Philippe had every reason to keep up a happy relationship with his resident masseuses.

Once she arrived at the stand, munching on some banana bread that Amnat made to please the European clientele, Thanikarn busied herself with the day's preparations. Like every morning, she took out her little mat and towels, oils and creams and began setting up for a day's work on her side of the stand, closest to the hotel swimming pool. Rinalda, the first and oldest resident masseuse, was already bent over a very plump blond in a fluorescent-blue bathing suit, massaging her client's meaty thighs. Sawitti was sorting through her nail polishes.

'*Sawadee*, Karn,' they both said in unison.

'Lots of new people at the hotel today. A group from Shanghai just arrived,' Sawitti added.

'Chinese?' Thanikarn asked. 'Not many Chinese tourists come here.' Philippe was French.

'No, not Chinese. Expats. Europeans. Spring vacation ...'

Thanikarn looked out toward the tiny island of Koh Matlang, as if the tourists had arrived from across that sea. She cocked her head pensively as she spread her towel out flat with her hands.

'Maybe we'll get good tips this week!' she said with a smile, nodding toward Rinalda's fleshy client, who was moaning with delight, confident that the woman didn't speak Thai.

Fifty meters away, Philippe gave the two women at the

massage stand a wave as he chatted with a young, pasty-white-skinned couple on the restaurant terrace. Sawitti and Thanikarn returned the gesture, adding a broad smile; they were both quite fond of their debonair boss.

Philippe was a tall, slender man with long salt-and-pepper hair and a perpetual tan. He had that rugged ex-hippy style many expats adopted once they became permanent residents on Koh Samui. He came to the island more than twenty years ago, fell in love with its good weather, silvery beaches, green hills, kind people, and a beautiful young Thai woman, who left him a year later for an affluent Westerner she'd met on the plane while going home to visit her mother, a trip that Philippe had offered her as a birthday present.

Not long after being discarded, drinking away his disappointment in a bar, Philippe met Bandit, a retired Thai boxer. They were both swigging bottles of Tiger Beer, bored with the crass night entertainment, and got to talking about their pasts, their plights and their plans. Like Philippe, Bandit was looking for some way to invest the money he had managed to put aside from his career. Along with what Philippe had saved from selling his graphic design firm, they were able to pool together their funds, set up a partnership and buy a small plot of land on the beach with a dozen rundown stucco bungalows, which they transformed into a hotel. They had the woodwork and trimmings painted bright pastel colours, making it look like a cross between Munchkinland in *The Wizard of Oz* and the Cinderella castle in Disneyland. Philippe advertised their hotel in some French travel guides and, bolstered by word-of-mouth and the support of some independent travel agents, the hotel became quite popular with Europeans travelling on a budget. The lodgings were clean and tasteful but less expensive than many of the classier hotels on the beach in Chaweng. Most of the hotel guests were families or couples, with only a few lone travellers, which is what Thanikarn liked about working at the Golden Gecko. The sex tourists tended to stay in seedy budget hotels near the bars or in the super luxurious hotels, if they could swing a paid business trip.

Thanikarn had barely finished setting up for the day. She was smoothing out her towel, plopping up a small cushion and going through her little box of oils when she heard a deep male voice. 'Hello.'

She looked up into the bluest eyes she'd ever seen. Captivated by their intensity, she couldn't avoid returning their penetrating gaze.

'Do you speak English?' he asked.

For a few seconds, she was too transfixed to flash her usual smile. He was so *lor*. One of the most handsome young men she'd ever met.

'Yes. A little English,' she finally said, finding her smile. She was wearing knee-length pants and an old T-shirt with a stain on the front, the first things she'd grabbed off the shelf that morning. She folded her arms over her T-shirt to hide the brown blotch.

'How much for a massage?' he asked.

'What massage you want?' And she pulled out the sign with the prices. He studied the sign and then said with a smile that made her feel like melting, 'I don't know. I've never had a Thai massage. What's best when you're really tired?'

Thanikarn looked at the sign as if she had to study it even though she knew it by heart. She was averting those hypnotic blue eyes. 'Maybe Thai oil massage. One hour. Three hundred baht. That okay?'

'Yeah, that's fine,' he said and smiled. She smiled back. They were both trapped in a silly silence, waiting for the other to say something.

'Massage now?' Thanikarn finally broke the mesmerizing showdown.

'Now? Well ... I haven't eaten yet. Maybe right after my breakfast.'

'Massage not good after you eat. Better later.' It was unusual for Thanikarn to give advice, especially for a potential client.

'Okay. I'll come back at one,' he half-asked.

Thanikarn gave a nod. The young man began walking away, then looked back and gave her a wave before heading toward the terrace restaurant.

He quickly joined his parents, Jacques and Caroline, and his younger brother, Arthur, finishing up their breakfast. Lucas was late.

'Couldn't find the restaurant?' his father asked sarcastically.

'Come on. We're on vacation,' Lucas replied, which elicited a nod from his mother.

Jacques looked out toward the horizon and, with great satisfaction, took in a deep breath of fresh air. He coughed, covering his mouth. 'I think I've still got some of Shanghai in my lungs,' he said, seizing a chance to justify their vacation.

Manee, a coffee-skinned waitress wearing tight jeans and

a close-fitting *I Love New York* T-shirt, arrived to take Lucas's order. She smiled at him sweetly, something he was happily getting used to.

The Mounier family had arrived from Shanghai via Bangkok late the previous night. Even though Lucas hadn't received his breakfast yet, his father was ready to move on and beckoned Philippe, who acknowledged him with a nod. Jacques wanted to get a little rundown from the owner: what to see on the island, the local activities and the best restaurants. Seconds later, Philippe arrived, and the usual banter between boss and customer ensued. Jacques was always delighted to speak with a fellow Frenchman, something he could seldom do in Shanghai where all the people he dealt with spoke Chinese, an impossible language, or English, always a struggle.

Lucas was paying little attention to their conversation, although his mother and younger brother seemed to be a bit more interested. Arthur was keen on renting some jet skis or any other sort of speeding motorized vehicle. Caroline was more eager to explore different parts of the island, some of the cultural sights like the Big Buddha, and perhaps a jungle trek on elephants. No one in the family had ever ridden an elephant. His father was looking forward to going fishing. What Lucas really wanted was to chill out, take some long, solitary walks along the beach, maybe drink some beer in a low-key bar, or find someplace where they had some good local music. One thing they all wanted was a break from the noisy, crowded and polluted city of Shanghai or, in Lucas's case, from the gloomy, grey skies of Paris.

In the ensuing moments, they all decided that the first day of their spring vacation would be spent exploring the area around the hotel, perhaps a stroll through Chaweng, an ocean swim and a bit of reading under a parasol. Just a free day to relax.

* * *

It was nearly one in the afternoon, but Lucas still hadn't budged from the table. He sat lingering over his coffee, scribbling some lyrics into his notebook, a song that had been in his head ever since he woke up. Arthur interrupted his creative session.

'Wanna go for a swim?' he asked, already changed into swimming trunks and carrying a beach towel. Lucas looked at his watch, 'No, sorry, *frero*, I'm going for a massage. But I'll walk down there with you.'

Thanikarn was working on a pudgy red-headed woman as they passed by the massage stand. She smiled at Lucas and held up her hand to show two fingers, which he assumed meant 'two minutes'. When Arthur saw his brother's prospective masseuse, he gave a knowing smile. 'Now I see why you wanted to get a massage.'

Once Thanikarn was free of her customer, she beckoned to Lucas. He came trotting over, wearing a T-shirt and blue loose-fitting shorts, his flaxen hair shining in the sunlight. 'Is like this okay?' he asked, looking down at his shorts. Lucas sat on the edge of the mat, and Thanikarn gently washed off his feet.

'Take off shirt,' she said when she had finished, and adopting her professional tone, she told him to lie down on his stomach.

She opened a new bottle of oil, doused some on the creamy-white skin of his back, and sensuously began spreading it around with her hands. Thanikarn rarely had customers with such white skin. Most of her clients spent the first few days of their vacation soaking in the sun, trying to rid any trace of a pale city dweller. But Lucas, who was so fair he could have passed for a Swede, didn't care. Ever since he could remember, he had to hide from the sun lest he burn red as a lobster. His friends used to make fun of his light-coloured skin every time he wore shorts or went bare chested, but he always laughed it off. His paleness became part of his persona. He was an artist, not a jock.

Thanikarn started with his upper back and shoulders. He was easy to massage, with supple muscles, not too locked up with tension. Some people were easier to work on than others, and Thanikarn took a special pleasure in massaging Lucas, pressing with her thumb into his spine, bearing down with the palm of her hands, then with big ample movements spreading up around his shoulder blades. It seemed like she'd never caressed such fair, smooth skin. Not a gram of fat on his slim body, which she imagined concealed unlimited energy.

'This feels sooo good,' Lucas said. If he were a cat, he would have purred. Thanikarn didn't comment. She was concentrating, trying to feel what he was feeling, the secret of a good massage.

Maybe he fell asleep, Lucas wasn't sure, but sometime later, he heard her say, 'Now time to turn over.'

As he rolled onto his back, he looked at her with intoxicated eyes. Thanikarn recognized the sleepy gaze. She continued smoothing her hands over his almost hairless chest and arms, taking unusual pleasure in her task. It felt like a slow dance to the music of the soft lapping waves and wind-rustled palm leaves. Lucas mostly kept his eyes closed but peeked from time to time to watch Thanikarn working.

She was too pretty, and he was too curious for him not to start a conversation, something Thanikarn wasn't used to. 'Have you been doing this for a long time?'

'You mean massage?'

'Yeah.' The question seemed obvious to Lucas.

Unused to such questions, Thanikarn was taken aback. She was reluctant to tell him, fearing it would make her sound old. 'Don't know how long. Massage my grandmother when I was young. Then, I go to school to learn better. Get a license,' she said, looking at her tawny hands moving over his pale skin.

'Well, you are an excellent masseuse,' Lucas said in a dreamlike state.

'Now, your face,' she said.

He opened his eyes, breaking her concentration.

'Close eyes,' she said, shutting them gently with her soft fingertips.

Lucas obeyed. Free from those hypnotic blue eyes, Thanikarn spread her delicate fingers up and around his broad forehead, cheeks and strong chin, with a slow, soothing motion. A soporific smile appeared on his face. He dared not speak, or it would break the spell.

When Thanikarn finally finished, she said, 'Okay, sit up.' Lucas felt like he couldn't move. As he opened his eyes, Thanikarn was on her knees behind him, performing the last massage movements around his neck and shoulders, stretching his arms up and over his head, a few thumps and a final 'Okay, done.'

Utterly relaxed, Lucas heaved himself up off the ground. He dug into the pocket of his trunks looking for money, which fell on the ground. He picked the bills up and handed her a thousand-baht note.

'Cannot change. Too early.'

'That's okay. Keep the rest.'

'No. Too much.' Sometimes she did keep big tips but only with regular clients.

'Well, then, I'll take another massage tomorrow. This is an advance. Okay?'

Thanikarn pursed her lips and took a few seconds to say, 'Okay. What time?'

'Same time?' he asked.

Thanikarn answered with a nod.

'See you tomorrow,' he said, hopping off the massage stand, then turned around quickly, taking her by surprise.

'By the way, what's your name?'

'Karn. Friends call me Karn.'

'See you tomorrow, Karn!' He added with a grin, 'I'm Lucas.'

As Lucas walked off, a silver-haired man with a pot belly was eying the price list. She explained the various options to her new customer, furtively watching Lucas as he headed for the beach.

Business was usually good when a new group of tourists arrived. A relaxing massage was one of the first things a travel-weary tourist wanted. Thanikarn, Sawitti and Rinalda chatted and gossiped in Thai, sometimes breaking into muted giggles as they worked on one client after another. There was a soft childlike quality to their melodious, muted voices as they spoke.

Rinalda was the most experienced of the three. She had been working at the Golden Gecko ever since it opened and always had entertaining stories. Despite her age, she was strong and resilient, never complaining or showing signs of impatience. Sawitti, whose finely defined arched eyebrows and permanently pink-tinted lips made her look like a precocious teenager, was the youngest. She was always the last to show up at work and the first to leave. Even though she had good training as a masseuse, she found it was too hard, and ever since Thanikarn had joined them, she had appointed herself as the resident manicurist. She made less money doing nails, but since she still lived with her parents, it wasn't a problem. Her present priority was finding a wealthy *farang*, a Westerner, to marry, and so she spent what little money she made on going out to clubs like the Reggae Pub, Green Mango and Henry Africa's, always sure to be packed with tourists. If none of her old school friends were available, she'd sometimes coax Thanikarn into joining her. She couldn't go alone – it would give a bad impression.

Being the prettiest masseuse at the Golden Gecko, Thanikarn was also the busiest, something she naively attributed to the fact that she was very good at her job. She was conscientious, had the suppleness of a contortionist, and had developed surprisingly strong arms and hands, given her petite size. She'd always been less loquacious than her two co-workers, with a tendency to daydream. They weren't dreams of a wealthy prince charming like Sawitti's, whose future beau would most likely turn out to be decades her senior. Thanikarn dreamed of getting out of her monotonous rut and leading a different life, having a career like the women she saw in American television shows, women who wore high heels and pantsuits, carried briefcases full of dossiers, and opened the doors to their own offices. She would often look at Rinalda and think that she didn't want to end up massaging until she was sixty.

When the sun began to set and a beautiful pink, yellow and purple hue lit the sky, it was time to go home. As usual, Sawitti had already packed up her manicure tools and was ready to leave.

'Karn, you want to join us tonight? I'm meeting Manee at the Green Mango at eight-thirty.'

'Tonight? No, I don't think so. I'm a little tired.' She was tired every night, so it was more of an excuse than a reason. Even though she liked Manee and the rock band at the Green Mango on Wednesdays, she was already resigned to a quiet evening at home and a sprint over to see her grandmother. It had been several days since she'd last seen her.

'You always say you're too tired. This is the time to go out and have fun, before you get too old,' Sawitti said. Her clumsy comment pricked Thanikarn where it hurt.

'Next time for sure,' Thanikarn said, trying to mean what she said.

After Sawitti left, Thanikarn began putting away her massage oils and gathering up the towels when she caught a glimpse of Lucas and another young man, perhaps his brother, on the terrace, now dressed for dinner, both wearing long pants and ironed shirts. They were soon joined by two older adults, their parents, looking casually elegant. The whole family had that indefinable

French flair that Thanikarn admired, one that said, *I'm from a different world, a sophisticated world of people who have good taste, money and time to shop.* She watched them with a sense of longing in her big, brown eyes. It seemed like they belonged to a private club that she would never be able to join. Still dressed in her shorts and stained T-shirt, she avoided their path as she scurried off to the washroom with her bundle of towels.

3

Lucas, Arthur and their parents were ready to go at seven thirty for their day of diving, too early for the breakfast buffet or an appetite. Coffee and cellophane-wrapped pastry did the job, filling them up enough to avoid seasickness. Once on the boat, the boys stretched out on the wooden benches, tucked their towels and sweatshirts under their heads and dozed on the boat ride to the little island of Koh Tao. Jacques stood, arms crossed, next to the helm, secretly wishing he was navigating. As an experienced sailor, he was happy the instant he set foot on any floating craft, from a canoe to a steamship. Caroline, who never got seasick, already had her nose in a book.

It was a beautiful day, a few cotton-puff clouds spotting the sky. Nothing less than perfect.

Once they arrived at their diving spot, the boys slipped easily into their wetsuits while Jacques uncomfortably stuffed himself into his. Caroline lathered herself with sunscreen, getting ready to go snorkelling in the warm, crystal-blue water while they were diving.

The boys and Jacques were looking forward to fantastic flora and fauna, but unfortunately, most of the coral was a bleached-out grey, and the only fish were several colourless schools of barracuda. When they came back from their dive and clambered onto the boat after only fifteen minutes, they complained to the two apologetic crew who explained in broken English that it was from the warming sea temperature, too much sea traffic and pollution. This sent Lucas, the family ecologist, into a rant about the damages done by stupid and selfish humans. The crew, used to such complaints, promised a better dive on the other side of the island after lunch.

The Mounier family's mood picked up with the delicious barbecued brochettes and a fresh fruit salad. At one o'clock, Lucas thought about Thanikarn working at the hotel. He learned about the boat trip too late to cancel his rendezvous and the fact that he was 'standing her up' gnawed at him.

Back at the Golden Gecko, Thanikarn was finishing a foot massage she was giving to a snoring octogenarian. She had to gently shake his feet to wake him up.

'Finished, papa,' she said. The groggy-eyed Frenchman paid and left without eye contact.

Thanikarn grabbed her bag and ran off to the service washroom. She splashed some cold water on her face, undid her ponytail, brushed her shiny dark hair and put it back up in a chignon, checking herself in the mirror. She returned to her post, feeling refreshed, and looked at her watch. One o'clock. She sat down and waited, cross-legged, gazing out toward the sea, where she spotted some fishing boats unloading a group of tourists who filed up the beach. Lucas wasn't among them. She pulled out her manicure box and began filing her nails. Ten minutes passed, then fifteen, and twenty.

'Your handsome boy not coming?' Sawitti asked her as she was massaging a woman wearing a bikini, who might as well have been naked, it was so skimpy.

Thanikarn didn't think her remark merited a reply. Her tummy began growling. She often snuck into the kitchen after lunchtime to mooch some leftovers from Amnat, but she didn't want to leave her spot unattended for that long. 'I'm going down to the beach to get some *khao niew moo ping*,' she told Sawitti. 'You want me to bring you something?'

Sawitti looked reflective, then shook her head no. 'Take your time,' she added. 'If he comes, I'll tell him you're coming right back.'

Thanikarn nodded with a smile and trotted off toward the sea, hailing a little old woman plodding along the shore, carrying across her shoulders two heavy baskets on the ends of a pole containing grilled pork skewers and sticky rice.

After the Mounier family finished their lunch, which Lucas found unbearably long, the crew pulled up the anchor, and putted off for the other side of the island. The afternoon plunge was more satisfying than the first; besides the usual schools of barracuda, there were some batfish, colourful angel and butterfly fish, and even an octopus. The coral had the colour of coral.

Then Lucas got his secret wish for a speedy wind-up of their excursion. They hadn't been in the water for long when the rubber strap on Lucas's mask broke and he had to hold it on with one hand, and Arthur lost a fin that dropped down to the ocean floor. The boys signalled to Jacques that they were heading back to the boat. Jacques, who was out of shape and tired, gratefully followed them. Before heaving himself up, he took off his fins, threw them on the deck and missing the bottom rung of the ladder, rammed his toe on the edge of the second step, crying out French expletives. Limping across the deck, he claimed it was broken. Caroline was already on board feeling too sorry for herself to give him any sympathy. She had brushed her leg against a rock covered with fire coral.

After the minor misfortunes, they were ready to call it a day. The crew revved up the stubborn motors, and the boat sped toward Koh Samui like a pony quickening its pace back to the stables. Lucas looked at his watch, three thirty. It would take an hour to get back, Lucas thought, still enough time to get in a massage with Thanikarn.

* * *

As soon as their boat returned to the shore, Lucas gathered up his wet clothes, slipped into his sandals and hopped off the boat, bidding his family a curt *ciao*. They were all too tired to notice. He jogged back to the hotel and headed straight for Thanikarn's stand. Massaging a young woman's face, she spotted Lucas in the distance. Sawitti saw her colleague's eyes light up.

'Ah. He didn't forget you, your charming prince,' she teased.

'Hey!' Lucas called out to her with a smile and a wave. She looked his way with an instant smile. As he approached, seeing she was busy, he slowed his pace. He arrived, still a little winded from running, and panted out his apologies, explaining his sudden obligation to go diving with his family. She listened, her face serenely calm, while her fingers continued circling over her customer's tanned forehead.

'So, you still have time for me?' he asked with a charming smile.

'Still have time. Come back, fifteen minutes.'

'Okay, I'll go get a coffee. Want me to bring you something to drink?'

Thanikarn smiled self-consciously, shaking her head no. This was the first time anyone had ever offered to bring her anything.

Instead of getting a coffee, Lucas headed back to his room to take a quick shower. He'd heard that local people said foreigners sometimes smelled like pigs, which was probably true, especially if they weren't used to the tropical heat and forgot to wash.

Feeling refreshed, he stopped for a quick espresso at the bar. Philippe was doing some accounting at the desk nearby and called out to Lucas.

'How was the dive?'

'Oh, great, yeah, really cool,' he lied. It was no use complaining, besides, what would he be complaining about if not modern humanity's destruction? It wasn't Philippe's fault the ocean was doomed.

Lucas waved to Thanikarn from where he was sitting at the bar. She signalled with a beckoning hand for him to come. He hopped off his stool and sauntered over.

'What kind of massage today?' she asked.

'I don't know, like yesterday. An oil massage is fine.' Tired from the dive, he was looking forward to a good rest. He stretched out his lanky body on her mat, stomach down, resting his head on a little pillow that Thanikarn had prepared. She poured some oil on his back and tenderly smoothed it into his skin. Within a few minutes, Lucas fell sound asleep, and while Thanikarn chatted quietly with Sawitti and Rinalda, their muted, mellifluous voices crept into Lucas's dreams. After an hour, his massage was finished, but Thanikarn didn't bother waking him up right away. She'd decided he would be her last client of the afternoon.

When she had finally finished arranging her affairs, she gently patted Lucas on the back. He stretched out his arms like a cat and yawned. 'Wow, that felt wonderful,' he said, rolling himself up to a sitting position. Thanikarn let out a little laugh. 'I think you fall asleep.'

'Yeah. I probably did.' He looked out toward the sea, as if he were trying to focus his thoughts.

'What are you doing tonight?' he asked without looking at her.

'Me?' She was flustered. 'Oh, I go home, eat some dinner, maybe go out with friends to a bar later.' She reddened, immediately regretting she'd made something up.

'Can I come with you? To the bar, I mean.'

She wasn't sure what to say. It wasn't the first time she'd been asked out by a client, but those men were always older and certainly expecting more than she was willing to give. Lucas could sense her hesitation and suddenly realized he might have been too brash. Maybe she had a boyfriend or maybe she was even married.

'That's okay if you want to be with your friends. No problem,' he added quickly.

'No, no,' she cut in. 'It is not special. I just meet Sawitti, and girlfriends.' She surprised herself, persisting in her little lie.

Lucas looked at her, expectation in his eyes. 'So, I can meet up with you?'

She had to think about it for a minute as she calculated how she would change her story about meeting Sawitti. 'I come pick you up later. After dinner ... Ten o'clock okay?'

'Perfect. I'll wait for you in front of the hotel,' he said, standing up. 'Oh, I almost forgot.' Lucas dug in his pocket and pulled out a five-hundred-baht note.

'No, no, no. You pay me already, remember?'

'Yeah. I guess I did,' he chuckled.

* * *

After a dinner of cold *pad Thai*, Thanikarn took a shower and washed her hair, smoothed some coconut moisturising cream on her face, trimmed and polished her nails. She dug through her limited wardrobe and tried on at least three different outfits, finally settling on a short, white, cotton skirt and a light-blue sleeveless top. Simple and discreet, but showing off her slim, firm body. There was no full-length mirror in her home, so she studied her reflection in the windowpane. She still wasn't satisfied, but there was no reason to fuss: this wasn't a date.

The Mounier family opted for an early dinner at their hotel after their tiring day out at sea. Caroline, who usually instigated their conversations, sat listlessly swirling the ice in her glass.

Arthur's head was about to fall to his plate. Jacques was especially tired, still grumbling about his sore toe and a possible visit to the hospital. Lucas was relieved that his parents and brother wanted to go back to their rooms for an early night in bed. Lucas announced with conviction that he would be going out with Thanikarn for a little drink in Chaweng. His parents couldn't protest, he wasn't a child, but they nonetheless reminded him to be careful, watch his wallet and not drink too much. His father dug into his pocket and peeled off a couple of five-hundred-baht bills and handed them to Lucas. As Lucas had anticipated, his patience and amiability during the day had paid off. 'Merci, Dad,' he said, giving him a kiss on top of his balding head, and headed off to his room to get ready for the evening.

4

Lucas was in front of the hotel at precisely ten o'clock. He didn't expect Thanikarn to be on time, girls never were, but he didn't want to keep her waiting in case she was. He was dressed casually but with a touch of French elegance – light cotton pants, a chic, short-sleeved T-shirt and impeccably clean sneakers. He kept a lookout, craning his neck to the right and left, and within a few minutes, as if from out of nowhere, Thanikarn sidled up on her pink Yamaha scooter. She looked much more feminine than during the day and quite sexy straddled on the still-vibrating bike. They exchanged admiring smiles, both pleased by the way the other looked. 'Jump on in back,' she said unceremoniously, and he hopped on. She made a sharp U-turn and they sped down the main road toward the centre of Chaweng Beach. Lucas clung closely to Thanikarn's body; his hands tightly gripped around her tiny hips as the bike swayed right and left through the dense traffic. He wasn't far from being terrified. The warm sea air covered their bare skin with a humid mist, and the wind-swept street dust made Lucas squint. Thanikarn's hair was swept up into a thick chignon and stayed perfectly in place as she sped along, holding her head high, weathering the moist breeze like a statue on the stern of a ship. The road noise made it too noisy for them to talk. As they approached the central part of Chaweng Beach, they slowed to a crawl in the bumper-to-bumper traffic. Clumps of tourists rambled down the sidewalk lined with rowdy bars, crowded terrace restaurants and a seemingly limitless number of massage parlours.

'Lots of people,' Lucas commented.

'Yes, every night like this,' she answered as she pulled her bike up into a row of other motorbikes so tightly crammed together they hardly had enough space to get off.

'Is this where your friends are?'

'Maybe,' she said casually. As they headed down the street. Lucas resisted the temptation to take her hand.

'There. The Green Mango,' she said, pointing across the street, 'Most famous in Koh Samui,' she added. 'Lots of tourists, drinks, music, dancing, Thai girls.'

'Okay, great, I'm up for anything,' he said, his eyes bright with anticipation.

They walked into a club that was obviously *the* place to be, with two huge rooms for dancing, each with its own DJ and music. One room was playing techno trance music; the other blasted out popular hits. Lucas spotted several scantily dressed young Thai women sitting on barstools, but for the most part, the two rooms were full of foreigners. The music was conflicting and chaotic. Lucas screwed up his face and sighed. This wasn't his kind of place. He didn't want to offend Thanikarn, but after about five minutes screaming into her ear to be heard, he asked her if she knew someplace that wasn't so loud and crowded.

'If you like. I know many places,' she was quick to reply.

'What about your friends?' he asked apologetically.

'No problem. Maybe come later, maybe go to different place,' she said with a smile, relieved that her little story was of no importance.

They walked down the street for a few blocks and entered a less crowded club. Even here, the music blared, while a DJ tested his speakers on the dance floor and several televisions posted on the walls squawked away. Several small groups of people of mixed ages were playing pool and drinking beer; long-haired bar girls sat on stools looking teasingly seductive, calling out to any lone male customer who entered.

'You buy me drink, mister?'

There were woven smells of cigarette smoke, sweaty foreigners and fried fish. It was an all-out attack on Lucas's senses that made him wince.

'Here not so many tourists,' Thanikarn said. A couple of girls she knew near the billiard tables spotted them and burst into surprised waves and smiles. Lucas recognized one of them, the young waitress who had served them breakfast. Thanikarn waved hello, and they soon jaunted across the room. The girls said something in Thai to Thanikarn.

'This is Lucas, from France,' Thanikarn said in English. Then gesturing toward her friends: 'This is Manee, and this is Ka.' They *wai*ed, bowing with folded hands, and giggled when Lucas playfully waied back.

'Can I buy you all a drink?' Lucas asked. Thanikarn smiled. Her young farang companion was courteous, and she knew this would make a good impression on her friends.

'No, we have already,' Manee said. 'With friends playing pool.' She pointed to a small group of Thais and a couple of foreigners across the room. 'We'll leave you alone with your handsome date,' she said to Thanikarn in Thai, and then to Lucas, with a heavy accent: 'Happy to meet you.'

'They are friends from hotel,' Thanikarn said once they left.

'Yeah, I remember. She's a server.'

'Manee. We call Manee the monkey.'

'The monkey? Why?' Lucas asked.

'Because she has dark skin,' she said nonchalantly.

Lucas blinked slowly. That would be *so* politically incorrect back home. 'She's okay with that?'

Thanikarn looked at him innocently. 'Why not?'

Lucas let it go.

Lucas led her over to the bar to order a drink. Thanikarn suggested a beer called Chang, which meant 'elephant', very popular with Thai people. As they drank and watched the incoming clients, the club became increasingly crowded; tourists and locals strayed in, ordered drinks, wandered around the large room, glasses in hand. The DJ was only warming up, but the decibel level was already barely tolerable to Lucas. A few people were on the dance floor, moving to the music, only some with any true rhythm.

'You dance?' Thanikarn asked.

'No, I'm no good at dancing,' he said, quickly adding, 'It's okay if you want to, though.'

'I stay here with you,' she said as she hiked herself up onto a barstool. Lucas felt like placing his hands on her coffee-cream thighs but knew that would be unseemly. She must have read his mind and tugged down her skirt, not wanting to give him the wrong idea. As the DJ music went into full throttle, it was becoming too difficult to talk without shouting. Like clubs everywhere, this one was designed for drinking, people-watching, dancing and hooking up, all of which made intimacy impossible.

Thanikarn watched Lucas discreetly, worried that he wasn't having a good time. Lucas was disturbingly quiet, and she was afraid he was already bored with her. She wasn't very good at conversation, especially in English, and looked around the room, feeling inadequate. After a few minutes, she felt she had to say something.

'Hard to talk here,' she said into his ear.

'Yeah, you know someplace where the music isn't so loud?'

'I know,' she said, thankful the noisy spot didn't suit him. 'Let's go.' She slipped off the stool.

Lucas put his arm around her back and cordially escorted her through the raucous crowd toward the door. She felt the eyes of some of the bar girls following them across the room. They were all younger than she was, some in their teens, but wearing makeup and dressed in black, the age difference was less obvious.

'I know a little bar, not many people, sometimes live music. More quiet,' she said, once they were out the door.

'Oh, good,' Lucas said, rolling his eyes with relief.

After searching for Thanikarn's motorbike, lost amid a tangle of others, they headed down the coast toward Chaweng Noi. Thanikarn turned left on a tiny street that led to the beach.

They parked easily and walked toward the shore to a tiny, isolated restaurant, Samui Soul, with a thatched roof terrace that extended over of the sand. It looked like something out of a 1950s beachcomber movie: wooden plank floor, bamboo bar, old photos and colourful pictures on the walls. There were only a dozen tables.

'Wow, this is cool,' Lucas said, his eyes lighting up.

'You like it?' Thanikarn asked, pleased with herself.

'Of course. You come here often?'

'No, just once, with farang. Not French. But I never see him again,' she said, quickly.

A small group of scruffy hippy-type musicians were playing a melancholic rock song on a cramped makeshift podium. The guitarist and bassist both looked European; the drummer and keyboard player were probably Thai. There were no loudspeakers, so there was no need to shout to be heard. Lucas glanced toward Thanikarn with raised eyebrows, bemused.

'They're not bad,' he said, nodding to the drumbeat. 'I like the riff.'

'The riff?'

'That's a basic melody that repeats,' Lucas explained.

'Oh, I never hear *riff*. Maybe a French word?'

'No,' he laughed, 'it's English. A word that musicians use.'

'You a musician?'

'Trying to be. Well, not exactly a musician. I play piano and bass, but I'm more of a composer.'

Thanikarn was too embarrassed to ask what a composer was, but fortunately for her, Lucas continued. 'I mostly write songs, but other kinds of music too.'

'Ah.' She said. 'You must study a long time.'

'Since I was seven; first private lessons, then the conservatory, and now I'm studying musicology at the Fac.'

Thanikarn nodded. She wanted to ask him what the Fac was, but she reasoned it must be a special kind of school. 'I think you must be very good.'

He shrugged. 'Good is relative. Actually, I'm never happy with anything I do.'

Thanikarn didn't know much about music, other than what she heard on the radio and TV or in the clubs. But she knew that Lucas was on another level, and she was impressed. 'You're the first *real* musician I meet. Before, I only know DJs, and maybe some who play guitar on the beach.'

Lucas smiled, satisfied that he had earned a point. 'I'll go get us some drinks,' he said and headed over to the bar.

Thanikarn followed him with her eyes as he strode across the room. He was by far the most handsome man she'd ever gone out with. She had no idea how the rest of the evening would go, but her skin tingled with enthusiasm, something she hadn't felt for years.

He came back with two Chang beers, and sat down on the cushioned bench, his thigh touching hers. She could feel the heat of his body emanating through his linen pants, exciting her to a point that made her feel embarrassed. She wondered what he thought about her and half-regretted the way she was dressed, wearing a short, tight skirt like a common *mia chao*, or prostitute. She pulled away a few inches so that her thigh was no longer touching his and sat upright, throwing back her shoulders, trying to look poised.

'Everything okay?' A banal question, he knew, but he sensed the change in body language. He smiled at her warmly.

'Yes, everything okay,' she replied. She told herself to relax and smiled.

'Maybe you're tired. It must be hard work massaging all day.' He took one of her hands in his and caressed it gently. 'Your hands are strong, but delicate, feminine.'

As he held her hand in his, Thanikarn felt as if it were on fire, and the fire ran up her arm and straight to her heart. Her face reddened like a little girl being paid her first compliment. He stroked her fingers and palm. Her hands were not as soft as his. Why didn't she think to put on coconut oil? She did it for her customers but not for herself.

He respectfully placed her hand back on the table. And then, she spontaneously took back his hand and looked at it. 'Your hands are strong. Piano hands.'

'Yeah, I guess you're right. I practice a lot, about an hour of scales every day,' and he mimicked the rapid finger movements on the table.

The band played a few more songs. The intense faces of the musicians in stark contrast with the indifferent customers paying little attention to the live music. Lucas was one of the few in the room really listening. Thanikarn eyes began to feel heavy. It would be so nice, she thought, if she could rest her head on his shoulder. The band announced it was their last song before finishing up for the evening. Lucas, still concentrating on the music, pulled a small frayed spiral notebook from his pocket and scribbled something down. Thanikarn pretended not to notice. 'Just jotting down some ideas,' he said, 'music ideas.'

When the band finished playing, there was a feeble applause from a few of the customers. Lucas popped up. 'I'll be right back,' he announced and glided over to see the musicians as they slowly packed up their instruments. After a short exchange with the bass player, he returned to the table accompanied by a young man in his early thirties with long, light-brown hair held back in a headband. He wore multi-coloured, flowing Indian pants, a '70s T-shirt with a picture of Bob Marley, and leather sandals.

'Thanikarn, this is Ben. I invited him to come have a drink.'

Ben waied.

'Nice to meet you, Ben,' she said courteously. It was a phrase she had learned by heart long ago. Ben pulled up a stool and sat across from them.

'Ben lives on Koh Samui.'

'And you like?' she asked.

'Been here about seven years now. I love it.'

'What brought you to Koh Samui?' Lucas asked him.

'Long story,' he said. 'Another time.'

Lucas nodded with a smile, then added, 'Well, whatever brought you here, it was a good choice.'

'To Koh Samui,' Ben said and raised his glass.

Thanikarn was drawn into Lucas's blue eyes as their glasses clinked. If their depth was any clue to his soul, it was fathomless.

Ben and Lucas chatted about music, their favourite artists and styles, and trod into technical trade-talk that left Thanikarn out of the conversation. After about ten minutes, Lucas realized he'd been ignoring his host. He often got carried away when he discussed music.

'Sorry, Karn, you must be bored with all this music talk.'

She smiled politely. 'No problem,' she said, though she was relieved when Lucas and Ben finished up their drinks. They exchanged phone numbers with plans to meet up the next day.

Lucas and Thanikarn walked out of the bar hand in hand into a refreshing misty breeze blowing in from the sea. 'It's a beautiful night,' Lucas said. 'If you're not too tired, we could take a little walk on the beach.'

'Not too tired,' she chirped. Thanikarn pulled off her sandals, and they walked side by side along the shore.

Thanikarn never walked on the beach at night; she seldom walked on the beach at all. Sometimes, at the end of a long, hot day massaging, she would go sit at the water's edge and let the waves roll over her legs and thighs, along with other Thais fishing for *hoi siap*, baby clams, but otherwise, the beach was for the tourists.

'I love the ocean,' said Lucas. 'It puts everything into perspective.'

She looked out at the calm sea. She thought she knew what he meant but wasn't sure. Noticing her silence, Lucas continued.

'I mean, when we look at the ocean, so big, so powerful, churning like that since the earth was born, we realize how small we are.'

Thanikarn nodded. 'It always makes my problems very little. And then I feel strong inside.' It was the best she could do in English.

'My mother told me that my middle name, Adrien, means "man of the sea". And I always joke with her about it because in French the word for *sea* is *mer*, written *m-e-r*, but when you spell it differently, *m-e-r-e*, it means "mother".'

'Same. Mother and the sea,' Thanikarn said.

'You wouldn't happen to be Buddhist, would you?' he asked with a playful smile.

'A little Buddhist ... My family all Buddhist.' She paused. 'And you?' she asked, looking up at him.

'Oh, I'm not anything. I never saw any reason for believing in something I can't understand,' he said tersely. They continued walking, their feet crunching the damp sand, gazing at the sea tented by a dark indigo sky pinpricked with stars. The moon's glow reflected in the sea's ripples.

After several minutes, Lucas broached a subject he was eager to know. 'I imagine you meet lots of men here on the island.'

'Not many. No time.'

Lucas heard his cue. He always thought that moving fast was the best tactic. He stopped walking and turned her face toward his, looked into her big brown eyes, wide with anticipation, and gently kissed her on the mouth. She was a little taken aback but gave no resistance. She lingered, savouring the tenderness. He kissed her more passionately. She felt the heat of his tongue firing up her whole body, ending up in a pang of yearning in the hollow of her groin. The kiss continued. She would not be the first to draw back; she wanted it to go on forever. Finally, Lucas stopped and looked at her intently. Thanikarn looked around her, embarrassed. Thais didn't kiss in public, but fortunately they were alone.

'It's late. You have to work tomorrow. We should go.'

She wondered if he was somehow disappointed, but he gently took her hand, and they headed back in silence.

As they rode back to the hotel, the streets had lost their former buzz. Some late-night DJ music continued to blare out of half-empty bars with a few straggling customers, but most business had tapered off. Arriving at the hotel, Lucas hopped off the bike and squeezed her hand. 'Can we see each other tomorrow night?'

'We can,' she said softly, feeling reassured.

'Same time?'

She answered with a nod and rode away without looking back.

As Thanikarn approached her flat, her thoughts were in a tangle. She tried to sort them out one by one. He was too young. She was too old. She'd been alone for a very long time. She always said no. This time she let herself go. Why now? Why him?

5

After a restless night of streaming dreams, Thanikarn woke at sunrise; the memory of that moonlight kiss kept her from falling back to sleep. Too restless to stay in bed, she decided to get up and go through all her clothes. She threw aside the stained T-shirt, another couple of misshapen and faded tops, some torn pants, old, ugly underwear and a never-worn skirt and stuffed them all into a plastic bag. It was time to make space. She put on some cute, knee-length, red pants and a light-blue cotton top with short sleeves and dug through a little box of hair bands, clips and barrettes. She found a tortoiseshell comb with rhinestones she seldom wore and used it to bind her glossy dark hair.

Thanikarn arrived at the massage stand earlier than usual, singing out a good morning to Rinalda, who took notice of her young colleague's unusually neat attire.

'Manee told me about last night,' she finally said with a suppressed smile,

'Told you what?' Thanikarn asked, sounding surprised.

'So, now you go out on a date with young customers?'

'Not a date. We just went out. He wanted to see the island nightlife,' she said, a little miffed that Manee spoke to Rinalda.

Rinalda tilted her head toward the terrace and said, 'Look over there.' Thanikarn turned her head around to see Lucas's family arriving for another late-morning breakfast. Lucas looked as if he had just rolled out of bed, hair uncombed and wearing a wrinkled shirt. He saw her immediately and held up a hand, hailing a good morning. Thanikarn strained a smile, blushed, and turned around again, looking troubled.

'Be careful, Thanikarn,' Rinalda said. 'You could fall in love with such a handsome young man.'

Thanikarn answered by shaking her head, chasing away such a silly thought. Rinalda knew as well as she did that those kinds of romances never went anywhere. The only opportunities Thai masseuses usually had were with men decades older, not a decade younger.

Thanikarn worked through the usual hot April day, and despite the sea breeze, her sleepless night was getting the best of her. If only she could lie down and take a nap ... but no time, too many customers. With too little energy to do anything else, tourists had no better idea than to get a massage.

As Thanikarn was finishing up her last client for the day, Lucas's mother arrived. Rinalda wasn't busy and invited her to lie down on her mat. While Rinalda's deft hands began pressing into her fair-skinned back, Thanikarn observed Lucas's mother out of the corner of her eye. She was in good shape for someone her age, a woman who probably had everything a woman wanted: a husband with money, a house in Paris, vacations, pretty clothes, a happy family ... a smooth, rolling ball of a life Thanikarn would never know.

Lucas was going to be gone all day. He had called Ben and arranged to meet him at his place for lunch, an address he'd jotted down the night before. Before leaving for Lamai Beach at the southern end of the island, he let Thanikarn know where he was going. She acknowledged with a smile, secretly touched that he bothered to let her know.

Travelling down to see Ben took longer than Lucas expected. It was the same street he'd taken with his parents two days earlier, and Thanikarn the night before, a busy road that circled the whole island, but it was quite a trek to Lamai. The rumbling songthaew he was riding got stuck in midday congestion. With so much daily circulation and no stoplights or police control, it didn't take much to block traffic for miles, especially during the tourist seasons.

Ben had told Lucas to keep his eyes open for a small tourist shop called Books and Things, right across the street from a Tesco. Ben's store blended in with similar shops along the peripheral road, but inside this one, along with a mix of souvenirs, local craftwork, beachwear, sunglasses and flip-flops, it had the added feature of a section in the back that functioned as a small library, lending and selling secondhand books in English. There were even a couple of old leather armchairs where people could sit and read for as long as they liked. Sometimes, Ben explained, when tourists came in to buy the ubiquitous island accessories and souvenirs, those who were bored or tired would peruse the book-lined walls, sit and rest their feet.

Soon after Lucas arrived, he and Ben went out to order a

takeout lunch next door and brought their plastic boxes of fresh-cooked pad Thai back to the pleasantly air-conditioned reading corner. Ben told Lucas how he had set up an unofficial partnership with a Thai musician, Kawin, a former drummer in their band. Kawin had given up his musical aspirations for a more practical future, taking over his older cousin's shop in Lamai. It was Ben's idea to turn part of the store into a corner bookshop. Even though there was almost no market for used books, his little shop earned a local reputation with expat islanders who made exchanges, turning his little enterprise into a library. Sometimes tourists would contribute too, unloading unwanted weight before returning home. And from time to time, he'd even sell a book or two.

While they were eating their noodle dish and chatting about musical references, Ben excused himself to help a couple of tourists pick out some sunglasses. Meanwhile, Lucas browsed through the bookshelf, tilting his head sideways to read the titles.

'I noticed lots of books on finance,' he told Ben when he'd finished with the tourists. 'Not exactly recreational reading.'

'Yeah, they were mine. I thought I might as well stick them in with the rest of the books. I was never going to read them again.'

'You were in finance?' Lucas asked with surprise.

'I *studied* finance. It was supposed to be my future.'

'That's quite a transition – from Wall Street to Koh Samui.'

Ben laughed. 'Sure was. But no regrets.' Getting up, he asked, 'Want a beer? I have some bottles in the fridge.'

'Yeah, I'd love one.' Ben headed to a back room and came out with two bottles of Tiger. 'You're wondering why?'

Lucas nodded, then added casually, 'Unless you don't feel like talking about it.'

'I don't mind.'

Ben took a sip of his beer. Lucas did likewise. There was a short pause, and then Ben spoke casually; this was a story he'd told before, and he wanted to get it over with quickly.

'I was born and raised in London, but then my family moved to Singapore when I was about fourteen. My dad was in finance. Well, actually, he started off studying philosophy and psychology, but then got recruited by the World Bank. They were looking for fresh creative thinkers. He worked his way up.' He drew a sharp angle in the air to show that he went up sharply. 'We used to come here on vacations, but even here, my dad never really relaxed. He was always on the phone, always all stressed out. He expected me to follow the same path, maybe get me set up at the World Bank. I went to all the best schools, got into Harvard Business School. Just before my final year at graduate school, I came here to meet my mom and sister for our annual summer vacation. I thought I'd stay on a bit longer and study for my last year's exams. It was quite a luxury, studying on the beach under a parasol. My dad couldn't come that summer, too many last-minute problems. A week after we arrived, he had a stroke and died.'

'I'm sorry,' Lucas said.

'Me too. Worked like shit all his life, made a lot of money and died young. I decided right then, I didn't want to go there. I didn't want to do that.'

Lucas studied him. He felt a kinship in his distaste for material success. 'Well, I guess if you changed your mind, you could always go back.'

'What for?' He gave a little laugh and took a big swig of beer. 'Rich people come here to find paradise. I live in paradise. I'm good here, bro!'

Lucas had nothing to add; it was all too familiar. His own father was like Ben's, a workaholic obsessed with earning money. It wasn't out of greed; he wasn't a greedy guy. But he was paranoid, always afraid of an economic downturn, or some world crisis, and he had to provide for the security of his family. Whatever he earned and despite all they had, it was never enough.

Like most musicians, who were ready to sacrifice commercial success to do what they really liked, Lucas just wanted to make enough to live off his music. His mother always said real success was being able to make a living doing what you loved, and he loved music.

* * *

Since Thanikarn had arrived early and worked nonstop, she'd earned enough to pay her day's rent and felt no guilt in being the first to leave. She wanted to be sure she had time to visit with her grandmother before going out for the evening. It had been two distracting days since she'd seen Preeda and Uncle Trin.

Thanikarn's former home was near Mae Nam, about a twenty-minute drive from the Golden Gecko. The old wooden house they'd built was two miles inland in the middle of a coconut forest. Thanikarn drove up the dirt road, avoiding wide holes, loose stones, and yapping stray dogs chasing her scooter, and finally stopped in front of a pale-pink stucco house suspended on top of four corner pillars of stacked concrete bricks. She didn't see Trin's bicycle when she arrived and figured he must still be at the market.

On her way in, Thanikarn pulled a bottle of strawberry Fanta from her purse, popped off the cap, stuck in a straw, and placed it on their *saan phra phuum*, the family spirit house. The shoulder-high structure was painted white with gold trim and, like many traditional Thai alters, decorated with an orange-flowered strand of *phuang malai* and little ceramic figurines, one being a miniature zebra she'd placed there in honour of her mother many years ago. Preeda used to keep their spirit house garnished with fresh fruit and plastic cups filled with juice or water, but for the last year or so, the job had been relegated to Trin, who tended to forget his weekly task.

Thanikarn tried to drop in to see Preeda every day. Even though her grandmother didn't live alone, she was still a great worry to her. Knowing that her uncle Trin lived with Preeda was both a comfort and a source of guilt. According to Thai customs, it was her duty to take care of the family, a duty she only half-filled, bringing home the better part of her pay but leaving Trin to do the rest.

Trin was a kind man and far from stupid, but all his thoughts stayed locked up in his head, and whenever he tried to have a conversation, the words and phrases came out disconnected. If Thanikarn believed in reincarnation, which she didn't, Trin would have been a reborn old sage. Her mother's brother had always lived alone and friendless in a little cabin growing vegetables and raising chickens, but when Thanikarn's father died, he moved in with Preeda, something he had probably been longing to do. Thanikarn was a little reluctant to have given up her room, which no one obliged her to do, but with so many woeful memories as resistant as the weathered furniture, she selflessly moved out.

'Yai?' she called as she came through the door. Her grandmother was sitting in an old wicker armchair by the window, fanning away the fatigue of a long, hot day. Thanikarn gave her a tender kiss on the forehead and proudly handed her a small plastic bag. 'Caramels, from England.' She said, 'My last client gave them to me.'

'Candy? For me?' Her grandmother asked, looking up at her with a warm smile. Preeda opened the bag like a curious child and pulled out a decoratively wrapped caramel that she immediately unwrapped and popped into her mouth. She savoured it and, missing several teeth, chewed it with some difficulty.

'Careful. They're sticky,' Thanikarn said as she headed toward the water cooler. She filled a large glass and took it back to her grandmother. 'Such a hot day. You need to drink more water.'

Thanikarn waited patiently as her grandmother concentrated on rolling the caramel around in her mouth, savouring the buttery sweetness. When Preeda finally finished her candy, she took the glass and lifted it up to her lips with two hands. Thanikarn sat down on the floor in front of her grandmother and gently took Preeda's swollen feet. She placed them on her lap and began to massage them tenderly.

'Has Trin been gone long?'

'I don't know, last time I saw him was at lunch. He made me

some *kuai tiao* with egg,' Preeda said, once she dutifully drank her glass of water. She remained silent, waiting for any conversation to come from her granddaughter. Preeda usually had little to say, except to talk about what she ate or what she saw on television.

'I'm going out tonight, so I can't stay too long,' Thanikarn said casually as she was massaging. She remembered her own mother doing the same thing for Preeda and never thought twice about carrying on the tradition.

'Trin will be home soon,' Preeda said. 'He's always back before dark. He is so good to me. He shops for me, feeds me, gives me my medicine.'

Thanikarn smiled. 'I know. You're lucky to have him,' she said. Her grandmother's constant reminder of Trin's devotion never failed to reawaken Thanikarn's guilty conscience.

While Thanikarn massaged Preeda's feet, her grandmother rambled on about a Thai soap opera she watched every afternoon, talking about the characters as if they were old friends. After twenty minutes, Preeda began nodding off. Thanikarn gently placed her feet on the floor, stood up and kissed her goodbye.

'Bye-bye, Yai; see you soon,' she said quietly. Eyes closed, Preeda responded with a tiny nod.

When she arrived home, Thanikarn showered and washed her hair. She never wore makeup, which would only drip and smear in the humid heat, but she did smooth on some moisturizing cream she'd bought at the supermarket to give her face a soft glow. She picked out the cleanest, newest clothes she could find. The best she could do was a sleeveless white cotton dress with lace trim, not too sexy ... but feminine.

She arrived in front of the hotel at exactly ten o'clock. Lucas was not there. She turned off the motor of her Yamaha and searched up and down the street, feeling conspicuous, all dressed up, waiting in front of a hotel. She looked down at her hands and picked nervously at her fingernails, worrying that perhaps he'd changed his mind. Then she heard running footsteps. Lucas arrived panting.

'Sorry,' he said and gave her a little kiss on the cheek. 'I forgot my wallet in my parents' room, and they weren't there. I had to wait for them to get back.' The truth was he was out of cash and had to wait to ask for a loan.

'That's okay,' she said. 'No hurry. We can make time,' though she wasn't sure what she meant by that. Then she flashed a wide smile, the only way she knew how to make up for her insufficient English.

6

'Where to?' Lucas asked as he hopped on the back of her bike.

'Like you want ... Drinking? Music? Dancing?'

'Yeah. All three. But you do the dancing.' He teased.

'We go find something.' She kicked her little scooter into gear, and they sped off on the same road as the night before.

As they approached a lively section near the centre of Chaweng, she slowed down, looking for a place to park. Thanikarn managed to slide her scooter into one of the last remaining spots in front of a place called Starz Cabaret. As soon as Lucas stepped off, he was immediately accosted by a beautiful woman in a long, ruby-red dress with slits and silver high heels that showed off her shapely calves. 'Wanna see a great show, handsome?' She was stunning: tall and slender, with a sculpted face, voluminous red lips, impeccably drawn-in eyebrows, and dark eyeliner accentuating her almond-shaped eyes. Her hair was swept up in a chignon held by a rhinestone clasp. She handed him a flyer and gave him a flirtatious kiss on the cheek. Lucas was only half-surprised. He was getting used to the assertive females strolling up and down Koh Samui's sidewalks.

Thanikarn sidled up to him, looking over his shoulder at the flyer. 'This is ladyboy show,' she said matter-of-factly.

'Ladyboy?' Lucas asked.

'You don't know ladyboy?'

He looked at her, thought a second, and realized he did. He'd often walked by cabarets in Pigalle, and though he'd never attended a drag show, he had a good idea of what they were like.

'Many tourists go see ladyboy shows. You like to try? It's free. Just pay for drinks.' Lucas looked toward the entry, where another attractive ladyboy was waving them in. 'If you like, we stay. You don't like, we go,' she added, seeing the temptation in his eyes.

With a shrug, he said, 'Sure, why not?'

When they walked into the club, it was already full of customers. Folding chairs were askew in front of a tiny stage as if they were expecting a crowd, but for now, most of the people were sitting at the bar or at some of the little round tables for two. Lucas looked around the room and spotted a free table on the side.

The stage décor consisted of a gold curtain as a backdrop and a couple of incongruous Grecian urns on each side of the platform. The scratchy sound system blared out the theme song from *Rocky*, and a couple of free-standing projectors with harsh spotlights lit up a trio of gaudily dressed ladyboys as they entered stage. While they waited for someone to take their order, Thanikarn studied Lucas, who was cringing in his seat, reacting to the crass music and observing the crowd slowly taking their seats to watch the show. After two minutes, he scrunched his nose as if he were suddenly put off by a bad smell. Thanikarn noticed.

'You don't like?' she asked, opening wide her big, brown eyes.

Lucas gave a little smile and cocked his head. 'This is not really my kind of thing,' he admitted.

'No problem,' Thanikarn said, already rising to her feet. They made a beeline for the exit. Lucas let out a satisfied sigh, and Thanikarn was secretly glad he didn't like the show.

'Where to now?' Lucas asked.

Taking a long breath, Thanikarn looked up and down the street, embarrassed by a lack of inspiration.

'Let's go there for a drink,' Lucas said, pointing across the road. He instinctively took Thanikarn's hand, and she trailed after him. They sat down at a table on the terrace with few customers and ordered a couple of beers. A gentle night breeze brushed a strand of hair across Thanikarn's face. Lucas reached over and gently tucked it behind her ear. Thanikarn smiled at him, embarrassed but pleased. He was so devastatingly handsome; such fair white skin and golden-blond hair, he seemed to glow even in the dimly lit night. She wanted to say something but couldn't find the right words. Her English got stuck somewhere between her brain and her mouth.

Right now, conversation was not on Lucas's mind. He would only be in Koh Samui for a week, and though he usually took things slowly when he met a girl he liked, there wasn't enough time for him to pass through all the stages of courtship. If anything were to happen between them, it would have to happen fast.

'You live far from here?'

'Not far. My house is near lake, close to hotel.'

'I'm a little hungry. We had a late lunch and skipped dinner.

How about you?'

'Me?' Her appetite depended more on her mood than her stomach, sneaking up at odd hours. Sometimes she forgot to eat; sometimes she was ravenous.

'Maybe a little hungry,' she said diplomatically.

'How about we get some takeout food and go back to your place to eat. I saw a night market on the way here.'

Thanikarn stared into his deep blue eyes looking back at her full of anticipation. She wasn't prepared for such a provocative proposition, and her heart began thumping in her chest.

Lucas realized his suggestion might have sounded too direct. 'But if you prefer, we could go to a restaurant. No problem.'

Thanikarn wasn't sure what to say. She didn't want to seem too submissive, but she didn't want to disappoint him either. She bit her lip while several seconds ticked by.

'Okay, we can go to my house.'

They headed north to a food market near the lake in Chaweng. As they strolled amid the various stalls, Thanikarn fought to hide her apprehension about inviting a man into her modest home. A first.

As usual, Lucas thought all the food looked fantastic. He was counting on her for suggestions, so Thanikarn led him to her favourite vendor. She pointed to a fresh-looking crisp salad topped with grilled beef.

'*Yam Nua* ... very good, but maybe too spicy for you,' she said.

'No, I love spicy.'

Thanikarn exchanged a few words with the haggard cook

behind the counter. Wiping the sweat from his brow, he looked at the blue-eyed blond next to Thanikarn and grumbled, 'Mai ped.' Lucas understood what he was saying; he didn't think the dish would be suitable for a farang's consumption. Lucas then pointed to some glossy grilled chicken on sticks. The vendor wrapped the satay kai up in paper along with a little packet of peanut sauce, deftly slid a big portion of the salad into a Styrofoam box, and put everything into a plastic bag. Lucas paid, and they wound their way through the crowd back to her scooter.

It was a quick ride to the dimly lit road leading to Thanikarn's flat, a pleasant contrast to the lights and noise of town. The only sound to be heard was a stray dog barking at every passer-by, as well as the distant deadened beat of disco music blasting out of a nightclub's speakers a couple of miles away. Thanikarn parked her scooter and locked it up for the evening. This was the first time she'd brought anyone to her home. How ironic that it was a young farang. She led him up the unkempt stairs to her door, and the starkness of her simple living conditions glared at her as they ventured in: the faded linoleum floor, the rude makeshift kitchen, the wobbling ventilator on the ceiling ... She worried that Lucas might find it stark and shabby.

Lucas saw there was nowhere to sit except for a little stool near the sink and the single mattress on the floor. Thanikarn took a couple of pillows and placed them on the edge of the mattress for them to sit on, hastily throwing a bundle of worn clothes in the corner to make space. He plopped down with a broad smile.

'I like your place,' he said spontaneously, 'It's ... cosy.'

She smiled at him. Either he was being kindly dishonest or

had low expectations. She took out a couple of plates and served up their dinner. He ate with such gusto that it gave her an appetite as well, and as they chomped away, Thanikarn was relieved not to have to talk. Beads of sweat began dripping from Lucas's forehead after biting into a couple of hot chilli peppers.

Thanikarn laughed. 'Spicy!'

'Yeah, very spicy ...'

She cleared away their empty plates, put them into the sink, and poured on some water, leaving the washing up for later. They had bought a couple of beers at Family Mart on their way to her flat, and they took a few sips in silence.

Lucas put his hand to his shoulder, squeezed a tight muscle near the back of his neck. 'I think my pillow at the hotel is too big. Stiff neck.' Was this a hint?

'I massage a little?' Thanikarn proposed. 'It's free.' She laughed.

'That would be great.' Lucas turned his back to her, and she gently massaged his shoulders. He moaned with pleasure.

'Anybody ever give you massages?'

'No time. Always busy with customers.'

'How about if I give you a massage? Sometimes I give my mom a little shoulder massage. She says I've got magic hands.'

Thanikarn didn't have time to give a reply. 'Your turn,' Lucas said as he turned her around. He began gently massaging her shoulders. Her whole body felt as if it was melting under the pressure of his strong supple hands. After a couple of minutes, his hands ventured around her chest and crept toward her breasts, gently caressing them. She tipped her head to the side, sinking into pure pleasure. He turned her head around and kissed her on the lips. He eased her down onto the bed; his caresses went down her body, her waist, hips, thighs and between her legs. He continued kissing her with a perfect balance of tenderness and desire that made her body tremble. She found herself pulling her dress off. He admired her small, firm breasts, her flat tummy and slender hips as he stroked her tawny, smooth skin. She was too excited to be self-conscious. Lucas pulled off his T-shirt and tore off his loose-fitting pants. He was stiff with excitement but took the precaution of slipping on a condom that he had dug out of the pocket of his pants.

Thanikarn drew him toward her, feeling his wiry muscles bursting with passionate energy. They were both breathing heavily. He continued caressing her body and quickly worked his hands in between her legs. With his nimble fingers, he caressed her like she'd never been caressed before, and he was driving her wild with pleasure. How could someone so young be so adept and sensitive to what pleased her. She was seized with spasms of ecstasy that made her feel like an erupting volcano, and she suddenly exploded as she heard herself screaming with a newfound pleasure. Her throat had become dry with desire, and she desperately wanted to feel Lucas inside of her. She pulled him toward her, feeling his taut body as he mounted her. Once he'd climaxed, they both collapsed, hot and sweaty. She kissed his mouth and cheeks, saying *thank you* over and over in her mind, but no words came from her lips. No words were needed, and they both silently sank into a deep sleep.

The next morning, a sliver strip of sun slipped through the

upper window, awakening Thanikarn. She was nestled up against Lucas, enclosed in his arms while he continued to sleep. She looked at him, blinking with incredulity, as if last night was some crazy dream, but it was all too real, and she felt a hungry pang of desire for more of the same.

She carefully pried herself out of his arms, trying not to wake him, and inched toward the edge of the bed. She felt a strong arm pulling her back down. 'No, don't go,' he said, half-asleep.

'I have to go work. Already late.'

'Okay. I'll let you go,' he said, 'but only if I can see you again tonight.'

She answered with a kiss on his cheek and stood up. She was naked.

Lucas looked at her slender silhouette illuminated by the morning sun. 'You're beautiful,' he said.

She wasn't used to compliments, at least not sincere ones. As she discreetly washed up in a corner shower with no curtain or door, Lucas gathered his clothes from the floor and slowly dressed. He was still only half-awake and took his time. He went to pee in an old toilet that flushed with a bucket of water.

They left her apartment hardly speaking a word, still inebriated from the passion of their first night together. As they rode back to the hotel, with Lucas's arms grasping her waist, a broad smile brightened Thanikarn's face as she thought about working through the day with the prospect of another wonderful night.

7

Lucas tapped lightly on the door of his hotel room and waited. He tapped again a little harder until he finally heard his brother's dragging footsteps. Arthur cracked the door open, squinting his eyes as the sunlight struck his face. With a reproachful glare, he grunted, 'What time is it?' The curtains were drawn, and it was dark inside the room.

'What time did you go to bed?' Lucas asked, pushing his way into the room.

'Not that late. I'm just really tired. I think I'm sick.'

'Maybe too much Game Boy,' Lucas teased.

'So, how'd it go?' Arthur asked.

'Okay ... Nice.' There was no need to say more between brothers.

'Are Mom and Dad around?'

'I don't know ... I just got up!' was the obvious reply.

'Well it *is* nearly eleven,' he said with big-brother authority and headed into the bathroom to throw some water on his face and comb his ruffled hair. He slipped into some shorts and a T-shirt and went out to find his parents.

They were comfortably installed in reclining chairs near

the pool. Jacques was reading a newspaper, and Caroline was absorbed in a book.

'Well, hello,' his mother said. 'Have a good evening?' she asked as she received a peck on the cheek from her son.

'Yeah, it was really nice.'

'I hope you're being careful,' she said with her eyes still glued to the book. This was not the first time he'd heard this.

'Of course I am.' Lucas said and went to give his father a greeting kiss.

And he was careful. Lucas always carried protection, just in case. The AIDS scare had spread to every part of the world and permeated every level of society, including the Parisian bourgeoisie. Beginning with his first sexual adventure at the age of fifteen, it had been tacitly understood that Lucas was expected to use a condom. There was an open understanding between Lucas and his parents that he was old enough to use his own judgment. Caroline and Jacques were progressive parents; his father had taken part in the famous French student revolution in 1968, and his mother was a former hippy from San Francisco, so it would be pure hypocrisy if either one of them was intolerant with Lucas experimenting with life.

'Don't forget we're leaving in a couple of hours to see the Big Buddha,' Jacques said.

Lucas had forgotten. 'What time do we get back?'

'I don't know, probably a few hours. But I also want to check out the driving range at the Santiburi Golf Course. We'll be back before dinnertime.'

As long as Lucas could do as he pleased in the evening, he was willing to go along with the family plans.

Lucas wandered over to the terrace restaurant thinking it was probably too late for breakfast and too early for lunch. Manee greeted him with a smile and an enchanting 'Good morning.' He sat down and asked for a coffee. All the girls working at the hotel seemed especially eager to serve him. He wondered if handsome young men were rare at the family hotel.

'Anything to eat?' Manee asked.

'If it's not a problem,' he said with a broad smile.

She came back in a few minutes with his coffee, a basket of breakfast rolls, butter, jam and a plate of fresh fruit. Apparently, Manee had kept aside some breakfast. Lucas dug in, unconscious of the special treatment. All he was aware of was how exceptionally charming Thai women could be.

* * *

Thanikarn was steeped in reverie as she worked at the stand. Sawitti and Rinalda chatted away, sneaking a glance toward her from time to time. They both noticed that she was less talkative than usual. As she worked away, their lilting voices, like everything else around her, drifted in and out of her dreamy mind, still intoxicated from her passionate night. Out of the corner of her eye, she saw Lucas eating his breakfast on the terrace. Her spontaneous smile did not go unnoticed by her co-workers.

'Your Paris boy coming for a massage today?' Sawitti asked teasingly. Thanikarn paid no attention to her. Rinalda remained silent, her eyebrows twisted into a sceptical tilt. She was wise enough to know that Thanikarn's little fling would lead to nothing.

Rinalda had seen too many disappointing affairs between young Thai women and foreign suitors. A Western man wants sex; an Asian woman wants security. He falls in love with her sweet beauty and faithful affection, and she falls in love with a newfound hope of a comfortable future. But then Thai tradition comes into conflict with what Westerners consider more important: freedom and independence. She has a family to honour, and when he discovers the Thai priority of *naam-jai*, a general obligation to return acts of generosity, not the least being a girl's duty to care for her parents, everything falls apart. Her lover expects he'll replace his girlfriend's family, not adopt it.

But, Rinalda thought, Thanikarn's handsome suitor was just a boy. Surely, she was level-headed enough to know not to expect much.

Lunchtime came and went quickly, and by early afternoon, as she had completely forgotten to eat breakfast, Thanikarn's tummy was growling. On her first little break of the day, she snuck into the kitchen to see if Amnat had anything left in one of his big pots.

'Ah, Karn,' he said as he was clearing up, 'you never have any more time to come see your friend Amnat. Maybe you forget me?'

'I could never forget you,' she said, lifting a lid up off a big, black pot on the stove.

'Oh, so that's why you come. It's for my food, not me,' he teased.

He dished up a bowl of *tom yam kung*, hot and sour soup with shrimps. She thanked him with her wide smile and sat down on a kitchen stool to eat while Amnat continued cleaning up.

Amnat reminded Thanikarn of her father: calm, deliberate, good-humoured and always available if she wanted to say what was on her mind.

'You know, Amnat, sometimes I wonder what I'm doing with my life. I don't know where it's going,' she said pensively.

'Hmm, serious talk for a lunch break,' Amnat mused. 'What's on your mind, Karn?'

'Would you say I was pretty, Amnat?' she asked, unabashed.

'No,' he said with his back to her as he washed a huge pot. She blinked away the hurt. He turned around and smiled. 'I think you are beautiful!'

Thanikarn blushed and sheepishly lowered her eyes, slurping up some more soup. After a few moments of silence except for the clanking pots, she asked reflectively, 'Would you say I was smart?'

'Why are you worried about being smart?'

'That is a man's answer,' she quipped.

'You ask me a woman's questions; I give you a man's answer.'

Thanikarn laughed, at herself more than Amnat.

'So, what does pretty or smart have to do with figuring out your life?'

'Most women my age have a husband. They have a family. Children.'

'Just live your life. You don't have to know where it's going,' he said, as if it was too obvious to discuss.

'Some people do – lots of people do. They plan their lives, build careers, have goals,' she said, feeling as if she was more reasonable than her friend.

'So, instead of thinking about what you have, you think

about what you don't have. That's a good way to make yourself miserable,' he said with no intention of mocking her.

Amnat the moralist. He sounded like her father many years ago, after her mother died. The problem was that Thanikarn had never been satisfied with who she was. And it was getting worse as she got older. She was conscious of the dissimilarities that stretched between her and the people she worked for. They had accomplished something: they had careers, families, freedom to travel.

Amnat noticed the dark frown on her face. 'Karn?'

'I know, Amnat,' she said, her face brightening once again. 'You're right,' she said. She had to accept her fate and chase away envy.

Heading back to the massage stand, she crossed paths with Lucas's parents. 'Good morning,' she said cheerfully with her naturally wide smile. They returned the greeting. It was only after they passed that Thanikarn's face clouded with worry. Did they know that she and their son had spent the night together? If they did, what did they think of her?

Returning to her work stand, Thanikarn's eyes widened with pleasure when she saw that Lucas was waiting for her.

'Hey. Hi.' He grinned, resisting the urge to give her a kiss. 'I'm going to spend the day with my family, to see the Big Buddha and Fisherman's Wharf, but I'll be back this evening. How about dinner?'

Thanikarn knew that both Rinalda and Sawitti were watching her. 'What time you like I come get you?' she asked quietly.

'Eight o'clock okay? I'll take you to a restaurant.'

She nodded. That was a nice gesture; one that meant it wasn't just about sex.

Eight o'clock would mean not spending much time with her grandmother, but she would make up for it later. Her grandmother and uncle would be there next week. Not Lucas.

She nodded. That was fine. Better one hour or so, but it was in just about...

Lucas could would rather not spending much time with his grand memai but she could not hope for reace. For grandmother and uncle would be there aged on ..., Not Lucas.

8

Lucas wasn't particularly keen on seeing the Big Buddha. He'd already visited so many temples in Asia; one more would have no cultural impact. But this temple, being touted as a tourist must-see, was a good excuse for his parents to visit another part of the island. The forty-foot golden idol was impressive, and it made for some fun family photos, but if the intention was to inspire a feeling of spirituality, Lucas found it missed the goal; he thought it looked more like a Jeff Koons sculpture than a religious symbol. Before heading up the long flight of white stairs gleaming in the sunlight, they wandered past dozens of tourist shops selling the typical island wares. It never ceased to amaze Lucas how young souvenir vendors were able to say, 'look here', 'beautiful' and 'very cheap' in every language on earth. He observed the multicultural tourists, who as usual, spent more time taking photos of the statue than looking at it. Lucas's father, falling in line, insisted that Lucas and his brother or mother turn around every three minutes for yet another snapshot.

Lucas was trying to take in the magic and get something positive out of the visit. He experimented with the ancient chimes that lined the open corridors on each side of the Buddha, but his thoughts were constantly drawn back to Thanikarn. Even though he appreciated his family's efforts, he would have preferred being on his own. He wished he could have rented a scooter, but his father said it was out of the question – too dangerous. Even on foot they had a hard time remembering that driving in Thailand was on the left side.

* * *

Thanikarn thought about the Big Buddha as she massaged a red-faced German man. She had ridden past the towering golden statue many times on her little scooter. She remembered that it was on the way to the last place her father worked. He sometimes stopped at the temple on his way home from the construction site, not to pray but to have a drink with a friend who ran a little food stand nearby.

Her father had been working all year on a series of high-class villas overlooking Sunset Beach under the direction of a slick promoter in Bangkok. He oversaw the construction team, a responsible position he was proud of. It was painfully ironic that he only went up once on the roof to check things out where his men worked daily, but he was the one to have a fatal accident.

In a way, she missed her father more than her mother. He was inept at guiding her through puberty, but he did succeed in giving her courage and ambition. He hoped she would become a modern woman, learn English, travel, have a job that made her feel proud of herself. Thanikarn regretted that she never asked him about her grandfather's odd prediction about her being childless. She still wondered if he knew something about her health, such as some strange problem she had inherited. Or was he just being cynical?

What she did know was that her periods stopped nearly as soon as they started, which she considered more of a convenience than a problem. The few times she had sex with men – a high school flirt, a young man she met at night school, a farang Sawitti introduced her to over a year ago, each time without protection – left her convinced that her grandfather was probably right – she would never be able to have a child.

The day dragged on for Thanikarn, with nothing novel to distract her from the monotony of work. She tried to concentrate but was less in tune to her clients than usual and massaged mechanically, like a mindless wind-up doll, while she replayed the previous night in her head. Thanikarn was jolted from her reverie by Sawitti.

'What are you doing for Songkran, Karn? Are you going to take the day off?'

Thanikarn had nothing special planned for the Thai New Year, which was the very next day. Like every good Thai, she usually spent most of the day with her family and, if invited, took a little time to go out in the evening for some music with friends. The idea flashed through her mind that this holiday would be a perfect reason to take a full day off, and she wondered if Lucas had any plans.

* * *

Lucas and his family returned to the Golden Gecko right after they watched the sun melting into the sea's horizon near Mae

Nam. He was surprised to see Thanikarn still working. She had decided to take on one last client. He trotted over to see her.

'You're working late,' he said.

She acknowledged with a smile, and she continued massaging. 'Still okay for dinner?'

She nodded.

'See you then,' Lucas said, holding up eight fingers and a gesture to say that he'd be waiting for her in front of the hotel.

* * *

Lucas didn't have to wait for Thanikarn that evening. She came rolling up on her scooter the moment he arrived. He hopped on the back of her bike like the night before, and they quickly took off toward Chaweng Beach. As they rode along in the overcharged traffic, Lucas cried out to be heard over the whirring motor of her scooter, 'You know someplace nice we can go to?'

'Yes, many places. What kind of place you like?' she answered.

'Thai food. Somewhere quiet where we can sit by ourselves and talk.' After a moment, he added, 'My treat. I'm inviting you, so choose wherever you like.' He was feeling he owed it to her. She had been working hard all day while he was just lolling around.

After a ten-minute ride skirting around cars and trucks, Thanikarn pulled up in front of a restaurant called Wild Orchid Café. It looked nice, Lucas thought. Thanikarn wanted to make sure that she wasn't going to put him in an embarrassing situation and asked the host to show them a menu. 'This okay?' she asked.

'Yes, looks fine,' he said, paying little attention to what he was shown. The prices in Thailand were so much cheaper than in Paris, even upscale restaurants seemed inexpensive.

He had no idea how special it made her feel. She seldom ate out at formal restaurants where she was seated and served. He held Thanikarn's hand as they were led to a cosy beachside table on the terrace. She looked around the room. There were no other mixed couples that she could see, and she wondered if anyone would notice that she was with a much younger man. Lucas, to her relief, was oblivious and since no heads turned, Thanikarn comforted herself with the idea that she looked very young for her age. In any case, Thai women who went out with farangs were as common as coconuts.

After a quick dinner of *tom yam kung* and *gang panang* beef curry, they wandered over to the Jazz Bar, run by an expat Frenchman, quite a flamboyant character who could have passed for a circus ringmaster. His unusually decorated dive was written up in all the guidebooks. Thanikarn had heard that it had good music and atmosphere. The club was crowded, like most of the clubs on the main street in Chaweng.

'More people out tonight,' Thanikarn explained. 'Tomorrow is Thai New Year's. Songkran.'

'I heard about Songkran. Ben told me it was a lot of fun, people running around throwing water on each other. He invited me down to his place.'

She was disappointed to hear he already had plans. She thought a moment then timidly dropped a hint. 'Tomorrow, maybe I don't work. Take day off.'

'That would be great. You could come with me. It would

be more fun with you … I'll call Ben tomorrow, and we'll work something out.'

She thought a moment. She had to go see her grandmother first; not visiting her would feel a like a betrayal. Songkran wasn't just for having fun, it was also the day of the elderly. But surely she could still find time to do so. She gave a nod. 'Okay.'

Lucas was becoming impatient with the noise, the smoke, the raucous crowd and the impossibility of intimacy. Downing his beer, he suggested they head back to Thanikarn's apartment. This was what she had expected, even, she realized, had hoped he would propose.

Once they arrived, their inhibitions vanished; they kicked off their shoes and Lucas began kissing Thanikarn. He pulled her down toward the bed and proceeded to undress her, slowly, caressing her creamy-brown skin and covering her body with kisses. He held his excitement at bay, taking time to allow her arousal to mount. Thanikarn wanted him like she had never wanted anyone. Lucas concentrated on giving her pleasure, something that she had never received from any of the men she knew before, and she felt her entire body trembling with desire. His body was firm and strong with passion, and as he pressed his fair skin against hers, she threw her arms around him, tossed her head back, and pulled him toward her in ardent surrender. As before, Lucas took the time to make sure she climaxed before he consummated his own pleasure. Once he did, they both collapsed. He rolled over and whispered, 'You're wonderful.' An odd feeling wavered in her mind, a feeling she didn't recognize. Maybe she was in love.

9

Waking up the next morning, Thanikarn moved slowly. She swept her long hair into a chignon, attaching it deftly with a tortoiseshell comb, and went to check herself in the little cracked mirror hanging on the wall next to the shower. Her cheeks were a radiant pink, her eyes glistened, and she smiled at the pretty girl looking back at her. Across the room, Lucas was still sleeping soundly. She watched him for a moment, taking a picture with her mind. She never wanted to forget him. This was probably the nearest she would ever come to a true romance, and it was one she knew wouldn't last.

Lucas opened his eyes slowly, still drugged with early-morning dreams. He hoisted himself up onto his elbows, looked at Thanikarn across the room, and gestured for her to come to him. She obeyed with a smile, dropped down on the bed, and began kissing him again.

'I need to take you back to the hotel,' she said. 'Your family maybe worry.'

'No, it's okay. I told them I might stay out late. And that I planned to go see Ben for the Songkran.' After another kiss on her inviting lips, he added, 'They're doing their own thing today. I just have to go back to the hotel and change.'

'Don't wear good clothes. You get very wet today. Everybody throw water everywhere. What time you meet your friend Ben?' Thanikarn asked, hoping it wouldn't be too early.

'He said around lunchtime.'

'I come pick you up at twelve thirty?' she ventured.

'Yeah, no problem. Ben's not a morning person.'

That was a relief. She wanted to get Lucas back to the hotel soon so that she'd have time to visit her grandmother and Trin. 'You hungry?' she asked cheerfully.

'A little hungry,' he said as he slipped on his boxer shorts. She put some sweet rolls on a plate that he recognized from the hotel.

'I take these for you last night,' she said. Thanikarn never ate breakfast at home. She usually stopped at the market on her way to work to buy some soya milk and *patongko*, deep-fried dough sticks, but she'd anticipated waking up with Lucas. She poured them some bottled water. 'Sorry, I have no refrigerator, not cold.'

'No problem,' Lucas said, guzzling down a glassful. She watched him eat his *patongko*, a satisfied smile on her face. It felt so strange, seeing a lover first thing in the morning.

As soon as Thanikarn dropped Lucas off at the hotel, she headed off to her parents' old house, stopping by the food market on her way to get some *larb gai*, a special New Year's chicken dish, to offer Preeda and Trin for lunch. Thanikarn would still have a couple of days to visit the temple and give alms to the monks, a tradition she carried on in honour of her mother, who never missed the occasion to go to the temple to make an offering, important for a good start to the new year. Like most Buddhists,

Thanikarn's mother went to the temple to pray, offer food to the monks, and bathe the Buddha statues with holy water.

Preeda's face lit up when she saw her granddaughter walk in. Thanikarn helped her grandmother and Trin clean up the house, as was the custom for New Year's, and when they'd finished, she sat Preeda down in her old chair by the window to bless her with makeshift holy water, which was really just fresh water scented with rose petals. She reverently poured some of the water over Preeda's hands and feet, massaging them tenderly for a few minutes.

'Your mother did this for me,' Preeda said. Thanikarn looked up at her with an acknowledging smile. She knew that Preeda would say that.

'And now it's me,' she said. When she finished, she got up and gave her grandmother a kiss on the forehead.

'I'm sorry, but I won't be staying to eat lunch with you today. Friends are waiting for me to go out for the water festivities.'

'If I were fifty years younger, I would go with you,' Preeda answered with a complicit twinkle in her eyes. She seemed to be in a particularly good mood.

Thanikarn was back at the hotel shortly before twelve and sat waiting on her scooter across the street. She wanted to avoid seeing Philippe and her friends, not because she didn't have the right to take the day off. She wanted to keep her outing with Lucas private.

Lucas came jogging out with a joyous 'Let's go', and they took off for Ben's shop at top speed, which was not all that fast on Thanikarn's aging pink scooter. With Lucas's arms wrapped around her waist, they weaved in and out of traffic, trying to avoid unavoidable splashes of water. Some people were armed with squirt guns, others threw cups or even casserole dishes of water that they dipped out of huge barrels. Some who worked in roadside shops had even hooked up water hoses. Songkran was especially enjoyable for the children, who squealed with glee since they had full permission to attack any passer-by.

Rolling up to Ben's shop, they saw him loading his partner's dilapidated pickup truck with buckets of water. He shouted out a zestful hello and greeted the two of them with a hearty bear hug. They jumped into the back of the truck, and Ben drove. He had turned up the speaker on the truck radio and played a CD of '70s rock songs, including the Doors and the Rolling Stones. It blared out as they meandered down the street. Lucas and Thanikarn playfully threw out bowlfuls of water, spewing it indifferently onto any hapless pedestrian. Their mischief was duly reciprocated. Some Koh Samui locals took the Songkran celebration to its silliest limit, and the traditional touch of talc on the cheek sometimes became fistfuls of powder thrown in wild abandon. After an hour of amusement, they were not only drenched but mired in chalky muck.

They all headed back to Ben's shop to get cleaned off. Giggling like children, they watered each other down with a garden hose in Ben's blue-walled courtyard behind the boutique. Both Lucas and Ben stripped down to their shorts, while Thanikarn watered herself down in her shirt and shorts. She looked down to see that her clinging wet T-shirt was a bit too revealing and tried to loosen it, pulling it away from her body. She hoped the sun would do the work of drying it off quickly. Ben disappeared inside, and Lucas and Thanikarn collapsed with fatigue onto an old, warped bench. Lucas suddenly grabbed her and smacked a big kiss on her full, round lips. He found her so irresistibly enticing with her bedraggled wet hair and clothes.

'You're beautiful!' he said. She smiled sheepishly, not used to compliments.

'I thought you two could use a cold drink,' Ben said, coming out with some bottled beers, and the *Herald Tribune* tucked under his arm.

'Somebody left this on the counter,' he said as he sat down on a paint-chipped metal stool. He unfolded the newspaper.

'Anything exciting?' Lucas asked.

'The usual. I try to avoid knowing what's going on around the world. It just gets me riled up.'

He held up a front page for him to see. It announced the dire statistics of civilian casualties in the bombing of Serbia, along with an accompanying photo. Lucas began lamenting the US interventions. He was an estranged American citizen, but it didn't keep him from criticizing America's foreign politics. Ben chipped in, saying everything was controlled by private financial interests, even the top dogs in politics, aka presidents and prime ministers. They went on to discuss all that was wrong with the world, from economics to ecology. Thanikarn listened, her eyes wide with curiosity, even though she understood only half of what they were talking about. She knew little about politics, foreign affairs or international economics. The boys' tirade lasted a good ten minutes before they realized they must be boring the hell out of Thanikarn as well as putting a damper on the New Year celebrative mood.

'So, what's the solution?' Ben queried rhetorically, referring to the world's bleak condition. Then, finishing up his beer and rising to his feet, he added, 'Whatever it is, we're not going to figure it out today.'

Lucas flashed a sympathetic smile to Thanikarn, and she smiled back but continued to sit motionless, like a cat patiently awaiting some attention. There was an awkward silence, Lucas wondering what to do next and Thanikarn waiting for his lead.

Ben must have sensed they might have wanted some time alone. 'Have you been out to the Hin Ta and the Hin Yai yet?'

'Hin Ta and Hin Yai?' Lucas repeated. 'Sounds like something to drink …'

'We can go there by scooter. Very famous on island,' Thanikarn said and then realized her proposition excluded Ben from coming with them. She started to speak again, but Ben cut her off.

'It's a beautiful spot – you'll love it. But better get going now, before it gets dark.' Thanikarn gave him a grateful smile.

'Sure, whatever it is, I'm up for it.' Lucas said.

The afternoon sun had practically dried them off, and they were ready to move on. Lucas and Thanikarn thanked Ben for the afternoon outing and gave him a hug goodbye. They hopped onto her scooter and headed south to the famous rock formations Hin Ta and Hin Yai.

The rushing wind felt cool on their still slightly damp clothes, so Lucas wrapped his arms tighter than usual around Thanikarn's waist. The warmth of his body made her feel all soft inside as she rode slowly down the side of the road. Fortunately, they crossed fewer locals wishing Songkran cheer on their way and managed to stay dry all the way down to the site.

Thanikarn turned left off the main route where a sign overhanging indicated Hin Ta and Hin Yai, and they motored down a narrow road toward the sea. Once parked, they wound their way through the souvenir shops and tourists, and Thanikarn led Lucas toward a mound of rock formations jutting into the sea. Most everyone was snapping photos of some of the huge rounded rocks. Thanikarn hadn't yet told Lucas anything about them and waited for him to figure out why. They stopped in front of a wooden post with a description of the well-known site and the myth explaining the origin of the rocks.

'Wow,' Lucas said with a little laugh. 'Now I get it.'

Perched on the tip of a cluster of boulders, on the cusp of the cape, Hin Ta, which meant 'Grandfather's Stone', pointed proudly toward the sky. It unmistakably resembled an erect male penis. Hin Yai, 'Grandmother's Stone', lay splayed out about forty meters away, a smooth, wave-washed cleft, easily comparable to a woman's sex.

'People always come take pictures,' Thanikarn said.

Lucas shook his head slowly, not so much because of the rocks, which needed a stretch of the imagination, but because of the numerous tourists machine-gunning them with their cameras.

'There is a story,' Thanikarn said. 'They say it is spirits of wind and water that make the rocks like this. Took many, many years. The wind made Hin Ta, and the water made Hin Yai. Many people come from Japan, Taiwan, and China. They call it feng shui.' Then she added with her youthful chuckle. 'Some come here to ask help for making babies.'

'Yeah, I already heard a lot about feng shui. Wind and water. But this is different, if they come to pray to your fertility spirits.'

'Fertility spirits,' Thanikarn repeated with a nod, as if committing the word to memory. Her grandfather's dire prediction flashed through her mind.

'You have a lot of spiritual beliefs. Like Songkran, and water washing away misfortune and sickness,' he said. 'I'm not knocking it. I think it's poetic.'

'Poetic?' she asked, with a tilt of the head. Though she wasn't familiar with much poetry, it sounded positive.

After a few minutes of exploring the rock site, manoeuvring themselves gingerly, which sometimes necessitated getting on all fours, they found a quiet spot to sit and watch the changing sky as the sun went down behind them. Lucas wrapped his arms around Thanikarn's shoulders, and she rested her head on his chest.

'We have to make a wish,' he said. 'Ever since I was little, whenever we watched the sun set below the horizon, we would stop and make a wish.'

'But here we can't see the sun go down,' Thanikarn said with disappointment.

'Doesn't matter – we can still make a wish,' Lucas said.

'I tell you my wish?' Thanikarn asked.

'No, you keep it a secret. Like when you blow out the candles on a birthday cake.' Then he added reflectively, 'Maybe you don't do that in Thailand.' She looked at him blankly, then acquiesced with a smile and nod, as if she knew what he was talking about.

It wasn't her place to ask questions, and she liked the idea of keeping her wish a secret.

They sat silently as the light faded, each making their own private request. After a few minutes, Lucas grabbed Thanikarn and gave her a long, romantic kiss.

'We better go,' he said reluctantly, 'I promised my parents I'd have dinner with them.'

Thanikarn stood up. 'Then we go. Takes maybe one hour to go back. Lots of traffic today.' Respecting the wishes of parents, *katanjoo*, was unquestionable.

After the long and circuitous ride back, dodging more attacks from well-wishers, she dropped him off in front of the hotel, as night was blanketing the sky. They agreed that she would pick him up again around ten thirty. Their mutual desire to sleep together had become a given.

* * *

That evening, Jacques had booked a table at their hotel. Every night, weather permitting, the Golden Gecko served a meal on the beach, where they set up gas-burning lamps and a half-dozen tables covered with red linen tablecloths, wineglasses and porcelain plates. It was the ultimate island dining experience: Western elegance while digging your feet into the sand under the table and enjoying fresh, grilled seafood.

During the meal, Caroline and Jacques seemed distant, both immersed in their respective thoughts. Lucas and his brother surmised that they probably got in some stupid argument during the day and were avoiding further confrontation. Lucas recounted his afternoon, the water fights, riding in the truck, and Ben's hospitality. By the time he finished describing the rock formations, he had everyone at the table laughing and his parents on speaking terms.

When they had finished dinner, Jacques asked, 'Going out again?'

'Yeah, have to take advantage. We only have two more nights.'

Jacques and Caroline exchanged looks, which Lucas read as worry.

'What?' Lucas asked defensively, and before they could say anything more, 'Don't worry – I'm being careful.'

'I hope so. I'm sorry to bring this up, but I hope your friend Thanikarn isn't looking for something more than a good time,' his mother muttered. She was a little tipsy.

'What does that mean?' he asked.

'Well, I've heard stories about Thai women getting foreigners in a tight spot.'

Lucas eyes sharpened with indignation. 'She's not like that! She's a really nice girl. She works hard, she's trying to make a good life for herself and she just wants to go out and have a little fun for a change. Anything wrong with that?'

'Of course not,' Jacques said. 'But it's normal that your mother and I are a little worried about you.'

'I trust your judgment, Lucas. I just don't want anyone to get hurt,' Caroline said with tearful eyes. She'd been overly emotional ever since they left on vacation. Lucas's regard softened. He got up and gave his mother a peck on the cheek.

'Don't worry,' he told her. She acquiesced with a forced smile.

'We have a 10 am pickup for the elephant trek,' his father called out as Lucas was leaving.

'I know,' he called back. 'I'll be on time.'

Jacques shook his head, sympathetic to his son's gallivanting. He had acted the same way at his age. Caroline knew what Jacques was thinking and gave him a knowing smile. Jacques poured the last bit of wine into her glass. She twirled it around and downed it in one gulp.

10

Thanikarn and Lucas arrived in front of the hotel at precisely ten o'clock the next morning. Looking as if he just rolled out of bed, clothes wrinkled, hair ruffled, creases from the bedsheets still imprinted on his fair cheeks, Lucas gave Thanikarn a goodbye peck on her lips and ran to find his parents. As he could have guessed, they were still on the terrace, finishing up their breakfast. When Jacques said ten o'clock, it meant ten thirty. It was his well-known strategy to make sure everyone would be on time. The stupid thing was, since everyone knew he was exaggerating, it defeated the goal.

'Hungry?' his mother asked with a smile.

'No, I'm okay,' he said as he grabbed a sweet roll. 'Do I have time for a shower?'

'Meet us in front of the hotel in twenty minutes,' his father said, impatiently fiddling with his camera. 'And tell your brother to bring his camera. Mine is full.'

'Don't forget a hat,' his mother called as he jogged off.

Thanikarn crossed Lucas on her way to the kitchen to see Amnat. They exchanged smiles but said nothing. Philippe was at the front desk, head bowed, going over the accounts, and waved good morning to Thanikarn as she went by. 'You're early,' he said. She answered with a smile. Despite his nonchalant attitude, he kept an eye on everything that went on around the hotel. If the room service was irreproachable, waitresses were polite, the masseuses paid their rent, and the clients were happy, he didn't meddle.

'You're early,' Amnat echoed when Thanikarn popped into the kitchen. He handed her a freshly baked roll. 'Missed you yesterday. Since when do you take the day off for Songkran?'

'Since …' She tipped back her head, raising her chin and looking up at the ceiling as if she would find a good reason hanging there.

'Since you fall in love,' he said.

'No! Why do you say that?' she said with mocking indignation.

'Look at you. You're radiant. Like a woman in love.'

'I have to go work,' she said evasively, holding up the roll in a gesture of thanks on her way out.

Being in love had never been in Thanikarn's vocabulary. The word *love*, yes. She knew what that meant – love for her family and her friends, love for nature, the lush plants, the crystal sky and endless sea … But *in love* was something different, something she'd only heard about in stories or seen on television shows. It seemed so mysterious, like a miracle that dropped from the sky.

Walking back toward her stand, looking out toward the horizon that announced a whole world across the sea, she realized that being in love explained why she suddenly felt so hopeful, why there was a knot in her stomach each time she saw Lucas arrive, why her body ached with emptiness as soon as he parted, the pride she felt when she sat next to him or held his hand, and the pulsing desire to be with him every minute of the day. The realization struck her like a crashing wave, drowning her fear. 'I'm in love,' she conceded with newfound hope.

Rinalda was already installed, sitting cross-legged, crocheting, as she often did when she had time between clients.

'You're early,' she said without lifting her head from her task.

'Sometimes I come early,' she said, a bit exasperated hearing this for the third time.

'You never come early,' Rinalda said, still concentrating on her needlework. Thanikarn smiled to herself, satisfied with her newly discovered secret, and began setting out her oils and creams. A customer arrived, asking for prices. Rinalda let Thanikarn deal with him. She was in no hurry to begin working.

* * *

At ten thirty, a white open-top jeep rolled up to the hotel to pick up the Mounier family for an excursion to the elephant park. It was scheduled as an all-day outing – riding elephants, a Thai lunch, a monkey show and a demonstration of rubber tapping.

'You will love riding the elephants,' their driver said with false exaggeration.

'Sounds like exploitation to me,' Lucas mumbled in the back seat, far from the driver's earshot.

'I hear they're treated well,' Caroline replied. 'Better than being in a zoo or a circus … and at least they're saved from being slaughtered by poachers.'

'Stupid Chinese,' Lucas said. They were aware of the incessant hunger for ivory.

'I think they're pretty well taken care of,' Arthur chimed in. 'Probably not as hard to carry around a bunch of tourists on their backs as a bunch of heavy logs with their noses.'

'Depends upon the tourists,' Jacques said with his usual touch of cynicism.

The ride to the park took nearly an hour, but it was beautiful and allowed them to discover the interior of the island as they wound through the dense inland forests. Invisible crickets buzzed in the lush forest of endless hues of green, cascading leaves and towering trees. It was like a Gauguin painting brought to life.

Lucas began the trip resentful at losing a free day, but once he was riding an elephant with his little brother, he let himself go and indulged in childhood silliness, pretending along with Arthur that they were Crocodile Dundees. After the trek, they fed the elephants and watered them down. Lucas caressed the elephant's skin, wondering if its thick skin kept it from suffering. If it did, he'd like to be an elephant.

Lunch was a delightful feast, but the day's activities seemed to drag on endlessly and by late afternoon Lucas feared he would get to the hotel too late to see Thanikarn. They hadn't made any plans for the evening.

Driving back in their guide's jeep, he mulled over the fact he'd soon be heading back home to Paris. While rolling over the hilltops, observing the tropical vistas, valleys of green and an indigo sky, a nostalgic phrase and simple melody crept into his mind. He pulled out his ever-present notebook and quickly jotted down words, feeling inspired by a myriad of images of Thanikarn, and by the time they reached the hotel he'd written a whole new song.

Once they arrived, Lucas was the first to jump out of the jeep. He ran down the walk, but as he approached the pool deck, he could see that the little massage stand was already abandoned. Thanikarn had left. He wandered toward the beach, looking right and left, as if he might find her somewhere, then walked sullenly back to his room. There was a note taped to his door. *I come get you at 8. You not there, I go home*, signed by a little heart encircling a big *T*. He tore it off and smiled.

His brother and parents trudged in behind him, bedraggled from their long, hot day.

'I need a shower. I smell like elephant everywhere,' Caroline griped, holding her arm up to her nose. Jacques silently traipsed past them, heading to his hotel room. Caroline followed him with her eyes, then turned toward the boys.

'I think your father is very tired … See you for dinner?' which was half a question, half a statement.

'I've got a date,' Lucas said, holding up the note.

'Ah,' she said knowingly. She could hardly protest; they'd spent the whole day together.

'So, we'll see you tomorrow.'

'What about me?' Arthur piped up.

'See you in an hour,' his mother said and kissed him tenderly on the forehead. She always tried to be fair, doling out her affection equally to each of her boys. Sibling rivalry had diminished with age, but it still hadn't disappeared.

Lucas looked at his watch. It was already seven thirty.

'Got to go get ready,' he said, kissed his mother on the cheek, and took off for his room.

* * *

Lucas was in front of the hotel at a quarter to eight, showered, dressed, and perfumed with a douse of Hugo Boss. He was reviewing the song he had composed in his dilapidated notebook, making a few changes, when Thanikarn startled him. She had arrived by foot, looking like a vision, dressed all in white, a sleeveless, cotton-lace dress and white rhinestone-studded sandals with tiny heels. Lucas kissed her tenderly.

'My scooter down the street. Leave for fixing. Ready in five minutes.'

'No problem. We can walk there?' Lucas figured that scooter problems must be frequent on the island.

She took his hand, leading him off across the road. 'Not far, maybe ten minutes.'

It was a balmy, star-studded evening, not a cloud in the sky. In fact, it had only rained once since they'd arrived. Lucas loved walking, always something new to discover.

'So, how your day with elephants?' she asked.

'Great. One of my favourite animals. But I felt a little guilty. They shouldn't have to cart around a bunch of tourists every day.'

'Sad for elephants. In Bangkok, men take babies from mothers, break them to work for mahout. But Koh Samui camp not so bad. Babies grow up with elephant family, mahout not so mean.' She smiled her serious smile.

'We need to go to Ben's bar,' Lucas said, changing the subject. 'I have a little surprise for you.'

'We go eat first?' she asked. 'You always hungry,' she added with a chuckle.

'You know me pretty well now ... How about the night market?'

Thanikarn frowned, concentrating on where to go. She knew so many outdoor markets. 'We go to good one I know ... Laem Din.'

Taking their time walking slowly, they sauntered up to a tiny grubby shop next to a 7-Eleven, where Thanikarn had left her scooter for repair. A mechanic with greasy black hands slowly got up from his stool and gave her the keys, and they sped away.

Good food was important to Lucas. He was such a gourmand that if he couldn't eat well, he didn't eat at all and often ended up skipping meals. After ordering their dinner at an unassuming food stall, they sat on a concrete bench outside the market while an incessant stream of cars and bikes rumbled by. Thanikarn watched him with big admiring eyes as he scooped up his *wai kôo*, an octopus coconut curry. She quietly ate her favourite noodle dish, *pei pat*, contemplating the rest of their evening together. She didn't want to expect anything, but she still felt all fluttery inside thinking about making love later.

'You eat everything,' she said, realizing she hadn't said a word since they sat down.

'Yeah. Anything that walks, swims or crawls, just like the

Chinese. As long as it tastes good, I'll eat it.'

As soon as they finished their dinner, they headed for Samui Soul, the beach club where they met Ben for the first time.

It was still quiet when they arrived, a few customers, beers in hand, sat on bar stools, as the band began to set up. Ben was unrolling some speaker cables when they walked in.

'There they are!' he cried out when he saw them coming. 'Here for the show?'

Lucas and Thanikarn gave him Western-style hugs in greeting.

'Yeah, I thought we'd hang out here for a while,' Lucas said. 'Can I buy you a drink?'

'A Coke for me,' Ben said. 'I've been overdoing the booze.'

'Would you mind if I borrowed your bass while you set up?'

'All yours,' Ben said. He handed over his trusty bass, then continued setting up the gear for his evening gig. Lucas sat down on the edge of the stage and plucked out some chords, quietly humming the tune he had been working on during the ride in the jeep. He stopped to pull out some baht, which he handed to Thanikarn.

'Karn, can you go get us a couple of beers and a Coke?' She went over to the bar, where she became engaged in a discussion with the bartender.

Lucas continued trying out the chords to his song on Ben's bass, oblivious to a small group of locals dribbling in. Thanikarn returned with their drinks and took a seat at a little table near the small corner stage. Ben sat down with Thanikarn while the rest of his band settled into place.

'Can I borrow a mic?' Lucas asked from his stage-side perch.

Ben pointed to a stand behind him, gesturing for Lucas to help himself. Lucas adjusted the mic and hoisted himself up on the stool and like the experienced entertainer he was, pronounced, 'This is for Karn ... I call it "Wakin' Up Blues".'

Ben smiled in approval. Thanikarn perked up in her seat, attentive and wide-eyed. Lucas began strumming the chords on Ben's bass and sang:

Wakin' up, with the sun in my eyes,
Cherishing this moment with you,
I find it tough to realize,
That you and me is soon to be through.

Riding on the back of your bike,
My chest is bearing with your perfume,
And in the sun, I realize,
My grip on your hips is soon to be through.

Never saw me coming, now you see me go.
If I knew when coming, and if I seemed to know.
That I'd have that something, feeling as if though,
I'm the one to bring you pain in missing joy alone.

Please don't cry, please don't make me regret
The perfect moments that we've been through.
And before I go, please realize,
These feelings and affections have always been true.

Lifting off, the shore drifts away,
The colours seem to fade with the rain.
And sure enough, the forecast of fate
Doesn't seem to matter in relieving the pain.

Walking up, the cold pavement streets,
My shoes are digging into the snow,
And comes a breeze, where we two can meet,
A warm and soothing memory of a whisper so low,

Singing, couldn't be together, not even if we tried,
But I'll still remember, the moments that we've lied,
One against each other, staring in our eyes,
A thousand dreams for a one-night glance, and the lessons
        of a million lives.

Not a word could make me forget,
That living isn't easy for you,
And not a day has gone by yet
When singing this song gets me thinking of you,

When singing this song makes me think about you ...

When he finished, Ben and the small crowd at the bar clapped politely. Thanikarn's eyes were glassy, and she sighed feeling as though she was in a dream.

11

Thanikarn woke up entangled in Lucas's arms like twisted ivy clinging to a tree. She felt as if separating herself would break off the fragile branches of her newfound love. Not just her body or her mood but her whole being felt different now that she had tasted real love. Sleeping with Lucas surpassed anything she'd ever known before. Their lovemaking not only awakened every sensual part of her body but also every dormant part of her soul. As she lay motionless in his arms, she decided she would not be the first to move. She would wait forever if necessary. Thanikarn shut her eyes again and let herself drift between dreams and daydreams until he woke.

It could have been minutes or maybe as long as an hour before Lucas opened his eyes. He slowly turned over and kissed her good morning.

'What time is it?' he asked groggily.

'Maybe ten o'clock. I don't know.' She was perfectly awake.

Lucas rolled over the edge of the mattress and picked up his watch from the floor.

'Oh shit, it's ten thirty. You'll be late for work.'

'It's okay. This time okay. Your last day.'

It didn't take Lucas long to get up and dressed. This was indeed his last day, and he knew he had to spend time with his family, but it was difficult to leave Thanikarn. He'd probably never see her again. The same thought had crossed Thanikarn's mind, but she didn't want to think about it. He had to be with his family, and she had to work.

* * *

It was a beautiful, windless, cloudless day, postcard perfect. Jacques and Arthur proposed a short fishing trip, taking advantage of the mild sea. Caroline wanted to go shopping. She felt compelled to spend the last day picking up gifts for family and friends back home, silly souvenirs that would probably be stowed away and forgotten. She was surprised when Lucas said he wanted to go shopping with her instead of fishing with his father and brother. The truth was, he wanted to buy a going-away gift for Thanikarn. He had in mind some jewellery, something nice that would last beyond their brief affair. He was hoping his mother would give him some feminine advice as well as pitch in a little extra money.

Caroline's souvenir shopping was overtaken by Lucas's mission. They visited every jewellery store in Chaweng. Lucas was probably one of the most indecisive individuals Caroline had ever known. She often teased him for being a typical Libra.

He finally settled upon a pair of gold earrings in the form of butterflies.

'Do you think they're too expensive?' Lucas asked his mother.

She took the hint. 'I can help you out a little,' she said.

'You think I'm being extravagant.' Lucas apologized.

'It's not that. I just wonder if you'll be giving her the wrong idea.'

'What do you mean by that?'

'I mean, she's a masseuse. She's a lot older than you are. You don't know anything about her.'

'It's not like I'm giving her an engagement ring!'

Caroline looked sheepish. 'I'm sorry.'

They arrived back at the hotel about the same time that Jacques and Arthur straggled in from their fishing expedition proudly bearing a two-kilo barracuda sticking out of a plastic bag. They headed straight to the restaurant to ask the cook to prepare it for their dinner that evening.

Lucas could not turn down a freshly caught fish dinner. He feared Thanikarn would be disappointed that they wouldn't be able to spend the evening together and procrastinated telling her by going for a late-afternoon swim in the ocean. The sea in front of their hotel was shallow, and the water was so warm it sometimes lulled him into lethargy, so he needed to wade out a long way before he could find cooler water.

Thanikarn followed him with her eyes as he wandered down to the shore, looking proud. Though Lucas was sometimes self-conscious of his untanned torso, the Thai girls loved his fair skin, such a contrast with their own coffee-coloured hue. Once he ducked into the small, rolling waves, she lost sight of him for a long time. Though busy massaging a sleeping client, her eyes never left the sea. After a few minutes, she began to feel panicky. Her heart began to beat like a hummingbird's wings. What if he drowned? She knew she was being silly but couldn't help worrying and wanted to sprint to the water's edge and cry out his name. So, this was what happened when you were in love. Constant worry. She continued applying pressure to the man's hairy back, trying not to think about Lucas, or love, or the fact he'd be leaving soon. Then she spotted his sinewy silhouette climbing up out of the sea, and the tension in her body melted away.

By the time he arrived at the massage stand, walking slowly so he could soak in the final moments of the sun-warmed afternoon, he was nearly dry.

'Hey,' he said nonchalantly. It was surprising how well they both hid their feelings from everyone at the hotel.

'Hey,' she echoed, still busy with her hairy client.

'Can I get a massage?' he asked.

'Ten minutes,' she said with a broad smile.

Rinalda sat cross-legged, crocheting, and knew better than to offer her services. Sawitti was hunched over giving a deluxe manicure with the concentration of a surgeon performing an operation.

Lucas wandered over to an outdoor shower next to the pool, doused off the salt water and stretched out on a lawn chair. Once Thanikarn finished with her hairy-chested client, Lucas took his place on Thanikarn's mat.

'Last time,' he said sadly.

'Last time,' she repeated, copying his melancholy tone.

Lucas lay down on his stomach; Thanikarn oiled her hands and began massaging him slowly, tenderly, lovingly, trying not to show how much she enjoyed it. Lucas finally broke the news.

'Karn,' he said softly, 'I'm sorry but I can't have dinner with you tonight.'

'That's okay,' she said quickly, almost as if she expected it. Perhaps it was better not to spend the evening together. She would have a hard time staying cheerful.

'But I can meet you after dinner,' he added.

Massaging without the least break in rhythm, she smiled. Rinalda, never lifting her eyes from her crocheting, followed the exchange.

'Is that okay?' he finally asked.

'Not okay,' she replied, adopting a surprisingly serious tone. Lucas propped himself up on his elbows to look at her.

'Just kidding,' she said with her girlish giggle. 'I wait for you.'

Finishing up the short back-and-shoulder massage, Lucas thanked her like any other client and paid her three-hundred-baht fee. They had to keep up appearances.

'We'll probably have an early dinner, since we're leaving tomorrow morning. I can meet you somewhere if you like. Around ten, I think.'

'Okay. I come get you.' If she wouldn't be spending the evening with Lucas, Thanikarn would take advantage of the window and visit her grandmother and Trin. She'd neglected them the last few days.

* * *

Thanikarn zigzagged up the hill to her grandmother's house, avoiding the loose rocks and gravel. She parked her scooter at the bottom of the steps and entered the house with a plastic sack of treats that she'd picked up at a small roadside grocery store on the way. Her grandmother and Trin ate frugally. Their meagre budget kept them from ever going to restaurants or buying bottled drinks or pastries. She lifted the bag to show it to her grandmother, sitting in her favourite chair by the window. Preeda looked up from her mending with a welcoming smile. She looked as if she had been sitting there all day, just waiting for her granddaughter to arrive.

'Did you see your uncle Trin? He's been gone a long time,' she asked wearily.

Thanikarn went over to the window behind her and looked outside. She spotted Trin sitting on his haunches, staring out at his chickens as they wandered around in senseless circles, as if mesmerized by their disorganized pecking.

'He's taking care of his chickens, Yai.'

'Ah,' she said knowingly. 'That's good.'

'Can I get you some water?'

'No. I drink too much water. It makes me go pee. I'm too tired to get up again and again.'

Thanikarn went to the sink, ran the water long enough for it to warm up, and half-filled a little plastic tub. She brought the tub of water over to her grandmother and tenderly placed her feet inside. Sitting on a small foot stool, she gently washed and massaged her grandmother's gnarled feet. Preeda closed her eyes, and her lips turned up into a dreamy smile. Relishing her massage, she almost inaudibly questioned, 'How is your boyfriend?'

'What makes you think I have a boyfriend?' Thanikarn was taken aback by a question that seemed to come from nowhere.

'I don't know. There's something ... something different. You remind me of myself, a time long ago, when I met your grandfather.'

Thanikarn continued massaging Preeda's feet in silence. She didn't know what to say. She didn't want to lie, but she didn't want to tell the truth either. A fleeting affair with a farang was irresponsible and would only upset her grandmother.

'I met someone, and we are going out, but nothing serious.' Sadly, she was telling the truth.

12

Neither Thanikarn nor Lucas had any desire to go out. It was nearly ten by the time she'd arrived, and Lucas had said his goodbyes to Ben and the local crowd at the bar the night before. Thanikarn was happy when Lucas proposed that they spend the evening alone. They skipped across the street and ducked into a Family Mart to buy some cold beer before taking the short scooter ride to her home.

As soon as they arrived, Thanikarn flipped off her sandals and sat down on the bed. 'You can sing me my song?' she asked with such an earnest tone that Lucas came close to feeling sorry for her.

'I don't have anything to play on,' he apologized.

'I have,' she said brightly. Thanikarn popped up, and from the corner of the small room she took an odd-shaped bundle wrapped in a worn and tattered sheet. She proudly pulled out an outdated guitar. Lucas took it, examining its condition, and struck a few chords.

'Whoa. A little out of tune.'

'My neighbour downstairs not play anymore. I ask him, and he give it to me.'

Lucas smiled. She was determined to have her song. Judging from the guitar's pathetic condition, it was no surprise the neighbour gave it away. Sitting on a weather-worn wooden stool, the only place to sit in the bare room, he began the arduous task of trying to tune it up. Once he started to sing, Thanikarn sat on the bed and with nary a blink kept her eyes riveted on him throughout the whole song. When he finished, he put aside the guitar and kissed her tenderly on the cheek. She looked away, trying not to cry, then turned her head around with a sudden request. 'You can write me the words?'

'Sure.'

'Now?' She almost demanded. She looked around her and, finding no paper, grabbed a book off the floor, the one on corporate law. 'You can write in this. Lots of empty pages in back.'

Lucas took it, looked at her curiously. 'You're reading this?' He flipped through the pages, glancing at the text.

'Before, I want to study law. Be a lawyer,' she said.

'A lawyer?' he asked, trying not to sound too surprised.

'Yes. Important job, and you help people.' Then she added with a sheepish smile, 'And make lots of money.'

'And now?'

'And now, I think too late. Too hard. No time to study,' she said, trying to dismiss the subject as irrelevant. 'You write in the book, so I don't lose.' She handed him a pen.

Lucas sat down on her bed, propped the book on his knees and, trying his best to write legibly, copied down the text on one of the blank pages. Thanikarn fetched their bottles of beer, put one on the floor next to Lucas, and sat down beside him. He wrote, stopping only to take a few swigs of beer, while she followed every stroke of his pen. Each time he put down a word she didn't know, she asked the meaning.

'What it means, *cherishing*?'

Lucas thought a few seconds. 'It means holding something in your heart.'

'And *grip*?'

He tightened his hand around her wrist. She acknowledged the meaning with a satisfied nod.

And then a few moments later: 'What it means, *pavement*?'

'Another word for *street*,' he explained, and so it went, until he had written out the whole song, and she had learned a half a dozen new words in English. Once he had finished, she took the book from his hands and looked at the results, holding the page in front of her as if it were a work of art.

'I forget to ask. Why you call it "Wakin' Up Blues"? It means what?'

'Oh, well, blues is a style of music. It can mean sadness. But a sweet sadness. One filled with memories. I called it "Wakin' Up Blues" because when I wake up, I think of you and how happy you make me feel, and I think about how I will miss you.'

'Oh' was all she could say, when in her heart, she ached to say so much more. She closed the book and laid it carefully on the floor next to her bed.

After they finished their beers in silence, they stretched out on the bed and studied one another, with a long intense gaze into each other's eyes. Lucas pulled off Thanikarn's shirt. She unfastened the belt of his pants. They proceeded to undress one another slowly and tenderly. Once they were both naked, they fell into an unrestrained and passionate embrace. Thanikarn felt a hunger for Lucas like she'd never known. She abandoned any control to hold back her desire and planted wild kisses all over his face, his chest and down to his groin; he was stiff, and she wanted him inside of her. With no hesitation, she climbed on top of him and slipped him inside her.

'Wait,' Lucas cried out in a loud whisper. He gently rolled her over on her back next to him and grabbed his pants that lay crumpled on the floor but, after several seconds of frantic fumbling for a condom in his pocket, found nothing.

'I don't have anything,' he said with frustration.

Thanikarn was desperate with an intense need for him to make love to her. She pulled him back toward her. 'It's okay – I am okay, not sick.'

He caressed her cheeks; her eyes were filled with yearning. She was breathing heavily, and her body trembled with a hungry, desperate need to surrender her entire body and soul, a silent scream that said, 'Take me!' Looking deeply into her imploring eyes, Lucas could no longer resist and saw no reason why he should. This was the last time he'd ever see her; he wanted to make the most of it. Lucas held back until Thanikarn finally came, when she must have cried out loud enough to awaken the whole city, and then allowed himself to climax as well with an intensity that left Thanikarn feeling as if the whole world had stopped. Exhausted, they lay there for a long time, breathing heavily until their heartbeats slowed and they could finally speak.

'You're so beautiful,' Lucas whispered tenderly.

Thanikarn wanted so much to tell him she loved him. The words throbbed in her heart, but she couldn't allow them to form on her lips. Not even in a whisper. She turned her head and began to cry silently. He gently wiped away her tears. He knew why she was crying but didn't know what to say. 'We can call each other,' he finally proposed.

This wasn't much of a consolation, and he knew it, but there was little more he could say without lying. He couldn't make a declaration of lasting love. He couldn't promise her he would stay or come back; he couldn't even say for sure he'd never forget her. He was too young for that. Then his thoughts turned to the present. 'I'm sorry about not having protection,' he said apologetically. He sounded like he was thinking about her, but he was really more concerned about himself.

'No worry,' she affirmed. 'I promise, I am okay.'

'I believe you, but ... that's not the only problem.'

She looked up at him through her eyebrows, unsure of what he meant, then realized. 'Oh. No, don't worry. I can't have baby.'

Lucas nodded, assuming she was talking about birth control.

They both remained silent, Lucas stroking Thanikarn's head, their eyes closed, until he fell asleep. Once she felt his hand fall limp by her side, she opened her eyes once more. She could have watched him sleeping all night. She stroked his golden hair. It would be the last time, she thought, and the tears began to well in her eyes once again. A tear dropped onto his cheek. She quickly wiped it away, wrapped her arm across his body, snuggled her head into his chest, and closed her eyes, determined not to think about it.

The alarm on Lucas's watch went off at 9 am. He opened his heavy eyelids and stared at the ceiling as if trying to figure out where he was. He looked down at Thanikarn, her arms wrapped around him as if she was protecting a precious bundle. She heard the alarm go off but pretended not to.

'I have to get up,' he said softly.

'I know,' she said, without stirring. She didn't want to let him go. He kissed her on the forehead and pulled himself gently from her arms.

She rose reluctantly, washed and dressed in silence, while Lucas lolled in bed a few extra minutes. He rose suddenly, determined to get moving. After pulling on his pants, donning his T-shirt and splashing some water on his face, he was ready within minutes. He knew his parents would start to worry.

'We have to go,' he said needlessly. Thanikarn gave a silent nod. She wasn't sulking, though it might have looked that way. She was simply so overwhelmed with sadness that she had no desire to speak.

They rode quickly back to the hotel, a ten-minute jaunt from her flat, and Lucas hopped off the scooter, anxious to reassure his parents that he was ready to leave.

'Wait here,' he said. They had decided the night before that Thanikarn would take him to the airport.

She turned off her scooter and sat upright, tightly clutching the handlebars, waiting with apprehension, while Lucas helped his parents and brother load their luggage into the hotel van. They looked preoccupied, paying little attention to Lucas, as they piled into the back of the van. Lucas waved them off and jogged over to Thanikarn.

'All ready. We can follow them to the airport,' he said.

13

At the airport, they were surrounded by a throng of people, some lined up to check in, others pushing through for boarding, some huddled in family clumps. The intimacy of Thanikarn's peaceful little flat was now replaced by a sea of strangers stealing her last precious moments with Lucas. They clung to one another, Thanikarn nestled in Lucas's arms. His parents and brother were only meters away, pretending not to take notice of them. Thanikarn felt robbed of her last chance to say goodbye in privacy. It was over now, and all she could do was bury her head into his chest. If she tried to speak, she would choke on the words she ached to say.

They were both aware they would never see one another again.

'I'll call you,' he reassured her.

'We can keep in touch … I can always come back,' she heard him say. His words resonated with a fatal emptiness, but she pretended they were true. It was the only way she could face letting him go.

'Oh, and I almost forgot again,' he said suddenly. He pulled out the gift that he had bought with his mother.

'I meant to give this to you last night.' He placed the gift into her hand, a small, unwrapped red box tied up with a gold string.

'A little souvenir,' he added. Lucas wasn't used to offering gifts to a girl, and Thanikarn was even less used to receiving them. She fumbled awkwardly, trying to untie the knotted gold bow, her fingers shaking in a way she had never known.

'You can open it later,' he said. She looked up at him with supplicating eyes, moist with pain. He gave one final, intense look and kissed her one last time, tender and discreet.

'I have to go, Karn,' he whispered. She blinked away the tears as she watched him leave, clutching his gift against her chest. Just before boarding, Lucas turned to look back, but she was already gone.

* * *

Thanikarn didn't feel like working that day, nor did she feel like not working. At least if she kept busy, she would have less time to wallow in her sorrow. She arrived at the Golden Gecko just after eleven, her usual time, attracting no attention from Rinalda, who was already comfortably installed, crocheting. Sawitti still hadn't arrived, no surprise. Thanikarn forced a good-morning smile.

'How is my Karn this morning?' Rinalda asked, looking up through her eyelashes.

Thanikarn emitted a faint 'fine' and forced an even fainter smile. She began setting up for the day, spreading out her large, pink towel, smoothing out every little wrinkle with her hands. She glanced up at the sky from time to time as she continued her morning preparations. Lucas's plane should be taking off soon.

Dark clouds loomed far away. The weather report had announced a thunderstorm in the afternoon, rare this time of year. It would be one of those welcome brief deluges, a temporary relief from the tropical heat.

Thanikarn was arranging her oils when she heard a plane overhead. She was suddenly possessed with a fear she couldn't control. What if the plane was caught in a storm, and what if it crashed? An overwhelming terror churned inside her stomach that reason couldn't calm. She looked around like a frightened cat, but the danger came from inside her head.

A tall, tanned, dark-haired man arrived; he might have been Italian, or Spanish. He was notably good-looking, probably a good ten years older than Thanikarn.

'Hi. How much for a massage?' He had a self-assured air that annoyed her.

'What kind of massage you want?' Her tone of voice was indifferent, almost dissuasive.

'Body?'

She pointed to the little sign that stood in front of the stand. 'Prices all there,' she said. He studied them for a minute.

'Full-body massage with oil?'

'Okay.'

He waited instructions that didn't follow. She was still thinking about last night, that morning, the looming clouds, the plane up in the sky.

'You lie down on stomach,' interjected Rinalda. 'There, on towel.' Thanikarn looked at her co-worker with dark eyes.

Rinalda was trying to be helpful but had no idea how reluctant Thanikarn felt, her stomach knotted up with grief. The first man she ever loved had just walked out of her life. Forever.

Thanikarn poured some oil on her handsome client's back and began spreading it out, smoothing it across his skin. He moaned with pleasure. Instead of feeling flattered, she frowned with irritation.

When she finished his massage, he asked her if she was married or had a boyfriend.

'Yes,' she replied, without her usual bright smile. The question wasn't unusual or rude, but it felt like an insult. She was in mourning. Her Mediterranean man didn't persist and handed her a few hundred baht that he peeled off from a wad of bills, puffed up his chest and headed for the beach.

'I think men smell things,' Rinalda said, pointing to her nose.

'What do you mean?'

'You know what I mean.'

Thanikarn stubbornly looked the other way. Even though she knew nothing about pheromones, she understood. Being in love made women more attractive.

'I will be back in ten minutes. Maybe Amnat has something for me to eat,' she told her companion. She didn't feel like conversation.

She wandered into Amnat's kitchen. He was cutting up some tiny red-hot chillies. His eyes were watery from their pungent fumes.

'You came to cry with me?' he asked sarcastically.

She pulled up a chair next to him, sat down and burst into

tears, burying her head into her arms.

'I was joking, Karn!!!' He immediately put down his knife and wrapped his arms around her. 'What is wrong, my little flower?'

'He's gone, Amnat. He will never come back,' she wailed.

* * *

As Lucas's plane headed toward Bangkok, the rain began slapping against the window. He thought about Thanikarn; watching the large drops run slowly down the windowpane reminded him of her tears as they rolled over her round cheeks. He heaved a sigh and closed his eyes, then opened them again, suddenly struck with an eerie feeling that he had left something behind. He looked in his vest pocket; he had his wallet, passport, cell phone. He dug his hand into the front pocket of his pants, only to find the condom he had looked for frantically the night before. *Ah, there it is,* he thought, remembering that he had decided last minute to change his pants before going out. 'Stupid,' he said to himself reproachfully.

Satisfied that he hadn't forgotten anything, his feeling of anguish evolved into regret. His island adventure, the blue skies, sandy shores, palm trees, sea breezes and Thanikarn's sweet smile would soon be far away. The memories of his trip would surely fade, but she was too lovely to forget. Before long, the announcement of their imminent landing came over the loudspeaker. The first in a series of landings, take-offs, and landings. Bangkok, Shanghai, then Paris and back to school, work and friends. The same old routine.

Once the brief storm had blown over, Thanikarn half-followed Amnat's advice and left work early. Although not to do something that would keep her mind off herself and how she felt, like he had said.

She threw her purse over her shoulder, jumped on her scooter, and sped down the busy main street charged with the usual five o'clock traffic toward Lamai. Her destination was a short hour away, and she wanted to arrive before sunset.

Once she arrived at the Hin Ta and Hin Yai parking lot, she marched deliberately toward the famous rocks. She sat down on the curved stone where she last sat with Lucas and studied the natural crevice of Hin Yai, with its rounded bifurcated surface splayed out in front of her. She pulled Lucas's still-unopened farewell gift out of her bag, then slowly and reverently untied the gold bow. Thanikarn gazed out toward the sea and, after making a futile wish, opened the red velvet box to discover the gold earrings. She caressed the delicate gold butterflies with her fingers while she tried to imagine Lucas going to the store, looking at all the jewellery, and picking them out just for her. No one besides her parents had ever bought her such a personal gift. He was a generous farang and would make a wonderful husband someday. If he wasn't so young, it might have been different. She sat there, her arms wrapped around her knees, and reminisced; her face glowing with affection, her eyes targeted the horizon, and she waited for the sky to take on its twilight hue.

As she rode back home that evening, Thanikarn thought

about Amnat's attempt to reassure her. She had silently repeated his consoling words like a sacred chant all afternoon. 'One never knows ... Sometimes life has surprises ... Love is stronger than you think ... Whatever happens, it's probably for the best ...'

When she got home and opened the door to her little flat, all she saw was a room without Lucas. She dropped down onto the bed and wrapped herself up in the sheet. She smelled his scent on the pillow and buried her head into it, searching for comfort, losing herself in images of their last night together. She finally pulled off the pillow, opened her eyes and faced the empty ceiling. All those stupid clichés were little consolation, and the tears began to slide down her cheeks. She wiped them away with a certain resolve, knowing full well that her only solace now was to go to sleep.

14

It had been a week since Lucas left. A twilight canopy was forming overhead as Thanikarn put away her affairs for the evening. She added her last customer's pay to a large wad of baht that she had stuffed into her little change purse. She took out the money and counted it once again. *I have enough,* she thought. She zipped up her savings, buried it into her big shoulder bag and left with a determined gait. She jumped on her scooter and drove down the road to a local shop selling cell phones. It was a major purchase, one that she had been looking forward to all week.

'I can call France with this?' she asked the young man for the third time. He assured her that the service she chose would allow her to call anywhere in the world. She looked at her new Nokia phone with a sceptical frown, finding it hard to believe that what looked like a plastic toy could connect her with another person across continents. Since Lucas had advised her to wait and call him when there was some way he could call her back, she learned that a cell phone was the best solution.

She went directly home with her mobile phone, immediately plugged it in as the vendor had instructed, and checked carefully to make sure it was charging. Two hours, he told her. Just two more hours, and she could finally make the call she had been anticipating all week. She began preparing her dinner, dumped half of a cup of rice into her rice cooker, poured in some water, clapped down the lid. She chopped up some lemongrass, chillies and a couple of tomatoes and fried them in a little oil with a pinch of salt and a couple of slices of galangal to be mixed in with the rice. Waiting for it to cook, she occupied herself with washing out her underwear in the kitchen sink. Her motions were automatic and thoughtless as she kept busy.

Thanikarn ate her dinner, chewing each mouthful slowly, half-watching a stupid movie on the television. Prolonging her meal, she picked nervously at every morsel and wiped the plate clean with her finger, looking at her phone every ten minutes to see if it was still charging, as if her constant attention could speed up the process. After she finished eating and washing the dishes, Thanikarn looked at her watch; it was nearly ten o'clock. Counting on her fingers, she calculated the time difference between Thailand and Paris. Maybe he was eating lunch now, she thought. Good time or bad time? Doesn't matter – he said to call anytime.

She unfolded the little piece of paper Lucas had given her with his phone number and pushed in the buttons with great deliberation, one at a time. After his phone rang six or seven times, she heard Lucas's voice.

'*Bonjour, vous êtes bien sur la messagerie de Lucas Mounier. Laissez-moi vos coordonnées et je vous rappelle dès que possible.* Hi, this is Lucas. Please leave me a message, and I'll get back to you as soon as I can.'

She held the phone at a distance. This was unexpected. She

pressed the phone to her ear and spoke timidly, 'Lucas, it is me, Thanikarn. You please call me back. When you want. My number is 080 804 3882.' She pushed the little red button to hang up, and her face darkened, her brows furrowed with worry. This was all so new to her. Would he get her message? Would he call her back? He could be at school, or working, or out with friends.

She tried to read a magazine. Reading usually relaxed her and often put her to sleep, but the words melted into a blur, taken over by images of Lucas, his smile, his laugh, his kiss. She tried to imagine his life back in Paris. She'd seen pictures of the Eiffel Tower, the Champs Elysées, Notre Dame, the tree-lined streets, famous stores, traffic circles with their tourbillion of cars. She wondered what it was like to live there. She heaved a heavy sigh, feeling so far away from everything he lived every day. It might be a long time before he called back. Or maybe he would never call her back. She shook her head, trying to rid herself of such sad thoughts.

She picked up her little phone once more and looked at it, then placed it on the floor next to her bed. She tossed the magazine aside and dropped onto her back. It was no use trying to read. She tried to let go of her tension, breathing slowly, letting her slight body sink into the mattress, tossing thoughts out of her mind until she finally dozed off.

Thanikarn slipped into a dream. She was walking down the sidewalk on a European street wearing high heels and a short skirt, trying to look like a city woman, but her steps were awkward, and she staggered clumsily, attracting stares. She wanted to take off those silly shoes and walk barefoot, but she couldn't reach her feet. Then everything started moving faster, and dozens of pedestrians sped by. They all had somewhere to go, somewhere they must be, while she stood still, frozen, listening to a strange tune that came floating out of her shoulder bag.

The ubiquitous Nokia melody repeated several times before she woke up and realized the sound was coming from her own phone lying on the floor. She grabbed it and frantically pushed the little green button. 'Hello? Hello?' Silence. Did he hang up? Nothing.

She fell back down on the bed, her head hitting the pillow with a heavy thud. *Now what?*

The unmistakable tune started again. She quickly pushed the little green button and held the phone up to her ear.

'Hello?'

'Karn!' Lucas cried out. 'So, you have a phone now. That's great!'

'Yes, I buy it today. So you can call me. I am very happy to hear you.' Her own words sounded strange to her. This was all so new, talking into a little handheld phone without wires, speaking to someone thousands of kilometres away. He was so far, and yet his words sounded so clear and close.

'How are you?' he asked.

'Good. Everything is good. But you are gone. So, I am sad.'

'I miss you,' Lucas said, knowing this was little consolation, but there was not much more he could add.

'And you? Happy to be home?' she asked.

'Happy? I guess. It's good to be back. I have lots of work to do, finishing up my degree and all. I saw some old friends, and that's always nice. I've got my parents' big apartment to live in, so I'm pretty comfortable. They won't be coming back to Paris until summer. But it's cold here, really cold. Wet and grey. Nothing like Koh Samui. I miss the sun and ocean.'

Thanikarn smiled sweetly, as if he could see her. Smiles came so naturally to her.

'Here the same. Always hot,' she said with her little-girl laugh.

There was an awkward silence. Thanikarn had little to say. Her life was so uneventful.

'Oh, I almost forget. Your present, so beautiful. I love my earrings. I wear every day.'

'I'm glad you like them. I thought they would look good on you.'

'Everybody tell me so pretty.'

'I'd love to see you wearing them. Maybe someone could take a picture of you.'

'I try. But I don't like pictures. Never look good.'

'Yes, you do! I had my photos of Koh Samui printed up yesterday. There's one my dad took of you giving me a massage. You look beautiful.'

'You just being nice.'

'No really,' he insisted. 'I can send you a copy if you want ...'

'I better like a picture of you. You send me one?'

'Sure. You'll have to give me your address.'

'You send me at hotel. More easy.'

'Okay. As soon as I have time to go to the post office. Well, listen, Karn. I have to go now. I have a composition class. But I'll call you back soon. What's a good time?'

'Me? Anytime.' Then she thought that was stupid. She couldn't talk to him anytime. 'Maybe after work time is good, night time.'

'Okay, no problem.'

More silence confirming the vast distance between them.

'I miss you, Karn. I think about you all the time,' Lucas finally said.

'Me too. I think of you.'

'Big kiss and talk to you soon. Bye.'

'Bye, Lucas. Thank you for kiss.'

She hung up, closed her eyes and, with a smile on her face, fell sound asleep.

15

Weeks dragged by, enlightened only by several brief phone calls from Lucas. Thanikarn looked forward to those precious interludes breaking the monotony of her job, but their conversations were short; he did most of the talking since she was limited by poor English and an uneventful life. At first, he called regularly, once or twice a week. He spoke about his school, his projects, his outings in Paris, a play he saw or a concert he attended. But with each successive call, she felt his concentration waning, as the images of their island romance gradually became a faint blur in his mind, while for her, they remained vividly alive. She began to feel that his nostalgia for the time they spent together was replaced by his enthusiasm for what he was doing now. It left a hurtful hollow in her heart, but there was nothing she could do.

During their last phone call, he told her he might go to the United States. He had some relatives in Los Angeles, and it would be a good opportunity to look for work in music. Los Angeles was another famous city she dreamed of visiting one day. She had seen countless pictures in magazines and scenes in television shows, usually consisting of convertible cars driving down tree-lined boulevards, towering buildings with glass panes, the Hollywood

Hills, movie studios and famous stars streaming in and out of famous places.

He would be meeting some commercial movie producers, he said, friends of his father. Exciting for him but distressing for her; she would surely lose her place in his heart. Koh Samui was no rival to Hollywood.

It had been six weeks since he left; forty-two sunsets and one full moon had come and gone. When she headed home that evening, the next full moon was looming high in the sky. It beamed with a magical brightness that filtered in through the window of her small flat. She sat cross-legged on her bed, reading her English book. She had to improve her English – it was important, especially for speaking on the phone. Her paltry vocabulary was good enough for foreign clients but far from sufficient to express the kaleidoscope of sentiments she felt for Lucas. It was a hot, sultry evening. She reached over to turn out the lamp next to her bed, too tired to concentrate, and felt a light pain as she stretched out her arm. She touched her small breasts, held them in her hands, massaging them lightly. They felt tender and sore. How odd, she thought; too many massages, perhaps. It was true that she'd felt tired the last few days, but a good night's sleep should put her back in form.

Unexpectedly, Thanikarn woke the next morning still feeling tired and out of sorts for no apparent reason. She dressed slowly, skipped breakfast, having no appetite whatsoever, and with little motivation, left for work.

She didn't even return Rinalda's smile when she arrived at the massage stand, preoccupied by an odd nausea in her stomach, a feeling that made her head spin.

'Oh, someone doesn't look well today,' Rinalda teased. 'Sleep badly with the big full moon?'

'No, I slept okay. Just a funny sick stomach,' she said, rubbing it. 'Maybe I ate something bad.'

'Go see Amnat. He might have a remedy for that.'

In lieu of a reply, Thanikarn stared blankly at her well-intentioned friend.

'Now,' Rinalda ordered, 'before you turn green.'

Amnat had the reputation of being like a wise old grandmother who always had some secret ingredient for whatever ailed you. Thanikarn walked to the kitchen, dragging her feet like a reluctant child, passing by Philippe who was going through his morning accounts. He mumbled a 'Good morning, Karn,' without lifting his head, which she answered with a feeble 'Good morning.' She wandered into the kitchen, pots of soup already fuming, Amnat at the stove, frying up some chicken.

'*Sawadee ka*, Karn,' he said without looking at her. 'Hungry?'

'No, but I think I should eat something.' She went over to a pot of simmering soup. 'Amnat, what is this? It smells strange.'

Amnat stopped flipping his browning chicken and shot a look toward her through furrowed brows. 'What is wrong with you, Karn? That fish came off the boat this morning.'

Thanikarn looked at him, confusion filling her eyes. 'I don't know,' she said with exasperation. Her legs felt wobbly, and she turned to look for a place to sit. There was a stool next to the chopping table. She plopped down and, feeling queasy, crossed her arms on the table and dropped her spinning head on top of them.

'Karn?' Amnat said, bending over her, caressing her hair. He lifted her head with his hand.

She opened her eyes with uncommon effort and looked up at him. 'I'm okay. I'm okay,' she repeated with a weak smile.

'Maybe you should go see a doctor, Karn; you look so pale.'

'No, don't worry. I think I need to eat, but the food smells bad.'

'The food smells bad,' Amnat repeated. He fetched her a bottle of water and brought it to her, stuck it in her hand.

'Drink,' he said firmly. 'You always have a good appetite, Karn. Maybe you caught a stomach bug from one of your customers.'

Thanikarn drank her water complacently and smiled.

'Here,' Amnat said, handing her a bowl of rice. 'You can't tell me this smells funny.' She took a few forkfuls and chewed dutifully but with no appetite.

Thanikarn was almost never sick. The last time she had to stay in bed, she was ten years old with the flu.

'If you don't feel better later, you come back and see me, and I'll take you to the doctor myself.'

Standing up, Thanikarn smiled and waied sweetly, despite her feeling weak and woozy, and staggered out. Amnat watched her leave, with doubt written on his face.

When Thanikarn returned to the massage stand, Sawitti was setting up, busily checking her stock of nail polish. She noticed Thanikarn's lack of energy.

'You look tired, Karn. Too much partying?'

'Karn is feeling sick this morning, maybe a bug,' Rinalda affirmed.

'Better now,' Thanikarn said, unconvincingly.

'Amnat gave you something?' Rinalda asked, as if verifying that she did as she was told.

'Nothing he could do. I didn't want to stay in the kitchen. The smell of food cooking made me feel worse.' Rinalda studied her with a frown. 'And another funny thing,' Thanikarn continued, 'that I didn't tell Amnat. My breasts,' she said, rubbing them with her hands, 'they feel very sore.'

Rinalda shook her head back and forth slowly, rolling her eyes. 'Karn. You are not sick. You are pregnant!'

Thanikarn looked at her incredulously. 'No, that's not possible,' she said with a nervous little laugh. Rinalda looked at her askance with raised eyebrows. Thanikarn looked out toward the sea with a pensive scowl. She was thinking very hard as if trying to figure out a complicated riddle. Rinalda and Sawitti exchanged looks. Seeing the distress splayed across Thanikarn's face, they decided it was best to say no more.

Thanikarn worked throughout the day, keeping very busy. She hardly spoke, steeped in reflection. Could the impossible be possible? If she didn't feel better tomorrow, she would have to go to the doctor, if for no other reason than to offset her friend's suspicions.

After work, she passed by the pharmacy and asked for a pregnancy test as Rinalda had later advised. As soon as she got home, she sat down on a stool next to her sink and opened the small blue-and-white box, pulling out the little stick that would certainly dispel all doubt. The contents of the box looked unreliable. How could such a little piece of plastic give her such awesome news? Still distrustful, she carefully followed the instructions. She laid down the indicator stick for the short wait, too anxious to do anything but tap her fingers on the table as if it would speed up the process. She stared at the little circular window on the indicator and saw a cross forming where she expected a straight line. Her eyes widened. There must be a mistake. Either that or her grandfather's prediction was all wrong. And she had been stupid enough to believe it ...

An instant of joy quickly gave way to worry. She had never even imagined being a mother. What would she do with a baby? A baby whose father was a young man she hardly knew. A pang of guilt churned in the pit of her stomach. This is what she wished for that day on the rocks of Hin Ta and Hin Yai. She had wished for Lucas to remain in her life forever.

Blurry thoughts and nondescript feelings made her feel dizzy. She sat and breathed in and out deeply, trying to slow down her pounding heartbeat. After a few moments, her stomach began to growl and Thanikarn realized she hadn't eaten all day. She got up and made the only thing she thought capable of holding down, some rice and a couple of fried eggs. She drank some water and fell into bed, her body heavy with worry. Thanikarn had forced herself to think less and less about Lucas, but now she couldn't help but think of him. If she was pregnant, it was because of her reckless encouragement their last night together.

Only one thought allowed her to fall asleep. Maybe the test was wrong. Tomorrow, she would go see a doctor.

16

Thanikarn sat glued to a cold, grey, metal chair in a nearly empty waiting room, knotted up with apprehension. Finally, the nurse came in to hand her the official results. Void of expression, she courteously gave her the dreaded information.

'You tested positive,' the nurse said in a clipped voice.

'But how it that possible?' Thanikarn asked with true incredulity.

The nurse looked at her with raised eyebrows, as if to say, *Are you serious?*

Thanikarn sensed her exasperation and looked for a defensive reply.

'But I never had my periods. They stopped long ago.'

'That's called amenorrhea, my dear. You are thin and probably quite physically active. But an absence of menses doesn't mean you can't get pregnant,' she said, softening her tone. She directed Thanikarn to a counter for outpatients. Another nurse, a middle-aged woman with a stern jaw and clenched lips, studied her file before she began typing up her report on the computer.

'You are single,' she affirmed formally while verifying the forms Thanikarn had completed.

Thanikarn nodded, but the nurse didn't look up from her work.

'Here you are. I've assigned you an obstetrician,' the woman said, leaking out a smile as she handed Thanikarn her file. 'Call us in two weeks for your first appointment.'

Thanikarn just stood there staring at her. Her legs weakened, and her head felt empty as the fluorescent-lit room darkened and filled up with little floating stars. Fearing she would collapse, she staggered back to her chair and sat down. Being pregnant was something she always believed impossible, and the prospect of becoming a single mother felt like jumping off a ledge. After a few moments fixing her eyes on the blue wall across the room, breathing slowly to quiet her spinning head, she returned to see the nurse.

'What if I can't have this baby?' Her calm question hid an inner panic.

The nurse's brows tilted quizzically. 'Are you talking about an abortion?'

Thanikarn lowered her eyes as if she deserved a slap in the face.

'It's illegal and very complicated. Unless you can prove this was a case of rape or incest. Or if it turns out that your pregnancy puts your health in danger.'

Thanikarn wanted to run and hide from the welling shame, but her lips formed a polite smile. 'Of course,' she said quietly and calmly left the room.

Still in a daze, Thanikarn went to work and quickly began her task of setting up for the day. She was happy to have a first client appear within minutes – anything to keep her busy. She worked with feigned concentration, avoiding eye contact with either Rinalda or Sawitti. Her sullen silence was a signal to them not to ask any questions, and her two colleagues chatted quietly between themselves.

Thanikarn had always considered that one of the advantages of her job was to have time to think or daydream, but today she would have preferred otherwise. She didn't want to dwell upon her predicament. As the day continued at its usual placid pace, she worked in silence, hiding the relentless turmoil charging through her veins. Questions marched through her mind in a ceaseless parade. Why had her grandfather said she would never have a child? Did he mean she shouldn't have one? How could she have been so naive? What would it be like to bring a fatherless child into the world? What would people think of her? Preeda and Trin, how would they feel? What would her parents have said if they were still alive? Would her child be embarrassed, not having a father? Could she live with the shame?

When Thanikarn went to visit her grandmother that evening, Trin was sitting on the front steps, grimacing as he whittled away on a bent twig. He often sat outside, watching over his chickens, cleaning up around the yard, or passed his time carving wood, winding string or bending wire into funny shapes.

'*Sawaee Ka,* Lung,' she said on her way into the house. He answered with a grin.

Her grandmother was in the kitchen preparing a cup of hot *naam* cha, or milk tea, and cutting up cucumber and fresh pineapple. This would doubtless be her evening meal. Preeda never ate much at night; to do so gave her funny dreams, she said. Thanikarn came up from behind her grandmother, wrapped her arms around her waist, and pressed her head against her shoulder.

'*Sawadee Ka*, Yai,' she said.

Without abandoning her preparations, Preeda smiled to herself. Thanikarn took the knife and finished cutting up the pineapple and arranged it decoratively on a plate.

'Come,' she said, leading her grandmother to the small square table in the kitchen. 'I'll join you.'

After a few moments of silence, Thanikarn looked at her grandmother. 'Why did grandfather say I would never have any children?'

'Did he say that?' Preeda asked, picking up a chunk of pineapple.

'Yes ... You don't remember?'

Preeda shook her head slowly. Thanikarn thought it might be true she didn't remember – Preeda's mind was getting quite addled. Or maybe she was never even aware of what he'd said. In either case, Thanikarn couldn't question her word. Her heavy chest rose, then dropped as she let out an inaudible sigh that caught her grandmother's attention.

'You can have children if you want to, Karn,' she said with no hint of irony.

'And if I did have a baby, what would you think?'

'Oh, that would be so lovely. But first you need to be married ... Have you met someone?'

This was no help. Her remark was like a punch in the stomach. Being pregnant out of wedlock would surely cast a dark shadow on the family.

As the days went by, Thanikarn ached to speak to someone, but she had so few friends and, except for Preeda and Trin, no family. She often turned to Rinalda for advice or Amnat for consolation, but for this, there was no one. She wasn't only guilty of flirting with a much younger man, she had been stupidly naive enough to think she couldn't get pregnant.

Then again, if she had the chance to end this pregnancy, she wondered if she could. There were ways, of course – she'd heard of them – but she shuddered at the idea, a horrible act that would come back to haunt her forever like a *phee*, a ghost entering your house in the night.

Thanikarn remembered something she'd seen when she went to the hospital for her last check-up. While she was in the waiting room, a young Thai woman with a toddler came in and sat down beside her. Looking at the fair-skinned child in its stroller, Thanikarn surmised that the father was a farang. With his two pudgy outstretched arms, the child beckoned his mother to pick him up. She lifted him onto her lap, dug through her bag, pulled out a little toy giraffe and handed it to him. He turned his mother's chin toward him and gave her a soft kiss on the cheek.

It was perhaps the first time Thanikarn felt that her misfortune could be a blessing; she had always feared she would never be loved and would live out the rest of her life alone. Now, it seemed, her body was preparing her for graciously accepting the idea. The tiny miracle growing inside her was beginning to take over, and every little change in her body, her growing breast, her queasy stomach, her unusual fatigue, reminded her with insistence that she would soon be a mother.

After a stream of customers, Thanikarn wearily wound her way up the dirt road to see her grandmother. On her way, she decided it was time to get it over with and confess the shameful truth.

When she arrived, she found her *yai* napping. Something she did more often these days. Trin was somewhere, probably outside. Preeda's frail body gave a tiny jump when she heard the front door shut. Thanikarn entered the room gingerly, the same way she would soon announce her pregnancy. She went to the kitchen, took a fresh coconut out of the refrigerator and deftly hacked open a hexagonal hole. She stuck in a plastic straw and took it to Preeda, ceremoniously presenting it to her with two hands. Preeda slowly sipped up the clear juice, thanking her granddaughter with a weak smile. Thanikarn pulled up a chair and sat next to her.

'Yai, I've come to talk to you about something very important.'

Preeda tilted her head, intrigued.

'I would like to move back in with you and Trin. I am going to need your help.'

'Oh, how nice. I've missed you.'

'I need to come home because I'm going to have a baby.'

'I see,' Preeda said, nodding solemnly. Even with her addled mind, she realized that her granddaughter was saying something momentous.

'Will you help me?' Thanikarn asked, trying not to sound

terrified of her reaction.

'Of course, dear. I am old, and Trin is … Trin, but we are family. We love you.'

Thanikarn felt the pressure release so that she could breathe again. She reached her two arms forward and dropped her head on her grandmother's lap, letting Preeda tenderly stroke her shiny dark hair. Thanikarn could have stayed there forever, motionless, nestled in her lap like a contented cat.

* * *

It was nearly July by the time a letter from Lucas finally arrived. Philippe held it up for Thanikarn to see as she passed by him on her way to the kitchen to see Amnat. She was going to fetch a snack and have a friendly chat. Thanikarn had forgotten Lucas's promise to send something, so the envelope from France came as a surprise. With the letter in hand, she wandered down to her favourite place near the hotel, a spot where an old fishing boat lay overturned under a couple of palm trees.

She sat down on the boat's hull and carefully pried open the letter, careful not to tear the corner with the French stamp she would offer to Trin. She pulled out the photo enclosed in a little note. *For my beautiful Thanikarn, with fond memories of happy times. Lucas Adrien (your man from the sea).* She gazed at the glossy picture taken by Lucas's father in which she was seated behind him with her two legs straddled on each side, giving him a massage. He was lying on his back, head propped up for the picture, flashing a grin. Thanikarn's bright face and brilliant eyes radiated joy as she smiled into the camera. People seldom took pictures of her, and when they did, she never found herself to be very attractive, but she had to admit, in this one, she looked beautiful.

Thanikarn slipped her fingers over the shiny image; the corners of her mouth turned up, and her eyes became moist. She rubbed her still-flat tummy. 'That's your daddy,' she said out loud. As she continued to study the picture, she thought about Lucas's porcelain skin and blond hair and, for the first time, wondered if their child would look like him.

Having received the letter, Thanikarn thought about calling Lucas. She had lacked the courage up till now, fearing it would only awaken all the memories she was trying to forget, but she also felt she ought to thank him for the picture. As Thanikarn pressed on the relaxed muscles of her last customer of the day, she felt her own muscles tightening with tension. She was afraid to talk to Lucas again, afraid of successfully hiding what she had vowed to keep a secret.

As soon as she returned to her little apartment, slipped out of her beach sandals, and poured herself some water flavoured with a slice of lime, she sat down on her floor mattress to phone Lucas. She listened to the usual six or seven rings she expected, followed by his recorded voice, relieved that she could just leave a message.

'Hello, Lucas. It is Karn. I want to tell you your letter come today. And the beautiful picture. I call to say thank you.' She had done her duty and half-hoped he wouldn't return her call.

Thanikarn used a bowlful of the previous day's noodles to fry up with some garlic, red peppers and the cooked pieces of chicken that Amnat had wrapped up for her and had begun preparing dinner when the phone sang out its familiar melody. Her heart jumped.

'Hello, Lucas. You call me back. Nice surprise.'

'Yeah. Sorry I haven't called lately, but I was busy studying for my final exams.'

Thanikarn was reminded of his young age. Still in school and the father of her baby. 'Finished now?'

'Finished but still busy. I'm doing a little composing for a friend's short film. And working on my songs.'

'What you do next?' she asked, just to make conversation.

'Good question. I have a couple of options I'm considering.'

'Options?'

Lucas tended to forget about her limited vocabulary. 'I have a couple of choices, and I'm not too sure which is the best.'

'You always make good choice,' she said, not knowing why.

'Well, one of my choices is to go to Los Angeles. I think I already talked to you about it. I have family there, and a friend of my father knows some people in music. A producer who works in commercials.'

This was an 'option' Thanikarn hadn't expected. Paris was far away, but Los Angeles was even further.

'And other choice?' she asked with a hint of worry. What if it was a return to Koh Samui?

'The other choice is to stay in Paris and finish my degree at the Sorbonne. But I'm getting tired of school. I don't think a diploma is going to make any difference for my music career.'

She thought about herself when she was his age. After losing both her parents, choosing between school and work wasn't an 'option'.

Lucas's voice cut off her self-pity. 'I'll probably go to LA,' he continued. 'I wish I could come back and see you before I go, but it would be too expensive. I have to save my money for the States.'

Thanikarn was relieved to hear he wasn't planning to come back anytime soon.

'Hello?' he asked. 'You still there?'

'Yes, I am here. I'm happy for you. America. Good luck,' she said, pulling out a common expression she'd learned.

'Thanks. I'll need it. I'll call you as soon as my plans are settled. I should know what I'm doing in a week or two.'

Thanikarn didn't know where to direct their conversation. In her heart, she wanted to hold on to him. She wanted to tell him how much she still loved him. She wanted him to know that she could never forget him now, even if he never came back.

'Listen, Karn. Whatever I decide to do, I'll let you know. We can always keep in touch, no matter where I am.'

'Okay,' she said, thinking that America or France really made no difference.

'I have to go now. We'll talk again soon,' Lucas said, trying to sound reassuring.

'Okay.' She didn't dare say more; she was doing her best to control the jumble of emotions churning in her head.

'Big kiss,' he said sweetly.

'Big kiss,' she echoed.

17

Another month passed and Lucas hadn't called back. Thanikarn was sad not knowing what 'option' he had chosen, but then again, it didn't matter. He was far away with no plans to return.

Thanikarn still hadn't said anything about being pregnant to her friends at the hotel. The day she came back from the hospital, no one dared ask any questions. Maybe it was the stone-cold colour of shock written all over her face. She could have said something later, but with fear and doubt clouding her mind, it took her weeks to decide what to say. And back then, there was the possibility of a miscarriage, a convenient way to avoid telling the truth.

Now that the hospital confirmed that the baby was well on its way, even though she'd exchanged her stretch tops for loose cotton T-shirts that came down to her hips, her bulging tummy and blossoming breasts couldn't be hidden much longer.

Thanikarn fretted over how to announce her imminent motherhood. She thought about leaving with no explanation, but Rinalda, Sawitti and Amnat were her friends. She couldn't just quit without saying why. Remembering how things unfolded when she'd told her grandmother, Thanikarn realized that telling the truth wasn't the end of the world. It would be best to speak first with Rinalda. Being a mature woman, she would be the most likely to understand.

Around five thirty, Rinalda was slowly folding up her towels. Sawitti, always the first to go, had left nearly an hour ago.

'Rinalda, I have something I want to tell you,' Thanikarn said as an overture.

Rinalda continued arranging her affairs, not indifferent but showing little curiosity.

'I'm going to have a baby,' Thanikarn continued.

Rinalda stopped her folding and looked at Thanikarn. 'I know that, Karn. We all know that.'

Thanikarn lowered her eyes and sighed. 'I'm sorry,' she said.

'Sorry for what? Being pregnant or not telling us?' There was a hint of irony in Rinalda's voice that put Thanikarn at ease. She looked up to see that she was smiling.

'Come here,' Rinalda said. Thanikarn lunged forward to receive an uncharacteristic hug.

'Thank you,' Thanikarn said, holding back tears. She hated feeling so emotional, but these days crying had become as uncontrollable as a sneeze and as frequent as a blink.

'So, I guess we're going to have to find you a new job soon,' Rinalda said, looking down at Thanikarn's tummy.

'I might be able to get my old job back at the supermarket, but I don't want to lose my place here.'

'Maybe we can figure something out ... You could talk to Philippe.'

'Does he know?' Thanikarn asked, eyes wide with fear.

Rinalda looked toward his reception desk as if he were there. She thoughtfully shook her head. 'I don't think so.'

Thanikarn dropped her tight shoulders and let out a sigh of relief. It was bad enough that all her friends knew. She would tell Philippe if she had to, but for now she just wanted to make sure she could keep her spot at the Golden Gecko until she found another job.

Work and money were stressful matters that Thanikarn wanted to figure out quickly. She'd always been naturally frugal, but ever since she'd renounced her education she'd lost any ambition to make more money than she needed. Her small savings at the bank, money that was left over after paying back Trin, wasn't enough to carry her through several months of pregnancy without work.

* * *

Thanikarn's plan to move back home was one way to save money, and now she was certain she would be welcomed. Her grandmother said she missed her, and Trin wouldn't mind sleeping in the living room or, as she imagined, on a cot outside with his chickens.

The more she thought about it, the more she found the idea a good one, not just to save money but to ease her tormented mind. She was afraid to face the coming months alone, feeling vulnerable as all those bubbling hormones threw her into mood spins ranging from peaks of elation to black holes of gloom. She glowed in the thought of being a mother but worried about her baby being normal and healthy. She felt courageous about her choice to raise a child on her own but was tormented about the stigma of having a baby out of wedlock, especially one who might look something like his father. The 'what ifs' pestered her like a persistent fly. It would be nice to have the baby, someone, around all the time, even if it was just for silent company or one-way conversations.

Thanikarn soon realized that living at home wasn't as inconvenient as she remembered. Trin spent most of his time outside with his chickens or at the market, and in the evening he'd sit on the front steps, whittling wood or concocting his little wired sculptures. Preeda piddled around the house taking a very long time to do very little – light chores like sweeping, washing the dishes, or mending – until she was too tired to keep going. And then she would suddenly stop to sit down in her big easy chair next to the window, attending to whatever might catch her eye outside: a flying bird, a stray dog digging through garbage, workers gathering coconuts in the field. After dinner, before sliding into bed, she would slip out of her surroundings with a silly television soap opera. Preeda never had been very communicative, but she now seemed more and more distant with a glossy gaze that accompanied her silence. It worried Thanikarn, but at least Preeda was always there.

Thanikarn slipped into a wait-and-see state of mind when it came to Lucas. If he called again, she would pretend nothing had changed, her life bobbing along like an empty bottle in a stream of monotony. If he didn't call, she could get on with her life as a single mother, resigned to the fact that he had walked out of it forever. Nonetheless, she kept her phone close, like everyone else did.

Now she had five phone numbers besides Lucas's in her list of contacts: those of Sawitti and Manee, who both had cell phones long before she did, the hotel reception and the hospital, which was the most important. She wanted to be sure a nurse and doctor were always a phone call away. And just yesterday, there was a new addition, Phong's number.

Phong was an old school friend, but neither one of them had made any attempt to keep up their friendship after graduation. Thanikarn remembered how he had always been the first in class, an unpopular nerd with few friends. She knew he had liked her, but he never made any advances, probably too shy. It made her feel sorry for him, something no boy ever wanted to know. Sometimes she sat with him at lunch or walked home with him from school, and she liked doing their math homework together, a subject Thanikarn was surprisingly good at. But he was a secretive type of guy, who seldom talked about himself, and after finishing high school they went their separate ways. She'd heard that he moved to Bangkok to study at university, while she took the first job she could find. Now, he had a career at the bank and she was a pregnant, unwed masseuse.

The last time she'd gone to the bank, Phong was working as a teller, but when she went to check her savings account, after a lapse of nearly a year, she was surprised to see him sitting upright with importance behind a large wooden desk. He looked different – maybe it was the new haircut, short on the sides and swept up like a wave across the top his head. She wandered over to say hello and saw that his bronze-coloured name plaque was followed by the title of financial advisor.

'Oh, Karn!' he said, looking up at her through thick, black-rimmed glasses. 'It's been a long time.'

She answered with a broad, bright smile and pretended not to notice the large rhinestone in his left ear. That was new. After ping-ponging banalities, he suggested they get together some evening for a meal. Thanikarn wondered why now and not before; he had all those years between high school graduation to ask her out. She felt a little hesitant, but flattered by the prospect of a friendly outing, a welcome change to her uneventful routine, she replied that she would be happy to get together. Thanikarn proudly pulled out her phone, feeling like part of the modern world. Phong typed in his number, and she gave him hers.

'You call me, anytime,' she said, half-expecting to never get his call.

* * *

For no reason, except that is wasn't the weekend, Wednesday night had become girls' night out. On the popular night strip in Chaweng Beach, every night was party night, but Friday and Saturday tended to be more raucous, when men of all ages, after one drink too many, crawled out from everywhere, with annoying cat calls and sloppy attempts at flirting. There were enough professionals on the island to handle them, but sometimes, after too much alcohol, they uncontrollably chatted up anyone wearing a skirt, including locals out on the town, like Thanikarn and her friends.

On this Wednesday, Thanikarn was at home going through her clothes, looking for something clean and concealing for her evening out, when her grandmother called her from the living room.

'Karn, there is music coming out of your bag.'

Thanikarn assumed it was Manee, calling to tell her where they would meet up for their weekly outing, and sauntered out of the bedroom to fetch her phone.

'*Sawadee ka*,' she said cheerfully.

'*Sawadee kap*,' Lucas answered with one of the few things he remembered how to say.

'Lucas!' she cried despite herself.

'Yup. It's me.'

'I did not think you call again.' She looked furtively toward her grandmother. Preeda was paying no attention to her conversation. 'I am very surprised,' Thanikarn continued.

'I'm sorry. It's been a while. But things have been kinda crazy for me. I wanted to let you know about my plans.'

'*Ka*,' she said, fully expecting that his plans wouldn't involve her.

'I'm leaving for the States soon. I've had a lot to do to get ready.'

She was right. 'When do you go?'

'Really soon, like in a week. I'll stay with my uncle until I find a job and a place to live.'

Thanikarn wasn't sure how to respond. It was normal for him to be thinking of himself and his career plans. He was oblivious to the tiny miracle that tied them together.

'I have a ticket for the fourteenth, but I may have to postpone it. There is still a lot I have to get organized.'

'Can we talk when you are in Los Angeles?' The telephone was their only thread of communication.

'Of course!' Lucas said cheerfully. 'I wrote another song about you,' he continued. 'It's in French. But I can send it to you anyway.'

'What is it called?' she asked.

'"*Tu Me Manques*." That means "I Miss You".'

Thanikarn smiled. 'You can sing it for me?'

'Well, not now. I need a guitar or bass, but maybe I could do a simple recording and send it to you.'

'Okay.' Her slight smile widened. 'And my other song too?'

'Yeah. Sure. Why not? I'll try to get it off to you before I leave … If I have time.'

'If you have time,' she echoed. Foreigners were always bringing up time. Never enough time, losing time, making more time. So different from her culture, where life was an endless circle, not a finite line.

'But how you send me your song?' she asked, as the little furrow between her brows deepened.

'Oh, I'll record it with my microphone, put it on the computer, and copy it onto a USB key or make a CD.'

'CD?' she asked. A USB key made no sense

'Yeah. You know, like the CDs you buy at the store.'

'Yes, I know. But I don't know you can make one.'

'I'm sorry I can't be there to sing it for you myself. A CD is the best I can do.' He was probably trying to be sweet, but she imagined this was something he would just crowd into his busy schedule.

'That would be nice,' she said, hoping he wasn't just trying to be nice.

'So, what are you doing tonight?' Lucas asked casually; perhaps he'd detected the melancholy in her voice.

'Just going for drinks with Manee and her friends. In Chaweng.'

'Ah, Chaweng. *Tom ka gai* soup at the night market, a Tiger Beer on the beach. I wish I could be there. Well, I hope you have fun, but watch out for those drunken tourists.'

She remembered how he had always been very protective when they went out, holding her hand, wrapping his arm around her waist. His gallantry made her feel special. 'No worry for me. I am a strong girl.' If only he knew how strong she was being. Hiding what she knew and felt took Herculean effort.

'Well, take care, Karn. Hopefully I can get that CD off to you before I leave. Anyway, don't worry, I'll call you from LA. So, big kiss and goodbye for now.'

He always signed off with a kiss. 'Goodbye, Lucas. Have a safe trip,' she added. Airplanes scared her. She would never forget his departure from Koh Samui during that threatening storm. She had no idea then how much he would continue to be a worry.

18

Lucas's CD never came, but Thanikarn did receive a text message, something new to her. *I'm fine, just very busy. Hard to call you with the time difference. Take care, kisses, Lucas.* With the help of Sawitti, who showed her how to use the phone for texting, she sent a message back. *I'm fine too. No worry about me. Kisses, Karn.*

Every time she had news from him, it caused a mental battle, the sombre voice of reason competing with her hopeful heart. Reason reminded her that Lucas would never come back, and even if he did, she would be faced with a horrible decision: either keep their child a secret or tell him the dire truth. He would be terrified to learn he was a father, and there was little chance that a young, handsome, talented farang like Lucas would ever settle down with someone like her in Koh Samui. It was only in fleeting moments when she forgot who and what she was that her heart played with a fairytale ending: Lucas gracefully accepting fatherhood, deciding to live and work on the island, or better yet, whisking her and their child off to Europe or the United States.

Thanikarn's little tummy continued to swell. Fortunately, she could continue massaging the steady flow of post-summer guests;

she was supple enough to lower herself down and get back up off the floor without effort and strong enough to lift limp bodies or roll them over with agility. But she knew she wouldn't be able to do this much longer. Her friends at the Golden Gecko agreed to help her find another job, but most of the people they knew worked in the hotel business, cleaning rooms or cooking. Those were taxing jobs, and in a short time she wouldn't be able to stay on her feet all day.

When Thanikarn had gone for her twenty-week check-up, the doctor advised her to find a job where she could sit down most of the time, something about plasma that she didn't quite understand. Minor, it seemed, but she shouldn't take any unnecessary risks, and as for most mothers-to-be, nothing in Thanikarn's life was more important than getting through her pregnancy without complications.

One alternative was to go back to her old job as a cashier at the supermarket, but that was a final resort. She looked back at that job with resentment: time lost in neon-lit boredom. Then she remembered her friend Phong; maybe he could help her find something. He knew lots of professional people through his job at the bank.

She mulled over the idea of calling him, hoping he would call her first. Their last exchange had only been a week before.

She would wait.

Thanikarn was a little surprised to hear from Phong a few days later, but then again, if she didn't know him better, the way he looked at her at the bank would have led her to suspect he was a man in pursuit of more than friendship.

Phong was early for their seven o'clock meeting at the Pizza Hut in Chaweng. Considering his choice of restaurant, Thanikarn concluded that his intentions were far from romantic. After pushing open the heavy glass doors, built to keep out the island heat, she quickly spotted Phong sipping a Coke at a table in the corner, a predictable spot for someone who had always been shy with girls. She gave a wave to catch his attention and beamed her wide smile. He self-consciously beckoned her with a raise of his hand and stood up to greet her.

'I hope this place is okay,' he said to Thanikarn, pushing up his dark-rimmed glasses. It was a nervous tick.

'Of course it's okay,' she said, taking a seat across from him.

'I like pizza,' he said, sitting down.

'Yes, I remember.' Thanikarn giggled, just like when they were both back in school.

After the waiter took their order, a hot and spicy pizza, they talked about former times, teachers, classmates, silly memories. All the while, she was trying to figure out why Phong wanted to get together again. He was so enigmatic; it always seemed as if his words hid what was going on inside his mind.

As they finished eating, she began to think about how she would wade into the murky waters of her predicament, eventually asking for his help, but there was no subtle way to announce she was pregnant and needed a job.

'Phong, I know we've both gone our ways, but we were good friends once and I know I can trust you. I have something to tell you.'

Phong looked at her without blinking until she found the

courage to speak.

'I'm going to have a baby,' she finally announced.

'Oh,' he said quietly.

'It wasn't planned,' she went on to say, 'but I want this baby, and I will do my best to be a good mother.'

'I'm sure you will be,' he said and seconds later offered a smile that seemed to be tacked on as an afterthought.

'Since I'm on my own,' Thanikarn continued, 'I'll need to find a new job. Something less ... physical. My doctor says I can't go on giving massages much longer. You meet lots of people at the bank. I thought maybe you might know someone.'

'Um, sure. I can't promise you anything, but I can keep it in mind,' he said. His reply sounded a little dismissive, and Thanikarn wondered if he was just being polite.

Phong quickly asked for the bill. Thanikarn offered to pay her share, but he refused. Leaving the restaurant, he was unusually quiet, and she feared his silence was judgmental, reflecting a loss of esteem. Before getting on her scooter, Thanikarn thanked him again for dinner, trying to sound cheerful, but her honest eyes must have betrayed her distress. After an awkward moment, Phong gently took her hand.

'Karn, I know that it was hard for you to talk to me about this. I'll do what I can to help you. And, if you like, we can see each other again.'

'Oh, well ... yes,' she said, a bit flustered. 'That would be very nice.' She squeezed his hand and smiled with relief. Her heart felt lighter as she mounted her scooter and sped off in the hot, humid night.

Thanikarn was surprised to get a phone call from Phong a week later. He had indeed found something: one of his clients at the bank, a woman who made and sold jewellery at the Iyara Shopping Plaza in Chaweng, was looking for an assistant. He sounded content with himself, and Thanikarn wondered how she would ever be able to repay him.

Thanikarn lost no time and contacted her potential employer the next morning. Konticha explained the job briefly on the phone. Thanikarn would help her put together some of the jewellery, gluing pieces in place and stringing beads, as well as replacing her from time to time at the jewellery stand in the Friday night market, both sit-down jobs. Though she would be making less money at first and no longer be her own boss, it was perfect. The only problem was losing her space at the Golden Gecko, where she wanted to return as soon as she could after the baby arrived.

Thanikarn dreaded discussing her situation with Philippe. She wasn't afraid of him; in fact, she felt very comfortable with her landlord. He was always kind and patient, but she hated asking for favours. They always involved being indebted. She knew she couldn't expect him to keep her place vacant, so, if she wanted to come back, someone else would have to take over to keep up the rent. Maybe he would know someone.

It was the end of a long, hot afternoon, and some heavy, grey clouds loomed above the horizon. Once they burst open with a drenching deluge, they would float happily away. Manee had just served Philippe a beer at the terrace bar, and he was relaxing with a smoke after a busy day welcoming a busload of guests from Brussels. The hotel was fully booked.

Hmm, good time or bad time, Thanikarn wondered. There was no reason to put off asking; it wouldn't change his answer. Growing up in a family struck twice by tragedy, she could deal with disappointment. First, have no expectations; second, be prepared not to get what you want; and third, if you're let down, pretend it was for the best.

'Philippe. You have some time for me?' Thanikarn asked, her tone serious but with no undue drama.

'Sure, Karn.' He sounded tired, and she had second thoughts about bringing this up now, but Philippe was seldom alone and relaxed. She had practiced her announcement, using her best English.

'I am very sorry, but I need to stop my work here for a short time. After, I want to come back, not lose my place,' she said, hoping not to explain why. Revealing motives or desires wasn't part of her upbringing.

He studied her silently for a moment. If he didn't propose something, she knew it was her problem and that was the end of it.

'I try to find someone to take my place, but for a short time is not easy,' she continued. Her throat was tight with intimidation.

It was certain that Philippe could live without her rent for a while; it was a significant amount of money for her but only a modest income for him. He drew on his cigarette and then slowly stubbed it out in the ashtray. Waiting for his answer, she began to ponder; maybe he already knew why she had to stop.

Maybe he wouldn't want her back again. She bit her lower lip, embarrassment welling up inside.

'Well, look, Karn, see what you can do, and if you don't find a replacement right away, I think we can get by without anyone for a while,' he said, casually taking another sip of beer.

She thanked him with a huge smile. She could have hugged him, but instead, gave a deep bowed wai. Philippe politely waied back.

'See you tomorrow?' he asked.

'Yes, I come a few weeks more. And I keep try to find someone.' She turned and left, then looked back over her shoulder, sending Philippe another thankful smile.

19

It was like losing an old friend. Thanikarn had to give up riding her little pink scooter to work or anywhere else. She loved zipping around the streets of Koh Samui, but it was too uncomfortable now that her tummy was bulging and, more importantly, much too dangerous. Fortunately, a passing songthaew was always at hand any time of day or night for getting around the island. The ride down to her new workplace in Lamai took a little over a half an hour, and now that she was unabashedly wearing her signature bulge, she was often offered a seat, one of the unexpected advantages of being pregnant.

Far from anything she could have imagined, Thanikarn found herself learning a totally new trade. Funny how a single unforeseen circumstance led to a chain of newness. It all began with a simple massage, an unexpected invitation, a night of imprudence, and now, living back at home, the prospect of being a mother and a new job.

Konticha was at least ten years older than Thanikarn and unmarried with no children. She was a free-spirited, self-declared artist. As soon as they met, Konticha, one of the most sophisticated Thai people Thanikarn had ever encountered, launched into an account of her adventurous life. She rattled off the list of places she'd visited, travelling on her own to Jakarta, Delhi and Singapore: bustling, big cities that rang of excitement and adventure. Konticha picked up new ideas for her jewellery creations wherever she went, spending most of her time gathering local materials, beads, stones, enamel and chains and turning them into lovely earrings, bracelets and necklaces. She had even gone on vacation to London and New York. Thanikarn was amazed. Konticha's life seemed as fanciful as the jewellery she made, a little bit of this and that, a colourful hodgepodge worked into a harmonious whole.

Thanikarn was good with her hands, but now she was using them in a totally new way, and it was quite a challenge. Massaging was all about body contact, smoothing oil on skin, pressing palms and fingers into muscles and tendons, deep, penetrating work. It required sensitivity, strength and endurance, but it was more about feeling and touch than mental concentration. With Konticha, she discovered a different way of using her hands, precise manipulation that kept her head bent, paying constant attention to what her fingers were doing. Everything seemed so small – little pearls, rhinestones and beads, thin filaments of wire and fine chains, tiny clasps and hooks. Thanikarn learned quickly, but then again, she wasn't given anything too challenging, mostly sorting the materials, stringing, and gluing according to Konticha's instructions. Thanikarn was pleased with herself, discovering that she could be competent at something besides massage work. Anything was accessible; she thought, it was just a matter of learning and persistence, and the more Konticha gave her challenging projects, the more she enjoyed it.

They worked together in Konticha's little workshop, a transformed apartment in a two-storey building. The atelier was on the ground floor and Konticha's living quarters were upstairs. Since it was in the back of a small courtyard behind an office building, it was quiet enough to work in peace, even with the windows open. Ben's hybrid souvenir-shop-and-library was a five-minute walk down the road.

Konticha had inherited the studio from her parents. Thanikarn doubted that Konticha really had to work at all, since the inexpensive jewellery she sold could hardly pay for her jet-set lifestyle. She surely came from a family with money. Konticha's situation reminded her of Lucas; she had the fortune to follow her passion, knowing that if things didn't work out, there was no risk of being obliged to take the first available job in order to help take care of a family.

Thanikarn tried not to compare herself with others, but there were times she wished her life had been different. Then, being taught that envy only led to frustration, resentment, and sorrow, she would doggedly chase such thoughts away.

Since Thanikarn didn't have regular working hours at Konticha's studio, she could arrive anytime before noon. Her new boss was a late riser, and even if Thanikarn arrived at eleven, Konticha would still be dressed in her flowing silk robe with huge red-and-yellow printed flowers, sipping a cup of milky coffee, a habit she took up while travelling and staying in Western-style hotels.

Unlike Thanikarn's taciturn grandmother, whose introversion

was becoming a distressing sign of a failing mind, Konticha never stopped talking. Since Thanikarn and her new boss spent the whole day together, they had plenty of time to learn about one another, although Thanikarn did most of the learning. Sometimes Konticha would wander around the room, looking for something she couldn't find, while flailing her arms and ranting about the disorder in her workshop. But even if quietly seated, she would stop what she was doing to talk, twisting her body and throwing up her arms. Sometimes long, bubbly monologues burst out like from an opened bottle of champagne; other times she asked rhetorical questions meant to include Thanikarn in the conversation. Thanikarn began to wonder if Konticha had hired an assistant to help her make jewellery or to have a captive audience for every thought, lamentation, aspiration or existential reflection that trotted through her head.

Eventually, Konticha wanted to know more about her employee. Thanikarn felt her paltry collection of experiences left her with little to say. Her past was uninteresting, her present embarrassing and her future a mystery, even to herself. A life without a plan.

Thanikarn appreciated Konticha's discretion in not asking about the father. She had probably assumed he was out of the picture. She knew that Thanikarn had worked as a masseuse, was now living at home and never mentioned a man. Despite her Westernized facade, Konticha was still Thai enough to know not to cause another to lose face.

'So, the baby is coming when?' Konticha felt free to ask.

'In January, maybe the middle of the month ... Will you still need me after January?'

According to Phong, Thanikarn was hired for only two months. Konticha had said she only needed an assistant to fill a Christmas season order for a client in Bangkok.

'Maybe. So, what do you think – a boy or a girl?'

Thanikarn was working on a pair of drop earrings. 'Doesn't matter. Just a healthy baby,' she said without looking at her boss. This was only partly true. Even if she knew she would love a girl as much as a boy, she'd always considered girls to have less freedom and opportunity. Boys could satisfy their own ambitions without guilt.

'Well, if you ask me, it's a boy,' Konticha said, vigorously sketching out an idea with a charcoal pencil on her pad.

'Why do you say that?' Thanikarn asked, looking up with hopeful eyes.

Konticha continued sketching. 'I don't know. Just a feeling.'

'Oh,' Thanikarn said inaudibly. Always looking for predictive signs, she wished Konticha had had something more substantive in mind.

'Have you thought of a name?' Konticha asked.

Thanikarn had thought of a boy's name, but until she gave birth, she felt it was inauspicious to say so.

'Still thinking,' she said.

Konticha suddenly tore out the sketch she'd been working on, crumpled it up and threw it in the trash. She went and grabbed one of the many fashion magazines she kept stocked in her workshop and began flipping through it, as if trying to flip through the pages of a catalogue of thoughts.

Thanikarn sensed tension in the room, regretting she couldn't be more talkative. Konticha often seemed eager for more intimacy, but she was her boss.

'I'd make a terrible mother,' Konticha said suddenly.

'Why do you say that?' Thanikarn asked, accepting her invitation to say more.

'I'm a worrier. I worry about everything and everyone. The most I can handle is a cat. Cats can get along on their own. A family is too much responsibility. And then once you have a child, you're stuck, no more travelling, no more going out whenever you want. With Indy, I can come and go as I please. I just ask my neighbour to leave out some cat food and water. 'Isn't that right, Indy?' she said, looking over at her fat, rust-coloured tabby.

Thanikarn nodded, even if she didn't agree. Even though a child would surely be a worry, she believed that anyone you loved was a worry. Thanikarn instinctively put her hand on her tummy as if she needed to reassure herself and felt a tiny kick, not the first, a little nudge that said, *I'm here.*

* * *

It was inevitable. Thanikarn had left Konticha's studio late one afternoon and was waiting for a songthaew to come rambling by when she practically ran into Ben. She knew that his shop was a short walk from Konticha's apartment, but it never occurred to her to drop in and see him. With her bulging stomach, there would be questions, questions she might not want to answer. Besides, he would just remind her of Lucas.

They simultaneously smiled, happy to see each other, and when they locked eyes, Thanikarn's big tummy completely slipped her mind. Ben walked forward with outstretched arms to give her a hug.

'Whoa! Thanikarn. This is a surprise!' he said, referring to her stomach more than the fact he hadn't expected to see her again.

'How are you, Ben?' she asked with a wide smile and a tender twinkle in her eyes. She was sincerely pleased to see him.

'I'm fine, and you … beautiful as ever.' He didn't call attention to the obvious.

'Yes, I am very happy.' She added proudly, 'Going to have a baby.'

'I can see that. Congratulations!'

The question she wanted to ask was burning a heavy hole in her stomach. There was an awkward pause. Ben wanted to ask the same question, but seeing her condition, he was sensitive enough to know it might embarrass her.

'I'm off to the post office, have to get there before it closes, but I'd love to get together if you're ever back in the neighbourhood …'

She hoped he wasn't being merely polite.

'Maybe I come see you. I work close here. New job sitting down. Can't massage with this,' she said with a giggle, hands on her big belly.

'Well, you know where to find me,' he said and started to turn away. Thanikarn's heart had stopped. She wanted him to turn around. She wanted to know more. Then, he turned back to say, 'By the way, any news from Lucas since he left?' Her throat tightened. What should she say?

'Not for long time.'

'Me neither. I only heard he was thinking about going to Los Angeles.'

She nodded in acknowledgment.

'Well, see you soon,' he said, pointing a finger as if it was an order.

'See you soon.' She smiled, waving goodbye, and climbed onto a newly arrived songthaew.

20

There were some paltry signs of Christmas on the island: a few coloured lights hanging limply across the main streets, some garlands and balls decorating the expat bars and restaurants, and twinkling lights in front of the upscale hotels, each with a decorated fake pine tree reigning in the hotel lobby. It was slightly more festive for Lucas in Los Angeles. Sure, there were all the commercial signs of Christmas: decorations everywhere, mostly the shiny, flashing-neon type; corny songs oozing or barking out of loudspeakers in mall shops and supermarkets; cashiers donning elf hats; and lookalike Santas wearing sunglasses and waving from street corners. But this was not the kind of Christmas Lucas was used to. He felt nostalgic for the family's modest country home back in France, an old farmhouse near Mont-Saint-Michel, with its huge stone hearth and a roaring fire to fend off the crisp, cold winter weather.

Things were going as well as they could for someone in a new city and a new country. Even though he was an American citizen, he'd never lived in the States, and despite having his passport, he had to face the culture shock of a foreigner. His first few months in LA were disappointingly occupied by everything but his music.

His uncle Albert, a lone widower nearly fifty years his senior, was an incorrigible hoarder; there was practically no place to sit let alone sleep, so the best Al could do was put him up for a few days at a seedy hotel in the eastern suburbs not far from where he lived. However, his uncle was also a bit of a lifesaver, lending Lucas an old Nissan pickup truck, one of the many vehicles he kept stored in the garage and back yard.

Then there was the problem of a driver's license. Driving in Paris was an eccentric nuisance, and Lucas never used his father's Peugeot, but after trying to take inefficient buses, he soon realized that having a car was a dire necessity in Los Angeles.

Through a chain of acquaintances, Lucas managed to find a place to share with a young film student. It was located downtown, in a Latino neighbourhood with low-riders cruising up and down the wide avenues and lots of young Mexican girls wearing short-shorts and platform high heels. The area had little to do with the glamour of Hollywood, but it was animated, colourful and cheap.

During those first few months, his time was eaten up by practical details: getting a local driver's permit, understanding the freeway system and finding a place to live. Lucas was frustrated with all the daily hassles, including new encounters, the need to communicate on a new level and contact the list of people his father had provided, people who would supposedly give him a job.

There was little time for thoughts of his island romance, although there were a couple of times he was reminded of Karn, such as when he met a young Thai woman selling cigarettes at the corner gas station or when he met a cute waitress at a little Thai restaurant near Koreatown. They served his favourite chicken coconut curry soup. Otherwise, all his energy was focused on trying to make a new life and turning his passion into a profession.

As soon as the signs of a disappointingly artificial Christmas began to appear, Lucas started feeling homesick and his parents lost no time in letting him know they would offer him a round-trip ticket to Paris for the holidays. There was nothing to keep Lucas in Los Angeles and despite vague promises and a few appointments after the holidays, no contracts or jobs, he had nothing to lose by going home for Christmas.

* * *

His parents and brother had just returned from Shanghai, and everyone would be reunited for the next two weeks. It was a truly joyous reunion, everyone convening in the warm nest of their comfortable Paris apartment, sharing stories of time spent away from home. Foreign adventures were rattled off with bubbly enthusiasm. Once Lucas was over jetlag and all the trials and tribulations of living abroad had been unloaded, he settled into his adolescent habits, which included holing up in his room. Everything he found there reminded him of the time he spent in Thailand: a Buddha head he'd picked up in Bangkok, a square silk scarf attached by four corners that drooped from the ceiling, his teakwood incense burner and a package of fragrant sticks that were still sitting on his nightstand, and on his bookshelf, a stack of photos from his trip to Koh Samui.

Despite all the usual holiday distractions, seeing old friends and members of his extensive family, gift buying and food shopping, the fact of being back in his bedroom looking at the old photos brought back memories of Thanikarn and a twinge of guilt. He hadn't even tried to call her once while he was in LA. The song he promised to record and send never even got recorded. But she was special. Recollecting those enchanting moments walking on the beach, riding on her bike, or cuddling in her bed rekindled his affection for her; he wondered if she still thought about him after all this time. She must have been disappointed, writing him off as another flirtatious farang taking advantage of a pretty, sweet island girl, sleeping with her and then stuffing her into a mental closet, like a souvenir bought at the market.

Then again, for him, it wasn't like that at all. He had become genuinely infatuated with Thanikarn. She was faultless: beautiful, sweet and charming. And, he believed, sincerely in love with him. But with so many differences, their brief affair could never go anywhere but nowhere.

Feeling despondent and still having trouble falling asleep, Lucas lay in his bed with his head propped up on a pile of pillows and began jotting out a new song. The melody was already there, something he had composed back in LA, and now that he was in a dreamy nostalgic mood, the words came quickly. Though he was a perfectionist, he was determined to make a compromise regarding his usual fastidiousness. He told himself to just get it done and forget about professionalism for once. A simple guitar-backed recording should suffice.

It was two o'clock in the morning; the house was quiet. Alone in his room, he sat on a stool, perched in front of a standup microphone, and sang three songs: 'Wakin' Up Blues', the song he had sung for Thanikarn that night in the bar; his French song, '*Tu Me Manques*', and his new one, 'Everything's Fine'. The latter two songs were a bit on the melancholic side, but he was a melancholic sort of guy. As an incurable romantic, he sometimes thought he was born into the wrong century.

Once Lucas finished recording, he tinkered with a quick sound mix and because it wasn't a polished version, reluctantly burned it onto a CD. If he got it to the post office the next day, Thanikarn might get it before Christmas, and even though he knew she was a Buddhist, it would be a holiday gift and a way to say, 'I'm sorry.'

As he did with his former letter, he addressed it to the Golden Gecko; she surely still worked there. Besides, it was the only address he had.

* * *

Philippe rarely went back to France at Christmas time or any other time, but this year would be an exception. His mother was nearly ninety-two, in declining health, and his sisters back in Lyon made a special request for him to attend what might be their mother's last Christmas. His former business partner, Bandit, whom he had bought out years ago, came to stand in for him at the hotel. Bandit knew how to do everything: general management, bookings and cancellations. The accounting could wait for Philippe's return, and the staff knew their daily routines. Lucas's letter and CD for Thanikarn arrived just before Christmas but ended up in a drawer with other odd mail that could wait for

Philippe's return in January.

Bandit new nothing of Thanikarn's rental deal with Philippe, so a few days after taking over, he remarked there was a surplus of customers and an empty space at the massage stand. He mentioned it to his niece, Jantip, who worked part-time at the Anantara Lawana Resort & Spa, suggesting she might rent the stand a few days a week for extra income.

The first day that Jantip showed up, Rinalda was a little miffed. She had become accustomed to the comfort of extra space and the nonstop work. Both she and Sawitti wanted to say something about it, but it wasn't their place to bicker with the boss's friend. However, they didn't hesitate to let Jantip know that according to Philippe, the vacancy was only temporary.

Jantip was Sawitti's age but had a know-it-all attitude that irked them. Maybe because she was used to better pay, having worked at an upscale spa with wealthy clients. As far as Sawitti was concerned, Jantip didn't massage any differently than she or Rinalda, or anyone else she knew.

'Just wait until Thanikarn finds out; then she'll be put back in her place,' Sawitti told her colleague.

'Thanikarn doesn't need to know. When Philippe gets back, he'll take care of it,' Rinalda said with her usual placid voice.

Always ready to denounce a rival, Sawitti reluctantly heeded her friend's advice, but she would call Thanikarn anyway, 'just to find out how she was doing.'

* * *

With only one month to go, Thanikarn looked like she was going to burst. On her last visit to the obstetrician, a weary-faced Thai man in his fifties, he'd said with a doctor's stoicism that whoever was in there seemed ready to pop out any time. Thanikarn had felt an unruly amount of activity lately; baby's tiny nudges became feisty kicks, which sometimes caught her off guard, causing her to let out a little squeal while she sat working with Konticha.

'You have to tell Baby to calm down, at least until we finish up this order. I promised to send off the latest series of necklaces this week,' she said with an amused smile.

'It will be finished,' Thanikarn replied softly, gluing little sapphire-coloured stones onto a gold-plated pendant. She worked fast and well. Her self-confidence reassured her unduly nervous boss, who, Thanikarn learned, was prone to panic. Konticha was a chronic worrier who reasoned that anticipating the worst kept it from happening.

'Don't worry, the baby won't come before January. Everything will be finished for your client,' Thanikarn said to calm her.

Konticha liked Thanikarn and, though she hadn't told her yet, planned to keep her on as an assistant and raise her salary after the baby was born.

* * *

When Thanikarn heard from Sawitti, she agreed to meet up after work for an ice cream at Swensen's. They hadn't seen one another for nearly two months, and Thanikarn looked forward to getting the latest news about Manee, Rinalda, Amnat and Philippe.

Sawitti showed up at six thirty with her cousin from Pattaya. Like Thanikarn's old school friend Melinee, Lek worked in one of the city's infamous pickup bars. Sawitti and Thanikarn weren't the only ones who had a friend, cousin, sister or aunt who worked in Pattaya, a haven for attractive women looking for an accessible way to make money, usually to help with family back home. Lek, wearing bright-red lipstick and too much mascara, looked as if she was barely seventeen. But it was hard to tell. Some very young Thai girls managed to look older than their tender years, while many others, being small and slight like Thanikarn, with bright eyes, silky black hair, and creamy smooth skin, appeared young for their age.

After a quick introduction, Sawitti wanted to know all about the baby's progress and Thanikarn's new job. Thanikarn described her new boss and the experience of learning a different trade as well as how refreshing it was to discover another world. Unless she was mistaken, she felt a tinge of envy in Sawitti's eyes. Thanikarn had found fortune in her misfortune.

Although Sawitti, nor anyone else, had ever dared to confront her with a possibly embarrassing question, Lek was unabashedly direct.

'Do you know who the father is?' she asked outright.

Thanikarn looked her directly in the eyes and, not missing a beat, answered just as frankly, 'Of course I do.'

'A farang?' Lek blurted out without a second thought. 'I know lots of Thai girls who get pregnant with farangs. They get a test at the hospital for DNA; then they tell the father he has to help pay for the baby. Farangs have money. For them, it's no problem. Sometimes they pay for you to leave them alone,' she said matter-of-factly.

Thanikarn's face darkened as she shot a defiant look at Lek. 'I don't need help,' she said firmly.

'Maybe later you'll change your mind,' Lek said, digging her spoon into her sundae.

Sawitti felt she needed to break the tension and began talking about Thanikarn's plans after the baby arrived.

'You will come see us, I hope. And don't forget, if you need any help, we are there for you – me, Rinalda, Amnat, even Philippe.'

'I know,' she said, masking her anger with a forced smile. She knew that Sawitti was sincere, and she knew that Lek was not speaking nonsense.

21

Christmas came and went so quickly, Lucas felt as though it were a fleeting daydream. He found it almost too pleasant to be back at home again. His clothes were washed and ironed, there was always something to eat in the refrigerator, and he only had to pop out the door and walk to the metro or a bus stop to get wherever he was going. Now it was time to head back to his autonomous life in Los Angeles. His parents were also leaving after Christmas, returning to China, so his brother could finish up his last spring semester at high school in Shanghai. Once his father's business venture was settled and sold, the family would move back to France.

It would have been easy to stay in Paris, if all Lucas wanted was comfort and security. Most of his old friends were continuing their studies somewhere near home. He could follow suit, get a university degree and become an accredited music teacher, but Lucas felt as if this would be giving up on an improbable but not impossible dream. His old friends, sticking to their conventional ambitions in finance or business, were not getting the big picture. France was not the centre of the world, and he had to crawl out of his comfort zone even if it meant struggling alone in a city where there was unlimited competition and a crowded market.

As he packed his bags for Los Angeles, going through the usual conflict of what to take and what to leave behind and how to get it all into one suitcase, he shuffled through the pile of photos from Koh Samui. He hesitated when he came to a photo of Thanikarn. She had never called him back about the recording he sent. The conclusion was easy. She must have been annoyed with him for not keeping in touch and had given up on him. He didn't blame her. The only excuse he had was to say he hadn't had time, a trite excuse that always annoyed him whenever it came from someone else.

He took the pile of photos, unceremoniously wrapped them together with a rubber band and stuffed them into a shoe box with a variety of other packs of photos: a ski trip with friends in the Alps, an autumn break on the Cote d'Azur, a weekend in London. Little piles of memories, segments of his past that would be otherwise forgotten. The only way to bring them back into focus was to pull them out again. He put the lid on the box and then, as if guided by guilt, or some silly superstition, took the lid off the box and shuffled once more through the photos from Koh Samui. Selecting a picture of Thanikarn, he stuck it into the side pocket of his suitcase. Maybe it was an unconscious attempt that would keep this story from ending like all the others, a youthful memory that would fade into obscurity.

* * *

There was no chance that the memory of Lucas would fade into obscurity for Thanikarn. It would come crashing back into her life with her baby's first wailing cry.

Two weeks ahead of schedule, Thanikarn woke up in the night startled by the dampness between her legs. She'd been warned this might happen; her water had broken, sending out a signalling gush, urging her to get to the hospital.

Everything was quiet in the house; the dark room was dimly lit by friendly silver stars that pierced through the clear black sky. 'Yai!' she cried, heedless of the hour, 'I think it's time!' She struggled out of bed, grabbed a towel to wipe off her legs, and looked for her phone. The number of an ambulance had been recorded in her list of contacts just a week ago by the chief nurse at the maternity ward.

'When it is time, my dear, you call this number,' she said, as she deliberately punched the number into Thanikarn's cell phone. 'The ambulance will come right away.'

Preeda calmly lifted herself out of bed, as if it was normal to get up at 2 am, and hiding her inner excitement, wandered over to a little closet and pulled out the overnight bag she had prepared for her granddaughter with loving care weeks before: a nightgown, soap, toothbrush, toothpaste and comb.

'The ambulance will be here in ten minutes,' Thanikarn said, hanging up the phone and throwing it into her purse. She dressed quietly, already beginning to feel the onset of painful contractions. Preeda, wide-eyed and smiling like a child anticipating Christmas, sat on her chair and watched her granddaughter get ready.

'Yai, I will call you as soon as I can. You should go back to bed now,' she said as she bent over to say goodbye. Preeda looked up at her granddaughter; her usually vapid eyes were bright with hope.

'*Chohk dee na luuk.*' Take care now, she said quietly and watched Thanikarn sluggishly hobble toward the door.

Sooner than expected, Thanikarn was wheeled into a private waiting room and hiked up onto a bare bed where she passed what could have been a few minutes or a few hours; the stabbing contractions were so strong they distorted all time. Once she was ready and settled on the delivery room table, her now familiar doctor asked her if she had chosen a name, which was perhaps an attempt to get her mind off the excruciating pain.

'Thalay!' she cried out between the pants.

According to Thai custom, names were often found by combining the first name of the mother and that of the father; if the combination sounded like a word, it became a new name. For Thanikarn, the choice was so obvious it seemed like fate. She had remembered what Lucas had told her that night on the beach, that in French, his middle name Adrien meant *mer*, 'sea,' and was a word that sounded like *mère*, 'mother.' *Tha*, the first part of Thanikarn's name, and *Lu*, the first part of Lucas's name, sounded like the word in Thai for the sea, *thalay*. That was destiny's name for their child.

The ensuing pain was much worse than she could have ever imagined; it felt as if someone were hitting her in the small of her back with a sledgehammer as she grunted through the interminable pushes. And then, after a final effort, she heard the strident cry of her baby. When the doctor placed her son on her belly, Thanikarn burst into tears. Sobbing, she admired the most beautiful thing she had ever seen. Thalay was cleaned off, wrapped up in a warm blanket, and placed beside an exhausted but radiant mother who had fallen in love for the second time in her life.

Preeda seldom left the house, but the next morning, she crept into Thanikarn's hospital room and quietly approached the bed. Her eyes widened as she discovered her great-grandson. Holding her breath, Thanikarn felt sure that her grandmother would notice that Thalay looked different; he had much lighter skin than most Thai babies as well as a headful of chestnut-blond hair. It would only be when Thanikarn came home with him that Preeda would also discover his incredibly clear-blue eyes.

'My great-grandson. *Naa-rak naa-chang*,' Preeda said softly, complimenting him in the traditional Thai manner for being both handsome and ugly, lest the ghosts come whisk him away. With moist eyes and a faint smile, Thanikarn reached for her grandmother's arm and placed a tender thank you kiss on the back of her wrinkled hand.

Thanikarn returned a few days later to her grandmother's home, where she would remain nursing her baby for the next two weeks, recuperating, resting, never letting Thalay out of her sight, as if she was afraid that her tiny miracle would disappear. Trin was captivated by his nephew, the only thing he ever took as much interest in as his chickens. He seemed mesmerized by Thalay's tiny hands and fingernails, touching them as if they were extraordinary fragile miniatures that might break, and he became frantic with distress whenever Thalay so much as whimpered. Whimpers that seldom broke into more than a feeble cry, since Thanikarn was always nearby, ready to place Thalay on one of her small breasts to nurse. For her, nourishing her baby with her own body seemed like magic.

* * *

Several weeks later, on a cloudy Thursday afternoon, Thanikarn finally felt strong enough to take Thalay to the Golden Gecko. Ever since she'd called Sawitti with the news, she knew they were all impatient to meet her son, but she still felt apprehensive. Proud as she was, she was worried about what they would say or think once they saw him.

As she could have expected, Thalay was received with smiles and joyous chatter, but as was customary, only well-measured compliments. Even though they might have suspected who the father was, they had the discretion not to mention him or to make any comments about Thalay's light skin and chestnut-coloured hair. However, Manee couldn't help commenting on his eyes. 'The colour of the sea,' she said, 'a gift from *faa*.' Amnat was especially kind and appointed himself honorary uncle, reminding Thanikarn that if she ever needed anything, she could rely on him to be there.

Rinalda and Sawitti were a little embarrassed to tell Thanikarn her place had been rented by Bandit's niece. They explained that it was only temporary and part-time, and they were convinced that she could talk Philippe into letting her come back. However, to their surprise, Thanikarn didn't seem to care. Nothing mattered right now, nothing but Thalay, or so she thought.

Philippe had returned from France looking weary, both from the trip and from the heavy burden of seeing his mother in such ill health, but he was nonetheless pleased to see Thanikarn and her new son and insisted on opening a bottle of champagne to share right then and there. He popped it open for her and the others to drink a toast to the new arrival. After pouring out six glasses, one for Thanikarn, each of her friends, and himself, he did something that surprised Thanikarn. He dabbed a little bit of champagne on Thalay's ear. 'French custom,' he said. For a moment, her heart skipped a beat. Did he know Thalay's father was French? Then, with the clink of glasses and a toast, she set aside the foolish thought. It was surely a coincidence. In any case, she appreciated the French tradition for assuring good fortune.

Before excusing himself to get back to work, Philippe asked Thanikarn when she wanted to come back to work at the massage stand, adding that there was no rush now that it was being rented by Bandit's niece.

'You are so kind, Philippe. But maybe better to wait for Thalay to be bigger, and I can leave him with Yai. Then, I like to come back.'

She knew she could continue working with Konticha, and as long as the rent money came in, she assumed it mattered little to Philippe who paid it.

'Of course, Karn,' he said, then suddenly remembering, added, 'Just a minute. I have something for you.'

He walked over to his reception desk and pulled out the small packet he'd received for her from France. 'It came for you a few weeks ago.'

He held it up for her to see and stuffed it into her open bag. Thanikarn's stomach knotted up. She knew it must be from the only person who would send her anything at the hotel. He had not forgotten her after all.

22

Thanikarn waited until she was at home to open the package from Lucas. Discovering something he'd sent was a solemn event she wanted to spend alone, as if it were a precious secret that needed to be protected.

First, she settled Thalay, who had, as usual, fallen asleep during their ride home in the songthaew, into his little makeshift bassinet, a large converted wicker basket Trin formerly used to take his eggs to the market. He had carefully cleaned and disinfected it for his nephew, and Preeda lined it with a small foam cushion and a soft flannel baby's blanket that dated from Thanikarn's childhood.

Then she sat down in her mother's chair, while Preeda was in the kitchen with Trin making dinner. She carefully peeled open Lucas's little packet, making sure not to tear it. She would add it to a flowered tin box with the rest of his correspondence that she kept on the top shelf of her clothes closet.

Inside the packet, she found a white sleeve with a flashy silver CD inside. She carefully pulled it out to discover three different song titles written with a heavy black felt tip pen. There was a handwritten note folded inside the little packet wrapped around the CD. Worried she wouldn't understand the English, she read it with focused concentration.

> *Dear Karn,*
> *I'm so sorry I didn't get this sent to you sooner. I hope you are not mad at me for my lack of news, but like the American saying, 'better late than never'. I'm sending you two songs I recorded (not a professional recording, but I did the best I could with my home equipment). I hope you enjoy them. Let me know what you think when you have the time. Take care of yourself.*
> *Lots of kisses, Lucas*

Thanikarn's face lit up with a smile, and her eyes glistened with contained tears as she folded and slipped the note back into the package. She looked at the CD as if it were some sort of alien object that fell from the moon, turning in over and over in her hand. Her face fell at the thought that she couldn't listen to it right away. All they had was an old cassette tape recorder for listening to English lessons, the little TV she brought from her apartment and a very old portable radio that Preeda and Trin never listened to. Thanikarn had never owned a CD player, but maybe, she thought, Konticha would have one. When she went back to work next week, she would ask to use it.

Thanikarn felt like calling Lucas to tell him she received his letter, but maybe she should wait. There was so much she didn't want to say, and she had to figure out how not to say it.

Konticha had kindly proposed that Thanikarn bring Thalay with her to work.

'I'm sure you'll have plenty of time to help me,' Konticha told her. 'Babies sleep all day. Like cats.'

Thanikarn never expected her boss to be so tolerant or encouraging. It seemed as if Konticha actually wanted her to come to work with her baby. As first Thanikarn thought it might be because Konticha wanted to make sure she remained loyal, but her repeated insistence led Thanikarn to believe she was truly excited about having extra company.

'So, this is Thalay!' Konticha said, as she took him in her arms, holding him close to her chest, just like she did with her cat, Indy. Thanikarn looked on with a smile of approval that hid her former apprehension. She was dreading a question or comment from Konticha about Thalay's fair skin and hair. His father was obviously a farang.

'I'll give you back to your proud mama' was all that Konticha had to say. Thanikarn took her son looking pleased.

They set up Thalay's egg-basket bassinet in a quiet place not too close but not too far from the air conditioner, and Thanikarn was able to work through the morning without a hitch.

Before going out to get some lunch, Thanikarn asked Konticha if she had a CD player. She did but never used it, preferring to play her radio at work. She liked listening to a popular expat station that diffused a bit of everything. It improved her English.

Konticha pulled the old CD player from a shelf and dusted it off with a rag. 'I'm not even sure it still works,' she said.

'Can I play my CD?' Thanikarn asked, holding it up. She could have waited, but she was impatient to listen to Lucas's songs. Engrossed in sketching out a new jewellery idea, Konticha answered Thanikarn with an indifferent nod.

Thanikarn placed the CD player on her work desk, loaded the disk, and pushed the recalcitrant start button several times. It was a temperamental old machine, Konticha explained.

The song began with a few introductory chords, and then she heard Lucas's voice singing 'Wakin' Up Blues'. It was as if he were magically brought back into her life. She listened, mesmerized, and her lips formed the words that she'd learned by heart. When the song was over, she hit the pause button, looked over at Thalay sleeping soundly.

'Nice song,' Konticha said without looking up.

Thanikarn nodded with distant eyes.

'Someone you know?' her boss asked as she continued working on her design.

'Yes,' was all she said.

She pushed the start button again to hear the next song, '*Tu Me Manques*'. She didn't understand a single word, but the melancholy tune convinced her it must be a love song.

'So, he's French, your singing friend,' Konticha said, intrigued.

'Yes,' she repeated. She felt as if this song must also be about her and tried to imagine him singing it hundreds of miles away. She pushed the button again to listen to a last song, a more upbeat tune sung in English. 'Everything's Fine' was the constant refrain. She couldn't catch all the words but found the tune comforting.

Konticha observed Thanikarn from her desk. The importance of the moment was written in Thanikarn's sad eyes, focused on an image only she could see.

'Does he know?' Konticha asked.

Thanikarn could have asked what she meant, but she was tired of avoiding the truth. 'No,' she said quietly.

'I'm sure you have your reasons for not telling him,' Konticha said as she began colouring in the spaces on her new design.

'It was sort of an accident.'

Konticha let that one go. It needed no comment.

'Could I take the CD player home with me?' Thanikarn asked, changing the subject.

'I've had that old thing for years. You can have it, if you like. I never use it.'

Thanikarn wanted to accept immediately, but as custom would have it, she had to refuse. 'No, I couldn't take your machine,' she said.

'Oh, Karn, please! I never use it,' she said, putting down her pencil. 'You take it home with you. A baby gift, if you like.'

Thanikarn answered with a smile and deferential bow of her head.

Her first day back at work went smoothly. Konticha was right – babies did a lot of sleeping. Maybe it was nature's little gift to mothers, conveniently giving them time to rest or do other things.

Thalay did wake up from time to time, letting out his hunger cry, but Konticha would immediately stop whatever it was she was doing, sweep him up into her arms, and hand him over to Thanikarn to nurse. It seemed as though she considered him a welcome distraction.

As dusk approached, Thanikarn gathered up her things to go home. She had discovered that moving from one place to another with a baby needed organization, and this evening, besides her purse, a baby bag stuffed with wipes and diapers, and his egg-basket bed, she also had Konticha's CD player.

'Take a taxi,' Konticha suggested.

'No. It's okay, I can manage.' Taxis were a luxury she could do without.

She wrapped Thalay up in her baby sling and attached him to her waist, put the CD player in the bassinet, hiked her purse on one shoulder and the baby bag on the other, and trudged out looking like a heavily laden refugee.

Thanikarn didn't have to wait long for a songthaew. They were frequent during rush hour, but they were also crowded. Even though she was confident she'd get a seat, she hated being jammed in and bustled about. Once she boarded, a middle-aged woman gave up her place on the bench. She must be a mother herself, Thanikarn thought as she politely accepted and sat down, thankful for a seat. She tucked the basket under her feet, slung her purse and baby bag over her shoulder, and firmly held Thalay in her arms.

It only took a moment of inattention. Thanikarn was usually careful with her belongings, but she lacked the reflex of distrust, and though she cautiously kept her purse zipped, she didn't worry about its most precious content. She didn't notice the young man's deft hand as it slipped inconspicuously into her baby bag where she had tossed her phone for easy access. It was a cheap, practically worthless cell phone, but for someone who probably had nothing, it was something.

Once Thanikarn got home that evening, she accomplished her motherly rituals of bathing, changing, nursing and putting Thalay to bed, smiling her way through her tasks as usual. She fixed herself some dinner, rice with vegetable curry, and took her grandmother some fresh fruit juice as well as a sweet pastry before Preeda fell asleep in her chair like she did most every night.

After she finished her dinner, Thanikarn stretched out on the bed, loaded the CD player lying on the floor next to her, and played Lucas's songs, lowering the volume so as not to wake up Preeda or Thalay, peacefully sleeping nearby.

Once she had finished listening, she felt she needed to thank Lucas for the CD, just a little text message would suffice. She went to fetch Thalay's baby bag and dug into it, looking for her phone. Her hand groped around, first with annoyance and then with a frantic empty feeling in her stomach. It wasn't there. A silent string of questions ran through her mind.

'What happened? Where is it? What did I do? I put it there, I'm sure. It's not there. Someone stole it? Who would steal a phone? I shouldn't have put it in my bag. How could I be so careless?'

It wasn't the phone she regretted. She could get another phone. It was the phone numbers. She scolded herself for not copying down his number somewhere else. *Stupid, stupid girl,* she thought. She now had no way to contact Lucas, and there was no way for him to contact her. Her only consolation was that this was surely meant to be.

23

It took Thanikarn longer than usual to get ready for work the next morning. Thankfully, Thalay was there to keep her mind off her distress while preparing for another day at the atelier.

When she got to work, she told Konticha about her stolen phone.

'Oh, Karn … I don't want to say I told you so, but if you had taken a taxi like I suggested, this wouldn't have happened.'

Thanikarn just stood there, avoiding eye contact, feeling like she did when she was a child, being scolded for losing her new school bag.

Konticha knew Thanikarn didn't take taxis because she wanted to save every penny she could. 'I'm sorry. But don't be upset. I'll buy you a new phone.'

'No, no, it's not that,' Thanikarn said, lowering her eyes. 'I can buy a new phone.'

Konticha waited for her to explain. Maybe it was post-baby blues or perhaps this was just one problem too many.

She took Thanikarn by the shoulders and pulled her toward her for a motherly embrace.

'Tell me, Karn.'

'It's just.' Thanikarn looked away. She was afraid of having to explain more than she wanted. 'I lost all my phone numbers.'

Konticha pulled back and studied her from arm's length. 'And these phone numbers. You can't get them again?'

'Not all of them,' she said, flashing a forlorn glance at Thalay.

Konticha gave a knowing nod. She had some idea what this was all about. 'Maybe you will find a way. Give yourself some time to think. I don't suppose there is any hurry?' It was advice rather than a question.

'No hurry,' she said, although she had already resigned herself to the fact that the fine thread of communication between her and Lucas had snapped.

She settled Thalay in his egg-basket bed and installed herself at her worktable. She quickly began sorting through the chains, beads, hooks and threads splayed in front of her. She had several long drop necklaces to assemble, meticulous work that would force her to concentrate on something besides her problem.

She thought again about what Konticha said. Maybe she could find a way. There was the Golden Gecko. Philippe might have some record of the Mounier family's address, someplace she could write to or a telephone number the family provided when they made their reservation. But how could she ask for such information? It was private, and even if he had it, he might not want to give it to her. And then, there was Ben. Maybe Ben had his number. He was only five minutes down the road. He would surely help her out. Her mood picked up as she thought about the various possibilities.

Having such a large order to fill helped Thanikarn get through the day. Around four o'clock, Konticha broke their silent work rhythm with a start. 'Oh my, I forgot. I had an appointment with Phong!' She bolted out of the room to get to the bank before it closed. Thanikarn watched her leave with a remorseful pang in her stomach. She hadn't spoken to Phong since Thalay was born. That was no way to express *luhm bun kun*. He had been so generous with her.

Konticha returned an hour later and as Thanikarn could have guessed, Phong had noticed her lack of communication.

'Phong asked about you,' Konticha said. 'I told him you lost your phone, so he gave me this,' she said, handing over his business card.

Thanikarn heaved a deep sigh. 'I never even told him about Thalay. I'll call him as soon as I get a new phone.'

'Good. That's exactly what I told him,' she said, making Thanikarn laugh. 'There is a little shop down the street that sells phones. He even sells used ones ... not too expensive. Who knows, maybe yours will show up there someday ...' Konticha added.

The thought of her phone being sold on the black market, made Thanikarn smile. What could she do to make *that* happen?

* * *

After work, Thanikarn wandered up the road looking for the discount phone shop Konticha knew, a little hole-in-the wall right between the 7-Eleven and the place on the corner where they sold sandals and sunhats.

With Thalay in her life, everything was more complicated,

even going into a store to buy something. If he was quietly sleeping in his wraparound, it was manageable, but if he was awake and squirming, it became a matter of putting him somewhere to free her two arms and hands. As soon as he was old enough to sit up by himself, she hoped things would get easier.

The store vendor was a young man wearing a low-cut T-shirt and funny silver-rimmed, yellow-tinted glasses. He had wavy, black hair and such a pretty face he could be a *kathoei*, a ladyboy. He greeted Thanikarn with a broad, sparkling smile and immediately cooed over Thalay. He happily agreed to hold him while she looked at the choice of phones.

'Oh, you happy baby, you,' he said, looking into Thalay's clear-blue eyes and rocking him back and forth. 'You want a good, cheap phone, little mama? I just got one in yesterday. A new model. That one, on the right,' he said, cradling Thalay in his arms and indicating the phone with a tilt of the head.

She took it out of the display case and studied it, wondering whose sack it had come from.

'I can call anywhere with this?' she asked.

He nodded, more interested in Thalay than in making a sale.

'Easy to use?' she asked, examining the phone.

'Very easy. I'll show you.' He reluctantly handed Thalay back to his mother and explained the manoeuvres.

'It's like the one I lost,' Thanikarn said in a subdued voice.

'Oh, you lost your phone. That's too bad. Maybe someone will find it for you and call a number of someone in your list of contacts.'

'No, I don't think so. I didn't really lose it. Someone took it from my bag when I wasn't looking.'

'Oh, poor little mama. Yes, I know, you have to be careful ... Happens all the time. Happened to me, to my friends, everyone,' he said with a sweet smile and a wave of his hand with purple polished fingernails.

Thanikarn looked at him squarely. 'I know that now. I lost an important phone number,' she confided with unusual candour.

'Me too once. A beautiful friend I met in a bar. He gave me his number, put it in my phone. I wanted to call him back the next day, but ... no more phone. Somebody must have taken it out my pocket when I wasn't looking. It was crowded. My fault for not being careful.'

Thanikarn gave another sympathetic nod. Theft was a shared responsibility.

'But, maybe for me it was better I didn't get to see the beautiful man again,' he said wistfully. 'I fall in love too easy. So, maybe it was meant to be.'

Thanikarn paid for the phone, complete with a new phone card and new phone number. He was right. Maybe it was better she and Lucas could no longer call one another. She had too much to hide.

24

The early morning sun slowly drew Thanikarn out of a dream about Lucas that was so pleasant she didn't want to let it go. There was nothing terribly romantic or exciting about the dream. That's what made it so troubling; it seemed real.

The sun's rays didn't motivate her to get out of bed. Thalay did. His morning hunger whimpers made the last trailing images of Lucas's smiling face fade into the land of forgotten dreams. She leaned over and swept Thalay out of his egg basket next to her floor mattress, the one she'd brought from her old apartment.

'Morning, baby. Yes, I know, you're hungry,' she said, putting him on her breast for his first nursing of the day.

Her grandmother, an early riser, was already preparing some rice soup for breakfast.

'It's time for you to start giving Thalay a bottle. He has to get used to it if you want to leave him home with me,' she said from across the room.

Thanikarn smiled. 'I know. It is just so wonderful to feed him myself.'

'Hmm, that won't last much longer,' Preeda said, pointing to her teeth.

Once finished, Thanikarn handed Thalay to her grandmother. 'Can you change him please?' she asked needlessly, as Preeda stretched her hands out to whisk him off to give him his morning sponge bath, part of the usual routine. Every morning, after Thanikarn nursed him, Preeda bathed, changed and dressed Thalay while Thanikarn washed up and got ready for work.

Trin usually woke up soon after. He dressed without washing, left the house without eating, and headed straight for the unfenced chicken coop to give his flock their morning meal. He greeted his twenty-two chickens and rooster cock as if they were his children, calling some of his favourites out by name. With wide gestures, Trin tossed out their morning meal, a mixture of leftover scraps of vegetable peels and day-old cooked rice, and watched with approval as his chickens scurried and pecked at their morning feast. Thanikarn always thought it was a shame he never married. He could have been a very generous and loving father, even if he was a bit strange.

Thinking about unmarried men, she remembered what Konticha had said about Phong. She should have called him long ago. *Sam-nuk-bun-kun* was one's duty to honour generosity and return favours, and she had been selfishly negligent. It struck her that maybe that was why she deserved losing her phone. She would call him today, without fault.

Thanikarn usually got to Konticha's at a little past ten. This morning, she arrived earlier than usual, and Konticha was still wearing her peignoir and smoking a morning cigarette in the courtyard, the only place she ever smoked. As soon as she saw Thanikarn, she dropped her cigarette to the ground and snuffed it out with her flip-flop like a guilty teenager. It was a principle of hers never to smoke around the baby.

'Morning, Karn, you're early.'

'I got a ride right away and no traffic.'

Konticha opened the door of the atelier. With an after-you gesture and an enigmatic smile, she eagerly let Thanikarn enter first.

'I got good news last night. Another big order. My Bangkok customer is very happy. He wants a new supply of our blue moon-drop earrings,' Konticha said once they were inside.

'Ah, yes ... very beautiful. Should I work on them first?'

'I'll get you set up right away.'

'Oh, and I have my new phone,' Thanikarn said cheerfully, holding it up for her to see. 'I went to the little store you told me about. A very nice man took care of me. Sold me a good new one.'

'This time, Karn, you copy down all the numbers.'

Thanikarn gave a firm nod. 'I have a couple of people to go see who might be able to help me out for getting some numbers back,' she added.

'But you won't have much time to take a break for the next few days. The order is for Friday.'

Thanikarn smiled. 'That's okay. No hurry.' A few more days made no difference. Not even a few more weeks. Or months.

Thanikarn worked almost nonstop all morning putting together half a dozen pairs of earrings before lunch. The work was repetitive, but she remained diligent and meticulous. It was important to Konticha that her handmade jewellery was worth the price she asked. When it was a little after one o'clock,

Konticha sent her next door to get some takeout food. This had become a midday custom; a free lunch was an unofficial part of Thanikarn's salary. Maybe it was also a way for Konticha to make sure Thanikarn would get at least one good hot meal a day. Thanikarn looked so thin and frail, it worried Konticha; little did she know how strong she really was.

Thalay was awake, and Thanikarn usually took him along, wrapped up across her tummy. But this time, Konticha said to leave him with her. 'You'll be right back ...'

Thanikarn took advantage of her time alone to call Phong. She apologized for her lack of news, quickly admitting that she had no good excuse. She had already thanked him for the job long ago, but since things were going so well ever since, she felt she owed him more than simple thanks.

'If there is anything I can do for you, Phong, please let me know. Anything.'

'Okay. Sure. Well, we'll see ... Maybe,' he answered enigmatically.

'You have my new number now. Please. Call me anytime.' Thanikarn doubted he would call back. Part of her wanted him to, so she could feel as though she'd repaid her debts, but something about the way he spoke made her feel wary.

When Thanikarn got back to the atelier, Konticha had a little surprise waiting for her. Thalay was half-seated and smiling in a little blue-and-white baby carrier on top of her worktable. Thanikarn's eyes widened with delight.

'That egg basket had to go, Karn. He needs to sit up now, so he can see you.'

It was always so hard for her to accept gifts. She didn't want to think that Konticha did this because she felt sorry for her.

'It was on sale, and I never gave you a year-end bonus,' Konticha said, as if reading her mind.

Thanikarn said thank you with her eyes. 'He looks very happy.'

Thalay smiled at his mother, flapped his pudgy arms, and kicked his tiny feet. Sitting up in the baby carrier would put a whole new angle on life.

* * *

It took three days to fill the order for the moon-drop earrings. Thursday afternoon Thanikarn asked Konticha to take care of Thalay for a short while, long enough for her to go see Ben.

She usually took him with her everywhere, afraid to let him out of her sight. But if she went asking Ben for information about Lucas with little Thalay in tow, he might jump to conclusions, and if Ben was still in touch with Lucas, he might pass on the news.

'Of course I can take care of him. You go do what you have to do,' Konticha said. She was in a particularly good mood these days with all the new orders, plus Thanikarn suspected there was more than business going on between Konticha and her mysterious Bangkok client. She'd overheard their long conversations on the phone that rambled on beyond the essentials. Konticha explained recently that he was a very successful businessman with a whole chain of jewellery stores throughout Asia. And, she added with a smile, he was a widower.

When Thanikarn arrived at Books and Things, she wandered in and searched the room for Ben. There were no other customers, and Ben's partner, Kawin, was sitting behind the counter playing a video game on a small handheld console. He looked up at her but didn't emit more than a nod and friendly smile.

'Is Ben here?' she asked in Thai.

'He just left for the post office. He should be back in a few minutes.'

'I can wait here?' she asked, hoping the 'few minutes' wasn't an exaggeration.

'Sure, no problem,' he said, barely paying any attention to her as he frantically pressed the buttons on his little console. She recognized Kawin, and she was pretty sure he remembered her too, but neither one of them had been formally introduced. Her shyness and his preoccupation with his game left it at that.

Thanikarn wandered over to the corner library and looked at the various book titles; almost all of them were in English except for one that seemed to be in German and another in Russian, or was it Greek? She wasn't sure about the strangely formed letters. There were some old paperback novels, quite a few business books, and some oversize hardbacks. One beautifully bound dark-green book embossed with gold lettering caught her eye. *Two Centuries of Great Composers*. She pulled it out, thinking that it might be the kind of book Lucas would have liked. There was even a little CD attached in a white plastic sleeve. She sat down on the old, brown, cracked-leather chair and began flipping through the pages. She only recognized two of the composers, Beethoven and Tchaikovsky. Lucas probably knew all of them.

'Hey, Karn!' She heard coming from behind her.

She sprang to her feet to give Ben a hug.

'I'm really glad to see you. How's it going?' he said as he plopped down in a chair across from her.

'Good, very good. And how are you?' she asked politely. He gestured for her to sit down again.

'Me? Not much to say. Same as always. Business is doing okay. I'm still playing down at the beach café four nights a week. But I imagine you've got more news than I have,' he said, noticing her flat stomach.

'Well, I have my baby.'

He looked at her inquisitively.

.'A boy,' she answered. 'Very happy.'

'Well, I'm not surprised, with a mother like you.' She blushed and smiled self-consciously. 'You'll have to bring him around some day.'

She nodded. Ben offered to get them a couple of beers from the fridge, and she gave another nod to accept. Feeling self-conscious, she continued looking through the book as she waited.

'Take it with you,' Ben said when he returned with two bottles of Tiger. 'You can bring it back when you get tired of it.' She lifted her chin and smiled a thank you. She wasn't sure how to approach the subject of Lucas and the missing phone number. Fortunately, Ben, who was more accustomed to small talk than she was, saved her from bringing it up.

'Have you heard from Lucas?'

'Yes a few times ... He called me.'

'Oh, wow! Well, that's more than I ever got. But that's

normal. Musicians are like that. We're a friendly breed, happy wherever we are, but we move around a lot, and we're not so good at communication,' he rambled on cheerfully.

Thanikarn's heart stopped, and she hoped the disappointment didn't show on her face.

'So, you have no address or phone number for him?'

'Nope. But if he called you, you should have his number ...'

She shook her head. 'I lost my phone.'

Ben tilted his head in sympathy. He could see the sadness in her eyes. She flipped through the book in her lap, avoiding his regard, feeling at a loss for words. She made herself look up at him and smile. He smiled back and, knowing about her short relationship with Lucas, guessed why she was there.

'Lucas is in Los Angeles now,' she finally said.

'LA! Yeah, right. He talked about moving there. That's a long way off. But who knows, he might be back here someday. Like I said, musicians move around a lot.'

She took that as encouragement but didn't know what to say. Her limited English was a terrible barrier between expressing what she felt and what she could put into words.

'I have to get back to work. Nice to see you again, Ben,' she finally said, lifting herself from the chair to give him a hug.

'Yeah, same here.' He picked up the book she'd left on the chair. 'Really, take it with you. That way I know I'll see you again.' She gave him a big smile that sank from her lips once she turned and went out the door.

25

Thanikarn was left with only one alternative if she was to ever contact Lucas again: the Golden Gecko. Since she wasn't working there anymore, she felt uncomfortable about going to see Philippe; asking for personal information on past guests seemed so unseemly.

On her way to the hotel, riding along in the songthaew with Thalay on her lap, she ruminated about how to approach Philippe. She still hadn't found a legitimate pretext for asking about Lucas's family. She tried to imagine the spectrum of reactions she might get from her former boss, from being kindly helpful to coldly dismissive, but most probably, Philippe didn't even remember them. As special as they were to her, they were just another family checking in and checking out for him.

Well, she reasoned, it was still worth a trip. It had been a long time since she'd seen her friends Rinalda, Sawitti and Amnat. Besides, it might be a good idea to check out her old spot at the massage stand. She was still planning to recover her space once Thalay was old enough to be left with Preeda.

As soon as she got off the songthaew, she felt dizzy from an onslaught of nostalgic memories. Walking along the stone path to the hotel, she noticed how nothing had changed – the same colourful bungalows, exotic plants and thatched roofing, and she took comfort in the familiarity. Manee was setting up the tables on the terrace for dinner, taking her time as usual; Rinalda and Sawitti were gathering up their belongings, stuffing things into their bags, getting ready to go home. Amnat, she thought, must be busy in the kitchen preparing for the evening meal. She could smell his tom yam kung wafting all the way to the poolside. Carrying Thalay in his baby sling, she walked past the pool, where a few straggling tourists were still stretched out on the deck chairs, catching the last minutes of sun.

'Ah, Karn, you came back to see us,' Rinalda sang out as soon as she saw her approaching the stand. Sawitti, shovelling some fried rice into her mouth, managed to emit an inaudible hello. Her eyes twinkled with pleasure at seeing her good friend. Once she swallowed her food, she asked Thanikarn if she was ready to come back to work.

'Maybe ...' Thanikarn said. 'I'm just waiting for Thalay to be old enough to leave at home with Yai.' She pulled him out of her baby wrap and hoisted him into Rinalda's outstretched arms. He was then passed to Sawitti, and then to Manee, who came to join them, with the usual smiles and cooing from his aunties as they bounced him up and down. Thanikarn spotted Philippe coming out of the office. He had poured himself a coffee at the bar and was relaxing with a cigarette on the terrace. This was as good a time as any, she thought.

'Can you watch Thalay a few minutes? I need to speak to Philippe,' she asked her friends.

There was little need to wait for an answer – they were all too engrossed playing with him to even notice her request. She slowly walked over to see Philippe, giving a cheerful wave on her way.

'Hello, Karn. Haven't seen you for a while ,' Philippe said as she approached.

'Yes. Long time. I miss my friends,' she said, looking back over her shoulder. Even though they weren't the main reason for her visit, it was true.

'Ready to come back to work?' he asked.

'Soon. I'm waiting for Thalay to be a little older, so I can leave him with my grandmother.'

'Well, whenever you're ready, I'll let you work it out with the girls.'

She waited a moment. She lacked any subtlety in English, so her request would have to be direct.

'Philippe, I have a question. Maybe you can help me.'

'Sure, Karn. If I can.'

'There was a French and American family here … last year, April …' As she said this, she was thinking that it was senseless to ask. Philippe drew on his cigarette, looked at her intrigued, and let out a slow puff of smoke. He was patient with her timidity.

'A long time ago now,' she continued. 'But I wonder if you maybe have their address or phone number in your reservation books.'

'Wow, Karn,' he said sympathetically. 'I don't save all my old email reservations. There are just too many.'

'Email?' She had some idea of what he was talking about, but she hadn't thought about it before. She had never even handled a computer, so *internet*, *email* and *websites* were familiar words attached to mysterious functions.

'Everyone reserves by email these days.'

She listened, pretending she knew what he meant. It became immediately clear to her that Philippe would be of no help.

'I understand,' she said softly.

He could read the disappointment on her forlorn face.

'Sorry I can't help you.' He was sincere, not because he knew why she wanted to contact a family who came to the hotel last April. He didn't really care, but he figured that being such a shy person, if she had the courage to come and ask, it was important.

'That's okay,' she managed to say, then changing the subject: 'I'm going to go say hello to Amnat. I know he is there – I smell his soup,' she said lifting up her little nose.

'He'll be happy to see you, I'm sure,' he said, going back to his cigarette.

Thanikarn looked over to her friends and held up a hand to get their attention. She gestured that she was going to the kitchen. Rinalda smiled and waved her off. She was apparently more than happy to babysit.

As Thanikarn wandered into the kitchen, Amnat had his attention on a pot, tasting his hot soup. When he saw Thanikarn, he put down his big cook's spoon and went over for a hug.

'How is my favourite mama?' he said, then holding her at arms' distance added, 'And where is my nephew?'

'He's here, with Rinalda.'

'Are you coming back to work soon?' he asked, returning to stir some more coconut milk into his pot.

'I think I will be back next month.'

'You've had enough with your jewellery job.' It was more of a confirmation than a question.

'A little. It's okay. My boss is very nice, but I miss working outside. Seeing you and the girls.'

Thanikarn grabbed a piece of sliced red pepper and chomped on it slowly, stalling. She wanted to talk. Amnat had always been her unofficial counsellor, but this time, she didn't know what she wanted to say. Why explain her dilemma? He couldn't help her.

'I hear you are staying with your grandmother. So, I think you must be getting good care, eating well, getting enough sleep.' Life's essential values for Amnat.

'Yes, Yai is a big help. It's nice to be home.'

'You are happy. A healthy son, comfortable home, good job.'

She couldn't contradict him. Except that a very important person in her life was missing, and now she had no way to reach him. She was still trying to decide what she would tell Amnat. No one knew the whole story. In fact, no one knew even part of it.

Uncomfortable with her own thoughts, she suddenly announced that she would go fetch Thalay. Physical movement, if nothing but a quick walk to the massage stand, seemed to help her think more clearly.

Rinalda was sitting cross-legged on her mat with Thalay nestled in her lap. Seeing his mother, he flapped his pudgy little arms like a baby bird trying to take flight. She scooped him up and said thank you and goodbye to her friends, adding that she would be back very soon to work with them again.

When she got back to the kitchen, she saw that Amnat had

served up two bowls of soup on the kitchen table. He gave his 'nephew' a little pat on the forehead, a gesture that went unheeded by Thalay, who was more interested in grabbing the big, shiny spoon next to the bowl of soup.

'Now, don't tell me you're not hungry, because I know you too well,' Amnat said.

She smiled as she took a seat and propped Thalay up on her hip, keeping him a safe distance from the hot, steamy soup. She slowly stirred her spoon around in her bowl. Amnat sat down across from her and, adopting a fatherly tone, said, 'Now you tell me what's on your mind.'

He knew her well … She took a deep breath and then slowly and deliberately told him everything she had been wanting to tell someone for a long time. She told Amnat about her short and passionate adventure with a too-young farang; the silly belief that she could never have a baby; her prayers to Hin Ta and Hin Yai; her miraculous motherhood that wasn't so miraculous after all; her shame for having told Lucas not to worry about anything, and her struggle to keep Thalay a secret from his father; the postcards and songs Lucas sent, the occasional phone calls; and now, the fact that Lucas had probably disappeared from her life forever because she lost her phone. Amnat listened in silence, spooning soup into his mouth with a regular rhythm and following her every word, looking up from time to time as Thanikarn presented her tale. Once she finished her confession, Thanikarn, looked down and calmly began eating her soup. It was as if by simply telling her story, she had already been acquitted.

Amnat squeezed her hand gently, then got up and put his

bowl in the sink.

Was that it? she wondered. Then again, there wasn't much he could say. At least it felt good to talk; it made her story seem less dramatic in her mind.

'And now?' Amnat asked.

'And now? I don't know …'

Amnat continued piling dishes into the sink. 'You're a grown-up woman. A mother. You have an important job to do. You don't have much choice.'

Thanikarn winced. That sounded harsh coming from Amnat.

Even though his back was turned, he must have seen the desperation in her eyes.

'Some people think they can control everything. Other people think they can't control anything. How about you?' Amnat turned around to say. He was smiling, and the sternness in his voice had softened.

'I don't know …'

26

Reluctantly, Thanikarn finally gave up nursing her growing son. Thalay adjusted to the severance better than Thanikarn. He was perfectly satisfied with Preeda's bottle feeding, but Thanikarn's breasts were sore during the day, and the physical pain translated into a longing to have him cuddled in her arms.

Thalay was not only crawling around now but hiking himself up on two feet wherever he could find something to hold on to, and then he would grab at everything he could reach, so there were countless occasions for him to take a tumble. Thanikarn figured it was good for her son to learn how to fall.

Thanikarn didn't like the idea of leaving him home all day. It wasn't that she didn't trust her grandmother, who applied the right balance of tenderness and firmness that Thanikarn sometimes lacked. It was hard for her to be stern. But she also knew that Thai women sometimes babied their sons so much that they never grew out of expecting to get whatever they wanted. Thalay could use Yai's soft discipline.

The extra freedom meant that Thanikarn could go back to her old job at the Golden Gecko. She missed working in the fresh air, chatting with her friends and, most importantly, being her own boss. It wasn't as if she was unhappy working for Konticha. She had even become quite fond of her boss. Konticha was a lot more sophisticated than her friends at the hotel and kept her entertained with her colourful stories that seemed as full of fantasy as her jewellery, full of shine and sparkle.

As Konticha rambled on, Thanikarn would sit and smile though her monologues, adding an admiring, 'Hmm' or 'Oh my' which encouraged Konticha to be even more dramatic. She talked about her vacation in a medieval castle, her ocean crossing on a five-star cruise ship, the time she met a real count and another when she had dinner with a famous Indian actor. Thanikarn didn't care that her stories were embellished. That is what made them so endearing. They reminded her of when she was a child, listening to ancient legends like the *Jataka Tales*, stories about the *yaksas*, ogres and ogresses, or of other mystical characters.

Work had slowed down lately with fewer orders from the mainland, and Thanikarn felt it was a good moment to talk about her departure. She probably should have made arrangements at the hotel to reassume her former massage job first, but she was fairly confident she could work something out with Rinalda and Sawitti, who were quick to remind her that Jantip only rented the stand temporarily.

Before Thanikarn could bring the subject up that morning, Konticha told her that she had seen Phong again.

'He's a very nice man, Phong. He seems to care about you a lot,' Konticha said.

It didn't surprise Thanikarn that Konticha was trying to play matchmaker. She was worried about Thanikarn raising a son on her own and had told her more than once that a growing boy needed a male role model.

'Why do you say he cares about me?' Thanikarn ventured. Her last meeting with Phong had left her intrigued, even if she didn't have any second guesses about their relationship.

'He asks about you every time I see him, so I just thought ...'

As Thanikarn could have guessed, this was just Konticha's wishful thinking. Phong was an old friend from high school, but their relationship didn't seem to have changed since.

Talking about Phong had distracted Thanikarn from her mission that morning. It was time to bring up the delicate subject of her leaving.

'Konticha, I need to talk to you about my work here ...' She paused. This was going to be harder than she thought. Konticha waited, tilting her head to the side, chin thrust upward, with a look that Thanikarn interpreted as impatience. Thanikarn continued, 'I like it here very much working with you, but I think I need to go back to my old job.'

'Thanikarn, you can't leave me now. I need you.'

Thanikarn hadn't been expecting defiance. She didn't think Konticha ever really needed her at all. She had always felt like she was hired more for company than work.

'But you can find someone else?' she half-asked, half-affirmed. 'Someone who works better than me.'

'Of course I can find somebody else. But I don't want somebody else.'

Thanikarn was surprised by her frankness, and it left her with a loss for words. She wondered why she couldn't be as direct as

Konticha when it came to saying what she felt. Thanikarn sat down at her worktable, a feeling of consternation, and worry furrowed her brow as she wondered how to appease her friend. She thought for a few moments while Konticha went to her desk and began going through her accounts.

'Maybe I can continue working with you ... part-time. In fact, I can only have my old job a few days a week. I can still come help you the other days.'

Konticha pursed her lips like a petulant child. She didn't say anything for a few minutes. Meanwhile, Thanikarn pulled out her task from last week and began threading green ceramic beads on a string. The quiet in the room felt heavy. Finally, Konticha broke her pouty silence.

'If it's a problem of your salary, I can maybe try to pay you more.'

'Oh no! It's not that, Konticha. It's true I need to make more money, but it is not because of that. I really do miss my old job. Being outside. It was hard work, but I liked it. I liked to see different faces every day.'

Konticha looked wounded, and Thanikarn immediately realized she'd been thoughtless. 'I don't mean I don't like seeing you every day. I like working with you too. Very much.'

Konticha looked up and forced a smile.

'Then you can work part-time. You pick the days.'

Thanikarn got up and went over to Konticha and gave her an appreciative hug. Maybe it was not her place to do so, but for once, she felt mending hurt feelings was more important than propriety. She'd been learning more from Konticha than how to make jewellery.

'It's settled, then,' Konticha said with a lukewarm smile.

Thanikarn nodded and went back to her table to finish her day's work.

* * *

That evening, after feeding Thalay, who now sat at the table in a high chair, Thanikarn got a call from Phong. He spoke without preamble. In fact, he spoke as though they were continuing a conversation.

'We can meet tomorrow night at the Mango Bar for a drink and then go to a nice restaurant for dinner. Can you meet me in front of the bank at six thirty?'

'Of course. That would be very nice.' She accepted with no hesitation.

Thanikarn hung up feeling a little confused. This sounded like a real date. She pulled Thalay out of his highchair as he was teething on a mango seed. As she wiped the orange gook off his pudgy face, she looked in his clear-blue eyes. She saw Lucas hiding deep inside, dimly lit by distant memories. She would never stop loving him, but she would have to put that love softly to sleep and wake up to her future.

27

It felt strange to be back at the Golden Gecko, as if it had been years instead of months. Rinalda still crocheted when there were no clients; Sawitti still arrived late each morning; Amnat still tempted her with freshly baked breakfast bread, and Philippe still sipped his morning coffee with his first smoke of the day. Nothing had changed except for the way she saw it. More than before, she relished the chance to be working outside. She'd forgotten how important it was for her to look out at the sea and feel the ocean's breeze.

Dressed in shorts and a worn-out T-shirt with her hair tied back in a ponytail, she massaged a sun-wrinkled Russian woman and smiled to herself, hearing the distant cries of children on the beach. Long ago she listened to those little voices with empty longing. Now she imagined her own son being out there with his friends someday. As she looked at the children playing at the water's edge, she remembered when she was young, doing the same thing while their mothers worked nearby. She and her friends would sit with their clothes on, sometimes lying on their backs or their bellies, letting the waves wind around their legs or wash up over their bodies, giggling as they rolled about. Thanikarn was the only one who could swim, and though she never went farther than a few yards, she did sometimes slide under the water, teasing her playmates, who worried she would be swept into the belly of the sea and disappear.

Someday soon she would bring Thalay with her to work and take him to the shore. He would surely enjoy it the way she did. Maybe she could suggest an outing with Phong. She hadn't called him since they had that strange conversation at dinner a month before.

* * *

As Phong had proposed, their evening together had started with a quick drink at the Mango Bar, a short walk from his apartment. Thanikarn arrived at exactly six thirty. Phong was there, waiting with a half-finished cocktail.

'Am I late?' she asked as she sidled up next to him at the bar. He pushed his glasses up on his nose. She was wearing gold sandals, a flouncy pale-blue skirt and a white cotton-lace top that dropped over her shoulders – a feeble attempt to dress up. As she looked like a charming young Cinderella, no one could guess that she was a thirty-year-old mother.

'I was here early,' Phong said, almost apologetically. 'I didn't want you to have to wait here alone.'

She gave him an appreciative smile. A lone girl at a bar was something to avoid in Thailand.

'I reserved dinner at Poppies. Is that okay?'

Thanikarn's eyes widened. 'Poppies? I heard that it is a very good restaurant.'

She would have felt flattered if she hadn't already felt so indebted for his help in finding her a new job.

Phong ordered her a drink. 'Just soda water,' as she had requested – not very elegant, but she feared drinking anything stronger. The Mango Bar filled up quickly. It was happy hour and the noise level mounted along with the crowd who gathered there to dance and get drunk. Having a conversation without shouting would soon be impossible, and Phong seemed impatient to leave. As soon as they finished their drinks, he proposed they call for a taxi. Thanikarn suggested taking her scooter instead, more practical at rush hour. Phong hopped on the back of her little pink scooter and wrapped his arms around her waist, and they sped down the road. She hadn't ridden with anyone behind her since Lucas, and she felt a pang of nostalgia that quickly disappeared as she focused on avoiding the smelly trucks, pushy cars and straggling scooters on their way to the restaurant.

As she and Phong were led by the hostess to a window seat, Thanikarn was again reminded of Lucas and the last time she'd been to a stylish restaurant. She deliberately chased away his image and concentrated on trying to appear as nonchalant as Phong did.

The slow service left them plenty of time to talk. Thanikarn asked about his job, more from politeness than curiosity. It was a profession that he brushed off as too boring to talk about. They quickly passed on to reminiscing about the past.

'You used to say that you wanted to be a scientist or a doctor. I remember how good you were in science,' Thanikarn said.

'I did, yes. But, you know, my parents told me that training for a career in science or medicine would take too long. They didn't have enough money to send me off to Bangkok for six years of university, so I went to business school to study finance instead. It was easy for me, and the jobs came very fast. No more worries for my parents.' He seemed to sum up his whole life in a few phrases.

'And you?' he asked Thanikarn. 'I remember you wanted to become a lawyer.'

She looked at him, her eyes wide with surprise. 'You remember that?'

'I didn't have many friends back then,' he admitted, then realizing how that sounded, gave a little cough. 'I mean ...'

Thanikarn dismissed his gaff with a little smile. 'I did want to be a lawyer, and I still thought about it a few years ago. I took correspondence classes at the Open University. But the more I studied, the more it seemed impossible, not just because of all the work you had to do to get a degree. It was what came next. Like finding an apprentice job when I'm so old. I decided it was too late.'

Phong looked at her with eyes that said he understood.

Their food came, it was delicious, and they drank white wine, something Thanikarn wasn't used to, and she found it made her feel pleasantly woozy.

'Were you sincere about wanting to do something for me?' Phong ventured. Their plates had been cleared away, and they relaxed over a last glass of wine.

'Of course.'

'You were honest with me, Karn. Now I want to be honest with you.'

Thanikarn sat upright, tilting her head to the side like a curious little bird.

'My family is very' – he paused – 'traditional. They expect me to be traditional. They expect me to marry a Thai woman.'

Thanikarn listened, trying not to show her bewilderment. Was this the beginning of a proposal?

'The problem for me is … I have a boyfriend.'

Thanikarn looked at him blankly. Within seconds, her mind went from confusion to comprehension. It was true that back in high school Phong never had a girlfriend; he never even talked about girls. He was a loner and kept to himself. And now, she learned, he had probably always been *len phuen*, 'playing with friends'. So, she thought, that was why he was so tolerant and understanding when she'd confessed her predicament. He too had a heavy secret to bear.

'What do you think?' he asked bluntly.

'I think … you need to find a way to be happy.'

He squeezed her hand in a way that said thank you.

'But I don't understand how I can help you,' she said in earnest.

'I thought that maybe we could work out some sort of official arrangement. For the sake of my family. And for you too. I make a good salary; I can take care of you and Thalay.'

So, this was a proposal. Of sorts …

'I know this might sound strange, but it's something I've been thinking about for a long time. You don't have to say anything now.'

That was a relief. She had no idea what to say.

After dinner, Thanikarn thanked him for treating her to such a nice restaurant and dropped him off in front of the Mango Bar. Neither one of them made any reference to the huge dilemma that was left hanging in the air. He simply took her hand and thanked her for spending a lovely evening. He said they could see each other again, whenever she wanted, whenever she felt ready. He was always free on weekends.

'Maybe a picnic on Sunday. I can meet Thalay,' he said timidly. She was touched and gave him a little kiss on the cheek.

'I will call you,' she said, thinking it would be a long, restless night.

* * *

The weekends at the Golden Gecko were always busier than the weekdays, which was the real reason Jantip insisted on keeping the stand on Saturdays, as well as Tuesdays and Wednesdays, when she didn't work at the upscale Anantara Lawana. Jantip had the luxury of taking Sunday off to spend with her boyfriend, something Thanikarn couldn't afford. So, she gratefully agreed to rent the stand the other days, even though Sawitti scolded her for not negotiating.

'You were here first. You should take the whole weekend,' she said, purposely within earshot of Jantip.

Thanikarn appreciated Sawitti's spirit, defiantly coming to her defence, but she was privately happy with the arrangement.

She knew that Konticha would be pleased to learn that she would continue to work with her at the atelier at least three days a week. This meant that Thanikarn would be working every day, but a seven-day workweek was nothing new to her or most people working on the island. The idea of taking off weekends was something you did if you had an office job, like Phong.

Konticha recently announced she would be flying to Phuket to see her mysterious widowed client, who Thanikarn thought sounded more and more like a boyfriend. When Konticha told her about her upcoming trip, she bubbled with enthusiasm like a teenager anticipating her first date. Thanikarn's eyes glistened as it reminded her of how she felt when she met Thalay's father. Konticha was so excited that when Thanikarn asked what she should do while she was gone, her boss told her to take a couple of days off. Thanikarn felt embarrassed by her generosity and dutifully declined the offer.

'I'm your boss, and you are my employee. I make the rules,' she said jokingly.

Konticha insisted that it was perfectly normal, while Thanikarn thought, *Normal for a woman in love*.

Thanikarn now had a chance to take Phong up on his offer to go on a picnic at the Hin Lat waterfall.

Her last conversation with him on the phone had been awkward. She had explained why Phong's parents would never accept a daughter-in-law with an illegitimate child that had been fathered by a farang.

'I'd still like to meet your son,' he'd said. She hoped his proposition wasn't just to show that he didn't hold it against her personally. But then again, Phong was too open-minded for that. He had his own dark secret to bear.

Phong insisted on picking them up by car. He had recently bought a new air-conditioned Nissan. Thanikarn had everything ready for Thalay's first day swimming: towels, a change of clothes, a bottle filled with juice, a floppy blue sunhat and sunscreen. She came prancing out with Thalay hoisted up on her hip and a big beach bag slung over her right shoulder. Phong got out of the car to greet them.

'Phong, meet Thalay. Thalay, this is Phong,' she said playfully.

Phong peered into her son's phenomenal crystal-blue eyes.

'The doctor said they will turn brown. I'm still waiting,' she said.

It had been a long time since Thanikarn had taken a day off, and she looked forward to a relaxed afternoon in the cool refreshing hills of Ang Thong. When she was young, she and her family used to go there for a picnic a few times a year.

Soon after they arrived at the Hin Lat waterfall, they wandered inland toward a wide basin brimming with water after the rainy months of monsoon. Phong found them a large flat rock shaded by trees, where they could spread out their mats and towels. Thanikarn stripped off Thalay's diapers and, wearing her shorts and a long T-shirt tied in a knot around her waist, waded with him into the basin until she was standing chest high. She lowered him into the cool water and let him kick his little legs freely as he giggled with glee, his big blue eyes looking as if they would pop with excitement. Then she held him flat out on his belly and let him paddle his arms, a first stage in teaching him how to swim.

After playing with him long enough to wear him out, she took him back and handed him over to Phong. She waded back into the water while both Phong and Thalay followed her with attentive eyes. Thalay let out a distressed whimper when he saw his mother disappear under the surface. Phong bounced him up and down, softly repeating *dee*, to reassure him, even though he wore a worried look on his face as well. Ten seconds later, Thanikarn popped her head out of the water at the opposite side of the basin and giggled like she had when she was a child teasing her friends. Thalay's eyes lit up, and he broke into a hearty chuckle.

Thanikarn waded back toward them and climbed out of the water, dripping wet. She scooped Thalay out of Phong's arms and planted a happy kiss on his rosy cheek. Thalay touched her dripping hair, then flapped his feet in the air, anxious to go back in the water himself.

'I was worried about you,' Phong said.

'Sorry.' She giggled. 'This is where my father first taught me to love the water when I was a few years old. Then when I was about five, I learned how to swim in a pool. One of the rental complexes my father worked on belonged to a man who owed him a favour for helping him get a construction permit. My father asked if he could use the pool a few times before it was put on the market so he could teach me how to swim, something he swore he would do after his little brother drowned in the sea many years before ...'

Phong handed her a towel to dry off and they sat down on their picnic mats. Phong began pulling out their lunch: a box of spicy noodles, Malaysian fried chicken, and a bag of cut-up mango and sticky rice he'd bought at the market that morning.

As she took a sip from a bottle of water, Thanikarn watched a small group of children playing in the water. 'I'm going to teach Thalay how to swim one day, like my father did for me. Then I won't ever have to worry.'

Phong sat cross-legged next to her, finishing up a piece of chicken. Suddenly, a look of consternation creased his brow.

'You were right, Karn – my parents wouldn't have approved of our marriage. I'm afraid it was a silly idea. I'm sorry.'

'No reason to be sorry. That's just the way things are.'

'What is sad is that we're both trapped by the way things are,' he said with unusual bitterness.

Thanikarn was pensive, looking through him. 'It's as if … the way things are gets planted inside you when you're young. And then they take root and keep growing. So even if we know things could be different, we can't do things differently. You can't marry your boyfriend … and I can't marry you.'

Phong looked at her with a twinkle in his eyes. 'I think you would have made a good lawyer, Karn.'

She accepted the compliment. They sat there for several moments in reflective silence.

'I'm glad we came here, Phong,'

'We can come again anytime. I mean, anytime we can.'

28

Lucas rolled over in his bed, a blue blow-up mattress on the floor, and looked at the plastic alarm clock next to his pillow, hammering in his ear like a pickaxe. It was eleven in the morning; he really should get up. He closed his eyes again, wanting to drift back into his morning dreams, trying to capture those last snapshot images that were beginning to fade. He turned over on his back again, pried his eyes open and looked up at the ceiling. His head began throbbing. Too much to drink again. But as usual, some of the customers last night offered him a beer instead of a tip, and more from conviviality than thirst, he accepted. Now, he hoisted himself out of bed, getting to his feet unsteadily, trying to keep his hangover under wraps. Maybe a cold shower would help. And a cup of coffee. But he could hear the water running through the paper-thin walls next to his room, so the shower would have to wait. He dug through last night's clothes lying on the floor next to the bed in a room that was just big enough for a mattress, a desk and his unfolded suitcase that served as a drawer. Lucas didn't mind the cramped bedroom. Roughing it made him feel worthy of whatever good fortune might come his way. But he hated sharing the bathroom. And there was only one for the whole house.

He'd been sharing an old California bungalow house near the Hollywood Hills for a few months now. It was the exemplification of a struggling artist's abode, but the hard-knock lifestyle was beginning to wear thin. In the beginning, his diet of pan-fried tortillas with grated cheese and chopped tomatoes or an occasional late-night taco from the taco truck was novel, but his guts told him he needed some variety. He didn't dare stock anything in the refrigerator. With four guys sharing the same kitchen, nothing good to eat lasted very long. The house rule was that each one ate his own stuff, but it was hard to respect when one of them came home hungry at three in the morning.

Lucas lived with two other struggling musicians and a college dropout disillusioned with his plans to study engineering. The fact that Taylor and Keith had already been trying to make it in the music world for over two years wasn't encouraging. However, since Lucas considered them less talented, he kept a flickering flame of hope that it might be different for him. They had a commercial-pop style that fit in with mainstream taste, which he figured worked both for and against them. Lucas's style was more reflective. As he liked to say, he didn't do happy. He knew that upbeat songs were easier to sell, but he was a stubborn nonconformist, resolved to swim against the current. This meant he would have to create his own public, which could take forever.

Lucas had a self-encouraging mantra: *I know it will be tough, but no sweat, no gain.* If he repeated it long enough, he thought he'd end up believing it, except that after nearly a year in Los Angeles, the mantra was wearing out. But he still wasn't ready to call it quits and head back to Paris. He was only twenty-one years old, and at least he was getting by without financial help from his parents. Twenty-one was a proud age in the US, when in addition to all the other adult privileges, you could finally buy alcohol and drink in a bar, an added thrill in the States; except that as a fair-skinned, blue-eyed blond with little reason to shave, he was carded everywhere he went, an amusing anecdote he boasted to friends back home.

It was probably Jeff in the shower, the college dropout, who worked late nights as a barman at the Kibitz on Fairfax, a well-known venue for musical entertainers. Now that Lucas could legally enter a bar, he could also entertain in one, so he took up Jeff's suggestion to play at the bar-lounge Monday through Thursday, when the room was seldom booked, a modest financial boost for Lucas that was more likely to get him drunk than rich.

The clientele at the Kibitz varied, everything from down-and-outs to yuppie west-siders. Lucas considered it a sort of laboratory to try out his songs. He attracted a few admirers, the 'regulars' as Jeff called them: Marlene, a very large redhead artist with one arm; a cool black guy of about forty who always wore black pants, a black shirt, and a black leather cowboy hat; and Noah, a gay Jewish man in his fifties who owned an antique store up the street. Other than Lucas's trio of fans, the paltry crowd tended to be lukewarm and stingy with the tips. They were there to hang out, drink and chat while the weekday entertainers provided background music.

Although Lucas's professional aspirations continued to be disappointing, he couldn't complain about his social life. He had always made friends easily, so living with three other young men with a large social net, he met lots of new people, including beautiful girls. Though he spoke English without an accent, there was something very French about him. Young women were often charmed by his European flair, and he quickly learned how to manoeuvre an evening so that it ended up with an invitation to spend the night. It wasn't his main goal, but he was happy to go with the flow.

Late morning, Lucas staggered into their big kitchen to find a sink full of dishes, open packages of white bread and an empty jar of peanut butter on the counter, the remains of Jeff's dinner, no doubt. While he sipped his first cup of coffee, Jeff, six-foot-two, walked in with a towel wrapped around his lanky waist. Unlike Lucas, he was good-natured whatever time of day.

'You were good last night. Nice crowd.'

'All ten of them?' Lucas asked sarcastically.

'Yeah, it was a little slow, but they were really into you, especially Marlene.'

Lucas just smiled. He wanted to make fun of the fact that his biggest fan was also one of the biggest in the room, and handicapped to boot, but that would have been politically incorrect. If he'd learned one thing in the States, it was that there was a list of things you couldn't joke about.

'Can you play again tonight?'

'It's Friday!'

Fridays were booked by the Simple Souls, a trio that had started out as an R&B band but migrated to hard rock, boosting their already good reputation. Before the band, a guitarist named Michael warmed up the audience, playing his own stuff.

'Michael can't come tonight, some phony story about his sister's wedding in Omaha. I thought maybe you'd like to fill in for him.'

Lucas hesitated. He was hung over, had a job to finish up composing some music for a friend's website, and he was tired. When Lucas was tired, he was depressed. And when he was depressed, he lost the little confidence he had as a performer. But then again, he could use the tip money, and even if he didn't get paid for playing at the Kibitz, he always got a free pastrami sandwich. Good food was important, and he loved pastrami.

'Yeah, I guess so. What time should I be there?'

'Eightish is good.'

* * *

Lucas arrived at the Kibitz groggy and unkempt since he'd fallen asleep on the cushiony old sofa too comfortable to resist while preparing his evening's song list. He'd brought his base, thinking that's what the public expected, though he preferred to accompany himself on the bar's old Roland keyboard. When he arrived, there were only a few couples, a party of eight sitting in a booth, and half a dozen people at the bar. It was still early. He took his time tuning his bass, connecting the cables, and adjusting his seat, still trying to emerge from his recent nap.

He started off with a couple of standard Beatles songs to warm up his voice and then began his personal repertoire. Lucas had about six original songs that he felt comfortable with, including one in French. The reception was tepid, the applause was polite, but he knew most of the hard-rock fans were waiting for the Simple Souls, who'd be on a little after nine.

Lucas ended his gig with 'Wakin' Up Blues', and the band members plus the growing group that had gathered gave him an enthusiastic applause. Lucas was packing up his bass when a man who had been seated at the bar came to see him. He was dressed city-slick, a white shirt unbuttoned at the collar, a dark silver-grey jacket, designer jeans, and black leather shoes.

'Hi. Nice stuff.'

'Thanks,' Lucas said with a broad smile. He was hoping for a tip, but even a compliment was welcome.

'You're French?'

'Yeah, from Paris. I got here about a year ago. But my mom's American, so I'm both, actually.'

'Well, listen. I'm always looking for something original. Here's my card. If you want, give me a call next week, and we can set up a meeting.'

That was unexpected. Lucas took his card and looked at it. 'Michael Goldenberg, Golden Entertainment.'

How corny can you get? Lucas thought. He'd always been a bit paranoid about producers and immediately figured this was a typical scam, someone offering promotional work and pseudo marketing or maybe even a fake label proposition for a 'minor fee'. But he thanked him politely, shook his hand and said goodbye. Lucas was hungry, and the most important thing right now was a hot pastrami.

29

What was it that one of Thanikarn's clients told her? She was a loquacious lady from Canada, a retired schoolteacher who came to Koh Samui every year to spend a month escaping freezing temperatures back home. She repeated what she'd read in a magazine, something about how time passed, fast or slow. She said that when you do many different things, time seemed fuller and lasted longer, but doing the same thing every day, time appeared to go by quickly. That was why, she explained, she busied herself each vacation doing as many things as she could, eating in new restaurants, discovering the island by scooter, getting massaged, swimming and snorkelling, shopping, taking cooking classes, practicing yoga, and the list went on. She had to make her one month seem like a year.

Thanikarn had little choice when it came to varying her activities, and she could confirm that time went by all too fast. Maybe it was because of Thalay. He was nearly three years old, and it seemed like he'd been born yesterday. She was now thirty-two and didn't even remember turning thirty. Unfortunately, Thanikarn couldn't do much about slowing time. She had to work every day, and whether massaging or working for Konticha, everything except for raising Thalay had become tedious. If only she could spend more time with her son, sharing the precious moments of his early childhood, all those little firsts: his first steps, his first words, the first time he used a spoon. She lamented that her memory couldn't hold on to every minute like a polaroid camera. The time between those memorable firsts was turning into a fast-rolling blur, and he was growing up all too quickly.

It wasn't that she wanted him to remain a baby. The older he got, the more she enjoyed him. His developing mind and growing affection always kept her smiling. She simply wanted more time to savour the transition. She scolded herself for not having taken pictures as she tried to remember what he looked like when he began walking or drinking from a cup. Now all those images were becoming lost amid a myriad of new ones.

With so much time spent working and spending nights at home, Thanikarn found that her nightlife had faded until it was a shadow of former times. Her mother and Trin were there to babysit whenever she asked, but since she was gone so long each day, she couldn't bear the thought of not spending time with Thalay in the evening. Her friends Sawitti or Melinee would often try to get her to join them for a late-night drink after she put Thalay to bed, but the thought of getting up early the next morning killed her incentive to go out.

There were a few times they managed to convince her to go, once to the Green Mango, which only reminded her of the first time she went there with Lucas. It cast a dark shadow on the whole evening. Another time, her friends dragged her to a new disco. Even though she could compete with any young woman in the room, she felt stupidly old and unattractive. Feelings that must have given bad vibes because not one man ever looked her way. Then there was the time at Soi Reggae, when she was approached by a young handsome Australian who smelled of beer and cigarettes. His nasal accent and rude hands rubbing her back made her cringe.

The only reason Thanikarn agreed to her friends' outings was guilt. She should be looking for someone to replace Thalay's missing father. Phong's offer two years ago made her realize that any potential partner would have to be a farang. No Thai man would accept marrying her, and she couldn't wait for some Western mystery man to show up at her massage stand the same way Lucas had.

Even though Thanikarn was lonely and missed being in a relationship, she had no illusions of meeting a prince charming. The most she could hope for was someone kind, someone she could count on to be a good husband and father. Maybe someone much older, like Sawitti suggested. An older man with money. He could offer security and would be less likely to run off with another woman, practical advice that made Thanikarn's future sound like a cliché. Isn't that what most of those older lone male tourists came to Thailand for? To find a young Thai woman in need of security.

Konticha was still pushing for Phong, but she knew nothing about his personal life and parental pressure. She was into pop psychology and harped on Thalay's need for a male role model. Thanikarn laughed at the irony of Konticha's choice, a closet homosexual.

Somehow, she wasn't worried about a father figure.

Thanikarn's biggest concern was what she would eventually tell her son about his real father. As soon as he started school, he'd surely realize that other children had mothers *and* fathers, and unless someone popped into her life soon, before Thalay was old enough to realize the difference, she would have to come up with an explanation.

* * *

Thanikarn had become fairly resigned to being a single mother, and thoughts of Lucas had been swept away so that she could get on with her life, but sometimes, something or someone happened along to remind her.

Finishing work a bit earlier than usual, Thanikarn had stopped at the Family Mart to buy a cold drink before heading for home. She recognized Ben right away as he was waiting to pay at the cash register. Her heart thumped, and her throat tightened. Ben triggered thoughts of Lucas like Pavlov's bell.

'Hey, stranger! How've you been?' he said warmly.

'You remember me?' she asked with an effort to smile.

'Of course I do. Though it has been a long time ...' He looked sincerely pleased to see her.

Thanikarn mentally calculated just how long it had been. 'Yes, maybe two years.'

'Well, you look the same, pretty as ever.'

Thanikarn was never good at accepting compliments about her looks and lowered her eyes.

Ben grabbed the Coke out of her hand and put it with his

groceries. 'Let me get that,' he said and pulled a few coins from his pocket. Thanikarn acquiesced with a nod. Connecting Ben and Lucas was unavoidable and put her at a loss of words. They silently walked out of the shop together.

'Hey, come down to the shop and drink this. We can have a little chat.'

Thanikarn hesitated, undecided as to whether she should rush home as usual or face up to ghosts from the past. But Ben might have some news about Thalay's father, and she couldn't resist her lingering curiosity about what had become of Lucas. She accepted his invitation with a smile.

No good at initiating a conversation, especially in English, she walked beside him quietly. Books and Things was only a few minutes away. He opened the door for her and gallantly gestured for her to go in.

'Take a seat,' he said, indicating the old leather chairs in the corner. 'I'm going to get a beer.' He was back in thirty seconds, popping the cap off the bottle.

'So, if I remember, the last time I saw you, you had just had a baby boy,' he said, plopping down in the chair across from her.

'Yes. Thalay. He is three years old now,' she said, sitting up straight and proud. 'I put him in day school soon.'

She didn't mention a father, and Ben knew better than to ask.

'So, what are you doing in my neck of the woods?' Seeing her confused face, he rephrased the question. 'What brings you around here?'

'I work down the street. I make jewellery.'

'Oh, that's right. I remember now. So, no more massaging?'

'Yes, I still do massage. But only three days a week. The other days I work with Konticha, my boss.'

'And you live around here now?'

'No, I live with my grandmother and uncle,' she blurted out honestly.

'A busy mom, I see ...' he said with a knowing nod. So, she was working every day, living with her grandmother; there was no father around to help her out. Thanikarn wondered if Ben suspected Lucas was her son's father; the timing might trigger a connection.

'And you, Ben, still playing music?' She was trying to be sociable.

'Of course. Every Friday and Saturday night. You should come by sometime. You'll be my guest. Drinks on the house,' he added with a broad smile.

She echoed his smile. 'Thank you for invitation, but ...'

'No buts, just come. It's not like the other bars you know. Just nice people who like good old-fashioned rock music.'

'I know,' she said, looking at him, trust in her eyes. 'I will try to come,' she said, even though she could never go back there again. Too many memories. 'Sorry, I need to go; it's getting late for me.' She rose to her feet. 'My grandmother is waiting with my son.'

'Well, hope to see you again, and don't forget my invitation,' he said, getting up to accompany her to the door. Then he stopped, 'Hey, before you go, I've got something you might like to have.' He went to get a carton sitting in the corner under the bookshelves. 'An American couple dropped off an old video player and a few

Sesame Street cassettes. It belonged to their grandson. He went back to the States with his parents. Maybe you could play them for your son?' She looked at him, completely perplexed. '*Sesame Street* is really cool. It is an American TV program for kids, teaching them their letters and how to count. You'll see – it's great for learning English.'

Those were magic words for Thanikarn, and her eyes lit up.

'I've got an old shopping bag we can stick them in, and you can take them home with you now.'

She didn't know what to say. Why was he being so nice to her? How could he possibly know she wanted Thalay to learn English? She felt confused as if she might have said something that she didn't remember saying. She tried not to show it and gave Ben a little kiss on the cheek.

'Thank you. For being such a good friend.'

30

Thanikarn had practically given up on the dreams of her youth long ago, but now, with Thalay to raise, they seemed as fantastical as the *Jakata Tales*. She was determined life would be different for her son. Though she would teach him Thai values, to be respectful and generous with his family and kind to others, she wanted him to have qualities that Western people had. She wanted him to learn independence, to be smart and successful.

Since Thalay parents came from two different cultures, Thanikarn decided it was important for him to adopt both, Thai and Western, and the latter began with speaking English. Konticha told her about a small, private bilingual school in Chaweng Noi, but it was hopelessly expensive, like all the international schools on the island. Thanikarn regretted she couldn't send him there, but she was convinced he would easily learn English somehow. She had some silly idea that speaking English was in his blood, as was his fair skin, blue eyes and light-brown hair.

For Thalay's schooling, the best she could do for now was a little Thai school with friendly staff near her grandmother's home on a verdant road leading to the Tan Rua waterfall. The Wat Phukhaothong School was not only free but practical, since it would be Trin's job to pick his nephew up after school. Like most Thai schools, they introduced a little English, but mostly old-fashioned grammar. Thanikarn was undaunted and determined her son would speak English anyway, and she counted on using Ben's cassettes.

Trin helped her hook up the cassette player to their little television, the outdated turquoise Sony she had in her apartment before coming back home. Even though her uncle's behaviour made him seem incompetent, he had a knack for anything that was manual. He liked taking things apart and putting them back together again, and his natural talent could be useful.

Though Trin had no real desire to learn English, he ended up watching every episode of *Sesame Street*. He soon hummed along with the opening song, bobbing his head like a five-year-old. Trin and Thalay were equally captivated by Ernie and Bert, the Cookie Monster and Kermit the Frog. Thalay's favourite was Elmo, and predictably, Trin was especially fond of Big Bird. Thanikarn encouraged Thalay to repeat all the letters and numbers and repeated them out loud with him, concentrating hard on getting the right accent. He caught on to the idea and soon repeated words and answered all the questions out loud. It turned into a lovely game, and he progressed with amazing speed.

Her son's Western education wasn't restricted to TV land and colourful puppets. When Thanikarn thought about Lucas, she remembered how important music was for him, and she wanted Thalay to appreciate music as well. It was like another language that could open new doors. She continued playing Lucas's songs, partly because Thalay seemed quite taken with them. Ever since he had been a baby, his eyes sparkled every time she played them, and his little lips turned up into an unexpected smile. Thanikarn never tired of listening to his songs either, but she was afraid that Preeda and Trin would get weary if there wasn't other music in the house. Sometimes she put on the radio, but most of the local stations seemed to consist of more talk than music, so Thanikarn often played the CD she'd found in the back of the book Ben had given her.

She knew nothing of classical music, but she imagined Lucas was an expert. He'd told her all about his long years of training in piano and his education at the conservatory. She imagined that one day when Thalay was old enough, she would have him learn to play an instrument. It seemed like something most Westerners taught their children.

The classical CD she played had many famous pieces. Even Thanikarn recognized a couple of them, like 'Beethoven's Fifth' and Tchaikovsky's 'Swan Lake'; maybe she'd heard them on the television. There was also music by Chopin, Bach, Ravel, and even some opera songs, Carmen's 'Toreador Song', Wagner's 'Ride of the Valkyries' and her favourite, Puccini's 'Un Bel Di Vedremo' from *Madame Butterfly*. In the book, there was a résumé of the story and the heroine, Cio-Cio-san, who was forced to give up her son to his American father. It reminded her of another Thai myth about Phi Tai Thong Klom, the vengeful ghost of a woman who killed herself when she was made pregnant but ended up being betrayed and abandoned by her lover.

Trin and Preeda never commented on Thanikarn's new habit of playing music, but sometimes her grandmother would turn up the volume when it was a piece she particularly liked, what she called a 'happy song.' She would smile and shuffle her feet a little off rhythm in an imitation waltz on their creaky wooden floor when she heard Strauss's 'Blue Danube'. It made Thalay giggle, and then Preeda would look at him with a proud smile, pleased with herself for making her great-grandson laugh.

Her grandmother's playful behaviour had become increasingly rare. She spent most of her time passively watching the television with unseeing eyes, paying little attention to the image, or sitting in her chair and looking vacantly out the window. Thanikarn missed talking with her the way she used to. Now it was mostly one-way conversations, Thanikarn telling her about work and Thalay's daily latest antics, or when she came up short on topics, she commented on her television shows, but all she ever got in return was an occasional nod. Preeda was slowly slipping away, going into that comforting place in her mind of empty thought. It was as if she was just passing the time, waiting. Thanikarn knew her grandmother's mind was going too quickly for her to hold on to, but there was nothing she could do.

As time went on, Thanikarn wondered who was more alert and responsible, her uncle Trin or her grandmother. Fortunately, they complemented one another. Trin gathered eggs and rode his dilapidated scooter to the local mini-market to buy groceries or into town to get medicine or sundries; her grandmother prepared lunch and washed up the dishes. Trin mended a broken table or repaired the leaky faucet, and Preeda did his laundry and hung it up to dry outside. They both took care of Thalay while Thanikarn was at work, and she was relieved, knowing that as a team, they were reliable.

Thanikarn had no idea how long she and Thalay could continue living with her grandmother and uncle. She couldn't imagine moving out, but she didn't see herself living there forever. She longed for a normal family, but that looked more and more like a fantasy.

Phong told her that being different was a good thing. He would. Like her, he was on the outskirts of what was socially conventional, something that brought them closer together. They'd developed a strange but strong friendship over the past year, sharing their woes, worries, and expectations.

When the occasion arose, 'Uncle Phong' would join Thanikarn and Thalay for an early dinner, and whenever Konticha was out of town, they went to the waterfall on the weekend. Thanikarn never did meet Phong's mysterious boyfriend. He liked to keep that part of his life to himself. He told her he was still looking for a solution that would satisfy his parents' concerns, but finding someone he could trust wasn't easy. It was a similar challenge for Thanikarn, hoping to find a farang that would fill the bill of honourable husband and faithful father.

31

Lucas was having a hard time sticking to his goal. In fact, he wasn't sure what his goal was anymore. For now, he was just trying to get along on his own, which meant making enough money to pay his rent, buy groceries and put gas in his car.

It was eleven in the morning, but he was just waking up. Another late night, or more precisely, early morning, to bed after hanging out with friends down the street. It was the usual LA scene, everyone sitting outside around a big garden table with beer, weed and coke. Lucas smiled to himself each time a trickle of fine white powder was lined up. He often thought he could have been a poster boy for 'say no to drugs'. While the others sniffed, he drank beer after beer and sometimes smoked a little pot at night, but when it came to anything harder, he passed it up. It wasn't from principle so much as fear, especially when it came to cocaine; he was a self-diagnosed obsessive-compulsive, and getting addicted to coke could mean the beginning of the end.

Two of their guests that night were friends who had already come to his place for a couple of BBQs. Peter was a history teacher, one of the few people Lucas could talk to about politics. Brad worked as a market analyst in some little start-up. He was with his girlfriend, who after smoking a couple of joints was practically sitting on Lucas's lap. He diplomatically avoided any trouble with the boyfriend by talking to a guitar player from Oklahoma, a short, stocky guy with a tentative moustache. He'd come to LA to check out the music scene while staying with some mutual friends near Echo Park. For Lucas, he was a dusty mirror of himself, another aspiring musician filled with long-shot dreams. Mr Oklahoma introduced himself as Buck, though Lucas surmised he made the name up to go with his new moustache and cowboy boots. Like most of the musicians Lucas had met in LA, he was a proud autodidact with puffed-up self-confidence. Lucas, riddled with self-doubt and plagued by reflective realism, envied Buck's optimism.

Lucas waited for it to stop raining outside before reluctantly dragging himself out of bed. It was a long way from the bed to the floor for his feet to travel, especially with a hangover. He staggered into the kitchen where Jeff was sitting with a cup of coffee, flipping through the pages of *Variety*, the iconic trade magazine, looking for some upcoming movie shoots. In Los Angeles, working as an extra was an easy way to make a hundred bucks a day.

'Have a good night?' he asked, as he continued turning the pages.

'Okay, I guess.'

'The guy who gave you his card the other night came again.'

'Oh yeah?' Lucas asked without interest, preoccupied by finding his can of gourmet coffee.

'He didn't stay long. Didn't seem interested in the group that was playing.' Jeff said, as he circled a casting ad, 'Did you ever call him up?'

'Nah,' Lucas said, stretching open his eyes to wake up.

'You should've. I heard he's for real. I mean, I heard he's worked with some good people.'

Lucas proceeded to fill his Italian mini-percolator with coffee and stuck a couple of pieces of wholewheat bread in the rusty chrome toaster.

'I guess I should. But what I really need right now is some cash. I think I've got thirty-two dollars left in my account.'

'Well, you never know. He might find you a couple of paying gigs. Or you could always come work on a shoot with me.' Jeff added with consternation, 'If I can find one ... You must be getting a little tired of pastrami.'

He wasn't tired of pastrami so much as he was tired of failure. If he couldn't make a living doing music, he might as well go back to Paris. So, yes, maybe as a last resort, he'd call the guy back. The problem was he didn't trust him. He didn't trust any promoter, manager or producer – too many stories about bad experiences, promises that didn't come through, musicians being misrepresented or even cheated out of their money. Lucas had always been paranoid about spending money to make money; however, in his case, he had no money to spend.

After finding other mindless things to do all day, like playing a video game, tuning his bass for the third time, and recopying his music, he reluctantly called up Golden Entertainment. He got an immediate appointment with Mr Goldenberg, who belted out a 'Hey, what took you so long,' when he answered the phone. To his amazement, Jeff was uncannily right. Mr Goldenberg proposed a paying gig in West Hollywood. Lucas wondered if he was expecting a percentage of his pay, but Mr Goldenberg – 'Call me Mike' – told him before he asked that it was an offer of good faith. He wanted to see how his material would go over with a more sophisticated crowd. Lucas was taken aback with the proposition. It put a little unexpected pressure on him as a performer as he wasn't sure about accepting a test run.

The crowd at the Somewhere Bar Thursday night was bigger than Lucas was used to. The stage was wide enough for a six-member band, so he felt conspicuous, and there was no upright piano to hide behind like at the Kibitz. He felt naked standing there with only his bass and a spindly microphone stand. He started playing at 10 pm. Mike sat at the bar with a glass of white wine, talking to a yuppie-looking woman wearing a business suit and high heels.

Lucas felt as if he were back at the Conservatory playing for his final exam, but this time, instead of Chopin for a panel of pretentious professors, it was his own stuff for a pseudo hip production manager and a crowd drinking margaritas and mojitos. *Just do it*, he thought as he began playing.

He got through the evening without any hitches, and each song got polite applause. He felt reassured with the last round of clapping, which seemed genuine and sincere. Mike stayed the whole time and invited him for a drink at the bar once he'd finished. It turned out that Mr Goldenberg was more on the level than he expected and wanted to help him get started. He wasn't going to make any promises, but he was willing to bet his time and a little money to promote him. He thought there was a niche.

Not the mainstream pop-commercial crowd, but one made up of people who liked good lyrics, melodies you could remember and an original voice.

'Too many marketable products and fabricated celebrities with mass appeal out there,' he said disdainfully. 'You've got quality merchandise,' he added with a thumbs-up.

Mike's compliments gave Lucas a timely boost in confidence.

'Come to my office tomorrow, and we'll write up a little contract,' he said before leaving. Any words of a contract made Lucas nervous, but the next day, when he saw the terms, 10 percent of his takings, the standard tariff, he figured it was fair enough and agreed to sign on with him for a year. It was better than the alternative of waiting tables or teaching piano to kids, jobs he had done back in high school.

Things moved quickly from there, some more small gigs at local venues and a couple of outdoor festivals. With a little money trickling in, Lucas stopped worrying about what he was doing in LA. Though it was far from a life of glamour and he still wasn't rich enough to move into a place of his own, he began to feel more confident as a singer-songwriter. The biggest thrill was seeing his name on a poster stuck on neighbourhood store windows, even if his was at the bottom of the list.

The next step, which came nearly half a year later, was when Mike offered to pay some musicians to form a band so that Lucas would have professional backup to record an album. Once they got a band together, they worked on fourteen original songs, including 'Wakin' Up Blues', the song he'd written for Thanikarn, and the other two songs he'd sent her. It took a few months of rehearsals to get them ready. Lucas was amazed what money and a little organization could accomplish. Mike managed to get some of the songs from Lucas's album played on local radio stations. Then he got a tour with a well-known band, Eden Rock, who were all the rage on the West Coast. To top it all off, Mike insisted on giving Lucas Mounier, his discovered artist, a new stage name: Lucky Moon.

It went all too fast. Heading into Lucas's second year working with Mike, he signed with a major label, and soon after, Golden Entertainment pulled some strings and got his songs placed on a few national radio stations. One of the songs from his album, 'Charming Prince', went to the top of the charts.

It turned out that Mike was a great promoter. He never asked for a penny more than what was in the original contract and continued to find him top exposure. Lucas became his preferred protégé, getting more attention than any of his other artists. Of course, managing Lucas and promoting his success was not pure altruism – Mike was making his 10 percent – but it was far from the exploitation Lucas had feared. Hopeless at organization and a disaster when it came to marketing, he never could have done it on his own.

Lucas avoided reading the critics and wondered how much success it would take for him to have true self-confidence. He knew the initial charm of a newcomer could wear off, and he could slide right back down to where he started, so he stayed superstitiously humble and continued working on new material. It was all pretty exhilarating, but Lucas tried not to let it go to his head – no fancy clothes or car and no bragging to friends back home. Most of all, he kept very busy, too busy to remember those tranquil days with his family on Koh Samui.

32

It was Thalay's first day at preschool; he was so excited that he skipped and jumped all the way to the front gate. While some preschoolers had worried eyes or grabbed on to their mother's legs, Thalay took the young teacher's hand and traipsed off without looking back. When Thanikarn went to pick him after school, Thalay didn't even turn his head when she called. Instead, he stubbornly finished assembling his coloured blocks. A good sign, she thought, a mark of determination.

Thanikarn still regretted that she couldn't have put him into a private bilingual school, but at least he seemed happy, and as for improving his English, she would find another way. Then, as if Hin Ta and Hin Yai were still looking after them, she didn't have to. Thalay met Julie, a little Thai-English girl who could have passed for his twin sister.

The first day of school, all the first-year children were told to sit in a circle on the floor for introductions. Julie was immediately drawn to another toddler who looked like her and, presuming he spoke English, pranced up to him.

'Hello. This is for you,' she said, handing him a little cushion to sit on.

'Thank you,' he said in English. 'I go here,' he continued and placed his cushion on the floor next to her.

This was the beginning of an inseparable relationship. Within a week, Thalay and Julie became best friends. Every time Thanikarn asked Thalay about his day, everything included Julie, whether it was what songs they sang, about their playground games, or what they ate for lunch in the cafeteria. Thanikarn was delighted that Thalay had made a friend so soon, and she was thrilled that Julie spoke English.

'What does Julie look like?' Thanikarn had asked the day the two children had met.

'Like me,' he'd said.

She couldn't have been more intrigued. 'Does her mother come pick her up after school?' Thanikarn took it for granted that she was a Thai woman married to a farang.

'I don't know.'

Since Trin had been assigned to pick Thalay up after school, Thanikarn would have to replace him if she wanted to meet Julie's mother. She could take off early from her massage stand, where business had been calm all week. Thanikarn knew Trin would be disappointed, being deprived of his favourite duty, and reassured him that it was for one time.

Thanikarn was there early, along with other family members waiting at the front gate where the children filed out. She finally saw Julie, whom she recognized immediately. Her son was right; they could have been sister and brother. The two of them wandered out with the small herd of chattering children. Julie was whispering something into Thalay's ear, her little hand hiding her mouth as if she were relating an important secret before she skipped off. Thanikarn watched as Julie quickly jumped into the arms of one of the most handsome Thai men she had ever seen. He was tall, with silky black hair held back in a headband. His face looked as if it had been sculpted, with high cheekbones, a strong chin, and deep-set creamy-brown eyes. Thalay saw his mother at the same time and, excited to see her instead of his uncle Trin, ran to give her a hug. With a still-radiant smile, he turned around and yelled out to Julie, 'Julie … My mama!'

Julie smiled and waved excitedly.

Thanikarn was curious about the man who had come to fetch Julie. Could this be her father? Then, as if he'd heard her, he came strolling toward them, holding Julie by the hand.

'*Sawadee kap*,' he said, a polite greeting in Thai.

'*Sawadee ka*,' Thanikarn returned.

'*Kaw thôt kap*, I don't speak Thai very well.'

'It's okay. My mama speak English,' Thalay said.

Thanikarn reddened. 'A little.'

'I'm Krit, Julie's father,' he said, holding out his hand, Western-style.

Thanikarn shook his hand. 'I am Thanikarn,' she said and spontaneously waied.

'We would like to invite Thalay to our house to have a little snack and play for a while. It would be great if you could come too.'

'You want us to come to your house?' Thanikarn wasn't used to being invited into the home of someone she'd just met.

'Yeah. We live right down the street. Julie's mom gets home

early today, at five. You can meet her too.'

Thanikarn turned to look at Thalay, who had already broken away from her grasp to take Julie's hand. They were both jumping up and down, delighted with the prospect of after-school playtime.

'Okay,' Thanikarn said, trying to hide her intimidation.

Julie's home was a ten-minute walk from the school. Julie and Thalay scampered ahead while their respective parents trailed behind. Krit offered an unabashed history of their family. He explained that he and his wife, Sarah, had come to live in Koh Samui when his father died a couple of years before. As an only child, he had inherited the house, a modern two-storey home in an upgraded Thai district, a neighbourhood with few fellow expats. Krit said his wife fell in love with Koh Samui, and they decided to stay, partly for Julie's sake. No pollution to irritate her asthma. Since most of Krit's journalistic job was done over the internet, he figured he could easily continue his work on the island, and so one day, they just packed up and left England.

When they walked up to the front of his home, Thanikarn's eyes widened with admiration. It looked as if it must have belonged to someone who had an important job, one that required an impressive residence. Krit showed her in through the tall, silvery gate, and they all went into the large, American-style kitchen, where he immediately put on an English electric kettle to heat water for tea. He pulled some packaged cookies from the cupboard and handed one to each of the children, who went scampering off to Julie's room to play.

Since Thanikarn had no desire to talk about herself, she was relieved to let Krit ramble on about their family. Westerners seemed so open to her, spontaneously serving up portions of their life that she kept concealed in a vault of intimacy. The only information she let eek out was that she was living with her mother and worked making jewellery. She left out the part about being a masseuse; it sometimes gave the wrong idea. As with Ben, she assumed that Krit didn't ask about Thalay's father out of politeness, or perhaps, she mused, he didn't care. Separations, divorces and single mothers were common in the Western world.

Krit was about to explain how he'd ended up in Birmingham, when he was interrupted by the clack of the front door and the appearance of Julie's mother. Wearing a white uniform, a short, cheery-faced, curly-haired blond with blue-green eyes strode across the room.

'Hello,' she said, slinging her purse onto the sofa as if to say, *My workday is done.* There was a questioning lilt to her voice when she greeted them.

'This is Thanikarn, Thalay's mom. The kids are playing in Julie's room,' Krit said, placing his arm affectionately around his wife.

'Well, I've been hoping to meet you. Our Julie seems to have a total crush on your son,' Sarah said, extending her hand as Krit had. Thanikarn wasn't quite sure what she meant by 'crush' but her wide-eyed enthusiasm gave her a vague idea. They shook hands.

'Julie has been talking about Thalay since the first day of school,' Krit added in clarification.

'Oh, Thalay too. He always talks about Julie,' Thanikarn affirmed.

Sarah plopped down on a chair across from Thanikarn and quickly served herself a cup of tea, as she probably did at the end of every workday.

'Krit says you move here from England,' Thanikarn said in a conscientious effort to be sociable, though her hands felt clammy on her mug of tea. She always envied Westerners for their natural gift of initiating conversations.

'So, did Krit tell you how we met?' Sarah asked, smiling, making little dimples pop up in her rosy cheeks.

Thanikarn shook her head no. This was a subject close to her heart, a culturally mixed couple.

'We met at the university. I was studying dentistry at the time, and Krit was in the history department. It was the typical double date, you know; our mutual best friends invited us to come along with them to the movies. We really hit it off, right from the first night.'

'You go to school in England?' Thanikarn asked, turning to look at Krit with surprise. Going to study abroad had always seemed like an impossible dream.

'My father sent me to England to live with cousins a few months after my mom passed away,' Krit said. 'I was still very young. That's how I ended up studying in Birmingham.'

'We came back here to settle his dad's estate a few years ago,' Sarah said, confirming what Krit had told her. 'I thought Koh Samui looked like paradise. If you ever saw Birmingham, you'd understand. I was the one who suggested we stay here. I found a job pretty easily at the International Hospital.' Then, looking at her husband: 'And Krit works from home.'

'You're a dentist?' Thanikarn asked, surprise in her voice.

'Not quite. I needed a quick job back in Birmingham and didn't have the time or money to become a dentist,' she added quite candidly. 'So, I ended up studying to be a dental assistant.'

Thanikarn smiled. This woman she just met was letting her in on her life's disappointments.

'But why do you put Julie in a Thai school?' Thanikarn wondered out loud.

'To learn to speak Thai! And private schools are too expensive. Maybe later, when she gets older, but for now, public schooling is fine.'

Thanikarn's felt her shoulders drop, realizing how tense she had been up to now. Perhaps she was reassured that they too had to economize, something she would have only admitted to a family member or close friend.

Thalay and Julie came skipping into the kitchen. Julie ran to her mother and climbed up into her lap.

'Can Thalay sleep here?' Julie asked.

'Oh, that's a nice idea Julie, but you have school tomorrow, and Mummy works in the morning. Maybe another night.'

Julie's mother kept her word. There would be another night, as well as many others.

33

For Lucas, looking back at his life before he became independent
seemed like looking through the wrong end of a telescope. It was
all so tiny and far away. It would be his birthday soon, and he'd
be turning twenty-two. This time last year, he was feeling sorry for
himself, spending the evening with superficial friends in a seedy
bar – finally being of legal age, getting drunk on margaritas, and
aching to be back in Paris with old friends and family. But since
then, with all the unexpected success, his pessimism had been
defeated by what some would call perseverance, others destiny.
Still insecure, Lucas told himself it was mostly just good luck.

Lucas was now comfortably settled into his own one-bedroom
flat in Santa Monica. It was a modest two-storey complex a
few blocks from the beach made up of a dozen one-bedroom
apartments. It spoke luxury to Lucas. He never imagined he
could afford something so chic at his age. Compared to his tiny
bedroom last year, this was five-star.

Sea Horizon Apartments was slightly set back from the
sidewalk, with a dark-green concrete facade and coral window
trimming that melted it into the banana trees and bamboo planted
in front. There was an inner courtyard with a heated swimming

pool that was seldom used, especially since there were no children in the complex. José, a moustached Mexican gardener, took care of cleaning the pool and trimming the surrounding tropical garden. It reminded Lucas of the Golden Gecko, maybe one reason he chose it.

When he thought of the Golden Gecko, his thoughts immediately conjured up a little image of Thanikarn and those luscious massages. It caused an accompanying pang of nostalgia for his beautiful island lover. He still thought that if it hadn't been for her, he wouldn't have been inspired to write 'Wakin' Up Blues', one of the most popular songs on his album. It was aired more often these days than 'Charming Prince', the song that got him on the charts last year.

Lucas had a few concerts scheduled for the following month, all of them in a line-up with other bands, and then the following month, he would be making a flash appearance on *American Idol*, a show he deplored. But his agent, Mike, was unforgiving when it came to promoting Lucas's career.

'No matter how much you hate the show, you don't turn down good exposure, especially on TV,' he said. Mike had no sympathy for his protégé's anti-commercial idealism or his stubbornly held philosophy that no one was really entitled to judge art.

More for convenience than to celebrate his birthday, Lucas's family would fly to Los Angeles. They hadn't been back to the States for a long time, and this year, his brother's school vacation birthday coincided with Lucas's birthday. His mother had found a great place to stay in LA, thanks to a fortunate chance meeting with an American couple at a dinner party in Paris. John and Tricia vacationed in Paris several months a year and generously offered to loan their half-empty house to Lucas's parents whenever they came to Los Angeles, or even share it if they were home. They had plenty of room now that their kids had moved out, and for the Mounier family, this west-side home was more convenient than staying with Caroline's brother in Orange Country.

John was a screenwriter for TV, presently working on a slowly dying comedy series. He'd also worked with a well-known French film director who happened to be a friend of Lucas's father. His wife, Tricia, was a makeup artist who freelanced for television and movies. They lived on a tree-lined street in Hollywood in a quaint old California Craftsman home with a gable roof and overhanging eaves.

John played the bass – just a hobby, he said – but his musical talent was good enough for him to perform in a long-standing club on Vermont in Silver Lake. He played with a middle-aged pop group consisting of a white-bearded ex-country rocker on the electric piano, a five-foot-four crooner who wore a toupee, and a brunette blues singer who wore layers of makeup and tight knit dresses that stretched down to the top of her knees. They got gigs because of, not in spite of, their corny '60s repertoire.

The Pattersons were anxious to meet Lucas and invited the whole family for dinner. Lucas got along well with John, both being old jazz fans, and after a vegetarian feast prepared by Tricia, they ended up improvising a little jam session, John on bass and Lucas playing on their oversize baby-grand piano, which took up a large chunk of the living room. The 'music corner' John called it.

John really enjoyed Lucas, and before going to bed that evening, he told his wife 'the kid has something.' He sensed a talent that went beyond singing and music, a charismatic presence that wasn't being sufficiently exploited.

The second time they got together to play some music, John asked Lucas if he'd ever done any acting.

Lucas's first experience acting, if one could call it that, was when he was selected to be in a series of taped 'classrooms' with other children who spoke English, to be played in schools around France. He only remembered having a crush on his fake schoolteacher, Mirabelle. Then he took drama lessons when he was in middle school, an extracurricular activity his mother encouraged to help him overcome his shyness. He was good at acting, and his drama teacher talked him into going to an audition for an Edward Albee play to be performed at the Espace Pierre Cardin. One of the cast members hooked him up with his agent, which led to playing a small role in a popular French *feuilleton* that aired weekly on television. But a career in acting took time and dedication, and preferring music, he'd dropped the whole acting gig long ago. However, thanks to the little acting he had done, he had relative ease in front of a camera.

John seemed intrigued by Lucas's experience and proposed they meet up again to talk about a little idea he had.

John had begun to get discouraged with the series he was currently co-writing and had started working on a new idea for a comedy series. He'd recently dropped the plot-line script for *My Upstairs Neighbour* on his boss's desk. It was in the same vein as some other shows that weren't doing too badly at the time: *Friends*, *Reba*, *Will and Grace*. The main story was about a plump, thirtysomething, outwardly cheerful but inwardly self-deprecating woman named Melissa, who worked for a dating company. She would be played by Rachel Wolf, a standup comedian who had recently become famous. Originally, John's script called for her co-star to be an Italian, an incurable romantic idealist dealing with modern American culture. After meeting Lucas, John got it into his head that the co-star could just as well be a young French guy.

A few weeks after the Mounier family headed back to France, John gave Lucas the script of the first episode and explained the basic plot. Rachel, secretly enamoured with her upstairs neighbour, kept strategically setting him up with other women on dates destined to fail. John was exploiting the cliché idea of the impossible romance, a theme Lucas said he could identify with.

John set up a test run the following week at the television studio in Universal City with the director, Derek Schwartz, 'a trying to look younger than his sixty years' man with a permanent three-day beard and a crop of bushy salt-and-pepper hair that seemed to have been styled with a firecracker. He'd been directing for television most of his adult life, and John trusted him implicitly.

When Derek greeted Lucas with a firm handshake, Lucas let his eyes drop down to the ketchup stain on Derek's T-shirt.

'Lunch,' Derek said with a grin.

Lucas smiled. 'Happens to me all the time.' He felt like this was a no-fuss guy he could work with.

Derek, who was familiar with Lucas's album, had also been filled in by John about his background in acting.

'Think you could pile on the French accent?' Derek asked before Lucas started the reading.

'Yeah, no problem.' He grinned. 'I do it all the time. Great for picking up girls.'

Lucas read through the lines, working with a stand-in for Rachel, a perky brunette with her hair swept back into a ponytail and wearing large, blue-rimmed glasses, whom Lucas thought he'd like to see again. When they finished the scene, Derek looked at John and gave him thumbs-up. Now it was a matter of convincing the producers.

34

Tourist season on Koh Samui was year-round. Wealthy and retired visitors came in winter, families and students in summer, lovers and newlyweds anytime. Whatever the season, Thanikarn had little idle time between customers. Her body looked frail, but her arms were packed with sinewy muscles, and her hands were as strong as a mason's. She could massage for hours, one body after another, many twice as big as she was, often propped up on her knees, or sometimes she even used her feet so that she could bear down with all her force.

Her massage work at the Golden Gecko was very different from what she did in Konticha's workshop, placing little stones in their silver settings, twisting tiny wires, attaching miniscule hooks, stringing delicate beads. For the past year she had been alternating jobs, making jewellery on Tuesdays, Wednesdays and Saturdays and giving massages the other days of the week. She liked the contrast and appreciated the steady work, but having two jobs robbed her of time she could spend with Thalay.

While massaging a tense, wiry, young woman, she looked over at Rinalda, old enough to be her mother. She'd been doing this all her life. Her face was beginning to show signs of weariness;

her hair was greying, and her muscles were becoming flaccid. As Thanikarn studied her, she could see herself in another thirty years.

She looked at Sawitti, younger in years and in spirit with the worry-free attitude of an adolescent. Like Thanikarn, she had become a masseuse because it was convenient; it was steady work that required little training. But for Sawitti, massaging was meant to be a temporary job and a convenient way to meet a man who would whisk her from her job and slide her into a life of comfort. Thanikarn wondered if she hadn't once had the same hidden expectations.

Before now, Thanikarn accepted life passively, not doubting who she was, what she did or why. She'd never indulged in existential reflection. But getting older, raising a child on her own, she began asking herself uncomfortable questions. How long would she be doing the same job? Where did she see herself in ten years? What would her son think about her when he grew older? What would she think about herself? Would he ask her why she never tried to do something else, never travelled or married?

Thanikarn's former passive resolve, accepting things the way they were, had started to trouble her. Facing her role as a single mother in a modern world, she began to challenge what she'd always learned, that desire and dissatisfaction only led to more desire and dissatisfaction like a dog chasing its own tail. But now, she thought about how she might be judged one day by Thalay, the only one in the world who really mattered. Thanikarn felt she needed to make some changes in her life, even though she didn't know what they were.

It was probably Konticha who prompted her restless reflections. She constantly reminded Thanikarn to think about marriage and finding a father for her son.

The last time she brought it up, they were both engrossed in their work, Thanikarn at the table sorting through some engraved silver spacers to add to a necklace and Konticha at her sun-drenched desk scratching out some new ideas.

'I suppose you are simply counting on Thalay to take care of you one day,' she said.

'Perhaps.' Family always took care of family. Everyone knew that.

'But it would make things easier for you now, and Thalay later, if you had a husband. You never know what might happen,' she continued.

True. Thanikarn took it for granted that Thalay would grow up to be smarter, stronger, and more successful than she was. It was her mission to make sure he did. But what if she failed? Or what if Konticha was right, and something unexpected happened?

'What about Phong?' Konticha buzzed on about the subject like an annoying fly.

Thanikarn was focused on threading the spacers between jade-coloured beads.

'Phong is a very good friend. But he comes from a family with money, one that expects him to marry someone educated,' she said, head bent over her work. She hoped this would quash her boss's nagging.

Konticha stopped sketching. She twisted her mouth, pensive, perplexed, as if something was not right.

'We'll see …'

* * *

Fortunately for Thanikarn, Phong would soon no longer be a subject of conversation. She hadn't seen him for weeks, Monsoon season kept them from going on their occasional weekend outings, but he called her several days later to say he had something important to discuss and suggested they see each other for dinner.

They met up in front of a popular Irish pub he liked when it wasn't too crowded. Friday and Saturday night could be a bit rowdy at Murphy's, when displaced Brits and Irish or other homesick Europeans often showed up for draft beer at the bar, but on Sunday nights it was quiet. There was often a lingering odour of tobacco smoke and a sweaty crowd from the night before, but Thanikarn liked the relaxing atmosphere, a dimly lit wood-panelled room with soft background music streaming from corner speakers.

The young European barman, who seemed to recognize Phong, led them to a small table near the bar, and Phong ordered draft Guinness. Thanikarn wasn't used to the odd, bitter taste and screwed up her face with the first sip. Phong laughed. She laughed.

'I have to get used to this,' Phong said, holding up his glass.

Thanikarn tilted her head, perplexed.

'That's what I wanted to tell you. I'm moving to Dublin.'

She waited for the explanation.

'My friend, Sean, is Irish. He's an architect. We met here,

while he was working on a hotel complex. He's moving back to Ireland.'

'What about your job at the bank? What about your family?'

'My English is good; Sean will help me find a job. I hope … And for my family, the pressure is off these days. My sister just had a baby – I mean, two of them. My parents are busy helping my sister take care of the twins.'

Phong never ceased to surprise her.

'I hope you will be happy,' she managed to say, smiling through her disappointment.

Phong had become a pillar for her and Thalay. She never imagined he would move out of her life.

'Thank you, Karn.' Phong took her hand and gave a gentle squeeze.

Their food arrived. Thanikarn bit into her roast beef sandwich, a little too thick to fit gracefully into her mouth. Phong dipped his nuggets of fried fish into both mayonnaise and ketchup and popped them in his mouth, smiling. Digging into their meal lifted the shroud of sadness they pretended not to feel. Suddenly, Thanikarn's eyes widened like a startled deer; she sat upright and whipped her head toward the loudspeaker above the bar from where the first familiar chords of 'Wakin' Up Blues' flowed into the room.

Finishing up the last nugget, Phong hadn't noticed.

She regained her composure and took another sip of her beer.

When the waiter came for their plates, Phong's wiped clean and Thanikarn's still holding an unfinished sandwich, she asked their young English waiter about the music. He explained that it was one of the owner's CDs, a recorded compilation of recent hits. She nodded as if she knew what he was talking about.

Phong cocked his head and looked at her with curious eyes.

'One of the songs that just played, I know it,' she conceded quietly.

Phong, either from discretion or indifference, left it at that.

35

Once she had put Thalay to sleep that night, Thanikarn lay awake in bed, eyes open, staring up through the darkness, her head spinning with wonder. If 'Wakin' Up Blues' was a hit, then she could find out more about Lucas.

Thanikarn went to Konticha's the next morning, knowing it would be hard to concentrate on her work. As she was adding clasps to a pile of purple jade necklaces, she suddenly thought of a plan. She would go see Ben. He played music; he would know about the song, especially if it was well known.

It was nearly six thirty by the time she finished her day's work, but she knew that Ben seldom closed before evening. When she slipped through the front door of his shop, he was perched on a stool behind the counter reading a magazine. His eyes lit up, and he bellowed out an enthusiastic greeting when he saw her.

'Well, there she is, Princess Karn!'

'Hi, Ben,' Thanikarn said as if it had only been a few days rather than a year since they last saw each other.

Ben got up, worked his way around the counter, and gave her a big bear hug.

'How are you?'

'I'm good. Just always so busy, with work and taking care of Thalay.'

'I bet you are. But you never came to see me at the club,' he added, pretending to scold her. 'Come have a seat in my salon,' he said, showing her the way to the store's corner library. 'Can I get you something to drink?'

'No. I'm fine. I don't have much time. I just wanted to ask you something.'

'Of course,' he said, sweeping his arm toward the easy chair. She sat down, and he patiently waited for her to speak.

'I heard Lucas's song in a restaurant last night.' The look in her eye made it sound like a question.

'Yeah. Unbelievable! He had a couple of tubes.'

'Tubes?'

'Big-selling songs. They're called tubes.'

She looked at him as if she'd just learned something very important.

'I heard somewhere he had an album out … Didn't try to buy it yet.'

Thanikarn consumed the information with eager eyes. She wanted to hear more.

'So, he didn't give you any news,' her voice dropping to the floor.

'He must be a bit of a celebrity by now. I don't think he's going to be contacting me anytime soon. Probably busy as hell.' He caught Thanikarn's forlorn expression. 'But that doesn't mean you can't find out where he is or maybe even get in touch with him.'

'How?' Her question rebounded from the floor.

'Internet.'

'Internet.' All she could do was repeat the word. Everyone was talking about it these days, but what it was and how it could help her was a mystery.

'Yeah, we don't have an internet connection in the shop yet, but maybe you know someone who does, or you could always go to an internet café.'

She did know someone, Philippe, and of course Phong, at the bank, but she was too shy to ask Philippe and felt she didn't want to get Phong involved. She also thought about Krit. He used a computer all the time for his work. But reaching out to him presented the same problem. This was something she wanted to keep to herself; but at least she left Ben's with a little more hope than when she arrived.

* * *

Unexpectedly, Jantip was at the Golden Gecko when Thanikarn arrived at work the next morning. Any animosity between Jantip, Rinalda and Sawitti had faded long ago. As for Thanikarn, she had always found their working arrangement to her advantage.

'Hi, Thanikarn,' Jantip said, 'I came to pick up a bag I forgot here yesterday. I hoped I might see you.'

'Me?'

'I wanted to ask you if you would like to replace me at the Anantara Lawana.'

Thanikarn had completely forgotten that Jantip also worked

at the Anantara.

'Oh, sorry, I can't. I have another job too.' She was proud to say that, but she was still curious, so she added, 'Replace you for how long?'

'I don't know. I'm getting married next week, so maybe for a long time.'

It seemed as if everyone was organizing their future. She wondered if Jantip had also found a foreigner. It wouldn't have been unlikely; she could have easily met someone while working in a big five-star hotel with wealthy tourists. Or maybe just a local Thai. Either way, marriage sounded good, and Thanikarn felt a tinge of envy.

'You know,' Jantip said, lowering her voice, 'I always thought you were too smart and pretty to work here. It's different at the Anantara. Very classy.'

What Jantip was downplaying was exactly what she liked about working at the Golden Gecko, its low-key family atmosphere.

'You make more money at the Anantara, and you have everything there: souvenir shops, spa, business centre ... Rich people stay there.'

Thanikarn figured she guessed right about Jantip's future husband being a foreigner. Then she pictured all the facilities at the Anantara. Her mental promenade took her through the hotel, past those souvenir shops, that spa, and finally zooming toward the business centre ... and computers.

'You know how to use the internet?' Thanikarn asked, as if Jantip had followed her imaginary tour.

Jantip raised her eyebrows. '*Dai* ...'

'Can you show me how to use it?'

Thanikarn imagined that Jantip was someone who would be savvy about computers and the internet. More importantly, she was someone who had no clue as to why Thanikarn wanted to use a computer.

'*Dai*.'

'Now?' Thanikarn asked. 'You have some time now?' Her work could wait another half-hour or so.

* * *

There was no shortage of internet cafés on the island. A new one seemed to open every week. It was Jantip's day off, so she compliantly jumped onto the back of Thanikarn's scooter, and after a five-minute ride down the main road they found an internet café in between a souvenir shop and a launderette. Thanikarn had explained on the way, yelling back through the wind and street noise that she really appreciated finding someone who knew something about using the internet.

Once they sat down in front of one of the wide computer screens, Thanikarn told Jantip she wanted to look up the name of a song and find out more about the singer.

'Can you do that?'

Jantip shrugged with another '*Dai*.' Thanikarn felt as though Jantip was limited in words as well as curiosity.

'It's a song called "Wakin' Up Blues",' Thanikarn said.

Jantip looked at her quizzically. 'Can you spell that? I need to type it in.'

'*Ka*,' she said, and Jantip gave up her seat in front of the computer and stared over her shoulder. Using one finger, Thanikarn slowly typed in the name. The search engine they used came up with a response of *unfound*. Thanikarn frowned.

'We need more information,' Jantip said, sounding like someone who knew what she was talking about. 'Who sings it?'

'Lucas,' she said.

'Lucas what?' she asked, becoming impatient with Thanikarn. This time it was Thanikarn who, in lieu of an answer, shrugged.

'Okay, we put in Lucas, and we put in the name of the song.' This time a couple of websites appeared for them to choose from. And with a simple click, his unexpected picture made her start. There he was, sitting on a chair and holding a guitar, looking like he did when he sang the song for her in bar on the beach.

'Oh, that's Lucky Moon!' Jantip shrieked. '*Mee chuee-seang*,' she said, recognizing that he was famous.

'You know him?' Thanikarn turned her head to ask.

'*Naae-non*,' Jantip said. 'He had a song that came out, a big hit called "Charming Prince". And then I saw him on a TV show I was watching with Steve – Steve is my *American* fiancé,' she added.

Thanikarn's head was spinning. All this information came too fast. Lucas … a hit song … a television show.

'So, you see, you can read and find out all about him and his album and his show,' Jantip said, scrolling down through the website. 'What do you want to know?'

Thanikarn couldn't say what she wanted to know; she wanted

to know everything.

'It's okay. I understand now how it works,' she said curtly. She had shared enough with Jantip already and had no intention of sharing anything more. Jantip sensed there was more to this than Thanikarn was willing to say.

'You saw him before? He came to Koh Samui?' she asked. Though Jantip lacked true curiosity, this was good gossip.

Thanikarn just nodded, still staring at Lucas's image on the computer screen.

'A long time ago,' she finally said, 'before all this.'

'You were lucky. You couldn't meet him now,' she said with clumsy honesty.

Then, sensing she might have hurt Thanikarn's feelings, Jantip tried to change the subject. 'I like your earrings,' she said, touching one of the little gold butterflies that Lucas had given Thanikarn over four years ago.

'Thank you,' Thanikarn said, giving a weak smile. 'They were a present …'

36

Ben was right; Lucas was 'busy as hell'. Ever since working on the TV series, he'd been immersed in a new world with its own reality, or as Lucas said, its own 'sur-reality'. He'd never watched much television back in France. There, it was sadly limited in quantity and quality. Television in the States was on a whole new level, ubiquitous, infiltrating life 24/7; it was played in homes, restaurants, bars and gyms. His brief experience appearing in a few episodes of a French *feuilleton* was nothing like the exhausting rhythm of starring in a Hollywood series.

Another thing that changed was his privacy. As a singer, he was seen less than he was heard and seldom recognized in public, but now, most everywhere he went, someone spotted him.

'Hey, you're that guy Pierre,' they'd say.

That was annoying. It was a name he had always hated, ever since one of his classmates in sixth grade, an obnoxious brat named Pierre, almost got him expelled. Pierre had been the producer's idea: 'A French name the public will recognize,' he said.

'So is Michel,' Lucas argued back – one of his best friends was named Michel.

'Sounds like a girl,' the director said. And so, it was Pierre.

Not only did people ignore his real name, they also sometimes confused him with his role, criticizing or praising him for something he'd said or done in the series. He blamed their mistake on reality TV.

Lucas felt a pang of nostalgia every time he heard about a local rock concert and missed going on tour with his band. Over the last year, his status as a singer-songwriter had to take a back seat to his rising career in television. He was on a roll, and even Mike, his faithful and trusted music producer, encouraged him to take advantage of the publicity the series was generating. Mike still handled everything concerning the sale of his album, and since Lucas's TV popularity was pushing up the sales of his albums, Mike was still making a small but unfaltering percentage.

Despite Lucas's antipathy for entrusting yet another person to represent his interests, he was obliged to hire an acting agent since Mike had the good sense not to take on managing Lucas's acting career. Getting a new agent came not as advice but as an order from his scriptwriter friend, John. He warned Lucas of the abundance of opportunists in the television and movie industry, where there was a lot more hypocrisy than sincerity, and a sensitive soul like Lucas needed protection. Lucas was 'a little Nemo in a world of sharks', John told him. He knew just the right person to defend his interests, a sharp, on-top-of-it guy named Dan Black. Dan also handled the young and lovely Crystal Jennings, who had been promoted to stardom for her role in a remake of *The Adventures of Nelly Bly*, a film about the audacious female pioneer in photojournalism. Of course Lucas had heard of Crystal.

My Upstairs Neighbour was getting top ratings, and coincidentally or not, ever since Dan had taken Lucas under his wing, there were rumours the show would be nominated for several Emmy awards. There was even a chance Lucas might be up for a bid as Best Supporting Actor in a Comedy Series. It was almost certain, if the show was in the running, that Rachel, the star of the show, would not only be nominated but win the category of Lead Actress. The upcoming awards would be Lucas's first glimpse of the Emmy experience, an event that he had never even heard of before moving to LA. But, as he quickly learned, it was a really big deal in the States, especially in Hollywood, where receiving an Emmy could have almost the same impact on an actor's life as an Oscar.

The success of *My Upstairs Neighbour* turned out to be much more time-consuming than Lucas ever imagined. It wasn't just doing the show, which included readings, rehearsals and full days shooting at the studio, but there were other obligations that came along with the job, such as interviews, appearances on talk shows and charity or fund-raising events. Dan made sure that Lucas was in the public eye as much as possible, arranging for him to appear in the right place at the right time and, most importantly, with the right people. Lucas's new duties included dining at the best restaurants, attending late-night parties and spending time with people Lucas would have been happy to avoid.

Except for Crystal.

Sharing the same agent, Lucas and Crystal met one day at Dan's office. She was less glamorous than she appeared to be on screen but just as beautiful, beaming with innocent charm.

He was surprised by her casual, natural air. Wearing jeans, an oversize, long-sleeved T-shirt and Converse sneakers, with her strawberry-blond hair tucked under a cap, she could probably go unrecognized in public. There was something about her that reminded him of Thanikarn. Maybe it was the discreet smile or the way she riveted his attention with her intense almond-shaped eyes.

Dan carried out a quick introduction – 'Crystal, Lucas; Lucas, Crystal' – since they already knew the other's identity. Unbeknown to both, crossing paths at Dan's wasn't a coincidence. Nor was the fact they both ended up at the same dinner party in Malibu a week later, as well as at a fund-raising visit at the Los Angeles Children's Hospital, where they were caught arm in arm by paparazzi on their way out. A photo or two appeared in *Rising Star Magazine* and *In Touch*.

The pictures got the gossips talking, and the false innuendos caught Lucas and Crystal off guard. They exchanged a couple of phone calls to figure out how to set things straight, which unfortunately meant not appearing in public together. After meeting for a private lunch at the studio, they agreed avoiding contact was 'a stupid shame'. Crystal casually invited Lucas over for a drink at her home, a bungalow tucked away in the Hollywood Hills, and getting to know one another, they realized that they had a lot in common, especially their shared interest in politics and world events.

Crystal was uncommonly sophisticated when it came to current affairs. Her father, an outspoken liberal, was a former ambassador in Lebanon, and having spent her teenage years there, she knew which country was which on a map of the Middle East, unlike many Americans. She and Lucas had the same opinion about the imminent war in Iraq and they were both ready to voice their protest. They also shared other liberal ideas, on everything from Greenpeace to same-sex marriage, and like other well-known Hollywood celebrities, they had publicly signed petitions or made statements in the media.

The Emmy awards came up in September, just before Lucas's birthday, and as had been rumoured, *My Upstairs Neighbour* was nominated for several categories. Crystal was nominated for Outstanding Actress for her role in *Goodbye Grace*, a two-hour movie she shot earlier that year. As predicted, she won the award that night ... and as a surprise, so did Lucas. Dan obviously had nothing to do with the judging, but he didn't miss a beat in getting them to pose together for some glamour shots after the awards show. A photo of the two of them, in which Crystal, wearing an elegant Jean Harlow-like white silk gown, had her arm wrapped around his neck, was in all the tabloids and fan magazines the next day.

This touched off another round of gossip, which unlike the first time, they ignored. Not only because good gossip was good publicity but because they knew it was a losing battle to fight it. Right after the Emmys, Crystal had to fly back to Brazil where she was finishing up an action movie, and as for Lucas, he was busy working on future episodes of *My Upstairs Neighbour* or reading scripts. Dan had received dozens after Lucas's Emmy win, and he handed them all over to him in a thick pile.

Crystal returned to LA in late November after an exhausting

film shoot, looking forward to a good rest. She and Lucas wasted no time in seeing one another again. But their reunion was brief. Christmas was coming up, and Crystal flew back to the East Coast to be with her family. Lucas regretted not having the same opportunity since he had a lot of work taking him right through the holidays.

Then the day after Christmas, there was a horrible earthquake in Iran. The city of Bam was destroyed, and thousands of people were crushed to death, injured and left homeless. Crystal's father still had friends and contacts in the Middle East, including Iran, and didn't hesitate to take the first flight he could. Crystal volunteered to accompany her parents, much to the disappointment of Lucas. Not only had they planned to spend New Year's together, but as a fellow humanitarian, Lucas was eager to participate in the action, which Crystal opposed.

'You're under contract, Lucas; don't start messing around with the rules. You'll pay for it later.'

'It just feels so superficial and stupid compared to what you're doing.'

'Don't worry – there will be other New Year's Eves. And plenty of other chances to help out somewhere in this crazy world.'

He wasn't sure about New Year, but for humanitarian crises, there would no doubt be others.

37

Thanikarn was soon back at the internet café, but this time without Jantip looking over her shoulder. She still felt strangely guilty and couldn't help looking around the room to make sure no one was watching as she relocated Lucas's web page.

As soon as Thanikarn had impatiently skimmed through his biographical information, tracing the steps of his career – his local club performances, his album recording, his tours, the television show and the Emmy award – she scrolled down to read about his private life. The first thing she saw was the photo of Lucas and Crystal posing after the Emmy ceremony. There were others: a paparazzi shot of them ducking into a restaurant, another one of them riding together in a convertible Mustang, and a posed picture of them on the pier in Santa Monica. Although all the captions were written in English, the photos needed no translation.

Thanikarn studied the pictures of Lucas, recalling his sparkling eyes, his boyish grin, that little lifted brow expressing unease. She remembered him telling her he didn't like to have his picture taken. She tried to read some of the longer comments, but her pounding heart and wrenching stomach kept her from concentrating. Every image and laudatory remark pointed to one thing: Lucas had entered another world that left her further behind.

Walking out of the shop, her head was clouded with grief as if she'd just learned that someone had died.

She dreaded spending the day massaging at the Golden Gecko. It was work that allowed her thoughts to wander, and today, they would surely be dark thoughts. Rinalda and Sawitti were their chatty selves, but nothing they said was compelling enough to keep her mind off her discovery. It highlighted the stark truth. She had had a brief affair with a young nobody who became a big somebody, and she was now raising his son. If he knew, he'd probably resent her, maybe even detest her for having fooled him. She had to take responsibility for her mistake ... a wonderful mistake she didn't regret but one she felt obliged to hide.

Before leaving that evening, she was lured to Amnat's kitchen where the familiar fragrance of coconut and citronella beckoned her like her mother's arms. When she walked in, Amnat was chopping ginger that he tossed into his soup.

'Hello, beautiful,' he said. He quickly noticed that his comment didn't elicit her usual smile.

Thanikarn leaned against the worktable, half-seated on the edge. 'I know now ...' she said. 'Thalay's father. I found out where he is.' She waited for Amnat to answer a question she hadn't asked. He began chopping up long green beans for a papaya salad.

'Thalay will ask me one day. He will want to know about his father ...' Thanikarn wasn't sure where she was going with this confession.

'I wonder if I should tell him,' she finally said.

'Thalay or his father?'

Thanikarn frowned. She was talking about Thalay, not Lucas. 'I don't know what to do.'

'And you want me to tell you?' Amnat wasn't cooperating.

'Thalay will ask about his father, and when he finds out his father never even knew he was born, what will he think?'

'You know the answer to that.' He started grating papaya.

'He will want to know why I never told him,' she said with solemn resignation. Thalay would soon realize his father was a farang. Should she lie to him? *Could* she lie to him? She regretted having discovered what had become of Lucas.

'His father is family,' Amnat ventured.

Thanikarn hadn't thought about it that way; she doubted that family for a farang meant the same thing as for a Thai. She'd seen too many movies; Western culture was all about independence and freedom. Lucas was too young; she was too old. She couldn't expect or even hope for anything from him or his family.

Amnat sensed her silent despair. 'Sometimes the best decision is no decision. Sometimes, things just work out by themselves.'

Thanikarn frowned. That was no help. Or was it?

That night, as she lay down next to Thalay, waiting for him to fall asleep, she decided to play Lucas's CD, something she hadn't done for months. Was she looking for comfort or punishment? As she listened to the song for the umpteenth time, she smiled with a new thought. She had the original copy of a hit song sung by a famous television star. If Jantip knew her secret, she would be jealous or, knowing Jantip, spiteful, like when she chided her for being lucky to know him before he was famous. She stroked

Thalay's light-brown hair and thought about his father. He could probably offer Thalay many things she couldn't.

Thalay's eyelids began to close, then opened halfway, as she struggled to stay awake. When Lucas's song was over, Thalay said, 'Mama, play the lady's song with the pretty voice.' She reached over for the CD of *Madame Butterfly*, and as Cio-san sang 'One fine day' Thalay's little eyelids finally closed. She gave him a goodnight kiss on the cheek and remained listening, thinking about Cio San's heartfelt lament when her American lover came to take away their beautiful son.

* * *

Thanikarn never needed a babysitter for Thalay since Trin or her grandmother were always available. But these days, she was becoming wary of leaving her son alone with Preeda. Her physical and mental strength was weakening as fast as Thalay's was growing. Thanikarn sometimes left Thalay with Julie and her father, but only for a few hours, and she didn't want to abuse their generous offer to have him over 'anytime.'

Thalay had a whole week off from school, and he begged his mother to spend a day or two with her at work. Thanikarn didn't say no but warned him he might get bored while she was busy massaging. Then again, he might enjoy a day outside, and she knew all her friends at the Golden Gecko would enjoy seeing him after all this time. Even though Thanikarn had taught her son how to swim, she still insisted he stay away from the shore and within eyesight. With Philippe's permission, he could play in the jacuzzi part of the hotel pool with an array of colourful tubes and toys, a four-year-old's paradise. Thanikarn looked on proudly as he chatted away in English with some of the young hotel guests around the pool.

She also let him visit with Amnat in the kitchen. Thalay was fascinated by Amnat's dexterity at throwing 'this and that' into pots and pans, that magically turned into delicious soups, salads and curries. Amnat helped Thalay prepare his lunch, fried *pad*, letting him help by adding his own selection of tofu, eggs, sauces and a fistful of peanuts. When it was ceremoniously served to him in the terrace restaurant by Manee, he sat chest puffed high, feeling like a prince. He waggled his legs with delight as he waved to his mother working at the stand nearby.

Shortly before sunset, after Thalay had taken an afternoon nap on a mat next to his mother, Amnat came to fetch him during his break between the lunch clean-up and the dinner preparations. He proposed the three of them go for a walk along the seashore. There were few clients at this hour, and Thanikarn enjoyed a chance to take a relaxing stroll.

Though the sunset was out of sight, there remained a pink-and-yellow glow on the horizon as the three of them strolled down toward the water's edge. Thalay skipped off and sat down in the wet sand, letting the soft, rolling waves splash up around his hips just like Thanikarn used to do. Amnat and Thanikarn stood nearby watching him play.

'I've been thinking about what we talked about yesterday,' Thanikarn said. 'I don't know when Thalay will ask me, but when he does, I'll have to tell him the truth.'

'Which is …?'

'That I never let his father know he had a son,' she said decidedly.

'You're not afraid he'll ask you why?'

'Of course. But if I explain why, he will understand.'

'Which is …?'

'That I was afraid that if he knew, he would come take him away from me …'

Without waiting for his reaction, Thanikarn skipped off to join her son playing in the waves.

38

Thalay had such a good time when he went with his mother to the Golden Gecko that he begged her to take him with her to Konticha's workshop as well. Thanikarn was afraid he would be disappointed. There was no one to see except Konticha there, and he would be shut in all day with nothing to do, no pool, sand or ocean waves to play in. But she could never resist a request from her son, and with a promise from him that he wouldn't complain, she agreed. Being forewarned, Thalay took the initiative to pack a bag of his favourite toys.

Konticha knew everything there was to know about Thalay – he was Thanikarn's main subject of conversation – but she hadn't seen him for a couple of years. She immediately raved about how much he'd grown. Thalay was equally impressed by Konticha, flamboyantly dressed as usual, in a long multi-coloured skirt and purple cotton-lace top, making over him like he was a star. The moment they arrived, Thalay trailed after Konticha like a curious puppy as she wandered around the room getting organized. She put a stool next to her desk and let him look on as she sketched out new jewellery ideas. After watching Konticha, he dragged over a stool, climbed up and sat next to his mother, watching as she carefully strung a necklace with a series of carefully chosen coloured pearls. His keen interest in their work gave Konticha an idea. She rummaged around in her closet and found a big shoebox of unused pieces of jewellery, various rejects that consisted of strings, chains, bangles and beads.

'You can have this. My hidden treasure chest,' she said as she handed the box to Thalay.

He sat cross-legged on the floor, opened the lid and was thrilled with the shiny array of goods that he quickly dumped out in front of him. He separated the chains from the beads as he saw his mother do. He struggled stringing some carefully chosen shiny beads and polished stones on a black string. After working for ten minutes in silent concentration, he took his creation to Konticha.

'Here. This is for you,' he said. She kissed him tenderly on the forehead and immediately tied it around her neck.

'Thalay, this is beautiful.'

Thalay smiled with sunny pride and went back to his treasure chest to set about making a necklace for his mother.

Early afternoon, Konticha proposed that the three of them go out for a hamburger at MacDonald's. This was a new treat for Thalay; his mother had never taken him to such a place. Her theory was that fast food was bad for a person's body, but she didn't object. Konticha, seemed determined to make this a special day.

'Just once, won't hurt,' Konticha said, guessing the reason Thalay had never been there.

After lunch, Konticha suggested they stop in a store she knew on their way back to the atelier. An untypically chic boutique with brand-name clothing was going out of business and having a huge sale on everything in the shop. Thanikarn almost never bought anything new; most of her clothes came from the shopping fair or an annual temple fair. As she feared, Konticha insisted on buying Thalay a new pair of shoes, 'a gift from Auntie Konticha.' She encouraged Thanikarn to buy a half-price, long, sleeveless, print dress, flared at the bottom that 'would look fabulous' on her. Thanikarn looked at Konticha as if she had proposed she jump off a cliff. She couldn't remember the last time she'd ever bought or even worn a dress.

'I don't need this,' she said. 'I almost never go out.'

'That's why you should buy it,' Konticha said. 'It will give you a reason to go out.'

Thanikarn bit her lips and averted her eyes, but feeling beholden and earnest to please, she went to try it on. When she came out wearing the dress and looked in the mirror, she had to admit, the effect was stunning.

'Mama, you look pretty!' Thalay said in English, which solicited a nod of agreement from Konticha.

'I'm buying it!' Thanikarn said.

When they got back to the workshop, Thanikarn swept up her hair as she always did before setting to work and realized one of her little butterfly earrings was missing. She gasped, and a look of panic clouded her face. The earring must have caught on something when she was trying on clothes. Konticha agreed to watch Thalay so she could run back to the shop to look for it.

Thanikarn searched everywhere in the boutique. She scoured the floor in the dressing room and frantically went through a pile of clothes in the sales bin. The salesgirl even fetched a broom and swept the floor, but the dusty pile of grit contained nothing but some hairpins, a paperclip, and a torn-up ticket to a boxing match. On her way back to the atelier, she didn't take her eyes off the ground, half-hoping she would find it en route.

Once Thanikarn arrived at Konticha's, she dropped into her chair with a thud and slowly took off the remaining earring. This was yet another sign, she thought; superstition had become a habit. Neither Konticha nor Thalay knew why the earrings were so important to Thanikarn, but her son didn't like seeing his mother upset, and he wanted to help. He looked around the room in distress, then went over to his little pile of jewellery scraps on the floor, scattered them about, and found a gold chain.

'Here, Mama,' he said, handing it to her. 'You can put the other earring on this and put it around your neck.'

Thanikarn smiled at her son.

Seeing that she wasn't convinced, Konticha took the earring and chain. 'A wonderful idea, Thalay. Let's do this right now.'

Thalay watched with fascination as she trimmed the earring wire and soldered it into a little circle that she could then thread onto the chain. It was done within minutes.

Thanikarn looked at the necklace that Thalay put in her hand and with saddened eyes put one remaining remnant of a precious memory around her neck.

* * *

Like everyone else she knew, Thanikarn had always aspired to a life of comfort. And now, she could claim her life, such as it was, was comfortable. But she still felt like something was missing. That gnawing feeling of dissatisfaction continued to eat away at her happiness, and despite her efforts to chase it away, it returned every night when she went to bed alone. She was too young to renounce romance.

Most of the joy in her life came from Thalay. His inquisitive mind grew every day as he asked endless questions, the hows and whys of everything he couldn't figure out. 'Mama, why does the moon look bigger and smaller?', 'Why don't the chickens fuss when we take their eggs?', 'What makes you ticklish?', 'What makes the wind blow?' Unable to answer, Thanikarn told him he would surely learn about such things in school. Thalay still hadn't asked the question she dreaded. Although she realized she would have to tell him the truth one day, she secretly hoped some magical something would happen to make the task easier.

Thanikarn went back to check on Lucas's website one more time. She didn't discover much. He had recorded a new love song, surely not written for her, and there was talk of him acting in a new movie to be shot in the summer. There was also a new picture of Lucas with Crystal that made her wince. She realized that she didn't want to see any more than she'd already seen. And, the less she knew about him, the less she would have to explain away.

It was tempting to dream, but just when she thought she had control of her emotions, her buried hopes crept back into her thoughts and grabbed her imagination. She sometimes indulged in a fairy tale fantasy like when she was a child, in which everything unfolded just as she wanted.

Lucas returns to the island for a nostalgic visit to get away from his harried hectic life in Hollywood: the cameras, the journalists, the fans. He wants to get back to nature and see old friends. He remembers the wonderful time they spent together and goes back to the Golden Gecko looking for her. She's there, massaging a client like the time they first met. 'Hi, can I get a massage?' he asks, with his big, sweet smile. She looks up and discovers it's him. She's so happy she can hardly breathe. She jumps up, and he wraps his arms around her. They kiss ... and then ... Her fantasy fades. Although she'd heard that there were no limits to your imagination, there were limits to hers. There would never be a happily ever after.

Sometimes, Thanikarn wished she could meet someone who would cause her memories of Lucas to disappear. She wanted the looming fear of never finding love again to end. But then again, how could she want to forget such a beautiful memory? One that stared her in the face every time she looked at her son.

39

A couple of weeks after their shopping spree, Konticha startled Thanikarn with a momentous announcement: she was leaving the island. Pran, whom Thanikarn had been told was nothing but a friend and client, had since become Konticha's fiancé and financier. Pran, a wealthy gemmologist in Bangkok, had a shop in Phuket Town on the picturesque Thalang Road, a street that attracted hundreds of tourists all year long. The shop had never really prospered, and he proposed turning the whole affair over to Konticha. She could feature her personal line of upscale jewellery using real gems that he would provide at cost. Konticha would not only have her own boutique but her own home. Pran owned a discreet colonial-style villa on the outskirts of the city that served as a secondary residence. They could spend time there together whenever he wasn't working on the mainland. Her beau also had plans to rent a second boutique in a five-star luxury hotel called the Sea Breeze Resort on Patong Beach. This was an opportunity no single working woman could resist.

'I'm not getting any younger, Karn,' she said, stating the obvious. 'If I'm going to make a change in my life, this is probably the last chance I'll have.'

'And what about your workshop and your house?' Thanikarn asked, her voice faltering. She was already feeling the threat of losing not only her job but a friend and confident.

'I can always rent out the workshop. And my house? It never really was my house anyway.'

Thanikarn remembered her saying that even though she had legally inherited the property, it really belonged to the whole family.

'You know, there's nothing to keep me here in Koh Samui, nothing I would regret.'

Her remark was like a punch in the stomach. Konticha played such an important role in her life, as boss, mentor, and much more. Thanikarn stood speechless.

'Don't look so forlorn, Karn. I'm not forgetting you. In fact, I'm offering you a permanent job. You can come and help me manage the shops.'

Thanikarn looked at Konticha as if the words she was saying made no sense.

'I can't handle two places on my own,' she continued in a bubbly voice. 'You'd be working full-time, managing the beach store. And I can offer you rent-free lodging! Pran owns a small apartment in the heart of Phuket Town that stays empty most of the year. He just keeps it for friends or family when they need a place to stay.'

'But Thalay ...'

'Thalay? There are plenty of international schools in Phuket. In fact, I already found one for you.' Konticha knew this was the carrot that would entice Thanikarn to join her.

'It's run by an American. Not expensive at all. I heard he was a retired millionaire who married a Thai woman. They offer partial scholarships to Thai children, probably his wife's idea, and I'm certain that Thalay would have no problem qualifying. Pran is a very important man on the island.'

Thanikarn's head was spinning. She felt as if Konticha was yanking her out of the ground by the roots. The thought of even trying to consider this was impossible.

'I'm not the only one who needs to make a change. We both know that if you don't do something soon, you won't be able to do anything at all. You'll just plod along, same work, same people, getting older. Getting old.'

Konticha began explaining how she would organize her departure, what she would take, how she would set up the new shop and her new home. Thanikarn wasn't listening. She was thinking about her grandmother and Trin. How could she abandon her family? And then there were her friends at the Golden Gecko and Julie.

'I know this sounds sudden. Just think about it.'

Thanikarn was far from convinced. Her distant eyes saw nothing but what she already knew, a tranquil life on the island. It took more than a list of good reasons for Thanikarn to decide anything. She acted on feelings, and everything she felt right now, her comfort and security, her trust and love, her confidence and hope, was all tied together in Koh Samui.

* * *

Thanikarn stowed Konticha's proposition somewhere in the back of her mind, or at least she tried to, hoping that something would come up so she wouldn't have to decide. She needed a sign; maybe something would happen, a fight between Pran and Konticha, or Pran's business collapsing, or someone getting sick, or …?

She never could have guessed that the 'something' would concern her and Thalay, not Konticha.

Thalay and Julie had a sleepover at Julie's on weekends, and even though Sarah was in Singapore for a three-day dental convention this weekend, Krit kindly offered to have Thalay over on Friday night as usual.

As agreed, Thanikarn picked up Thalay and Julie after school on Friday and walked them to Julie's house. Thanikarn dropped her son off thinking that Krit might regret his offer. She knew how rambunctious two four-year-olds could be, but he seemed confident about his childcare skills.

'I can stick them in front of a movie – I just bought *The Lion King* – then I'll feed them some noodles for dinner and put them to bed early. No problem.'

Thanikarn took advantage of a free evening and went out for ice cream sundaes with Sawitti in Chaweng before spending a quiet night at home with Preeda. She was just clearing up in the kitchen after serving her grandmother a light dinner, when she got a phone call from Krit. It was around 9 pm. He explained that Thalay wasn't feeling well and had changed his mind about sleeping over. 'Nothing serious,' he added.

Nonetheless, Thanikarn was worried. It wasn't like her son to complain, especially when it came to a sleepover at Julie's. She feared he must be very out of sorts to ask for his mother to come fetch him.

When Thanikarn arrived, Krit opened the door with a smile, looking nonchalant.

'So sorry, Krit,' Thanikarn said as she entered, scanning the room for her son.

Krit held a bottle of local rum in one hand and a glass with some ice in the other.

'Join me for a drink?' he asked, holding up his glass.

'Oh no. Thank you. I think I should take Thalay home.'

'No rush. He's asleep.'

Perplexed, Thanikarn looked up at him; he was easily a head taller than she was.

'Yeah, when I was putting them to bed, he said he didn't feel good and wanted to go home. Then I read them a story waiting for you to come, and both the kids fell sound asleep.'

'Maybe I go see him,' she said, heading for Julie's room.

'No rush.' Krit gently took her arm, holding her back.

Trapped between politeness and worry, Thanikarn stopped.

Krit looked into her eyes. 'Have a drink with me first,' he said with kind insistence.

She answered with an unsure smile and, as he headed into the kitchen, she called, 'Just a glass of water!'

Thanikarn sat down on the living room sofa, feeling a little anxious. Krit wasn't acting like his usual self; this was apparently not his first glass of rum that evening.

He came back with two half-filled glasses of rum and sat down next to her, inches away. Thanikarn took a glass, and he held up his, gesturing that they make a toast. She reluctantly clinked her glass with his but immediately put it back down on the coffee table.

'You are a very pretty girl, Karn.'

Krit's remark caught her off guard. She looked away.

'Ever since the first time I saw you, I've wanted to ...'

He leaned over, pushing her shoulders against the back of the sofa, and stuffed his tongue into her mouth with a forceful, wet kiss. She squirmed, afraid to make any noise – the children were sleeping in the next room. She struggled to turn her head and move out of his grip. He proceeded to push her down flat on her back, and while trying to resist him, she frantically kicked her legs, knocking over the table along with their glasses that went crashing to the floor. The jarring noise stopped Krit in his tracks. He sat back, his head wobbling as if he'd just been slapped. Thanikarn sprang to her feet and stood facing him with contained anger just as Julie came stumbling in half-asleep.

'Daddy?' she said, running to him.

He swept his daughter up into his arms. Julie seemed not to notice Thanikarn.

'It's nothing, baby, just a little accident,' Krit said, stroking Julie's head.

Burning with embarrassment, Thanikarn turned on her heels and went into the bedroom to check on Thalay. He was sound asleep. Her first impulse was to wake him up and take him home with her, but she stopped in her tracks, not wanting to make matters worse than they already were. Krit strolled into the bedroom, carrying his sleepy daughter, and proceeded to put her back to bed.

Thanikarn turned and furtively left the room. Once she was on her scooter speeding home, angry teardrops swept down across her cheeks.

40

It wasn't long after that horrible evening at Julie's that Thalay began begging his mother to go over to her house again. Thanikarn couldn't bear the thought of seeing Krit. She had sent Trin to fetch her son after school the following afternoon and for the rest of the week. It was the only place she might cross Krit's path.

Thanikarn made a few feeble excuses to Thalay, but eventually, it wouldn't seem normal not to let him visit his best friend.

Thanikarn was still trying to digest the whole situation. Even though she had received a short message from Krit – *Sorry. It won't happen again.* – she remained terribly angry, not just because he made such a clumsy pass at her but because he was so disrespectful to his wife. Thanikarn had taken Krit and Sarah for the perfect couple, and now, he had put an ugly crack in her picture of a happy Thai-Western marriage.

She was still in the process of figuring out how she would handle this when she got an early-evening call from Sarah.

'Hello, Karn,' Sarah said, sounding less perky than her usual self.

Thanikarn's heart skipped a beat. *Did she know?*

'Julie's been asking me for Thalay to come over, but it seems you've been quite busy lately.'

'Yes. Very busy.'

'I haven't said anything to the children yet, but I'm taking Julie back with me to England this summer.'

'Oh ...' Thanikarn said. She wanted to ask why, and if 'I' meant the whole family, but didn't dare.

'The children won't be seeing each other for a long time, so it would be nice if they could get together a couple of times before we go. How about this weekend? I could always come and get Thalay if you don't have time to bring him over.'

'It's okay; I can ask Trin.'

'Sure, if you like, but I'd like to see you again, too, before we leave.'

'Oh. Yes ... me too,' she lied, afraid to face her ever again.

* * *

When Thalay told his mother that it was only Julie and Sarah who would be going back to England, Thanikarn suspected something wasn't right. It could be that Sarah had something to take care of back home, but more likely, Thanikarn thought, this was about Sarah and Krit. Julie's mother needed to take a break from her husband.

Either way, Thanikarn felt this was the sign she needed to help make a decision. She thought about Phong, who had left for Ireland. And now, Julie and her mother would be leaving too. She was still torn between the *greeng jai* she had for her little family and the *greeng jai* she held for Konticha, someone who had done more for her than anyone else in her life. Konticha as well as her family deserved her gratitude. But maybe it didn't have to be a choice. She could keep the balance of *sam-nuk-bun-kun* by honouring her debts to both. By accepting Konticha's offer, she wouldn't be turning her back on her family. On the contrary, she would be making much more money in Phuket and could send home a portion of her salary every month to make her family's lives more comfortable.

The more Thanikarn thought about telling Preeda and Trin about leaving, the more she felt it was senseless to worry. Preeda was slowly receding into that comfortable land of forgetfulness. She no longer mentioned Thanikarn's grandfather, or her mother or father, whose early deaths had left her in such grief. And she never went out anymore, not even to take a walk to the local market. Although she did take good care of Thalay when he was a baby, it was as if nature had a sixth sense, and the more her attention waned, the more he grew independent. Now Preeda spent most of her time in vapid contemplation, staring out the window while she sat in her threadbare easy chair. Sometimes she would get up, wander around the small, three-room house, looking for something to keep her busy, simple chores like washing or sweeping. And most every evening she sat in silence, mending clothes in front of the television, barely lifting her head to watch the show.

Trin had always lived in his own world. Thanikarn felt that he loved her, and she liked to think that he found joy in taking care of his nephew, but his introversion made it hard to be sure. His way of avoiding pain had always been denial, so when something made him feel uncomfortable, it didn't exist. She feared that once she and Thalay were gone, he would forget them just like Preeda had.

Thanikarn's friends at the Golden Gecko were surprised when she told them she was leaving. Rinalda said she understood why but was sceptical about Thanikarn being happy in Phuket. She'd heard about the low-life, riffraff tourists. Sawitti was a little jealous, but Thanikarn assured her that moving to Phuket didn't increase her chances of meeting a prince charming. Philippe said it sounded like a good idea, but she knew he was just being polite. He had no reason to care. They all echoed Konticha's argument when they told Thanikarn that it would be good for her to make a change. Even Amnat encouraged her to go.

'Our lives are good here. But you are still free enough to try something new,' he told her.

'Something new isn't always something better,' Thanikarn argued. She was looking for a better reason from her trusted friend.

'You can always come back, Karn. Nothing will have changed here,' he said with a slight air of melancholy. 'You're still young enough to take chances ... You have nothing to lose.'

Her Buddhist upbringing, which had become engrained by osmosis rather than by anything she'd been taught, often left her feeling confused, especially when it concerned deciding about her future. She had learned that it was useless to run after happiness, since it was always fleeting, but now she was being encouraged to try, and even though she believed in accepting her lot in life, she felt a compelling lure to do something to improve it.

The last thing that Amnat said before she left made it easier. 'Today you are saying goodbye to old friends, but soon you will be saying hello to new ones.'

Thanikarn might have been limited in ambition, but she was intrigued by the unknown.

41

Getting ready for their move to Phuket, Thanikarn spent much more time packing up Konticha's things than her own. Not only were there cartons of jewellery, tools and drawing materials but there were also all her personal belongings.

Konticha scolded herself as they folded her clothes. 'I don't know why I keep so many things,' she said. 'I never wear them.'

But that didn't keep her from filling up one box after another with dresses, tops, skirts and shoes. Thanikarn thought it was a good thing Konticha was moving into a furnished house or there would have been even more to pack. Konticha gave a few things to Thanikarn to take home for her mother: a new rice cooker, a gold-framed picture of the king, a pretty hand-woven floor mat. Konticha would leave anything Thanikarn didn't want for whomever would be renting the house. 'And if they don't want it – well, they can just throw it away,' she said.

Ever since Julie had left for England, Thalay had been restless and a little cranky. He was no longer used to playing alone. Trin even had to remind Thalay about feeding the chickens, a chore he'd always looked forward to. Before she left, Julie's mother had given Thalay a shoebox full of DVDs as well as an old DVD player, a small but certain consolation for losing his best friend, but he didn't like watching movies alone. Thanikarn was distressed and unsure how to entertain him. She told him about their imminent move, but changing homes was little comfort to a four-year-old. However, as soon as Thanikarn explained that they'd be flying in an airplane to go to Phuket, that was all he could talk about.

The day before their departure, Thanikarn filled a couple of canvas bags, one for herself and one for Thalay. Her wardrobe was limited to shorts and T-shirts, a couple of skirts, two blouses, the dress Konticha insisted on buying, flip-flops, a pair of nice sandals and a pair of low-heeled shoes. There was still space for the CD player Konticha had given her – which she wasn't sure she needed, but just in case – and Lucas's CD, with the photos and letters he'd sent all carefully sealed in a plastic bag. She sadly realized that these were the only personal possessions worth taking.

Thanikarn had been on a plane only once herself, when she and her parents had flown back to Bangkok to see her terminally ill paternal grandfather, a sad affair that spoiled the excitement about taking a plane. So, this time, despite her anxiety about moving, she took a vicarious pleasure in her son's enthusiasm for the trip.

As she anticipated, their departure evoked little reaction from either Preeda or her uncle. Shortly after breakfast, Thanikarn zipped up the two bags and gave her grandmother a big hug and goodbye kiss that she answered with a smile. She had been quietly sitting in her chair watching her granddaughter skit around the house getting ready to go. Then, as Thanikarn and Thalay piled into the taxi, they waved goodbye to Trin, who was puttering around in the yard outside, perhaps avoiding a formal farewell. He gave a brief wave back, as if they were going off to the beach.

She was fighting back tears, but when she saw Thalay smiling and wide-eyed with excitement, she realized she had no reason to be so dramatic. Phuket was only an hour away, and it wasn't as if she and Thalay would never return. As soon as she began making more money, they could come back whenever they liked. And when they did, Preeda would probably still be sitting there in the chair and Trin would still be outside tending to his chickens. But it wasn't the distance that troubled her or the idea of making a change. She was bothered by something she couldn't describe. Thanikarn turned and looked out the window at her parents' home with the eerie feeling she would never come back.

* * *

It was a short ride to the Koh Samui airport, an airport so small that it melted into its tropical surroundings, and in a matter of minutes they boarded their midday plane. Thalay clenched the arms of his seat during take-off and bounced up and down, giggling with glee as the plane lumbered into the air. He kept his head glued to the window during the whole trip, marvelling at the sea below and the clouds that seemed close enough to touch. When they arrived at the airport in Phuket, his little heart was still pounding as he skipped along beside his mother on their way to a taxi.

After a half-hour ride, their taxi pulled up in front of the address Konticha had written down on a yellow sticky note. Thanikarn's jaw dropped when she saw the house located on a tree-lined suburban street just outside of Phuket Town. It was an elegant two-storey villa painted yellow with rose-white shutters and eaves. A white picket fence surrounded the lush front yard dotted with tropical plants and fruit trees.

Konticha spotted the taxi when it pulled up and strolled out to greet Thanikarn and Thalay at the gate. 'Welcome to Phuket,' she said with a radiant smile. She led them through the living room filled with stylish colonial furniture to a little patio in the back where a man who must have been Pran was seated at a round wrought-iron garden table sipping what looked like a mojito from an ice-filled glass. He politely stood up to receive them.

'Pran, this is Thanikarn ... and this is Thalay,' Konticha said, placing her hands on Thalay's shoulders.

Thanikarn waied, as did Thalay.

Pran appeared to be at least twenty years older than Konticha, a short, stout man with a gentle, round face and thinning, black hair carefully combed over a bald spot. She quickly noticed his polished black shoes and crisply ironed shirt. His keen eyes squinted with discernment as he examined his guests, and she shifted uncomfortably. But then he smiled warmly and bent down to shake Thalay's hand – an unexpected gesture that immediately put Thanikarn at ease.

'I have heard many good things about you from Konticha. I'm pleased to finally meet you,' he said, offering her his outstretched hand. He was obviously someone who was used to dealing with Westerners. Thanikarn shook his hand timidly, daring to let her eyes meet his.

'You are so kind to invite us ... and let us stay in your apartment ... I don't know how to thank you.'

He turned to look at Konticha. 'Your presence seems to be very important to Konticha. That is thanks enough.'

A man in love, Thanikarn thought. She placed her hand on her heart and lowered her eyes, her head dipping into a respectful bow. Thalay studied the adults around him, not sure what to think, but since everyone was smiling, he smiled too.

Pran pulled some keys from his pocket. 'So, let's go see your new home.'

The four of them piled into in his dark-blue Audi A8 with beige leather seats. Thanikarn leaned back into unfamiliar luxury. He drove them to Phuket Town, crossing through the centre, and finally pulled up in front of a modern apartment building with a granite facade. The front door was made of glass, and Pran punched in a code to enter. The bright entry hall and staircase going up to the third floor were spotlessly clean. When Pran opened the door to the two-room apartment, Thanikarn's eyes widened with surprise. It was much nicer than anywhere she had ever lived. There was an open kitchen with electric burners built into the countertop, a microwave oven and a shoulder-high refrigerator. It had a separate bathroom with a walk-in shower and a toilet that flushed. The apartment was sparsely furnished, but there were decorative touches to make it look lived-in, a modern TV, potted plants, framed pictures on the wall, extra cushions on the sofa and a Chinese rug on the floor.

'I think you'll be comfortable here,' Pran said, casually casting an eye around the place. 'I had someone come in and get it ready last week – clean sheets and towels – so you can move right in.'

Thanikarn was speechless.

'Is this where we are going to live, Mummy?' Thalay asked, speaking Thai but saying *Mummy* in English just as Julie did with her mother.

'Yes! What do you think about that?' Konticha asked.

'Very, very good,' he said, wrapping his arms around his mother's legs with a gleeful hug.

Pran handed Thanikarn the keys. 'Here you are, *Thur* Karn. You must be tired, so we'll let you get settled in.'

'Call me in the morning,' Konticha added, looking over her shoulder as they left. 'I'll show you the shop.'

* * *

After taking a little nap on the spacious double bed, Thanikarn and Thalay ventured out to discover their new neighbourhood. She spotted a launderette across the street and thought about how that would be practical. Most of the other shops were predictable for an urban residential street: hairdressers, household goods, fresh produce stores, a few restaurants and takeout eateries. It all felt very familiar, except that instead of seeing faces she knew, she saw only strangers. She and Thalay strolled down the street, and they stopped in front of a Häagen-Dazs ice cream store. She proposed they share a cup, which took Thalay a long time to choose. It was a rare treat to end an exciting day. His mother found a little supermarket and bought some fruit and porridge for breakfast, then ordered some takeout food from a stand nearby to heat up for dinner. She was too tired or perhaps too excited to even think about cooking.

It took a while for Thanikarn to figure out how to work the television and DVD player, but despite Thalay's 'help' she finally mastered the unfamiliar technology. She put on one of Thalay's favourite movies, *Fievel Goes West*, and they settled on the sofa together. Cuddled up with her son, Thanikarn leaned her head on his shoulder. Her mind drifted, settling on the familiar faces of those she had left back home.

'Are you okay, Mummy?' Thalay asked.

She kissed him on the cheek. 'Of course,' she said and quickly chased away images of Preeda and Trin. She needed to concentrate on their new life. It lay just on the other side of a good night's sleep in their big double bed.

42

Lucas had spent the last two months in South Africa acting in a film about the end of apartheid in the 1990s. As a blue-eyed blond, he was cast in the role of Lars, the son of a National Party member who rebelled against his family to fight for the African National Congress. It was a secondary role, but he loved playing the part of a revolutionary character. It corresponded with his own rebellious nature.

Meanwhile, Crystal was in London performing in a theatre piece, a revival of Ibsen's play *A Doll's House*. She was serious about her acting career and relished the opportunity to work on the stage. Dan, their ambitious agent, had a hard time going along with her choice. It meant turning down a lead role in a new high-action movie, but Crystal argued that she had already been in too many commercial Hollywood movies.

'But this is huge,' Dan said. 'Another sequel to *Superman*!'

'And where will that get me?'

'Tremendous exposure, fans and a million dollars.'

Crystal shrugged, regretting her rhetorical question. Even if Dan was right, Crystal was burnt-out playing superficial roles and she needed a break. Besides, she explained, she would never be taken as a legitimate actor if she didn't do something more demanding, like appearing on stage in front of a critical British audience.

Arriving back in LA from South Africa, Lucas was expecting to sign on for another season of *My Upstairs Neighbour*. But Rachel Wolf, because of what she called conflicting interests, had quit the show. The producers didn't want to risk going on with another actress. 'Rachel *is* the show,' they said. Even though Lucas found their attitude a little disparaging, he saw their point, and the fact that the show *Friends* was ending that year as well put them in the same boat.

Dan reassured Lucas that he'd have no problem finding him another job, but Lucas wasn't in a hurry to jump into another acting commitment. For nearly three years he'd been tied down with Hollywood contracts, and he hadn't been looking forward to another season of *My Upstairs Neighbour*. It paid the bills and made him a familiar face, but he had been itching to break out of it. What Lucas really wanted to do was his music, and he missed performing before a live audience. Dan was doubly disappointed, first Crystal and now Lucas, both called to the lure of the stage.

Dan's loss was Mike's gain. Lucas's former agent couldn't have been happier.

'Lucas, you made my day!' Mike said, talking into his cell phone while lunching in a trendy restaurant on Melrose. 'Come see me tomorrow – I've already got something lined up. It's as good as done.'

Lucas popped over to Mike's Hollywood office the next day to get the details. What Mike had in mind was an Asian tour.

Another big band he represented, the Pink Pirates, all-female heavy metal, had to opt out of their upcoming engagement. Their lead singer, Paula Plunder, had overdosed and been sent into rehab.

'Get your guys together. Start rehearsing yesterday,' Mike ordered.

Lucas began looking for his former band members, and in a matter of days he had tracked them all down. As he could have guessed, no one was too busy for a six-week Asian tour and a handsome salary. After a couple of months of rehearsal, Lucky Moon would be back on the road.

Before flying to Tokyo, the first city on their tour, Lucas wanted to spend a week in Paris with his family and then stop in London to see Crystal.

While they were both working, Lucas in Cape Town and Crystal in London, they had phoned each other every few days, sharing their respective woes and joys. He talked about the constant summer showers and 'weather days'; she pouted out loud about the city traffic and exorbitant housing prices. He raved about the fresh seafood, and she complained about the bland pub food. But phone conversations couldn't make up for the hugs and kisses they both missed. It had been months since they'd seen one another, and neither one wanted to wait another six weeks for Lucas to finish his tour.

Crystal knew she couldn't expect a declaration of love from Lucas. He only seemed capable of expressing his feelings in the songs he wrote. Ironic that someone who came across as an incurable romantic could be so hermetic in a face-to-face relationship. But, she reasoned, maybe he was just shy, finding her star status too intimidating. She decided that as soon as he came to London, she'd have to make the first move in their relationship, or they'd never get beyond the 'really good friends' stage.

When he called her from LA, she explained that she had no free time in the evenings, except for Sunday, which was a dark night at the theatre, and she'd have small errands to run during the day, but he still 'had to come.'

'Why?' he asked naively.

'Because I miss you!'

After a full five seconds that seemed to her like an hour, he finally spoke. 'Crystal, I miss you too. All the time.'

She smiled, feeling warm inside. That was monumental coming from Lucas. 'So, when are you coming?'

'Just as soon as I can. We've got two months of rehearsal. It will probably be the end of November, right after I go see my parents in Paris ... Can I stay at your place?' he asked, immediately realizing that was a dumb thing to ask.

'Of course. You're not going to stay in a hotel. I have a really comfortable sofa in the living room.'

'Great,' he answered, not sure if she was teasing or serious.

'So, how long can you stay?'

'Well, we have to be in Tokyo the eighth of December. So, a week?'

'I'll take what I can get,' she said with a sigh.

* * *

The band rehearsals went smoothly. Everyone was more than ready when Mike gave the band members their visas, flight schedules and hotel bookings. He was an excellent organizer and left nothing to chance, especially with a foreign tour. It was a tight program, first stop Tokyo, then Hong Kong, Manila, Kuala Lumpur, Singapore, and finally, Bangkok, with only a few days of rest between each gig.

Lucas spent a week at home with his parents, his father now semiretired and his younger brother starting his first year at the Sorbonne. It was a short, nostalgic visit, and Lucas slipped right back into his teenage habits, hanging out with old school friends in the evening and sleeping late in the morning. He missed Paris and decided that if he ever settled down, it would be in France. The States was no place to raise a family.

He took the Eurostar to London and arrived at St Pancras station late afternoon. He put his big suitcase into checked luggage and headed out with only his backpack. It was a hefty walk to Covent Garden, but Lucas hated taking taxis and felt he needed the exercise. He arrived in time for a bite to eat before Crystal's show. She had left a VIP invitation for him at the counter, and they'd agreed to meet backstage after the performance. It would have been too perturbing for her to see him before she went on stage.

After the play, followed by several long curtain calls, an attendant led him to Crystal's loge. He knocked on the door.

'Crystal?'

'Come in!' she said, taking the pins out of her hair. He entered gingerly. She immediately went to close the door behind him and then threw her arms around his neck. He responded with a long-awaited kiss.

'What did you think?' she asked once they managed to pull themselves apart.

'You were great!'

'Really?' she asked with earnest eyes. Despite all the positive reviews, she wanted his approval.

He tilted his head teasingly, as if musing over his reply. Then he said, 'Of course, really. You were fantastic!'

She rewarded him with a kiss.

Once she took off her makeup and changed, they took a big black London taxi back to her apartment, a small, second-floor flat she was renting in Camden Town. Lucas scanned the living room. 'Is that my bed?' he asked, looking at the sofa.

'Could be,' she said, pouring two glasses of red wine. They made a toast to her success and sat down on the sofa for a long chat. Once they finished their drinks, Crystal said she had to get some sleep. Lucas looked at her blankly. She shook her head in dismay, thinking how hopeless he was when it came to taking initiative.

'Come on,' she finally said, leading him to the bedroom.

* * *

Crystal performed six nights a week plus two weekend matinees, but she decided to spend all her free time with Lucas. He'd only been to London a couple of times with his parents, too young to remember much, so he enjoyed touring the city with a beautiful, charming guide. They walked for hours, did some shopping at Harrods, strolled through the parks, visited the museums, caught a couple of expositions, and whenever their feet got tired, stopped for a draft beer or fish and chips. They didn't have the same media coverage in England as they had in the States, so they were free to walk around hand in hand or stop for a kiss on the street without looking over their shoulder for lurking paparazzi.

The short week nourished their growing affection for one another, and parting was more difficult than Lucas had imagined. When it came time to say goodbye, he felt as if he was being wrenched away from something vital. Their relationship was like wet clay that had been sculpted into form but was not yet solidly set.

At Heathrow Airport, just before his flight to Tokyo, it was a mixture of insecurity and pride that kept Lucas from saying what he really wanted to say. Crystal, a good actress, hid her wistful yearning for him to tell her he loved her. She'd shown enough initiative already and decided she wouldn't be the first to declare the L word.

'Dan left me a message this morning. He's excited about my return to LA,' Crystal told him just before he headed off for passport control. 'He's already trying to set something up and told me to expect a couple of scripts next week.'

'I think he's given up on me,' Lucas said.

'Don't be so sure. You're still a pretty hot product.'

Lucas rolled his eyes. She was right, but she voiced exactly what he *didn't* like about Hollywood.

'You'll call me?' she asked.

'Of course.'

'Well, goodbye,' she said, trying to mask the expectation in her heart.

'Goodbye,' he said and gave her a big kiss.

He walked away without looking back. *You're such a coward,* he thought, shaking his head. He should have said it. *Stupid jerk.*

Once he settled into his seat on the plane, he took out his phone. Crystal had just sat down in a taxi. She heard a short *bleep* and pulled her phone out of her bag. *I forgot something ... I love you,* he sent.

She typed a reply. *Next time I'll be sure to remind you.*

43

Thanikarn never had to set her alarm. Thalay always woke her up when daylight first seeped in through the window. But this morning, exhausted from the excitement of their trip, he was still sound asleep when her phone rang.

'Karn, I'm on my way. Meet me downstairs,' Konticha said.

They just had time to wash, dress and munch on some store-bought rolls before scuttling downstairs.

Konticha's future jewellery shop was a fifteen-minute walk from Thanikarn's new apartment, giving them a chance to discover their new hometown. It was still early; the sun's rays hadn't yet heated the paved streets, and there were few tourists exploring the town. As they wound their way through the narrow streets, turning up one and down another, Thanikarn absorbed her new surroundings, admiring the facades of colourful two-storey shops and elegant colonial-style buildings, while Konticha explained what she knew of Phuket Town's history.

'Over a hundred years ago, this was a rich city,' she said, feeling a bit proud of her new community. Tin!' she said with a decided nod, as if this explained everything.

'What's tin?' Thalay asked.

'A metal that comes from the ground that everyone wanted to buy,' she said. 'You can make lots of things from tin,' she added.

'Like what?' Thalay persisted.

'Like ...' She searched for a reply. 'Cans!' she announced with a self-satisfied smile. 'Anyway, lots of Europeans came here, merchants, traders, the British, and lots of Portuguese, who built these little shophouses,' she said, flinging her arm toward a brash, pink, two-storey building. And then the Chinese. They built those big mansions,' she added, pointing to a huge, ornate residence across the street.

'And now?' Thanikarn asked. The architecture was impressive, but she saw no egregious signs of luxury.

'Now, there are tourists who come to Phuket Town when they get bored at the beach. And they spend their money in shops like mine.'

The three of them came to what seemed to be a popular street with more tourists – strolling along the sidewalks, peering into shop windows, or sitting at tables installed outside of eateries.

'This is Thalang Road; the next street over is Dibuk. That's where my shop is.'

She picked up her pace as they turned left, walking past various stores. Konticha stopped in front of a shop with two large display windows, sandwiched between a clothing store and a chic bohemian café with little round tables set in front.

'Here it is,' she said, pulling out some keys. 'The future Konticha's Treasures,' she announced, opening the door and ushering them in.

The rectangular room had shelves on one side and long

wooden tables stacked with empty glass cabinets on the other. The boxes Thanikarn had helped Konticha pack were piled on top of one another in the back of the room. There were two separate doors. One opened into a small bathroom and the other, a dark empty room, slightly smaller than the store, had two little windows in the back.

'That will be the workshop,' she said, pointing to the back room. I still need to put in overhead lighting, buy some worktables and stools. The salesroom still needs fresh paint and a new floor.' She proceeded to describe how everything would be set up and her plans for decorating. Thanikarn looked around, trying to imagine herself working there. This was a long way from Konticha's little stand at the night market in Koh Samui.

'When will everything be ready?' she asked.

'Oh, a couple of weeks at the most. But we can set up the boutique at the Sea Breeze anytime. I'll take you there tomorrow.'

* * *

The Phuket Sea Breeze Resort and Spa was a five-star luxury hotel catering to wealthy tourists from around the world. It had everything a reputable five-star resort should have: a spa offering professional, quality service; a tourist agency; a gym; yoga classes on the semiprivate beach; multiple swimming pools; four restaurants, including Mediterranean, Thai and Japanese; three bars, one planted in the middle of the central pool; and a hair salon with local beauty products. The Sea Breeze was on the west coast, just south of Patong and north of Phuket's second-most-popular beach in Karon. The hotel complex faced the beach on one side and the main road on the other, where there was an impressive gated driveway leading up to the lobby.

As he did for the jewellery store in Phuket Town, Pran had arranged for Konticha's boutique at the Sea Breeze. He was a long-time stockholder in a chain of luxury resorts, one of which was the Sea Breeze, and it was no problem for him to work out a deal with the owner.

'The boutique is still being set up,' Konticha explained as they crossed the vast, marble-floored lobby. It was in the left wing of the hotel, right next to another small store selling beachwear, sunglasses, suntan lotions and other accessories. She unlocked the glass door of her future store, already furnished with a desk, shelves, and tables.

'This used to be a souvenir shop, selling rare shells, crystal rocks and local artists' paintings on velvet ... waterfalls, elephants, that sort of thing,' she said, rolling her eyes. 'They didn't do very well.'

After a brief tour of the resort and all its amenities, Konticha took them to lunch in the hotel's terrace restaurant next to the pool. It specialized in Western-style food.

'I don't know quite how we're going to work all of this out,' Konticha said, taking a bite of her teriyaki beef salad. 'You'll be managing either the Sea Breeze boutique or the store in Phuket, or maybe one shop one week, the other shop the next.'

'But what about making the jewellery?' Thanikarn asked, curious about her former job.

'I'm hiring some local people to do that.'

Thanikarn cocked her head, wondering if she was being downgraded.

'I've got to have someone I can trust, someone who understands the business and can carry on if I need to travel ... someone like you,' Konticha added.

Thanikarn blinked. This was a promotion!

'We'll have to find someone to take care of Thalay after school. There are buses to bring him home. If it's not a school day, and you're working at the Sea Breeze, you can send him to the Kids' Club where he'll have other children to play with. He'll love it.'

Thalay was following the conversation with wide eyes, trying to make sense of it. The only school he'd ever known was a fifteen-minute walk away, and the only place he ever played with other children was in the school courtyard. He continued munching on his junior hamburger, dripping with mayonnaise and ketchup, confident that Konticha had everything worked out.

Right after lunch, they wandered over to the Kids' Club located on the other side of the hotel's central swimming pool, which was shaped like a puzzle piece, with hidden alcoves surrounded by lush green vegetation. The Kids' Club was furnished with low tables and little chairs, shelves stocked with all kinds of games and books, and a full collection of toys. A sliding glass door led to an enclosed yard with slides, swings and a large wooden play gym.

When they arrived, two little girls were seated at a table, filling in their colouring books, and a few toddlers were playing on the floor. A very attractive, young Thai woman was speaking in perfect

English to a blond lady wearing white stretch pants, a halter top and high heels, her hands resting on her son's shoulders. Once the woman and son left, the Thai woman, who called herself Jennifer, came to greet them. Konticha explained that Thanikarn would be working in the new jewellery boutique, leaving Thalay from time to time after school as well as some weekends. Accepting children of staff members was not normal hotel policy, but Jennifer had already been briefed on the arrangement by the manager. Pran had thought of everything.

Jennifer bent over to welcome Thalay and said hello in Thai.

'Thalay speaks English,' Konticha added, speaking as if she were his mother.

'Oh, he does!' Jennifer said, pretending to be impressed.

'Yes, I do,' Thalay said in his best English.

Jennifer took Thalay by the hand. 'Come with me, Thalay. I want you to meet Andrew.' She led him outside, where a very handsome young man was playing ball with some young boys. Konticha and Thanikarn trailed behind them.

'Hey, Andy,' she called out, waving him over.

Andrew was a handsome Eurasian in his early twenties. He had a slender frame, chestnut-coloured hair, and light-brown eyes. He trotted over to them with a playful smile.

'This is Thalay, and his mother, who is going to be working in the new boutique.' Thalay looked up at Andy.

'Hi, Thalay. Give me five,' Andrew said, holding up his hand for a tap. He was obviously used to being with children. Thalay laughed and gave him an energetic slap with his hand. 'Want to come play ball with us?'

Thalay didn't wait for permission and bounced off behind Andy. Konticha and Thanikarn went back inside to chat with Jennifer. She explained that she and Andrew were graduate students at Chiang Mai University. That's where they met.

'He was in permaculture, and\I was in puericulture,' she added with a little laugh.

Neither Konticha nor Thanikarn got the joke.

Jennifer noticed and quickly added, 'I'm here doing an internship because I specialize in early childhood education, and since Andrew is working on his doctoral thesis – he's studying biological solutions to improve the ecology – he came along to help out. We're planning to get married as soon as we finish university.'

'Oh,' her new acquaintances said in unison.

Thanikarn wasn't sure what a doctoral thesis was, but she thought how smart they must be, both getting university degrees. As Konticha chatted with Jennifer, Thanikarn watched Thalay playing outside with Andy. Someday, he too would go to university, maybe meet a girl like Jennifer, get married and be successful. In any case, she would do everything she could to make it happen.

44

Konticha's shops were ready to open sooner than they expected. Within a week, the main store in Phuket Town was freshly painted and decked with a new wooden floor. Thanikarn helped Konticha fill up the cabinets with her latest collection of bracelets and earrings and tack up her long, wraparound necklaces on the wall displays. They spent a whole day working on the storefront window, going for a mix of local charm and modern chic. The backroom workshop was now brightly lit with overhead lighting, important for working on the jewellery, and furnished with a couple of large rectangular tables, stools, and storage cabinets. Pran had a built-in safe installed, now that he was providing semiprecious gems to be incorporated into her new collection.

The boutique at the Sea Breeze didn't require much renovation and took only a couple of days to prepare, one to haul over some boxes using Pran's car and another to arrange the jewellery on the shelves and tables.

Konticha planned on running both boutiques every day, but in the beginning, kept one store closed while working with Thanikarn in the other. That way, she could teach her how to handle either one of the boutiques on her own. Once Thanikarn had learned where everything went and how to replace stock, use the cash registers, take credit card payments, write up receipts and deal with fussy customers, she would take over at the Sea Breeze full-time, since Konticha preferred staying in Phuket Town, so she could be close to Pran, whenever he was there. If Konticha had to take a few days off for travelling, Thanikarn could close the Sea Breeze, where there was likely to be less business and run the main shop.

They had been using Pran's car, but Thanikarn would be going back and forth across the island on her own, so Konticha insisted on buying her a new scooter.

'I'd be happy with a used one. I have enough money,' Thanikarn said.

'You need a new one – it's more reliable. Anyway, I'm paying for it. Part of business expenses.' There was no arguing with Konticha.

Konticha told Thanikarn that according to Pran, they would have to prepare for more orders. He was not only Konticha's boyfriend, client, patron and investor but her counsellor as well. An expert when it came to marketing, he'd hired a professional photographer to take beautiful pictures of her best-selling jewellery to advertise in some in-flight magazines. They had a promotional catalogue printed up to distribute in his stores and send out by mail. Pran had orders coming in already. And once Pran had the website up and running on the internet, they could expect even more business.

Konticha quickly hired two young women to help make the jewellery. She insisted that everything should continue to be handmade and remain under her artistic scrutiny. This gave Thanikarn yet another job, one of supervisor, helping Konticha with what she called 'quality control', Thanikarn had no experience in telling anyone how to do anything and didn't like criticizing someone else's work. Fortunately, Nataya and Ailada were quick learners and assiduous workers, needing little more than gentle suggestions.

Thanikarn's confidence as a manager came slowly with each incremental accomplishment, like successfully filling out orders, replacing stock, taking the initiative to modify the jewellery displays or even advising customers in their choices. Konticha was always very supportive and continued to encourage her.

At first, Thanikarn was completely confused and embarrassed by Konticha's kindness, but as time went on, she began to understand. Konticha had a generous nature and a lot to give but no one to give to. She was well past the age to have children, her parents had passed away long ago, and her only family was an estranged brother who lived in Jakarta, married to an Indonesian woman who had managed to convert him to Islam, estranging Konticha from her nephew and nieces.

Konticha knew that Thanikarn had lost her own mother when she was young and been left to discover womanhood and motherhood on her own. Thanikarn's loss created a vacuum in her education that Konticha felt compelled to fill. As a self-made entrepreneur, she enjoyed giving advice on a young woman's place in the modern world.

'Times have changed,' Konticha told her. 'It's not because you're a single mother that you can't make something of your life.'

Thanikarn hadn't even a tenth of Konticha's ambition. Konticha had gone to college, studied design and travelled when she was young. Her father was a successful businessman and her mother an accountant. She had inherited property and had enough money to start a business. If Thanikarn hadn't lost her parents and had continued school instead of working, maybe things would have been different, but things were what they were.

'You take what you have, and you make the best of it,' Konticha said, trying to be encouraging.

Thanikarn appreciated Konticha's concern and effort but sadly believed she could never fulfil her boss's expectations. However, she would do her best to reciprocate, and she swore to herself that given the chance, she would do anything she could to show *tob-taen-bun-kun* and return her favour one day.

Now that Thanikarn had a place to live and a more responsible job, the only thing that needed to be settled was Thalay's schooling.

* * *

The Euro-Thai International School had several grades, starting with preschool and continuing to twelfth grade. It had a reputation as one of the best international schools on the island and promised graduating students entry to the top universities. From first grade on, all the major subjects were taught in English, but students were also required to learn a bit of Thai language and culture. The ETI School's beautiful campus was located midway between Phuket Town and Patong Beach, attracting students from the

334

entire lower half of the island.

School would be starting the first week in September. Thanikarn had filled out the forms Konticha had given her and sent them in for processing the enrolment. Once notified, all that was left to do was to go for a short interview with the director to test Thalay's English level.

When they arrived at the school for the first time, Thanikarn gawkèd at it with awe. It was a five-star campus – with sleek, modern buildings, a vast, manicured yard, a swimming pool, a running track and even tennis courts. They were quickly guided to the administration department and the director's office on the second floor. The director's secretary showed Thalay in to see Mrs Hoffman for his interview. Thanikarn sat and waited in the reception room, trying to concentrate on reading a magazine. Konticha had assured her that there would be no problem, but everything had been going so smoothly, she superstitiously worried that something had to go wrong somewhere. The interview was taking a long time, and she wondered if that was a good or bad sign.

The door finally opened, and Mrs Hoffman, an all-business-looking woman in her fifties, perfectly coiffed, and dressed in a classy pantsuit and stylish shoes, came out with Thalay. She introduced herself to Thanikarn, who looked down at her own mismatched attire. Though she had made sure Thalay was wearing long pants, a clean, ironed shirt and brand-new sneakers, she'd forgotten about herself.

Mrs Hoffman was holding a file and called out to her secretary, a small, round Thai woman who sat behind a desk full of folders, typing away on a computer keyboard. She looked as though she must have been working there forever. Thanikarn held her breath; neither Mrs Hoffman nor Thalay showed any signs that announced success or failure. The director finally turned to Thanikarn and smiled.

'We had a very nice chat,' she said. 'Thalay told me all about Koh Samui, his grandmother and uncle and the chickens ... and his best friend Julie.'

Thanikarn was still waiting for a verdict.

'When he told me how much he missed them, I assured him he'd be making lots of new friends here at the school.'

Thanikarn felt her tight shoulders drop. 'So, everything is okay? His English is okay?'

'Of course.' She shook Thanikarn's hand and smiled again. 'Khun Chan will help you now. She can answer any questions you might have.'

'Thank you!' Thanikarn said and waied deeply, an automatic reaction.

Mrs Hoffman gave a little nod. 'See you next week,' she said to Thalay with a smile and disappeared behind her office door.

Thanikarn and Thalay went to see Khun Chan for the administrative work. She gave them a booklet with the school's policy, class schedule, school calendar, bus information and directions for buying a uniform. There were papers to sign and a few details to work out. Thanikarn was relieved that they could talk about all of this in Thai.

'And what about the scholarship? Does it cover all the expenses?'

Kuhn Chan looked puzzled. 'Scholarship?' she asked.

'To pay for Thalay's classes,' Thanikarn said, becoming a little worried. If there was no scholarship, she couldn't possibly pay.

'The classes have already been paid for,' Khun Chan said, flipping again through the papers in Thalay's dossier. 'Kuhn Konticha Kahlang transferred the money weeks ago.'

Thanikarn looked at her blankly. Once she understood, she was dumbfounded. There never had been a scholarship. Konticha had made it all up. Thanikarn knew that her stubborn boss would refuse her money even if she had it. How could she ever repay such generosity?

Thanikarn tucked the file of papers into her bag. They thanked Khun Chan and said goodbye. Once they'd left the office, Thalay looked up at his mother.

'Mama, what is a scholarship?'

'A scholarship is what they give to children who don't have enough money to pay for the school.'

'Who is "they"?'

Thanikarn thought a minute before answering. She wasn't quite sure. 'The people who run the school.'

'And where do the people who run the school get the money?'

'From people who have lots of money and want to help students who don't have money,' she explained.

'Nice people ... like Konticha,' he said naively.

'Yes. Like Konticha,' she echoed.

45

After a couple of months, the stress Thanikarn had felt in her new management job sloughed off like old skin. She settled into a comfortable routine, getting up early every weekday, helping Thalay get dressed and fed, riding her scooter with him in the morning, dropping him off at school, and then travelling another twenty minutes to the Sea Breeze. She usually went for a coffee once she arrived, a recent habit she'd picked up from Konticha. She enjoyed going to the outdoor pool bar, where she was served by Bill, a handsome young man from New Zealand with bulging biceps and a golden tan. He had asked her to teach him a little Thai, and in exchange, he kept her smiling with silly jokes and amateur magic tricks. After her coffee, she opened the lobby boutique. The hours posted on the front door said from 10 am to 6 pm, but this was Thailand, and promptness in a beach resort was more an exception than the rule.

Within the first few weeks, Thanikarn found time to discover Patong Beach and Soi Bangla, its main thoroughfare, which was lined with 'girly bars', cheap beer, souvenir shops and a myriad of restaurants, night clubs and discotheques. Its superficiality stared her in the face. When she left work in the evening, Patong's flashing neon signs, bar-club hawkers, dozens of young working girls, and raucous tourists felt like an aggression, one she had to flee lest its ugliness seep into her soul. Fortunately, she escaped the nightlife before it really began, speeding away on her little scooter back to Phuket Town for an evening with her son.

It had been easier for Thanikarn to meet men when she was a masseuse, but they were often men with the wrong idea. Although she was proud to hold a more respectable job, she sometimes missed her old one – her friendly chats with Amnat or gossiping with Rinalda and Sawitti.

Feeling nostalgic one day, when business was slow because of a rowdy pool party offering free fresh fruit shakes and live music, Thanikarn closed shop and strolled over to the spa. It had titillated her curiosity ever since she'd arrived. She looked around the reception area and picked up a little card with a list of services. A charming young woman who looked as if she could be Thanikarn's younger sister came over to greet her. She was wearing the hotel's uniform, a coral-pink tunic with her name, Nantida, embroidered on her shirt.

'Hello. Can I help you?' she said in automatic English.

Thanikarn shook her head no. 'I'm just having a look. I work at the hotel,' she answered in Thai.

'Oh,' she said, pleased to be speaking to a colleague. 'Where?'

'I run the jewellery boutique,' Thanikarn said, unaware that it may have sounded pretentious.

'Yes, I've seen it. Very nice.' Nantida said. 'I work here at the spa reception in the afternoon. In the morning, I do massages outside ... at the pool stand.'

'That was my old job,' Thanikarn said with a smile.

'In a hotel?'

'I rented a stand next to a small hotel in Koh Samui. For almost ten years.'

'*Dai!*' Nantida affirmed, a little surprised. 'I just started. It's hard. I get tired too fast.'

'I did too, at first. But don't worry, you learn to pace yourself.'

Nantida nodded in agreement. Thanikarn casually looked at the list of services and prices.

This was a luxury spa, and services were much more expensive than what she charged.

'I'll come see you at the stand sometime,' Thanikarn said, surprising even herself. She was curious or perhaps lonely. She glanced at the clock on the wall, nearly 5 pm. She wanted to make an inventory before closing time.

'Well, I have to get back to the store. See you soon ...' Thanikarn said.

Nantida gave a wave goodbye.

As she headed back to the boutique, Thanikarn thought about the irony of her new life, a job that offered her more security and money but less freedom and friendships. That night, she decided to call her grandmother and Trin. It was always an effort to call home, and she found she had less and less desire to do so. Although Thanikarn missed Preeda, calling had become more of a duty than a pleasure. It was wearisome to carry on a one-way conversation knowing that anything Thanikarn told her grandmother would be confused and forgotten.

'Will you be home before I go to bed?' Preeda asked.

'No, Yai. I'm too far away.'

'You don't have your scooter?'

'Yes, I have my scooter, but I have to take a plane or a train to come see you.'

'Oh,' she would say, with utter disappointment. 'Maybe tomorrow.'

'Yes, maybe tomorrow.'

It was no use trying to explain. Distance and time were notions too abstract for Preeda's dwindling spirit. Thanikarn pictured her grandmother spending most of her day alone in her chair, wistfully waiting for time to pass. It would never get any better.

After ten minutes of chatter, talking about her work at the store, Thalay's school, and what she cooked for dinner, she became tired of her own voice and passed the phone to Thalay so he could say hello and whatever else popped into his head.

Then, they both sent Preeda a kiss and a hug before saying goodbye. The hardest part was hanging up, when Thanikarn heard the crestfallen tone of her grandmother's voice tugging at her like a small child begging to be picked up and held.

* * *

It was Saturday, the busiest day at the boutique, but Thanikarn had to take the morning off. Thalay needed some vaccination shots and blood tests, school requirements. She could have sent him off with Nataya or Ailada, but Thalay hated getting shots, and it was with a new doctor in a new town. If the doctor saw Thalay right away, she could still get to the Sea Breeze by ten thirty. It wasn't as if she couldn't be late, but Thanikarn was beginning to feel the weight of professional responsibility.

While waiting with Thalay in the reception room, she picked up a *People* magazine lying on the chair next to hers. Someone must have left it behind. She casually flipped through the pages, recognizing very few of the so-called celebrities. Then she fell upon a full-page picture of Lucas singing into a microphone with his band behind him. *Lucky Moon – Asian Tour*, was written in big red letters across the bottom of the page. Her heart began to thump, and she felt an empty hole in her stomach. She hadn't given Lucas a thought since their arrival in Phuket.

Even though the waiting room was empty, she kept the magazine folded as if reading something unseemly. Thalay was fiddling with a transformer toy as he nervously awaited his vaccinations, paying her no attention.

'Thalay?' the doctor's nurse called out. Thanikarn rolled up the magazine and tucked it into her bag.

Once they arrived at the Sea Breeze, she accompanied Thalay to the Kids' Club, and he ran off to join Jennifer and Andy, his dreaded shots long forgotten. Thanikarn managed to open the boutique in plenty of time to prepare for weekend customers, who seldom arrived before eleven. Alone in the shop, she pulled out the magazine. Despite her shortcomings in English, she got the gist of the text. Lucky Moon would be performing throughout Asia with a final booking in Bangkok during the Christmas weekend. In a couple of weeks, he would be just an hour away by plane.

She could hardly concentrate at work that day, her head

spinning with speculations. Perhaps he would need a little rest. Perhaps he would go back to see Ben and maybe even look for her. Would he go to the Golden Gecko? Or had his new life left him completely indifferent about his fling in Koh Samui?

All the buried memories – how they met, their dates, their lovemaking, the last time she tried to contact him, the fact that she lost her phone and never spoke to him again – came rushing to the surface. She couldn't stop imagining all sorts of possible scenarios that took her back years ago when she still held hope that Lucas would return.

46

'I still think it's shitty to work on Christmas,' Freddy said, cleaning off his drumsticks. 'Did Mike have to schedule our last gig tonight?'

'Come on, Freddy – its normal. It would have been stupid not to. Anyway, people here are Buddhist. They don't give a shit about Christmas,' Lucas said, his legs swung over the arm of an old leather chair, going through their song list. 'We can celebrate after the show, and you can sleep in tomorrow. All day.' He sipped up the last drops of his watermelon shake through a straw.

'Yeah, great. Champagne and a cold turkey dinner.'

Lucas was used to Freddy's complaining and changed the subject. 'What time is your plane tomorrow?' he asked.

'Late afternoon, I think,' Freddy said with a sour face.

'So, you'll get home a day late. My family celebrated last night. We always do a big dinner on the twenty-fourth.'

'When are you leaving?' Freddy asked, his gruffness fading.

'Sunday night, late,' Lucas said.

The band members had all planned to head home after the tour. Freddy was flying back to Chicago; Nick, the bass guitarist, and Russell, lead guitar, were returning to Los Angeles; and Lucas would be going back to Paris for two weeks before flying to LA.

'But I might change my flight. I already missed Christmas, and it would be nice to chill a couple of days on the beach,' Lucas said, combing his blond hair back with his fingers.

Ever since they'd landed in Bangkok, images of his first trip to Thailand had been swimming through his mind: the sight of pretty Thai girls, the lilting sound of the language, and eating spicy, fragrant food …

'In Thailand?' Freddy asked.

'Yeah. I know a great place. An island called Koh Samui. I went there about five years ago with my family … had a super time. Thought I might go back, see if it was as good as I remember.'

'Sounds cool,' Freddy said with a nod of his chin.

The tour had been going well, no hitches, except for a problem with the sound system in Tokyo and some confusion with ticket sales in Kuala Lumpur. But Lucas was exhausted, too many airports, crowds, noisy cities and late nights. Even though he'd feel a little guilty about not going home right away, a few more days away wouldn't hurt. He imagined drinking beer in a beachside restaurant and hanging out with his buddy Ben – if he was still there. And getting an outdoor massage. With Thanikarn?

What he wouldn't give for one of her wonderful massages. He closed his eyes and smiled, remembering her magic hands massaging his shoulders and neck, her soft touch stroking his face – not to mention their hot nights in bed. She was special.

He regretted losing contact with her, but then again, she was the one who never got back to him after his last letter. Was she angry with him because he left or because he was such a lousy correspondent? He stopped asking himself long ago. There was no use in trying to keep up a long-distance relationship that had no future.

He took out his phone and dialled Mike's number.

'Hi, this is Mike,' the recording said, 'I'm not able to answer your call, as you can hear. Leave me a message, and I'll get back to you just as soon as I decide if it's worth it.'

'Hey, Mike, Lucas. We're doing our last show tonight. Don't panic. Everything's fine. I just wanted to ask if you could change my flight back to Paris for the twenty-ninth. I'd like to stay in Thailand for a few extra days. Thanks in advance and Merry Christmas.'

There. That was settled.

* * *

As in any Thai resort, Christmas Day in Phuket didn't feel like Christmas. There were some familiar signs stuck up on shopping mall windows and sparse decorations in the big hotels – a few garlands, a fake pine tree decorated with shiny red balls, or an automated Santa doll – but they were timid tokens that went mostly unheeded. Tourists in Thailand during the holidays were happy to exchange a traditional Christmas for clear blue skies, a shining sun, stretches of pure white sand and a daily swim in the sea. Nonetheless, for some local shops like Konticha's, the holiday season meant extra business. Many vacationing tourists couldn't resist buying a little something for family members, lovers or friends, and as a last-minute gift, original, handmade jewellery was the perfect choice.

The jewellery supplies at the hotel boutique were emptied out by Christmas Day, and Konticha wanted to restock quickly to take advantage of a fully booked hotel. She proposed bringing over a carton of replacements Sunday morning, so she could get back to open the Phuket store by ten.

Thanikarn had been bringing Thalay with her every day to the Sea Breeze while he was on Christmas vacation. He enjoyed his time at the Kids' Club where he got special attention from Jennifer and Andy, his new 'best friends'.

The last day before vacation, his school had held a little Christmas party. They gathered around a huge decorated tree, and all the children received a little bag of imported chocolates, and all his Western friends talked about what they would be getting from Santa Claus. Though Thanikarn wasn't very familiar with the tradition, she did assure him he would be getting a little surprise from his mother.

Thanikarn wanted to leave early Sunday morning, knowing Konticha would need help restocking the boutique. She and Thalay woke up at eight, washed, and ate a quick breakfast. Just before leaving the house, Thalay asked if he could take the bag of Christmas chocolates he received to share with the other children at the Kids' Club. His mother agreed it was a very nice idea and congratulated him for his thoughtfulness. He grabbed the chocolates, and they scampered down the stairs, Thanikarn in more of a rush than usual.

'Can I eat one now?' Thalay asked before getting on the scooter.

'Just one,' she said. He fished two out of the bag before she tucked it into his backpack.

He climbed on, sitting between her legs, holding a chocolate in each hand.

Thanikarn and Thalay arrived at the hotel a little after nine. Thanikarn parked her scooter in the staff section of the hotel parking lot, and they hopped off.

'Thalay,' she moaned, looking down at her crisp white shirt. There was a huge chocolate stain.

'Oops! How did that happen?' he asked.

'How did that happen?' she repeated, shaking her head.

First things first. She'd take Thalay to the Kids' Club, and then she would see about getting the chocolate stain out of her shirt.

On their way through the west wing of the hotel, Thanikarn bumped into her new friend Nantida on her way to the spa, carrying a pile of clean folded towels.

'*Sawadee ka,*' Nantida said.

'*Sawadee ka,*' Thanikarn echoed. Noticing her pile of laundry, she had an idea.

'Go ahead, Thalay. I'll be right there.' Thanikarn knew he was itching to join his friends.

'Nantida, maybe you can help me. Look,' she said, showing her soiled shirt to point out the obvious. 'Do you have an extra tunic I could borrow? The time to get my top washed and dried?'

'No problem. We all have extra uniforms. So hot, you know. Sometimes we need to change twice. Come with me.' She led Thanikarn to the spa staff's locker room. Nantida pulled out a clean coral tunic from a shelf and handed it to Thanikarn in exchange for Thanikarn's soiled top.

'I'll throw it in with the next batch of towels. You can come get it in a couple of hours.'

'*Khap koun ka*,' Thanikarn said with a gracious smile.

'If I'm not here, just ask Siriluk,' she said, indicating the young woman behind the reception counter. Siriluk gave a little wave.

When Thanikarn joined Thalay at the Kids' Club, Katy, a young German girl, was sitting on the floor playing with some dolls while her parents were off for a sea-dive. Thalay was on the floor with Colin, a boy his age, pulling giant Lego bricks out of a carton. Jennifer was sitting on a little stool, rearranging books and board games on the shelves.

'Good morning, Jennifer,' Thanikarn said, as she crossed the room. 'How was your Christmas?'

Jennifer looked at her coral top. 'Changing jobs?' she teased.

'A little accident. My top is in the wash.'

Thanikarn was waiting for Jennifer to mention her Christmas gift from Andy, a long necklace with a purple jade pendant that he'd bought at the shop.

'Great. And I loved the necklace!' Jennifer said. 'I bet you helped him pick it out,' she added with a wink.

A Russian couple appeared at the door: a stocky man with a bulging stomach hanging over his swim trunks, a heavy gold chain adorning his thick neck, and his much younger blond wife, wearing a see-through sarong over her bikini. She was pushing forward their son, a shy little boy of about seven.

'Hi, Alex,' Jennifer said, bending down to the child's eye level.

'Have a good time, darling. We'll come get you for lunch,' his mother said, quick to turn her back and leave with her impatient husband.

Jennifer whispered to Thanikarn that they dropped him off every morning so they could relax by the pool, 'undisturbed'.

Just then, Thanikarn got a call on her cell phone. It was Konticha, running late as usual.

'Hi, Karn. Where are you?'

'I'm at the Kids' Club to drop off Thalay. And you?'

'I just parked the car,' Konticha said, short of breath, carrying a cumbersome carton as she walked. 'I'm heading over to the beach bar for a coffee with Bill. Come join me when you're finished.'

'Okay. Maybe ten minutes?'

'No need to rush. I need a rest.'

Thanikarn turned to Jennifer, putting away some books left strewn on the floor. 'Where's Andy?' she asked, realizing she hadn't seen him yet.

'Oh, he's up in the business centre, doing some research for his doctoral thesis. He'll be down in an hour or so.'

* * *

Andy sat upstairs working on a large outdated computer, completely engrossed in analysing some research data. He got up to retrieve a pile of papers slowly filing out of the copy machine, which sat on a table next to a large, open window. As he waited for the last paper to roll out, he casually looked out toward the beach. The odd landscape caught his attention. He leaned out the open window to get a better look. The sea had retracted farther than he'd ever seen, leaving a bare beach that stretched out like a broad swath of desert sand. Some curious tourists were pointing toward the strangely retracted sea while others were scouting along the bared shore for seashells. Then his eyes widened with fright. He caught sight of a long, white crest that had formed on the horizon.

He stood transfixed as he realized that the seawater was rolling back inland with slow but constant determination as it sent a cluster of little fishing boats bouncing and tossing about as if they were made of matchsticks. 'Tsunami!' he whispered. Andy dropped his papers and dashed out of the room. He ran through the long hallway, his heart pounding, to the stairs leading to the Kids' Club. He stumbled and almost fell as he scampered down the steps.

Jennifer was changing a young toddler with Katy looking on. Thanikarn was just saying goodbye to Thalay, sitting on the floor with Alex and Colin amid a pile of Lego. She gave her son a quick kiss on the top of his head.

'See you for lunch, Thalay. Konticha's waiting for me.'

As Thanikarn headed out of the room, Andy almost knocked her over as he came running in. 'Get everyone upstairs!' he shouted. 'Tsunami,' he cried, trying to control his voice. 'We all have to go. Now!'

Jennifer immediately began gathering the children.

'I have to go get Konticha,' Thanikarn said.

'No!' Andy ordered.

'Only two minutes. I'll run.'

'You don't have two minutes. A huge wave is coming ... fast.'

'I can swim,' she said and ran off before he could stop her.

47

Wearing her favourite long paisley skirt, Konticha sat on a barstool sipping her coffee while she watched some squealing children playing in the pool. There were fewer people than usual lounging on the deck since many of the hotel guests had attended last night's Christmas party and were sleeping in late.

A gentle but strangely ominous breeze shook the bamboo leaves, and a few distressed voices carried by the wind came from the shore, but the excited voices of the children playing in the pool drowned them out. Katy's parents were blithely jogging through the palm trees, laughing as they dodged around the tall, wind-bent trunks, huffing and puffing, their eyes glued to the ground. Nantida was at the open-air massage stand with her back to the sea, occupied with her first customer, a plump Chinese woman lying on her stomach. Agitated birds fluttered overhead. Bill was busy preparing a cappuccino for a sun-wrinkled woman wearing a straw hat and sunglasses to cover her bloodshot eyes. She causally flicked her cigarette ash on the ground as she read the morning newspaper. Bill had put on one of his favourite old Queen CDs and was lip-syncing to 'We Will Rock You'. The rhythmic music and the hissing milk steamer stifled the distant screams coming from the beach.

It was a matter of seconds before the angry sea, awakened by an underground earthquake 300 miles away, would come crashing through the row of palm trees and barge uninvited into the unsuspecting guests around the pool.

Thanikarn had dashed out of the Kids' Club and was running as fast as she could toward the pool bar. 'Konticha!' she screamed and lurched toward her just in time to grab Konticha's fragile hand.

Konticha turned her head to see the enormous wave break over their heads and let out a terrified screech that was immediately stifled as she took in a gulp of foamy seawater.

Tons of water surged past as it tore up everything in its path. Thanikarn and Konticha were instantly captured by the ponderous wave, churned and tumbled in circles as if in a huge washing machine. Floundering, Thanikarn felt pure panic, her vision blurred by the murky seawater; the taste of salt seeped into her mouth as she stubbornly held on to Konticha's hand. Determined not to let go, Thanikarn flailed her other arm and kicked her legs with all her might, battling with the surging current. A tree branch bashed into her calf, ripping into her skin, but she felt no pain, just terror, as the relentless wave caught them in its deadly surge.

Thanikarn could think of only one thing, getting them up and out, but in such clouded water, she didn't even know which way was up. Then suddenly, Thanikarn's fierce and desperate momentum was cut short. Konticha was stuck. Thanikarn had no idea what was holding her back. Seeing only blackness, she continued to tug at Konticha with all her might, now using both hands. Then she felt a violent thrust from something speeding along through the opaque water like a battering ram. Whatever it was, it knocked into her body with such a force that her tenacious grip on Konticha's arm was snapped loose.

Almost out of breath, Thanikarn flailed her arms, trying to get back to Konticha, but the wave pushed her onward, tumbling her around like a broken doll. She began feeling an intense, deep pain in her chest spreading up into her back. She was running out of air after what had seemed like an eternity. *Get to the surface. Get some air.* As her eyes searched desperately around her, she saw a glimmer of light coming from what she thought must be the sky. She kicked and pushed toward the light, and with a final push with her tired arms, she popped her head through the water's surface just long enough to take in a desperate gulp of air, before the powerful wave dragged her back inside as if it were a vacuum.

Thanikarn was a good swimmer, but she never had to swim in water teeming with broken tree branches, lounge chairs, umbrellas, wooden carts and shattered glass. The massive current dashed all sorts of debris into her body, bashing into her back and sides, and scraping against her skin. She fought off the objects, flailing her arms and kicking her legs as if she were being viciously attacked. She struggled to keep afloat, but the twisting torrent clouded by dirt and sand kept pulling her back down into its belly. Her strength was beginning to run out as she was tossed around in what seemed like endless circles. Determined not to give up, she again saw light shining through the top of the wave. She stretched her arms up over her head and thrust them backward in a last valiant effort to propel herself up and out.

The instant her head burst through the surface, she coughed out the water and gasped for air. She continued to heave in loud gasps as her broken body bobbed along as the water continued rolling inland. She realized with relief that the wave's surge had gradually begun to lose force as it carried her along. She allowed herself to hope that the worst was over, and she was going to be okay. Then suddenly, sneaking up from behind, a floating coffee machine banged into the back of her head.

Almost no one on the beach had had time to realize what was happening. Most of them had no time to fight, think, pray or regret: Nantida massaging her first customer, Katy's parents jogging along, the fat-bellied Russian worth millions and his sexy, young wife sitting by the pool, Colin's parents preparing for their dive, Bill singing 'We Will Rock You', his body built like an ox but which snapped like a twig, and the gleeful children playing in the pool. The relentless wave took everyone down with the same cold cruelty, tourists who had travelled from afar and locals who had been living there all their lives, young and old, rich and poor, strong and weak. Disaster struck with blind indifference.

* * *

Just before the first wave hit, Jennifer had quickly scuttled the children upstairs while Andy ran around the lobby warning everyone within yelling distance to get to higher ground. Once upstairs, Jennifer stayed with the children in a room on the inland side of the hotel as far from danger as possible. Andy, as well as every able-bodied man or woman, was trying to rescue those who came close enough to the edge of the building for them to help. They extended a hand, held out a stick, dropped over a sheet, torn curtain, or anything they could find that a passing victim could grab. They managed to pull a dozen or more people from the current. Some were badly injured; others were in a state of shock as they were hoisted up from the swollen sea.

Those lucky enough managed to grab onto the edge of a building or the trunk of a tree. But most of those who were on the beach that morning were pulled under by the current, crushed by the water's weight, trapped by the turbulent wave or knocked unconscious. Adding to what was already catastrophic conditions, most Thais didn't know how to swim.

Considering all the noise, screaming, and traumatic confusion, the children cloistered in the room with Jennifer were surprisingly calm; perhaps they were paralysed with fear. Only Kira, a baby girl, had been sobbing for the last thirty minutes. Once the children's initial shock waned, Katy began crying to see her parents. Alexander remained crouched in a corner with his head buried in his arms. Colin sat next to him, holding on to a blanket, sucking his thumb like a two-year-old. Kira finally fell asleep from exhaustion.

Thalay looked at Jennifer with questioning eyes. She knew what he wanted to ask, and despite his young years, he knew she had no idea. She took him in her arms and hugged him tightly. She wanted to say everything would be all right, but she didn't know how to make a false promise. She just held on to him, compulsively brushing back his soft hair. When Andy came back into the room, exhausted from trying to fish out as many people as he could, he walked slowly toward them. Jennifer looked at him with the same inquisitive eyes as Thalay. With the weary face of defeat, Andy slowly shook his head.

* * *

Less than an hour had gone by when the current finally lost its momentum and began to subside. The island had been struck by two successive waves, and although the islanders sensed the worst was over, no one knew what to expect. While many people didn't dare budge from safety, others began to venture out, wading through the water by foot or using whatever they could find that would float, like a broken door, to look for stranded survivors. The wreckage was overwhelming, and those who had been violently separated from family, friends or loved ones desperately began trying to find them.

Ambulances could soon be heard in the distance. They got as close as possible to the ravaged area. Those who were unharmed pitched in to attend to the wounded, bandaging up cuts with sheets or towels, using parts of the furniture to make splints, covering people in shock with blankets, and generally trying to keep a sense of calm.

Chakorn worked as a gardener at the Sea Breeze. When the wave hit, the scrawny, sun-weathered man was trimming bushes along the entrance driveway and managed to scamper up a tree and hold on to the upper branches as the water surged around him. Once the water had subsided, he climbed down and went out looking for his wife who worked in the hotel laundry room. He scoured the immediate area of the hotel, where she was usually stationed; then he looked in the water-soaked lobby and the ground-floor rooms, lifting shattered furniture and debris, calling out her name. Judging from the tremendous force of the wave, strong enough to have tossed a car into the swimming pool and a boat onto a roof, he figured she could be anywhere.

After an hour searching around the hotel, he headed toward the centre of Patong. Wading through the knee-high water for a good ten minutes, he sighted a body in a coral tunic lying on top of a clump of tree branches. He began trudging through the cluttered water as fast as he could. To his disappointment, it wasn't his wife. He checked to see if the young woman was still alive. Her limp body was warm, and though completely unconscious, she was still breathing.

Chakorn was small and lean, but the young woman was light enough for him to carry. He swept her up into his arms and walked another fifty feet to where a group of people had gathered around a rescue truck collecting people too wounded to walk. He passed the unconscious body to two hefty men helping injured people onto the truck.

'Family?' a nurse standing in front of the truck asked. She was holding a clipboard in her hand, writing down the names of anyone who could be identified.

'No, I don't know who she is, but she works at the Sea Breeze.'

The nurse looked at her tunic and wrote, *Nantida. Sea Breeze staff*.

48

The cell phone under his pillow was stubbornly vibrating. Lucas reluctantly reached underneath and answered.

'Lucas. It's Crystal. Did you see the news?'

'What news?'

'The tsunami. In Thailand, Indonesia – half the coast in the Indian Ocean. Wiped out!' she cried.

It was noon, but Lucas was sleeping in late. He felt his head pounding as Crystal spoke, a hangover from their little Christmas party the night before. He tried to make sense of what she was saying as he propped himself up in bed.

'I just woke up,' he said groggily, rubbing his eyes and trying to focus.

'You're in Bangkok,' she affirmed.

'Well, yeah. We just did our last concert.'

'You have to go to Phuket,' she ordered.

'Phuket?'

'My mom's best friend is on vacation there with her husband. We can't get through to them. All the phone lines are down. You're right there. You can do something,' she said, her voice trembling.

'Give me a few minutes. I got to bed really late last night. I'll call you right back.'

After a quick trip to the bathroom to throw water on his face, Lucas grabbed the remote control on the nightstand and flipped on the television. *Breaking News* appeared on the screen with the devastating images of the tsunami that had just hit the west coast of Thailand. He stared at the TV with disbelief. It took him a while to digest what he was watching.

Once he understood what was going on, he called Crystal.

'I can't believe it. It's horrible,' he said, truly shaken.

'I know. I've been crying for the last hour. Can you go? Can you get to Phuket right away? They need all the help they can get. Please! I'd go myself, but I can't just pick up and fly across the world. I'm shooting all week.'

'I was planning to go to Koh Samui for a few days, but forget that … I'll call the travel agency and see what I can do.'

'I'll send you all the information about my mom's friend … And, Lucas. Thank you. Thank you so much!'

* * *

All the planes and boats going from the continent to Phuket were overbooked with people, many of whom were on their way to find relatives, friends or loved ones. There were also droves of rescue teams, doctors, nurses, and forensic specialists on their way. The earliest booking Lucas could get was on Monday. Meanwhile, he gathered as much information as he could, the latest reports on the damage as well as the number of wounded, missing and dead.

Crystal was right, getting through by phone to the hospitals and shelters was nearly impossible, and he couldn't find out anything specific about anyone.

The catastrophic scene in Phuket was like many other regions stuck by the tsunami. It seemed that the worst damage was in Indonesia, but the whole west coast of Thailand was destroyed, especially in Kao Lak to the north. Some areas were harder hit than others – it all depended upon the landscape and the sea bottom. As it turned out, Karon beach was one such place, and everything located there, including the Sea Breeze and the hotel where the friends of Crystal's mom were staying, had been hit hard.

In Phuket, the hospitals had filled up quickly. Despite the arrival of extra doctors and nurses, the staff were still overwhelmed. The extra beds brought in were not enough, and people who were only mildly injured or in shock were lying on blankets on the floor.

So many dead bodies were found with such frequency that people had to improvise; they wrapped them in sheets of plastic and carried them tied to rods like freshly hunted game to be piled into trucks and hauled off to a receiving centre. Laid out in rows, the bodies were covered with dry ice to keep them from decaying in the heat. As soon as possible, the victims were put into refrigerated trucks that served as temporary morgues. Forensic specialists were frantically trying to collect DNA from the unidentified bodies before they were hauled off, but so many came all at once that some, especially local Thais, were taken off to be incinerated without being fully identified.

A data research centre was set up by the beginning of the

week, and volunteers came in from all around the island and the mainland. They set up computers that began running day and night. Information boards were posted in the centre of Phuket Town with a 'wall of the missing', which was quickly covered with impromptu photocopies of passports or printed photos of happy, smiling faces taken on vacation. In sharp contrast, there was a 'wall of the deceased' with macabre photos taken of bodies that were bloated and discoloured almost beyond recognition, leaving their identity a mystery unless they could be identified by some item of clothing or jewellery.

Thousands were dead or missing, vacationing couples, families, lovers, friends, foreigners and Thais. Many parents had lost their children, caught off guard and swept away, but there were also many children, like Thalay, who had lost their parents.

Tents had been set up outside to receive the misplaced and homeless. The unclaimed children were assembled and lodged in a camp near the hospital. Aided by other volunteers like Andy and Jennifer, self-appointed caretakers made sure the children were fed, kept clean and got a modicum of sleep and comfort. Keeping up their morale was difficult. Whether the children's parents were missing or declared deceased, they needed courage and consolation. Some could still hope, while others, barely old enough to understand, could only grieve, waiting for relatives to arrive and rescue them.

As the days passed with no news, Andy and Jennifer found it increasingly difficult to reassure Thalay that his mother would be found. Jennifer had posted a picture of Thanikarn on the wall of the missing. She got it from Nataya, Konticha's assistant at the atelier. She had no idea how Nataya obtained it; it didn't matter.

Thalay had remained quite calm despite all the chaos and distress. Even the adults were hoping for miracles, so for a five-year-old, anything was possible. The news of a young English girl swept away on the beach and found alive days later, two kilometres inland, spread rampantly through the camp. It renewed faltering faith that until a missing body was found, there was still hope.

The tsunami had wrought terrible damage along the entire coast, but since there was much more devastation in the north, the survivor camps pitched up in Kao Lak urgently needed extra help. Andy and Jennifer decided they were needed there more than in Phuket Town. On Tuesday, Andy went to see Thalay after breakfast to let him know they would have to leave him for a short while to join the volunteers in Kao Lak.

'When are you coming back?' Thalay asked.

'Just as soon as we can.'

'Can I go with you?' Being abandoned by his best friends had him worried.

Andy shook his head no. 'I'm sorry.'

'So, who will help me find Mummy?'

Andy was devastated. He'd lost hope but he couldn't let it be contagious. 'There are lots of great people here to help you.'

Thalay reached up his arms for a hug. Andy picked him up and held him tightly. 'I promise we'll all do our best,' he repeated, whispering into his ear.

* * *

The truckload of injured Thais, including Thanikarn, whom Chakorn had unknowingly rescued, was taken to Vachira Phuket Hospital. She was registered and admitted with the identity the nurse had noted on her clipboard, Nantida, Sea Breeze staff. The first doctor who examined her concluded that besides a broken shoulder bone and some internal bleeding, she was in a deep coma. The reason was unclear, perhaps a lack of oxygen or, judging from the huge bump on her head, a blow to the head, which was quite worrisome since it could indicate brain injury. The chief surgeon had selected her along with other critical patients to be flown out by helicopter to Bangkok and placed in an intensive care unit in Klang Hospital. There was more room in hospitals on the mainland, and it was better equipped for further testing.

Meanwhile, the data centre in Phuket Town had retrieved a list of staff names at the Sea Breeze along with other major beach hotels along the damaged area. Since all employees at the hotel filled out an information file, the volunteers were able to track down Nantida's closest relatives, an aunt and uncle who lived in Lampang province.

Her aunt was completely confused when she received the phone call. The last time she'd even heard from Nantida was over a year ago, and she had no idea she was working in Phuket.

Her aunt struggled to make sense of it all when Dr Sukwana's secretary read out the medical report.

'She's had a CT scan and an MRI; apparently there's no brain damage. Normal pupil reaction, and she's young, so there is a good possibility of recovery.'

Nantida's aunt explained that she and her husband ran a little dry goods store and wouldn't be able to come see their niece right away. The doctor's secretary reassured her that there was no need to come immediately. Until their niece came out of her coma, there was little they could do.

'When will that be?' her aunt asked.

'Too early to say. Every brain is different. But we'll let you know as soon as we see some progress,' she said dismissively. Thanikarn was just one among thousands, and there was no time to go into detail.

49

Lucas landed at Phuket Airport slightly before nightfall. He'd booked a hotel in Phuket Town near an information centre set up in the middle of the city, joining many other foreigners there who'd come for the same reason. The atmosphere was heavy with remorse. When people crossed one another, there were attempts at polite smiles, but many kept their heads down, weighted with worry, or hid their eyes, red and swollen from crying. As he worked his way downstairs to the restaurant for breakfast the next morning, he heard wails of distress seeping through hotel room doors.

After a quick cup of coffee and toast, he headed out to the information centre, a short walk, to see what he could find out about the friends of Crystal's mother. Ever since Crystal's last phone call, they still had no news of the Wests, and their family was anxiously waiting to know something ... anything.

There was already a big crowd when he arrived, foreigners as well as Thais. Some people were huddled in front of the information boards, while others were queued to get help from volunteers manning the computers in the data centre. Lucas got in line, hoping that it would be the quickest way of getting reliable news.

After a ten-minute wait, he was received by a young English woman with a Liverpool accent. Her wide eyes indicated that she recognized who he was, but in these circumstances, she pretended not to.

'Can you fill this out for me?' the woman, named Tess, asked, handing him a printed form and a pen while avoiding eye contact.

'Sure,' Lucas said. She blushed as she read his name out loud.

'Let's see what we can find,' she said pensively, biting her lips as they stared at the computer screen while she scrolled through a list of names.

'Here they are, Mr and Mrs West,' Tess said with satisfaction. 'They're both registered at the Phuket International Hospital.' She handed Lucas a photocopied paper with the address and directions for getting there.

'It's not too far from here,' she added.

'Thanks. Thanks a lot,' Lucas said.

She smiled at him, avoiding those deep blue eyes but following him with a steady gaze as he walked away.

When Lucas got to the hospital, he quickly explained his mission to the receptionist, who informed him that Rob and Mary West were in a recovery room on the second floor. When he finally found the Wests, he introduced himself and explained why he'd come. They apologized for having caused so much distress to their friend, but since they'd lost everything – travel documents, phones and all their credit cards – communication was nearly impossible. They had only contacted their own family yesterday.

After the tsunami hit, Rob explained how they'd both gone

into shock, but lucky for them, their injuries were minor. Rob had a broken arm and lots of bruises; Mary had some nasty flesh wounds that needed to be stitched and treated for infection. They were looking forward to leaving the hospital at the end of the day.

'Let's all go out for dinner,' Rob proposed. 'It's the least we can do for all your trouble, coming all the way to Phuket just to check up on us.'

That evening, they met up at the Wests' hotel where Lucas called Crystal, who immediately called her mother so that she and Mary could have a little chat. After a tearful conversation between long-time friends, Rob, Mary and Lucas went next door for dinner.

The Wests explained that they'd known Crystal ever since she was a baby and were appointed by her parents to be Crystal's unofficial godparents. They also told him that they'd already heard all about him from Crystal's mother. And … they were big fans of *My Upstairs Neighbour*.

'Too bad they cancelled the show,' Mary said.

'It was none too early,' Lucas said with a smile. 'I felt like I was trapped in a time warp, like *Groundhog Day*.'

Despite their ordeal and all the tragedy that surrounded them, they all enjoyed their dinner, and Lucas even managed to get them laughing again.

'So, now that you've accomplished your mission, are you heading back to LA?' Rob asked before saying goodbye.

Lucas thought a minute before answering.

'Maybe not right away. I don't have any work lined up right now. I might stay on here a few days and see if I can help out.'

Mary took his hand. 'I know Crystal would be here doing just that, if she could.'

That clinched his decision.

* * *

The following day, Lucas went to visit the coastal area. The damage was overwhelming; it looked as if the whole coastline had been destroyed by an atomic bomb. Rescue operators were still finding bodies after almost a week of searching; sometimes they were so decomposed, mixed in with the debris, that the only way to locate them was by the putrid smell of decay. He returned to his hotel that afternoon feeling exhausted from sadness. He decided he needed to help any way he could.

Lucas had no experience when it came to humanitarian aid, but neither did most of the people helping. He went to the information centre early that evening and talked to a Mr Harrison, the impromptu director of rescue and aid operations; he was an English ex-nurse who'd moved to the island five years before, when he retired.

'We've already got all the people we need working the computers. And you've got no medical experience. But there is something you can do,' he said, concentrating on a list of names on a clipboard.

'Do what you do best,' he suggested, finally looking at Lucas. Lucas looked back at him blankly.

'I'm a singer and an actor,' Lucas said, shrugging.

'I know. Go see people. Talk to them. Listen to their stories.

They need someone to talk to. Reassurance. You're a good actor. Make them believe in something positive.'

'Okay,' he said, less sure of himself than the director.

'Anne can give you a list of the hospitals and camps,' he said, pointing to a woman sitting at a desk behind a pile of papers.

'Oh, and one other thing ... We're doing a memorial service on New Year's. We're going to have refreshments after. I was going to play that Eric Clapton song at the end of my talk ... "Tears in Heaven". I never really liked that song ... but seems appropriate, doesn't it?' Lucas nodded. 'Maybe you could sing it for us instead. Got a guitar?'

'I'll find one.'

* * *

Lucas did exactly as the director suggested. He began with Patong Hospital the following morning, then Bangkok Hospital in the afternoon, Phuket International the next day and, finally, Vahira Phuket Hospital on Friday. He mainly visited with tourists, since most of them spoke English. Though there were countless Thais, they were more likely to receive visits from family or friends.

Lucas was received with unusual joy by an elderly French couple, relieved to speak in their mother tongue. He helped them communicate with their doctor, explaining that the husband was diabetic and his wife had some serious allergies. Then the couple spent a good hour telling Lucas about their harrowing experience. Up until now, they had had no way to communicate with their family, but thanks to Lucas, they were able to make a few phone calls to their children, using Lucas's cell phone.

The victims Lucas visited were all different, but their stories were much the same. Family members, newlyweds, retired couples, students on vacation, or groups of friends – all ripped from a dream vacation and cast into a nightmare.

Lucas was particularly touched by a silver-haired Canadian woman. She had been going to Phuket for the last ten years, renting the same little bungalow in Kao Lac. This year she'd brought her granddaughter Alicia with her to settle a feud between the child's divorced parents, who couldn't decide who would have her for the Christmas holiday. Though the frail old woman had survived, she had no news about her granddaughter. With tears in her eyes, she squeezed Lucas's hand. 'Please help me find her!'

'I'll see what I can do,' Lucas promised.

Alicia wasn't the only name on his list. He had others written on scraps of paper or noted on his phone, most given to him by those who were injured and unable to leave the hospital to look for themselves.

The next day, Lucas went back to the information centre with his list of names and descriptive notes he'd taken. Tess was still there manning the computer, more than happy to help in any way she could. They scrolled through the data and found a few of the people on Lucas's list – two were in hospitals and one in a relief camp – but they couldn't find the name Alicia Altman anywhere. They turned toward another register with names of the deceased and photos of the unidentified.

Lucas was almost afraid to look at the pictures of the bodies. As they filed through the macabre series of snapshots, he finally spotted the body of a young girl with long brown hair wearing a yellow sundress.

'Stop there. That one,' he said quietly. He felt a wrench in his stomach, and tears welled up in his eyes. 'I think that's her. Alicia.'

Tess noted the reference number of the photo and said she would do a follow-up. Lucas waited until the end of the day for a confirmation, but as he dreaded, it was Alicia's body. He felt sick at the thought of announcing her death. Her grandmother and Alicia's feuding parents would blame each other and blame themselves for the rest of their lives.

Lucas had never been so closely involved with death. The overwhelming heartbreak of so many people weighed upon him like a fallen sky. He felt their pain as if it were his own, a pain he would never forget.

50

After Thalay bravely waved goodbye to Andy and Jennifer, he couldn't help feeling abandoned.

Jennifer was replaced by her friend Parisa, a short, round Thai woman with rosy cheeks and glossy, black hair, who looked much younger than her fifty-some years. Good with children and having worked as a kindergarten teacher for three decades, she was the perfect person to take over. She'd also raised two children of her own, now young adults, busy working the computers in the data centre.

Parisa had limitless patience and tenderness and wore a constant smile as she tried to keep the children occupied, finding whatever activity she could to take their minds off their loss, but it was a constant battle, and she had to wipe away many tears. Jennifer had asked her to take special care of Thalay, who had lost the only people he knew on the island, and Parisa promised she would do the best she could.

Since Jennifer and Andy's departure, Thalay had stopped talking or interacting with the other children and barely touched his food. He spent most of his time playing alone with Playmobil or drawing pictures in a large sketchbook that a tourist named

Albert had given him. Albert was a tall Dutch man with blond hair and blue eyes who'd lost his daughter and wife. He had slept in late that fateful morning while they had gone for a walk on the beach. Albert and Thalay exchanged no more than a few words, but they didn't need to.

It had been a week since the tsunami hit. There were a dozen other children in Thalay's group, most of them foreigners who had to be retrieved by relatives, but since many family members had to travel from halfway around the world, the children had no choice but to wait. The only other child still left from the Sea Breeze was Katy. She was waiting for her grandparents, off on holiday themselves; they had been tracked down only a day before.

The Thai children in the group had all been placed with relatives, but it was different for Thalay. The data centre had contacted his grandmother and his granduncle Trin, and quickly found a social worker on the island of Koh Samui who could go see them to announce the sad news in person. The social worker informed the relocation director in Phuket Town that Thalay's relatives were incapable of coming to get him. She also said that even if they could come, they weren't responsible enough to take care of him if he was sent home.

* * *

With each passing day, the odds mounted against finding those who were still missing. And if they were found, they were seldom found alive. Thalay was constantly told, 'You just have to wait.' Difficult advice for a five-year-old.

Parisa decided to take Thalay along with the rest of the children in her group to the memorial service held in the lobby of the Phuket International Hospital. She hoped it would comfort them to hear some inspiring words and share the day with others. None of the children were enthusiastic, not knowing what a memorial service was, but at least it was something new to do. Thalay obediently tagged along but asked to sit on the floor in the back of the room rather than joining the rest of the children seated in front of a makeshift stage. Parisa didn't insist that Thalay join them; she let each child deal with his or her grief as they wished.

The director had prepared an unofficial talk. He wasn't very good at public speaking and didn't want this to resemble a religious service, so it was difficult for him to find the right approach. He stood behind a little podium equipped with a microphone that he ended up not using. He had a hearty voice that carried, and he wanted to keep this as intimate as possible. There were about a hundred and fifty people gathered in the hall, some in wheelchairs or bandaged, others still waiting for news about the missing, and many who were there to mourn. There was also a group of nurses, doctors, administrators and volunteers, taking a little time off from their daily duties.

The director knew he was reduced to repeating banalities, but he was sincere when he tried to reassure those who lost their loved ones that the greatest honour they could do for them was to carry on living and appreciating life to its fullest.

Lucas sat and listened, looking at the floor, raising his head from time to time to observe the crowd, many with handkerchiefs wiping away tears, others burying their heads, overwhelmed with grief. When the director had finished, he beckoned Lucas to come and sing. Lucas reached down and picked up the guitar he'd borrowed from one of the hospital attendants, strapped it around his neck, and took his position next to the director. With no introduction, he slowly began strumming the familiar chords of Eric Clapton's 'Tears in Heaven'. The music had a stronger cathartic effect than the director's speech, drawing out tears from those who had managed to control them up until now. The little group of children, some of whom had been squirming with impatience during the talk, sat up straight in their seats and craned their necks to see Lucas singing. Thalay, who had been sitting cross-legged on the floor in the back, suddenly raised his head, eyes wide with recognition when he heard Lucas's voice. He stood up and slowly walked forward through a forest of legs toward the podium. He placed himself in front of the crowd and stood listening, staring at Lucas until he finished the song. The director gave Lucas a thankful nod, and he solemnly unstrapped his guitar and placed it on the chair behind him.

Once he turned around again, Thalay had walked up to him and unexpectedly threw his arms around Lucas's legs. Touched by such a surprising display of affection, Lucas bent over and hoisted him up onto his hip. Parisa immediately stood up and ran toward them.

'Thalay,' she called out, then looked at Lucas with an apologetic smile.

Lucas shook his head as if to say, *No problem.*

'So, you're Thalay,' he said, smiling.

'Can you play the other song?' Thalay asked.

Lucas looked at him, rather puzzled. 'The other song?' he asked.

'My mummy's song.'

'Is that your mom?' he asked, looking at Parisa standing nearby.

Thalay shook his head no. Parisa looked at Lucas with sad eyes, and he understood.

'Come see,' Thalay said, squirming out of his arms. He hopped down and grabbed Lucas by the hand, tugging him toward the hallway. He then sprinted off to where there was a large display panel with photos and names of the missing. He pointed to a picture of his mother, the very picture Lucas had taken years ago of her sitting under a palm tree on the beach in Koh Samui. Lucas turned white. He felt a wave of disbelief, as if a ghost from his past had appeared to say hello. He stared at the photo, squeezing Thalay's little hand. A slew of questions churned in his head.

'And your dad?' Lucas asked, fearing his reply.

Thalay shrugged, then looked up into Lucas's brilliant blue eyes as if they held the answer. Somewhere mixed in with the distant memories swimming in Lucas's mind, they did.

Lucas stood up and turned to Parisa and asked, 'No news?'

She shook her head slowly, sadly.

'And what about his family?' Lucas vaguely remembered Thanikarn talking about her grandmother and uncle and wondered if they had been swept away with Thanikarn.

Parisa turned to Thalay, 'Would you like to go get us something to drink, Thalay?' She pointed toward a little buffet set up in the lobby for the commemorative service. Thalay looked hesitant; he didn't want to let go of Lucas's hand.

'I'd love a can of Coke,' Lucas said, and Thalay sprinted toward the drink stand.

'We contacted his mother's family in Koh Samui. His great-grandmother is in the last stages of Alzheimer's, and his great-uncle, well, he has problems. We'll have to keep Thalay here with us until we find a solution,' Parisa said.

'There's no chance of finding his mother?'

'Alive?' She paused and then added, 'It's been a week now.'

Lucas gave an affirming nod. He thought for a moment, a long, anguished moment that made his head spin. He looked across the room; a volunteer worker was handing Thalay a can of Coke and a box of juice.

'Maybe I can help,' he said, his eyes fixed on the little boy he had just met.

Parisa looked at him. His face was so solemn, she sensed that this was more than a simple offer to give a hand to a stranger.

'Help is always welcome,' she said, just before Thalay came trotting back with the drinks.

* * *

That evening, Lucas could think of only one thing: what he would do. He could get on a plane and leave the next day, and no one would ever know. He could go back to his life in LA, be reunited with Crystal, go on as if none of this ever happened. Thalay would survive without him; he'd be put in a foster home and eventually be adopted. There was no reason anyone would suspect he could be his father, and Lucas could keep this a secret his whole life.

If he turned his back on all of this, he would have to.

That night, Lucas couldn't sleep. He cursed Crystal for having flung him into this situation; questions whirled through his mind as he tried to make sense of the morass of problems he'd fallen into. Was Thalay the result of a reckless moment in his past come back to haunt him? Had Thanikarn lied to him, or had it been an accident? If it was the latter, why hadn't she told him? And most important, was Thalay really *his* son?

Lucas must have finally fallen asleep; he was slowly awoken by a stream of light seeping in through the window curtains. He pulled the covers over his head, not wanting to face the day. He knew what he had to do; it must have taken possession of him sometime during his restless sleep. He had to know if Thalay was his son.

Lucas was sure that with all the forensic doctors and DNA equipment on hand, it wouldn't be hard to arrange for a simple saliva sample to be taken from him and Thalay. That meant he would have to speak to Parisa about it first and furnish some sort of explanation. He couldn't let personal embarrassment get in the way of knowing what he had to know.

After a quick breakfast, he found Parisa where he'd last seen her in the hospital courtyard that had since become a makeshift playground. She greeted him cheerfully, happy to see he hadn't left. Her gentle disposition made it easy for Lucas to be direct. He quickly got to the point, and avoiding too many details, he told her that yesterday, when Thalay had shown him his mother's picture, he'd recognized her immediately; in fact, he was the one who took it. He was only nineteen when he met Thanikarn, who was a masseuse at the time. They had a two-week romance, and he felt that there was a good possibility that he was Thalay's father. But it was important to know for sure, and he needed confirmation, that is, a DNA test.

If Parisa was surprised by his story, she didn't show it. Either she was demonstrating Thai discretion or it simply wasn't that surprising.

Thalay had no idea what was going on when Parisa took him to see the doctor for 'a little check-up,' she said. But he didn't seem curious about it. Ever since the disaster, since so much of his familiar life had changed, nothing seemed out of the ordinary.

Lucas went back to get the DNA results that afternoon. The last time he'd felt such trepidation was a couple of years before, after a little 'accident' back in LA, when he went to get tested for AIDS. But on that occasion, he was just being paranoid. This time, the results, he feared, were more likely to be positive than not.

'No doubt about it. The DNA matches up,' the doctor said with no prelude.

Now what? Lucas asked himself. He had no plan, no guide, no answers, and no one he could talk to. Well ... maybe there was one person, two, in fact. Even though he was an independent and successful adult, he needed to talk to his parents.

He would have preferred not to have had to explain such heavy news over the phone. Once he did, it sounded bizarre enough to have been made up. His parents' first reaction was disbelief, then acceptance, then worry. But if Lucas was still unsure about what should be done, his mother had no doubt.

'Lucas, if this child is your son, that means he's my grandson. There's no way I'm going to abandon him at a time like this. I don't know exactly what we can do, or how, but we're coming out there. And we'll deal with it one way or another.'

Maybe this was what Lucas needed to hear. A call to moral duty that he had a hard time answering.

Once Lucas got back to Parisa with the news, she was more than willing to help.

'What do you want to do?' she asked.

'I don't really know. But I want to help. He's my son.'

Before they made any plans, they needed to know a little more about Thalay's alternatives, and that involved some extra detective work. Parisa began by contacting Jennifer and Andy, who were still in Khao Lak.

Jennifer, Parisa learned by phone, knew little about Thanikarn's personal life. She was new to Phuket. But Jennifer did know a thing or two about Konticha.

'Konticha wasn't just her boss. They were really close. Like sisters,' Jennifer said.

Parisa found out from the data centre that Konticha's body had been found. Her family in Jakarta had been quickly informed of her death, but it was Konticha's fiancé Pran, who came to identify the body and arranged for a cremation ceremony. He had since returned to Bangkok, consumed with grief, Parisa was told.

Jennifer and Andy were worried about what would become of Thalay. 'Things are being worked out,' Parisa told her and promised to let them know once something had been decided. She purposely omitted telling them about Lucas, not wanting to say anything until she knew what he intended to do.

Meanwhile, Lucas had to set things straight with his son, partly by his own conviction and partly because of what his parents advised. But it was delicate. How did you tell an unsuspecting four-year-old who just lost his mother that you were his missing father? This was the first question he asked his parents the last time they spoke by phone.

'There's no easy way. All you can do is tell the truth,' Caroline advised.

Afraid that some things might get lost in translation, Lucas asked Parisa to help him out. This was too important to screw up.

The three of them went out to have a little drink on a restaurant terrace not far from the hospital. Lucas began with a simple question in English.

'Did your mother ever talk to you about your father?'

Thalay shook his head no. This left Lucas the job of filling in the missing pieces in a way a young child could understand.

'Thalay, I met your mother about five years ago. Before you were born. We didn't know each other for very long, but we loved each other very much. Then, I had to go back to my home in France, a country very far away. Your mother never told me she had a baby. You! I don't know why she never told me. But now, because I'm here, and because I saw a picture of your mother, and because of what the doctors told me, I know that I'm your father.'

Speaking Thai, Parisa asked Thalay if he understood. He nodded. Parisa continued talking to him in his native language. Lucas wasn't sure, but he figured she was re-explaining things to make sure everything was clear. When she'd finished, Thalay looked wide-eyed at Lucas as if he were seeing him for the first time.

'You stay here now?' Thalay asked him.

The question ripped into Lucas's heart. He looked at Parisa with searching eyes, but it wasn't her responsibility to furnish an answer.

* * *

It wasn't long before Lucas got another call from his parents. Ever since they discovered the news, they had been in constant contact.

'Did you tell him?' his mother asked.

'Yeah. I told him. It felt so weird. Surreal. Parisa helped me out, explaining everything.'

'And?'

'I guess it went okay. I mean, I don't really know what was going on in his head. But he was really cute. He asked me if I was going to stay with him. I didn't know what to say.'

'We booked a flight to Bangkok. We arrive Thursday.'

Lucas didn't protest. In fact, he was relieved. This whole thing was probably going to affect them as much as him.

'Meanwhile, I suggest you take advantage and get to know your son.'

'You make it sound like a punishment,' Lucas said. He felt bad enough as it was.

His mother sensed the hurt. 'I'm sorry, Lucas. I didn't mean it like that. The poor child has lost everything. He must feel so heartbroken and confused. Spending some time with him is the least you can do.'

'I know,' Lucas said. 'The thing is, I'm afraid of what comes next.'

'What comes next? We figure out how we're going to take care of him. What do you think we're coming to Thailand for?'

51

Lucas walked down the sidewalk with a smiling Thalay propped up on his shoulders. For now, the heavy weight of responsibility was proving to be fun. Getting to know his son had been a little awkward at first, but Lucas had always been good with children. He liked them, and they liked him back. Even as an independent adult, he'd never lost his playful side, making light of things, joking around. In fact, given the chance, he still liked putting together Lego. The idea of being a father hadn't yet registered, but if nothing else, he felt that he and his newfound son were becoming good pals.

After spending a second day together, Lucas asked Parisa if Thalay could spend the night with him at his hotel; it seemed the next step. That afternoon, Lucas took him out for a bit of shopping in Phuket Town. He bought a DVD of *Star Wars* as well as a toy lightsaber, thinking a movie with prop would be good evening entertainment. He could only imagine how intimidating this whole experience must be to a young child. Thinking back about how he was at that age, he realized he'd probably have been terrified. But Thalay went along with everything Lucas proposed.

Soon after they got settled into Lucas's deluxe double room, the only room available when Lucas checked in, the first thing Thalay noticed was the guitar Lucas had borrowed propped up in the corner He went over, examined it curiously, and timidly plucked a few strings.

'Have you ever played a guitar?' Lucas asked.

Thalay slowly shook his head. 'Can you play my mummy's song?'

Lucas picked up the guitar, sat on the bed, and tuned up a couple of chords. 'I think you mean this one,' he said, and patted a place next to him for Thalay to come sit down. He looked at is son with a knowing smile and began to play.

> Wakin' up, with the sun in my eyes,
> Cherishing this moment with you,
> I find it tough to realize,
> That you and me is soon to be through ...

Thalay listened, silent and attentive while Lucas sang the entire song. When he finished, Thalay simply smiled. He'd heard what he needed to hear and looked at Lucas as if he knew what he needed to know. Lucas put the guitar down and gave him a tender little kiss on the forehead.

After a quick Western-style dinner downstairs in the half-empty hotel restaurant, they returned to Lucas's room. He put on the *Star Wars* DVD, and the two on them snuggled up on the bed to watch the movie. Exhausted from all the newness, Thalay fought to keep his eyes open and continue watching the movie, relishing the comfort of his father's tender embrace, but he lost the battle and reluctantly fell sound asleep.

After Lucas tucked Thalay under the covers, he looked at his watch and made a mental calculation of the time. This was a good time to call Crystal back in California; she wouldn't have started work yet.

He still hadn't broken the news to Crystal. In fact, they hadn't even spoken to one another since he'd located her godparents over a week ago. At the end of their quick call, Lucas had announced his intention to stay on and help with the relief efforts, and Crystal, proud of his decision, asked that he keep in touch, but he knew she was busy shooting all day, every day and probably hadn't even noticed he hadn't yet called back.

Lucas figured there was no good way of telling Crystal that he was the father of a recently discovered orphan. It was unfortunate that it had to be over the phone, just like with his parents, but he knew that if he didn't tell her now, she'd find out later, and then she'd be furious for not having found out sooner. Better to get it over with, he thought.

With the preamble 'You're not going to believe this ...' he began his story by recounting his strange encounter with Thalay during the memorial service, which led back to an explanation of his island adventure five years ago. Even if he was only nineteen at the time, he didn't want to make it sound like he was just an innocent victim and quickly added that he accepted his part of responsibility. He said he was also fully aware that the consequences didn't only affect him but his parents and her as well.

Once he'd finished, Crystal was at a true loss of what to say.

'Give me a little time to let this sink in.'

Though he couldn't have expected more, Lucas was disappointed. He was hoping for at least a hint of empathy.

* * *

While waiting for the arrival of his parents, Lucas toyed with the idea of making a trip to Koh Samui so that Thalay could see his great-grandmother and great-uncle one last time. Parisa had told him that they'd been informed of Thanikarn's disappearance. Their situation was esteemed inadequate for taking care of Thalay, and though they must have felt deep sorrow for what had happened, they hadn't expressed any desire to see Thalay. It was as if they had taken it for granted that everything had already been settled.

'If you and your family are planning to take care of Thalay, maybe it would be better not to remind him of what he left behind. With time, he will forget,' Parisa said.

'Maybe,' Lucas said. 'But it doesn't seem right not to go see his family. It might be reassuring for them to know he has a father and a new family.'

'Will it make a difference?' Parisa wondered out loud.

'Maybe not,' Lucas said. 'But I would feel guilty being so close and not going to meet them myself.'

Parisa conceded with a smile.

* * *

Arriving at the little Koh Samui airport, Lucas was charged with old memories. It was the last place he'd seen Thanikarn, and he could still remember their long goodbye kiss.

He hired a taxi, and as they wound up the narrow dirt road leading to Thalay's former home, the familiarity lit up Thalay's eyes. Lucas began to wonder if this wasn't a mistake.

'Does your great-uncle or *yai* speak any English?' Lucas asked as they were pulling up to the house. Thalay shrugged. It was surely something he had never thought about.

'I'll let you do all the talking,' Lucas said with a smile.

They climbed out of the taxi, and Lucas asked the driver to wait for them.

Lucas had never seen the family home, a simple wooden structure, old and worn, precariously balanced on concrete bricks. He spotted Thanikarn's old pink Yamaha scooter parked along the side of the house, the one they rode on years ago. Thalay knocked on the front door, but no one answered. He pushed it open, peered in and saw Preeda staring out the window with her head tilted to one side, as she sat sunken into her tattered wicker chair. Lucas followed Thalay inside.

'Yai?' Thalay asked softly. She turned around and looked at him.

'Oh, hello little one,' she said. 'I remember you ...'

She opened her arms, and Thalay ran to her for a hug. She looked hard into his eyes as if trying to make sense of exactly who he was; then she stared out the window again, still holding on to her great-grandson's hand.

'Trin is outside with the chickens,' she said, softly speaking to herself.

'I'll go tell him we're here,' Thalay said.

He took Lucas by the hand. 'Come see Trin.'

They circumvented the house and crossed the backyard to the unfenced chicken patch.

'Trin!' Thalay called out. Trin turned around and looked at him but calmly continued his task.

'Do you want to come feed the chickens?' he finally asked.

Thalay walked over to where he was dispersing the feed, took a handful of grain from Trin's blue plastic pail, and began tossing it out to the chickens like his great-uncle.

After a minute, Trin asked, 'Who is your friend?'

'He is my *phor*!'

'Oh,' Trin said, his voice calmly trailing off.

'He came to get me. He's going to take care of me until we find *Mae*.'

Trin nodded as if this all made perfect sense and continued to watch his chickens pecking on the ground.

Trin said nothing more. He finished his chore, put down the pail and headed back into the house. Thalay looked up at Lucas, who gestured with a tip of his head that they should follow his uncle back into the house. Once inside, Trin took down a little plastic basket from the kitchen shelf, rummaged through it and pulled out a tiny object he had crafted with chicken wire, a miniature chicken. Trin handed it to Thalay. 'For you,' he said, then stood back and said, 'You can go now.'

Thalay slowly walked over to his grandmother. Preeda looked at him with her glassy absent eyes.

'Yai, this is my *phor*. He will take care of me until we find *Mae*,' he repeated what he'd told Trin.

She nodded slowly. Her lips turned up; her eyes shone with a distant tenderness that said she understood. Thalay gave her a hug and then reached up to touch her cheek. 'Goodbye, Yai,' he said. Preeda stroked his hair again and gave him a sweet smile. It was a sombre moment, and Lucas observed silently as if in a place of worship.

'You will come back?' Preeda asked.

'When they find *Mae*,' Thalay said with conviction.

Preeda kissed him on the forehead and then resumed her dreamy stare out the window.

Trin had begun fiddling with an old radio.

'I'll take good care of him,' Lucas said to them just before they left. Thalay didn't bother to translate. It wasn't necessary.

52

Under normal circumstances, the Mounier family would have had to wade through a lot of red tape before leaving the country with Thalay. But these were desperate times. There was so much devastation, thousands and thousands of injured and homeless, that whatever might lighten the tremendous load on the administrative organizations, hospitals and placement services was a blessing.

Another fortunate factor for the Mouniers concerned Konticha's fiancé, Pran. Parisa had contacted Pran when she'd learned that Lucas and his family were willing to take responsibility for Thalay. She knew Pran was a member of Thailand's wealthy and influential elite. He could surely help and, if willing, he could make things happen.

Lucas timed a trip to Bangkok so that he and Thalay would arrive the same day as his parents. They agreed to all meet up at the Miramar Hotel in the centre of the city. It was an emotional moment for everyone, one that began with hugs and tears from his mother, leaving Thalay taken aback by all the fluster.

'Don't worry – those are happy tears,' Lucas said.

Caroline found Thalay irresistibly adorable but restrained

herself – she didn't want to intimidate him with a deluge of compliments. Lucas's father stayed his sober and cautious self, even though he was as moved as Caroline. 'Never count on everything going smoothly,' he said as an aside to his wife.

Pran agreed to meet Lucas and his parents the next day and welcomed them into his twenty-sixth-floor office on Ban Mo Road. He said he would do what he could to help, sincerely convinced that this is was what Konticha would have wanted. Since Lucas had proof of being his biological father, it was just a matter of a few phone calls to get Thalay a Thai passport and an emergency visa for France. Things could be followed up at the Thai embassy once they were back home.

As soon as they had everything they needed, they booked a flight to Paris. Caroline went shopping in one of Bangkok's mega shopping centres and bought Thalay a set of warm city clothes. It was hot and humid in Thailand but bitterly cold in France.

Thalay couldn't have imagined the enormous change he was about to experience. Lucas had bought a little tourist book of Paris at the airport and showed him pictures of where he'd be going. He explained that the people there spoke French, but most of them could also speak English. Thalay felt a knot in his stomach that made him feel a little sick. If he had been an adult, he could have recognized it as stress. He'd lost his mother, Konticha, his great-grandmother and Trin and was about to fly far away from everyone and everything he'd ever known.

Thalay slept most of the eleven hours back to Paris. When he woke up, he was in a different world. Everyone was speaking a language he didn't know. Walking out of the airport, a brisk winter air chilled his cheeks.

'It feels like a refrigerator,' he said to everyone's amusement. During their drive into Paris, he looked out the window. The sky was a misty steel grey, and the highway was lined with barren trees, a stark contrast from the lush green vegetation he'd always known.

Delighted to have suddenly assumed a new title, Uncle Arthur was ready and waiting for him when they arrived home. He'd been practicing a few words of Thai, so he could greet his nephew in style.

'*Sawadee kap. Sabai-dee-roo?*' Hello. How are you?

Thalay's face lit up with a curious smile.

'Did I say that okay?' Arthur asked with a grin.

After meeting his young uncle, who had worked his characteristic charm, Thalay was shown to his new room. Before their arrival, Arthur had been instructed to dig out old toys and video cassettes stashed away in the storage cellar, and Lucas's old room had been transformed into the way it had looked twenty years ago. Thalay immediately scampered to a huge toy chest and like a child opening presents on Christmas, pulled out everything that had been inside as quickly as he could.

Lucas and his parents had been deliberating for the past few days about how to manage integrating Thalay into a new life. Even though Lucas had no work set up right away, Dan had called to say he was being considered for a major role in a new TV series and had to 'hightail it back to LA' before the end of the month.

Unless he wanted to say goodbye to his career, Lucas couldn't stay in Paris. And it wasn't practical for Thalay to go with him to

Los Angeles.

Even without considering Lucas's growing career, his parents couldn't picture their unsettled son as a full-time father. Unlike the fictional characters he played, this was a real-life role, and Lucas hadn't had enough rehearsal time. Thalay's best option was to live with his newfound grandparents, at least for now. Lucas would come back when he could, and maybe Thalay could visit him in Los Angeles.

It would be a challenge to help Thalay feel at home in Paris, and the family drew up a list of priorities. School, they all decided, could wait until the fall. Meanwhile, they could help Thalay learn French while his English would continue to improve quite naturally. In the last few days, his vocabulary had already doubled.

Though Caroline mostly worked at home doing translations, she decided it would be a good idea to hire some help, someone who spoke Thai. It would surely be a comfort for Thalay to have somebody around who shared his culture and language.

Kat, the owner of a little Thai takeout restaurant just around the corner, agreed to help them find someone. Kat had an extended family in Paris, and surely, she said, she could find a family member or friend to come work part-time.

In a little over a week, Thalay had adjusted with surprising speed. Perhaps, Caroline said, it was because of all the love around him. Pei, Kat's sixty-year-old aunt, had shown up for an interview for the nanny job. She turned out to be perfect, the next best thing to a real Thai grandmother. She would cook Thalay his favourite foods, read to him and talk about her own life back in Thailand.

In just a short time, Thalay and Lucas had created a special bond, although Lucas felt more like a big brother than a father. He dreaded having to announce his departure, especially since Thalay's adaptation was slow to come. Thalay would often curl up in a little ball, hugging a pillow, and escape his sorrow the only way he could, by falling asleep. And almost every day, he would ask when his mother would be coming to get him. No one had the courage to tell him the answer.

* * *

Dr Sukwana was becoming increasingly concerned after the last visit he made to his comatose patient, Nantida. She showed all the necessary physical signs of progress: her flesh wounds had healed, her broken shoulder bone had set and, most importantly, she showed no signs of brain damage. She should have regained consciousness by now, and it was troubling that she still wasn't waking up. He decided she could use some emotional stimulus, and strongly advised that her family be summoned.

Nantida's aunt took the long train ride alone, leaving her husband to tend to their dry goods store in Mae Mo. It was an all-day trip, getting her to Bangkok in early evening. Before visiting her niece, she received a short briefing from the head nurse, a petite woman wearing wire-rimmed glasses, with her hair cut short like a man's. As they walked down the corridor, she spoke curtly, as if she could only afford a few seconds.

'We never know just how conscious our patients are. Sometimes a first contact with a family member can provoke a dramatic reaction. Just speak normally. Try to be gentle and encouraging, even if you think she can't hear you,' the nurse explained.

Nantida's aunt, weathered with age, timidly approached the hospital bed with anxious eyes. She bent over Nantida and peered into her face, then screwed up her own face into a confused frown. She turned toward the nurse. 'This is not my niece!' she said shrilly.

The head nurse's lips twisted into a knot, and her eyebrows slanted down. 'Are you sure?'

'Of course I'm sure,' she spit out, annoyed that she'd come a long way for nothing.

The head nurse sighed. 'I'm so sorry,' she said. 'These things happen, especially these days.'

There was little more to say. Ever since the tsunami, there were so many patients pouring in. This was not the first nor would it be the last case of confusion.

Now the head nurse would have to write up a report and contact the authorities responsible for unidentified persons. Meanwhile, there was nothing to do but wait for their unidentified patient to regain consciousness.

* * *

Supatra, a young night nurse barely out of her teens, was particularly distressed by the news. She had been caring for Nantida ever since she arrived, changing her dressings, washing her, monitoring her condition on the life support machines. She was highly devoted and worried that if her patient didn't wake up soon, it would be too late for complete rehabilitation. Since her identity was now a mystery, the chances of finding a family member could take weeks or even months.

Supatra knew it might have been against hospital protocol, but she decided to try something a little unconventional. She looked through the nightstand next to the bed and found a plastic bag with Thanikarn's personal items: the clothes she wore the day she was found, cleaned and folded, and a little gold necklace with a butterfly pendant. Supatra took out the necklace and studied it. She remembered a scene she'd seen in a movie once. A woman suffering from amnesia after a car accident was given a string of prayer beads, and once she held them in her hand, they immediately sparked forgotten memories. Maybe, she thought, the little gold necklace could work the same magic. Taking Thanikarn's limp hand, she placed the necklace in its palm and held Thanikarn's fingers closed over it, waiting for a little miracle. It was worth a try, but after several minutes with no reaction, she gave up, but rather than putting the necklace away, she lifted Thanikarn's head and fastened it around her listless neck.

* * *

It was Thalay's fifth birthday, a day that Lucas wanted to celebrate before heading off to Los Angeles. No one knew how Thalay spent his former birthdays, but the family wanted to make this one special. They'd planned a birthday cake with candles and a surprise present: tickets to Paris's Disneyland for the whole family.

That afternoon, Caroline came home with a bag of groceries. Pei was in the bathroom doing laundry and Thalay was sitting cross-legged on the floor with his lightsaber on his lap watching *Star Wars: Episode II* for the third time. Caroline went over and gave him a hello kiss and then headed for the kitchen.

'Come help me,' she called.

Thalay jumped up and trotted after her. This was the first time she had ever asked for his help cooking. They pulled the groceries out of the bag.

'We're going to make a carrot cake for your birthday. Your father's favourite.'

Thalay knew little about cooking, and this would be his first experience baking. To keep his attention from waning, Caroline let him push the button on the food processor to grate the carrots, crack the eggs, measure the flour, sugar and oil, and mix everything up in a big bowl, allowing him to stick his finger in 'just to taste', which he did at least five times.

That evening, the whole family ate an early dinner so that Thalay would still be alert enough to enjoy it: a simple meal, roast chicken and potatoes and a green salad. Skipping the usual cheese, they got right to dessert.

The lights were turned off, the cameras were ready, and Lucas ceremoniously brought out the cake lit with five tall candles as they all broke into the traditional happy birthday song. From the fascinated look on Thalay's face, this was apparently his first experience with a Western-style birthday.

'First you make a wish, and then you blow out the candles,' Arthur said once they finished singing.

'A wish?' Thalay asked.

'But don't tell us what it is! If you blow out all the candles, your wish will come true.'

Lucas shot Arthur a reproachful look, and Arthur sheepishly sunk back in his chair. He realized too late that was a stupid thing to say.

'One ... two ... three!' They all chimed. Thalay blew out all the candles, and everyone clapped their hands while Thalay, quite pleased with himself, bounced up and down in his chair.

* * *

Lying in her hospital bed eight thousand miles away, Thanikarn opened her eyes with a start. Gradually stretching out her stiff fingers, she turned her head sluggishly to the side, where she focused on the monitors next to her bed as they emitted a soft, regular beeping sound. Her right hand moved slowly over the sheets. *A hospital*, she thought. Her eyes closed again. She felt so weary. Then her right hand crept slowly upward until her fingers felt the gold necklace placed around her neck. Her lips turned upward. Hearing footsteps, she slowly opened her eyes again and turned her head; it was a woman bringing in a change of sheets. Supatra stopped in her tracks as she heard Thanikarn's frail voice.

'Where is Thalay?'